_____ Lynn, is a *New* _____ay bestselling author. She is _____ e bestselling Lux and Gamble _____ and the Covenant series. When she's _____ y writing, which is almost never, she can be _____ nd procrastinating on Twitter or messing with her dog, Loki. She lives with her husband in West Virginia and is addicted to 5-Hour Energy Drinks.

J LYNN

BE
WITH ME

HARPER

Harper
An imprint of HarperCollins*Publishers*
77–85 Fulham Palace Road,
Hammersmith, London W6 8JB

www.harpercollins.co.uk

A Paperback Original 2014
1

A catalogue record for this book
is available from the British Library

ISBN: 978-0-00-753099-1

Typeset in Meridien by Palimpsest Book Production Ltd, Falkirk, Stirlingshire

Printed and bound in Great Britain by Clays Ltd, St Ives plc

Dedicated to my brother,
who shares a birthday with Be With Me *release day.*
Happy Birthday, Jesse James.

Chapter 1

Sweet tea was apparently going to be the death of me.

Not because the amount of sugar could send you into a diabetic coma after one slurp. Or because my brother had nearly caused a triple-car pileup by winging his truck around in a sharp U-turn after receiving a text message that contained two words only.

Sweet. Tea.

Nope. The request for sweet tea was bringing me face-to-face with Jase Winstead—the physical embodiment of every girlie girl fantasy and then some that I'd ever had. And this was the first time I was seeing him outside of campus.

And in front of my brother.

Oh sweet Mary mother of all the babies in the world, this was going to be awkward.

Why, oh why, did my brother have to text Jase and mention that we were on his end of town and ask if he needed anything? Cam was supposed to be taking me around so I could get familiar with the scenery. Although the scenery I was about to witness was sure to be better than what I'd seen so far of this county.

1

If I saw another strip club, I was going to hurt someone.

Cam glanced over at me as he sped down the back road. We'd left Route 9 years ago. His gaze dropped from my face to the tea I clutched in my hands. He raised a brow. 'You know, Teresa, there's a thing called a cup holder.'

I shook my head. 'It's okay. I'll hold it.'

'Okaaay.' He drew the word out, focusing on the road.

I was acting like a spaz and I needed to play it cool. The last thing anyone in this world needed was Cam finding out why I had a reason to act like a dweeb on crack. 'So, um, I thought Jase lived up by the university?'

That sounded casual, right? Oh God, I was pretty sure my voice cracked at some point during that not-so-innocent question.

'He does, but he spends most of the time at his family's farm.' Cam slowed his truck down and hung a sharp right. Tea almost went out the window, but I tightened my death grip on it. Tea was going nowhere. 'You remember Jack, right?'

Of course I did. Jase had a five-year-old brother named Jack, and the little boy meant the world to him. I obsessively remembered everything I'd ever learned about Jase in a way I imagined Justin Bieber fans did about him. Embarrassing as that sounded, it was true. Jase, unbeknownst to him and the entire world, had come to mean a lot of things to me in the last three years.

A friend.

My brother's saving grace.

And the source of my crush.

But then a year ago, right at the start of my senior year in high school, when Jase had tagged along when Cam had visited home, he'd become something very complicated. Something that a part of me wanted nothing more than to

2

forget about. But the other part of me refused to let go of the memory of his lips against mine or how his hands had felt skimming over my body or the way he had groaned my name like it had caused him exquisite pain.

Oh goodness . . .

My cheeks heated behind my sunglasses at the vivid memory and I turned my face to the window, half tempted to roll it down and stick my head out. I so needed to pull it together. If Cam ever discovered that Jase had kissed me, he would murder him and hide his body on a rural road like this one.

And that would be a damn shame.

My brain emptied of anything to say, and I so needed a distraction right now. The perspiration from the tea and my own trembling hands was making it hard to hold on to the cup. I could've asked Cam about Avery and that would've worked, because he *loved* talking about Avery. I could've asked about his classes or how he was back in training for United tryouts in the spring, but all I could do was think about the fact that I was finally going to see Jase in a situation where he couldn't run away from me.

Which was what he'd been doing the first full week of classes.

Thick trees on either side of the road started to thin out, and through them, green pastures became visible. Cam turned onto a narrow road. The truck bounced on the potholes, making my stomach queasy.

My brows lowered as we passed between two brown poles. A chain-link fence lay on the ground, and off to the left was a small wooden sign that read WINSTEAD: PRIVATE PROPERTY. A large cornfield greeted us, but the stalks were dry and yellow, appearing as if they were days away from withering up and dying. Beyond them, several large horses grazed behind a wooden fence that was missing many of its middle panels. Cows roamed over most of the property to the left, fat and happy looking.

As we drew closer, an old barn came into view—a scary old barn, like the one in the *Texas Chainsaw Massacre*, complete with the creepy rooster compass thing swiveling on the roof. Several yards beyond the barn was a two-story home. The white walls were gray, and even from the truck, I could tell there was more paint peeling than there was on the house. Blue tarp covered several sections of the roof, and a chimney looked like it was half crumbling. Red dusty bricks were stacked along the side of the house, as if someone had started to repair the chimney but grew bored and gave up. There was also a cemetery of broken-down cars behind the barn, a sea of rusted-out trucks and sedans.

Shock rippled through me as I sat up a bit straighter. This was Jase's farm? For some reason, I pictured something a little more . . . up to date?

Cam parked the truck a few feet back from the barn and killed the engine. He glanced over at me, following my stare to the house. Unlocking his seat belt, he sighed. 'His parents had a really hard time a few years back and they're just now getting on their feet. Jase tries to help with the farm and stuff, but as you can see . . .'

The farm needed more help than Jase could provide.

I blinked. 'It's . . . charming.'

Cam laughed. 'That's nice of you to say.'

My fingers tightened around the cup in defense. 'It is.'

'Uh-huh.' He flipped his baseball cap around, shielding his eyes. Tufts of black hair poked out of the back rim.

I started to speak, but movement I saw out of the corner of my eye caught my attention.

Racing out from the side of the barn, a little boy seated in a miniature John Deere tractor hooted and hollered. His chubby arms were bone straight as his hands gripped the

4

steering wheel. A mop of curly brown hair shone under the bright August sun. Pushing the tractor from behind was Jase, and even though I could barely hear him, I was sure that he was making engine noises. They bounced along the uneven gravel and ground. Jase laughed as his little brother shouted, 'Faster! Go faster!'

Jase appeased his brother, pushing the tractor so it zigged and zagged to a stop in front of the truck as Jack squealed, clenching the steering wheel. Plumes of dust flew into the air.

And then Jase straightened.

Oh wow-wee.

My mouth dropped open. Nothing in this world could've made me look away from the splendor before me.

Jase was shirtless and his skin glistened with sweat. I wasn't sure what ethnicity he had in his family background. There had to be something Spanish or Mediterranean, because he had a natural tan skin tone that remained that way all year-round.

As he walked around the tractor, his muscles did fascinating things—rippling and tightening. His pecs were perfectly formed and his shoulders were broad. He had the kind of muscles one got from lifting bales of hay. Boy was ripped. His stomach muscles tensed with each step. He had a very distinctive six-pack. Totally touchable. His jeans hung indecently low—low enough that I wondered if he had on anything underneath the faded denim.

It was the first time I ever saw the full extent of his tattoo. Ever since I'd known him, I'd caught glimpses of it peeking out from the collar on his left shoulder and from under a shirtsleeve. I never even knew what it was until now.

The tat was massive—an endless knot shaded in deep black, starting at the base of his neck, looping and twisting over his left shoulder and halfway down his arm. At the bottom, two loops opposite each other reminded me of snakes curling up and facing each other.

It was a perfect fit for him.

A flush spread across my cheeks and traveled down my throat as I dragged my gaze back up, mouth dry as the desert.

Sinewy muscles in his arms flexed as he lifted Jack out of the driver's seat, holding him in the air above his head. He spun around in a circle, laughing deeply as Jack shrieked and flailed.

Ovaries go boom.

As Cam opened the driver's door, Jase sat Jack down on the ground and yelled at my brother, but I had no idea what he said. He straightened again, dropping his hands onto his hips. His eyes squinted as he stared into the truck.

Jase was absolutely gorgeous. You couldn't say that about a lot of people in real life. Maybe celebrities or rock stars, but it was rare to see someone as stunning as he was.

His hair, the color of rich russet, was a mess of waves falling into his face. His cheekbones were broad and well defined. Lips were full and could be quite expressive. A hint of stubble shaded the strong curve of his jaw. He didn't have dimples like Cam or me, but when he did smile, he had one of the biggest, most beautiful smiles I'd ever seen on a guy.

He wasn't smiling right now.

Oh no, he was staring into the truck, head cocked to the side.

Parched as I was, I took a sip of the sweet tea as I stared through the windshield, absolutely enthralled by all the baby-making potential on display before me. Not that I was in the way of making babies, but I could totally get behind some practice runs.

6

Cam made a face. 'Dude, that's his drink.'

'Sorry.' I flushed, lowering the cup. Not that it mattered. Wasn't like Jase and I hadn't swapped spit before.

On the other side of the windshield, Jase mouthed the word *shit* and spun around. Was he going to run away? Oh hell to the no. I had his sweet tea!

In a hurry, I unhooked my seat belt and pushed open the door. My foot slipped out of my flip-flop, and because Cam just had to have a redneck truck, one that was several feet off the ground, there was a huge difference between where I was and where the ground was.

I used to be graceful. Hell, I *was* a dancer—a trained, damn good dancer and I had the kind of balance that would make gymnasts go green with envy, but that was before the torn ACL, before the fateful jump had put my hopes of becoming a professional dancer on hold. Everything—my dreams, my goals, and my future—had been paused, as if God hit a red button on the remote control of life.

And I was about to eat dirt in less than a second.

I reached out to catch the door but came up short. The foot that was going to touch the ground first was connected to my bum leg, and it wouldn't hold my weight. I was going to crash and burn in front of Jase and end up with tea all over my head.

As I started to fall, I hoped I landed on my face, because at least then I wouldn't have to see the look on his face.

Out of nowhere, two arms shot out and hands landed on my shoulders. One second I was horizontal, halfway out of the truck, and the next I was vertical. My feet dangled in the air for a second and then I was standing, clutching the cup of tea to my chest.

'Good God, you're going to break your neck.' A deep voice rumbled through me, causing the tiny hairs on my body to rise. 'Are you okay?'

I was more than okay. My head tilted to the side. I was up close and personal with the most perfect chest I'd ever seen. I watched a bead of sweat trickle down the center of his chest and then over the cut abs, disappearing among the fine hairs trailing up from the center of his stomach. Those hairs formed a line that continued under the band of his jeans.

Cam hurried around the front of the truck. 'Did you hurt your leg, Teresa?'

I hadn't been this close to Jase for a year and he smelled wonderful—like man and a faint trace of cologne. I lifted my gaze, realizing that my sunglasses had fallen off.

Thick lashes framed eyes that were a startling shade of gray. The first time I'd seen them, I had asked if they were real. Jase had laughed and offered to let me poke around in his eyes to find out.

He wasn't laughing right now.

Our gazes locked, and the intensity in his stare robbed me of breath. My skin felt scorched, like I'd been standing out in the sun all day.

I swallowed, willing my brain to start working. 'I have your sweet tea.'

Jase's brows crept up his forehead.

'Did you hit your head?' Cam asked, coming to stand beside us.

Heat flooded my cheeks. 'No. Maybe. I don't know.' Holding out the tea, I forced a smile, hoping it didn't come across creepy. 'Here.'

Jase let go of my arms and took the tea, and I wished I hadn't been so eager to shove the tea in his face, because maybe then he'd still be holding me. 'Thanks. You sure you're okay?'

'Yes,' I muttered, glancing down. My sunglasses were by the tire. Sighing, I picked them up and cleaned them off

8

before slipping them back on. 'Thanks for . . . um, catching me.'

He stared at me a moment and then turned as Jack ran up to him, holding out a shirt. 'I got it!' the little boy said, waving the shirt like a flag.

'Thanks.' Jase took the shirt and handed over the tea. He ruffled the boy's head and then, much to my disappointment, pulled the shirt on over his head, covering up that body of his. He looked at Cam. 'I didn't know Teresa was with you.'

A chill skated over my skin in spite of the heat.

'I was out showing her the town so she knows her way around,' Cam explained, grinning at the little tyke, who was slowly creeping toward me. 'She's never been down here before.'

Jase nodded and then took back the tea. There was a good chance that Jack had drunk half of it in that short amount of time. Jase started to walk toward the barn. I was dismissed. Just like that. The back of my throat burned, but I ignored it, wishing I had kept the tea.

'You and Avery coming to the party tonight, right?' Jase asked, taking a sip of the tea.

'It's the luau. We're not missing that.' Cam grinned, revealing the dimple in his left cheek. 'You guys need help setting it up?'

Jase shook his head. 'The newbies are in charge of that.' He glanced over at me, and I thought for a second that he'd ask if I was coming. 'I've got a few things to take care of here first and then I'm heading back home.'

The stinging disappointment rose swiftly, mixing with the burn in my throat. I opened my mouth, but immediately snapped it shut. What could I say in front of my brother?

A small hand tugged on the hem of my shirt and I looked down, into gray eyes that were both young and soulful.

'Hi,' Jack said.

My lips stretched into a small grin. 'Hi to you.'

'You're pretty,' he said, blinking.

'Thank you.' A little laugh escaped me. It was official. I liked this kid. 'You're very handsome.'

Jack beamed. 'I know.'

I laughed again. This boy was definitely Jase's little brother.

'All right, that's enough, Casanova.' Jase finished off the tea and tossed it into a nearby garbage can. 'Stop hitting on the girl.'

He ignored Jase, sticking out his hand. 'I'm Jack.'

I took the little hand in mine. 'I'm Teresa. Cam's my brother.'

Jack motioned me down with his chubby finger and whispered, 'Cam doesn't know how to saddle a horse.'

I glanced over at the boys. They were talking about the party, but Jase was watching us. Our gazes collided, and like he'd been doing ever since I started at Shepherd, he broke eye contact with a distressing level of quickness.

A pang of frustration lit up my chest as I returned my attention to Jack. 'Want to know a secret?'

'Yeah!' His smile grew big and broad.

'I don't know how to saddle a horse either. And I've never even ridden one before.'

His eyes grew as wide as the moon. 'Jase!' he bellowed, spinning toward his brother. 'She's never ridden a horse before!'

Well, there went my secret.

Jase glanced at me, and I shrugged. 'It's true. They scare the crap out of me.'

'They shouldn't. They're pretty chill animals. You'd probably like it.'

'You should show her!' Jack rushed up to Jase,

10

practically latching himself onto his pants legs. 'You could teach her like you teached me!'

My heart lurched in my chest, partially at the proposition of Jase teaching me anything and due to my fear of those dinosaurs. Some people feared snakes or spiders. Or ghosts or zombies. I feared horses. Seemed like a legit fear considering a horse could stomp you to death.

'It's "taught" not "teached," and I'm sure Tess has got better things to do than ride around on a horse.'

Tess. I sucked in a breath. It was his nickname for me—the only person who ever called me that, but I didn't mind it. Not at all. While Jack demanded to know why I had told him my name was Teresa and Jase explained that Tess was a nickname, I was sucked back into the memory of the last time he'd called me that.

'You have no idea what you make me want,' he said, his lips brushing my cheek, sending shivers down my spine. 'You have no fucking clue, Tess.'

'Mind if I use the john before we get out of here? I've got to get back,' Cam said. 'I promised Avery dinner before the party.'

'I'll show you,' announced Jack, grabbing Cam's hand.

Jase arched a dark brow. 'I'm sure he knows where the bathroom is.'

'It's okay.' Cam waved him off. 'Come on, little bud, lead the way.'

The two of them headed off toward the farmhouse, and we were officially alone. A hummingbird took flight in my chest, bouncing around like it was going to peck its way out of me as a warm breeze picked up, stirring the hairs that had escaped my ponytail.

Jase watched Cam and Jack jog over the patchy green grass like a man watching the last life preserver being taken as the *Titanic* started to sink. Well, that was sort of offensive,

11

as if being alone with me was equivalent to drowning while being nom nom'd on by cookie cutter sharks.

I folded my arms across my chest, pursing my lips. Irritation pricked at my skin, but his obvious discomfort smarted like a bitch. It hadn't always been like this. And it definitely had been better between us, at least up until the night he'd kissed me.

'How's the leg?'

The fact that he'd spoken startled me, and I stuttered, 'Uh, it's not too bad. Barely hurts anymore.'

'Cam told me about it when it happened. Sorry to hear that. Seriously.' He paused, squinting as the line of his jaw tightened. 'When can you get back to dancing?'

I shifted my weight. 'I don't know. I hope soon, as long as my doctor clears me. So fingers crossed.'

Jase's brows knitted. 'Fingers are crossed for you. Still, it sucks. I know how much dancing means to you.'

All I could do was nod, affected more than I should've been by the genuine sympathy in his voice.

His gray eyes finally made their way back to mine, and I sucked in a breath. His eyes . . . they never failed to stun me into stupidity or make me want to do crazy-insane things. Right now his eyes were a deep gray, like thunderclouds.

Jase wasn't happy.

Thrusting a hand through his damp hair, he exhaled deeply. A muscle in his jaw began to tick. The irritation inside me turned into something messy, causing the burn in the back of my throat to move up to my eyes. I had to keep telling myself that he didn't know—that there was no way he could've known and that the way I was feeling, the hurt and the brutal wound of rejection, wasn't his fault. I was just Cam's little sister; the reason why Cam had gotten into so much trouble almost four years ago and why Jase

12

had started making the trip to our home every weekend. I was just a stolen kiss. That was all.

I started to turn, to go wait in the truck for Cam before I did something embarrassing, like crying all over myself. My emotions had been all over the place since I injured my leg, and seeing Jase wasn't helping.

'Tess. Wait.' Jase crossed the distance between us in one step with his long legs. Stopping close enough that his worn sneakers almost brushed my toes, he reached out toward me, his hand lingering by my cheek. He didn't touch me, but the heat from his hand branded my skin. 'We need to talk.'

Chapter 2

The piece of hair that Jase had reached for blew across my cheek untouched as those words hung between us. My stomach dipped like it did those seconds before I stepped out onto the stage. Fear had always formed an icy ball in the center of my chest when I stopped before the judges and poised, waiting for the music to begin. No matter how many competitions I had entered or how many recitals I performed in, there had always been a second when I wanted nothing more than to run off the stage.

But I hadn't run away all those times and it was the same with Jase. I wasn't going to run from this conversation. Long ago, I had been a coward. Too scared to tell the truth about what Jeremy—the ex-boyfriend from hell—had been doing. I wasn't that girl anymore. I wasn't a coward anymore.

I took a deep breath. 'You're right. We do need to talk.'

Jase lowered his hand as he glanced over his shoulder, toward the house. Without saying a word, he placed a hand between my shoulder blades. Unprepared for the contact, I jumped and then flushed.

'Walk with me?'

'Sure.' The hummingbird was back with a vengeance, pecking a hole through my chest.

We didn't end up walking that far as we were still in plain view of the house. With all this land, I figured there were places that offered more privacy, but he steered me to the nearby split-rail fence surrounding the pasture opposite the field where the horses grazed.

'Sit?' he asked, and before I could say standing was fine, his large hands settled around my hips. I gasped as he lifted me up like I weighed no more than his little brother and sat me on the top rail. 'This has to be better for your knee.'

'My knee—'

'You shouldn't be standing around.' He folded his arms.

I gripped the rough wood, only relenting because the last thing I wanted to do was talk about my knee. He didn't say anything as he stared at me and I wanted to sit there mute, forcing him to broach the subject.

My silence lasted all of five seconds before I blurted out the first thing that came to my mind. 'It's stupid.'

'What?' He frowned.

'The name of the town.'

He knocked the longer strands of brown hair out of his face. 'You're mad over the name of the town?'

'Is Spring Mills even a town? You kind of live in Spring Mills, right?' At Jase's confused stare, I shrugged. 'I mean, isn't it really just Hedgesville or Falling Waters? Just because you build a super Walmart, that doesn't make it a town.'

Jase stared at me a moment longer and then he laughed deeply—the sound rich and yummy. God help me, but I loved it when he laughed like that. No matter how irritated I was with him or how badly I wanted to karate kick him between the legs, when he laughed, it was like the sun was shining in my eyes.

He leaned against the fence and as tall as he was, we were at eye level as he reached over, draping an arm over my shoulders. He tugged me in close—close enough that if I lifted my head, our mouths would be inches apart. My heart literally did several pliés in my chest. If talking about fake towns and Walmarts got him in the hugging mood, I'd start naming other places like Darksville and Shanghai and—

'Sometimes I don't think you're right in the head.' He squeezed me as he dropped his chin to the top of my head, and my breath caught in my throat. 'But I like that—I like you. I really do. Not sure what that says about me.'

Pliés? My heart was now a ninja. Maybe this conversation wasn't going to make me want to go rock in the corner. I relaxed. 'That you're awesome?'

He chuckled as his hand slid down my spine and then was gone. He hoisted himself up beside me. 'Yeah, something like that.' There was a stretch of silence and then his gaze settled on me again. His eyes were almost a pale blue now. 'I do like you,' he repeated, voice softer. 'And that makes it so much harder to figure this out. I don't know where to really start, Tess.'

The ninja in my heart keeled over dead. But I had a good idea of where he could start. How about why he hadn't returned a single e-mail or text since that night a year ago? Or why he stopped coming home with Cam? I didn't get the chance to ask those questions.

'I'm sorry,' he said, and I blinked as the air went out of my lungs. 'What happened between us? It shouldn't have, and I am so very fucking sorry.'

My mouth opened, but I couldn't make a sound. He was sorry? It felt like he'd punched me in the chest because to be sorry meant he *regretted* what he'd done. I didn't regret it, not one bit. That kiss . . . the way he had kissed me

16

proved to me that there really was a such thing as uncontrollable attraction, that yearning for more could be painful in the most delicious way, and that there really were such things as sparks flying when lips touched. Regret it? I'd lived off that kiss, holding it up high and comparing everyone in the past, which was not many, and everyone after him, which was even fewer, to *that* kiss he regretted.

'I'd been drinking that night,' he continued, that muscle in his jaw thrumming along with my heartbeat. 'I was drunk.'

I snapped my mouth shut as those three words sunk in. 'You were drunk?'

He looked away, thrusting his hand through his hair again as he squinted. 'I didn't know what I was doing.'

A horrible twisty feeling coiled in my tummy. It was the same feeling when I had come down from my jump wrong. That horrifying, sinking sensation that had been a warning before the burst of pain that had come next. 'You drank like two beers that night.'

'Two?' He wouldn't look at me. 'Ah, I know it had to be more than that.'

'Had to be?' My voice squeaked as a different kind of emotion started to fester inside of me. 'I remember that night *clearly*, Jase. You barely drank two beers. You were not drunk.'

Jase didn't say anything, but his jaw worked like he was about to crack his molars as I stared at him. Apologizing was bad enough, but claiming he was drunk? That was the worst kind of rejection.

'You're basically saying you wouldn't have kissed me if you hadn't been drinking?' I slid off the fence and faced him, resisting the urge to plant my fist in his stomach. He opened his mouth, but I rushed on. 'Was it really that disgusting to you?'

17

His head swung toward me sharply and something flared in his gray eyes, darkening the hue. 'That's not what I'm saying. It wasn't gross. It was—'

'Damn straight it wasn't gross!' There were a lot of moments in my life when Cam would tell me that I didn't have the common sense to keep my mouth shut. This was cooking up to be one of those moments. '*You* kissed me. *You* touched me. *You* said I had no idea what I made *you*—'

'I know what I said.' His eyes flashed an angry quicksilver now. He looked me dead on as he hopped off the fence with the kind of grace that was almost predatory. 'I just don't know why I said those things. It had to have been the beer, because there is no other reason why I would've done or said any of those things!'

A red-hot burn replaced the hurt. My hands closed into fists. No—no way did two beers make him do those things. 'You're not a lightweight. You'd been in full control of yourself. And you had to have felt something when you kissed me, because you couldn't kiss like that and not feel anything.' The moment those words jumped off my tongue, my heart lurched. Thinking that was one thing, but saying it out loud showed how . . . how *naive* the words sounded.

'You've had a crush on me for how long? Of course you'd think it meant something amazing. Jesus Christ, Tess, why do you think I haven't talked to you this entire time? I knew you would think there was more behind it,' he said, and heat poured across my cheeks. 'It was a mistake. I'm not attracted to you, not like that.'

I jerked back as if I'd been slapped. And God knows I knew what it felt like to be slapped. Part of me would've taken that over this. I should have run when he said he needed to talk. Or at least limped back to the truck. Screw being brave and confrontational. Hurt and embarrassment crawled up my throat, filling my eyes. Apparently, I was as transparent as a window, so I was thankful for the sunglasses hiding my emotions, but he must've seen something in my expression, because he closed his eyes briefly.

'Shit,' he cursed low, the skin around his lips a shade paler. 'I didn't mean it like that. I—'

'I think you did,' I snapped, taking another step back. Jase was right. That night had been a mistake—a stupid kiss that I had attached feelings to and built up in my head during his absence. I don't think I'd ever felt more foolish than I did in this moment. 'You couldn't be any more clear.'

He cursed again as he crossed the distance between us, dipping his chin and causing several locks of waves to tumble forward. 'Tess, you don't understand—'

I barked out a short laugh as mortification burst through me like a dam breaking. 'Oh, I'm sure I understand completely. You regret it. Got it. It was a mistake. You probably don't want to be reminded of it. My bad. And it doesn't matter. Whatever.' I was rambling, but I couldn't stop myself from trying to save face in the worst possible way, and as I went on, I didn't look at him. I couldn't, so I focused on his grass-stained sneakers. 'It's not like I'm going to be here for long anyway. As soon as my knee is cleared, I'm out. And that will be sooner than later. So you don't have to worry about running into me for long or me bringing any of this up again. It's not like you're the only guy that's—'

'Kissed you?' At the sharpness in his tone, I looked up. His eyes were narrowed until only thin, silvery slits were visible. 'How many guys have you kissed, Teresa?'

Not many. I could count on one hand and only needed two fingers to count how many went beyond that, but pride had sunk its claws in me. 'Enough,' I said, crossing my arms. 'More than enough.'

'Really?' Something flashed across his face. 'Does your brother know this?'

I snorted. 'As if I would talk to my brother about that. Or like he actually has a say on whom or *where* I put my lips.'

'Where?' he repeated, head cocked to the side as if he had to work that single word through his mind. The moment he decided on what that could possibly mean, his broad shoulders stiffened. 'Where are you putting your lips?'

'Uh, like that's any of your business.'

His stare sharpened. 'It's totally my business.'

Did he live in an alternate universe? 'I don't think so.'

'Tess—'

'Don't call me that,' I snapped, sucking in a deep breath. Jase reached for me, and I easily dodged his grasp. The last thing I needed was him touching me. Determination settled into his striking features. 'Where are you—?'

The door to the front of the house slammed shut behind us, saving me. Jase stepped back, drawing in a deep breath as his little brother raced across the grass and gravel.

From about four feet away, the little boy launched himself at Jase, screaming, 'Superman cape! Superman cape!'

He caught Jack and slung him around, latching his little brother's arms around his neck. Jack hung down his back, sort of like a flesh cape.

'Sorry it took so long.' Cam grinned, unaware of what felt like unbearable tension to me. 'Your mom had lemonade. And applesauce cake. Had to get me some of that.'

Jase smiled, but ducked his chin at the same time. 'Understandable.'

I stood there like a statue. A bird could've pooped on my head and I wouldn't have moved. My fingers felt numb from how hard I was clenching my hands.

As Jase turned to the side, Jack smiled at me. 'Are you going to learn to ride?'

I didn't realize what he was talking about at first, but

when I did, I didn't know what to say. I doubted Jase wanted to see my face on this farm again, even if I had the lady balls to get on one of those things.

Cam was staring at me, brows raised, Jase was staring at the ground, his jaw tense, and Jack was waiting for me to answer.

'I don't know,' I said finally, voice hoarse. Willing myself not to make more of a fool out of myself, I forced a smile. 'But if I do, you're going to help me learn, right?'

'Yes!' Jack beamed. 'I can teached you!'

'Teach,' Jase murmured, hooking his arms around Jack's legs. 'Like I said, little bud, she's probably got better things to do.'

'Nothing is better than riding a horse,' Jack argued.

Holding on to his brother, Jase straightened and glanced at me. His expression was shuttered, and I wished I hadn't mentioned the horseback riding. Jase probably thought I was being serious and trying to find a way to see him.

After this, I honestly never wanted to see his face again.

That hurt to realize I felt that way. Before the kiss, we had become friends—good friends. Texting. E-mailing. Talking whenever he came with Cam. And now that was ruined.

I will not cry. I will not cry. That was my personal mantra as I shuffled back to the truck and climbed in, using my good leg to propel me up. *I will not cry over the jerk.* I also told myself to stop staring at Jase, but I watched him with his brother up until mine returned.

'You ready to head back?' Cam asked as he closed the driver's door.

'Ready.' My voice was unnaturally thick.

He glanced at me as he turned the ignition. He frowned. 'Are you okay?'

'Yeah,' I said, and cleared my throat. 'It's allergies.'

The doubtful look on his face was expected. I didn't have allergies. My brother knew that.

Cam dropped me off in front of the West Woods complex. After asking him to tell Avery I said hi, I *carefully* exited the truck and headed up the narrow walkway toward Yost Hall as I dug out my key card.

I'd gotten lucky with the dorm situation. Because I was a late registration, all the rooms in Kenamond Hall and Gardiner Hall, dorms usually reserved for freshmen, were full. I almost didn't get a dorm. The day before classes had begun, I showed up at the residential life department, praying they could put me somewhere—*anywhere*. My only other option was to live with Cam, and as much as I loved my brother, rooming with him was the last thing I wanted.

Tears were shed. Some strings were pulled, and I ended up in a West Woods suite-style residence hall, which was so much better than the tiny matchboxes called rooms in the other halls.

Using my card, I slipped into the cool air and headed for the stairwell. I could've taken the elevator to the third floor, but I figured the walking and climbing were good for my leg since I hadn't been okayed to really do anything more active. I would be soon, though. I had to be, because if I was going to get back into the studio in the spring, I needed to get my ass back in shape.

I was panting by the time I reached the door leading to my suite. It blew my mind how my body went from being the Terminator to Sponge Bob in such a short period of time.

Sighing, I swiped the card and stepped into the living room of the suite. I wanted nothing more than to climb into bed, shove my head under the pillow, and pretend today never happened.

But that would be asking for too much.

I blew out a breath when I saw the hot pink scarf dangling from the doorknob to the bedroom. Closing my eyes, I groaned.

Pink scarves were code word for enter at your own risk. In other words, my roommate was getting some sweet, sweet lovin'. Or they were inside quietly fighting, and if they were quietly fighting, they would soon be loudly fighting.

At least I still had access to the bathroom.

I hobbled over to the worn brown couch and plopped down with the grace of a pregnant mountain ram, dropping my purse beside me. Kicking my bum leg up on the coffee table, I stretched out, hoping to relieve the dull ache in my knee.

A thump on the other side of the wall caused me to jump. I glanced over my shoulder, frowning at the wall. No more than a second later, a muffled moan raised the hairs on the back of my neck.

It didn't sound like a happy moan on the verge of the big O kind of moan. Not that I knew what that sounded like. The few times I had sex ultimately ended with me cursing every romance book out there that led me to believe I'd be sailing through the clouds. But it didn't sound right.

Keeping my leg on the table, I stretched up, straining to hear what was going on in the room. Debbie Lamb, my roomie, was a junior and seemed like a really sweet girl. She hadn't crucified me for ruining what would've most likely been a semester not sharing a room until I showed up, and she was really smart and quiet.

But her boyfriend was a different story.

A few seconds passed, and I heard a very distinctive male grunt. Cheeks burning, I whipped around so fast I almost gave myself whiplash. Grabbing a pillow, I shoved it over my face.

They were most definitely having sex.

And I was sitting out here listening to them like a creeper.

'Oh God.' My voice was muffled. 'Why am I in college?'

A dull pain flared in my knee as a reminder.

Slowly, I lowered the pillow. The door across from me, leading to the other bedroom that shared the suite, remained closed. I hadn't seen our suitemates, not once, since I started school. I was partially convinced that they were invisible or were llamas or under the witness relocation program, forced to hide in their rooms. I knew they weren't dead because I heard them sometimes while I was in the living room. They always quieted when they heard me moving around in the suite.

Weird.

Propping the tan pillow against my chest, I reached into my purse and pulled out my cell phone. I briefly considered texting Sadi, but I hadn't spoken to her since I left the dance studio in July. I hadn't spoken to any of my friends since then.

Most of them were in New York City. Sadi was starting at the Joffrey School of Ballet, the same school I had a full scholarship to attend. They were living my life—my dream. But the scholarship hadn't been canceled. The instructors had placed it on hold, promising me a spot next fall if my injury was healed.

I dropped my phone back in my purse and then leaned back, holding the pillow close. Dr. Morgan, the specialist at WVU who'd done my surgery, believed I had a ninety percent chance of healing completely, as long as I didn't suffer another injury. Most people would think those were good odds, but that ten percent scared the crap out of me, and I refused to even consider it.

Forty-some minutes passed before the bedroom door opened, and Debbie stepped into the suite, running a hand

24

through her shoulder-length brown hair, smoothing the ends down. She saw me, and her face flushed red.

Debbie cringed. 'Oh! You haven't been out here too long?'

'No. Just a couple of minutes . . .' I trailed off, taking a closer look at Debbie while she straightened the hem of her floral blouse. Her eyes were red and puffy. They'd been fighting. Again. They must've made up, but they fought so much I wondered how they had any time for anything other than arguing and makeup sex.

Erik appeared, his fingers flying over the screen of his cell. His short, dark hair stuck straight up. He was good-looking, I'd give him that, but I didn't understand his appeal. At all. He was big in the frat that Jase belonged to, was somewhat of a local basketball star during his high school years, but he had the personality of a cornered hyena.

Sliding his phone into his jeans pocket, he smiled at me, but it was a nervous smile, one that made me antsy.

'Are you okay?' I asked her.

'Of course she is,' Erik answered, laughing.

I stared at her pointedly, ignoring him, but she nodded quickly. 'Yeah, I'm perfect. We're going to get something to eat before we head to the party. You want to come?'

My mouth opened, but then Erik also answered for me. 'She looks like her knee is bothering her, so she probably wants to stay here.'

I snapped my mouth shut.

Debbie looked uncomfortable as Erik started to usher her toward the door. 'You coming to the party?'

I hadn't really been invited, but I knew if I showed up, no one would say anything—no one except Jase, and I didn't want to see him. I shrugged. 'I'm not sure yet.'

She lingered. 'Okay, well—'

25

'Babe, come on, I'm fucking hungry.' Erik grabbed her arm, causing the flesh under his fingers to indent. 'It's getting late.'

A low burn started in my stomach as I looked at that grip. How many times had Jeremy grabbed me like that? Too many to count. Seeing that made me feel nauseated. Made me want to think about things best left forgotten.

Debbie's wobbly smile faltered. 'Text me if you want . . . or need anything.'

Erik grumbled something under his breath, and then they were gone. And I was sitting there, with my leg propped up on the coffee table, staring at the door, but my thoughts had skipped back a couple of years.

'You know I'm fucking hungry,' Jeremy said, leaning over and grabbing my upper arm. He squeezed until I cried out. The car suddenly felt entirely too small. There wasn't enough air. 'What were you doing that took so long? Talking on the phone?'

'No!' I knew to remain still, to not pull away, because that only made him madder. 'I was only talking to Cam.'

He relaxed, his fingers loosening their hold. 'He's home?'

I shook my head. 'I was talking to him—'

'On the phone?' In a second, his features turned from cute to monstrous. I winced as his fingers dug in through my sweater. 'I thought you weren't on the phone?'

I shook myself out of the memory, happy to discover that all I felt was the residual anger. For the longest time, I would get sick to my stomach even thinking about him, but those days had long since passed.

Jeremy had been an abuser, but I was no longer a victim.

I was over what he'd done to me. Over. Over. Over.

Pulling my gaze away from the door, I squeezed the pillow until my arms ached. I didn't have proof that Erik was hurting Debbie, more like a sixth sense about it, and I knew that most bruises wouldn't be visible. Not if Erik was smart, like Jeremy had been.

26

I spent the rest of the evening eating out of the vending machine from down the hall and thumbing through my history text before crashing early. As I lay there, floating in the la-la land of almost sleep, I felt pretty damn lame. Here I was, a few months shy from turning nineteen, it was a Saturday night, and I was almost asleep before ten.

Lame didn't even cover it.

Rolling onto my side, facing the wall, I drifted off to sleep wondering if Jase's rejection would've hurt so badly if I hadn't ruined my leg.

The ding from my cell phone sounded far away when it woke me some time later. I blinked my eyes open, confused. Green light from the clock on the nightstand flashed a quarter after one in the morning. The ding came again.

Smacking around until I reached my cell, I picked it up and squinted at the message. I read it once. Thought I was still dreaming. Read it twice. Thought I forgot how to read. Then I sat up, blinking the sleep from my eyes. The dark room came into focus enough for me to see that the bed on the other side of the room was empty. I looked down at the phone again.

I need to talk to u

It was from Jase.

The second text read *I'm outside*, and my heart sped up. Jase was here.

Chapter 3

I had to be dreaming.

At least that was how it felt as I found my flip-flops, slipped them on, and then grabbed my key card. For a brief moment I considered ignoring his text, but my body seemed to have a mind of its own.

I was definitely going to want to karate-chop myself in the morning for this.

As I left my suite, I began to fear that this was some kind of joke because how did Jase know which dorm I was in? Even if he knew it was in West Woods, there were six buildings that made up the complex. I doubted he'd asked Cam.

My stomach dipped and twisted into complicated little knots as I walked down the stairs, clutching the railing. Darkness seeped in from the windows on the landing. Maybe I was really dreaming and this would become a nightmare. The railing would turn into a snake—God, I *hated* snakes—total Beetlejuice style.

Cringing, I pulled my hand away from the smooth metal of the railing and limped my way to the first floor. The lobby was silent with the exception of the soft hum and whirl of a dryer located in laundry services.

As I stepped into the night, tiny bumps spread over my flesh. I wished I'd had the foresight to grab a cardigan. There was a surprising chill to the night air.

I stopped on the porch, clutching the key card until it left little indents in my hand as I scanned the walkway and trees lining the path. All the benches were empty. There was no one out here. Besides the chirps of crickets, the only sound was distant laughter and faint music, punctuated every so many seconds with a happy shout.

My heart turned over heavily as I stepped off the porch, pushing my hair out of my face with my free hand. This was a joke. Or maybe he meant to text someone else and was waiting outside of her dorm. My skin prickled at the thought of him texting any other girl at one in the morning, which was stupid.

I shuffled several feet down the walkway, peering between the trees and thick hedges. The hollows of my cheeks started to burn as I stopped in the middle of the pathway. I shifted my weight from my aching leg to the other. What was I doing out here? I didn't even bring my phone with me. It had to be a mistake or a joke or a—

A thick shadow broke free from under the trees, moving between the hedges. The form was tall and solid and as it stepped into the pillar of light cast from the lamppost, my mouth dropped open. It *was* Jase, but what was he doing back there? As he turned toward me, his hands left the zipper area of his jeans. Oh my God.

'Jase?' I hissed, hurrying the rest of the way toward him.

His chin lifted at the sound of my voice. 'There you are.' He said it like he'd been waiting forever and a day for me. One side of his lips kicked up. 'You're here.'

There was a flutter in my chest at the sight of his half smile. Recalling what he had said to me earlier helped me ignore the dumbass butterfly in my chest. 'Were you just peeing?'

The half grin spread. 'I had to use the bathroom.'

'In a bush?'

'Someone needed to water it.'

My lips twitched as I stared up at him. The unruly mop of hair fell across his forehead, brushing the edges of his eyes. The old, vintage style T-shirt he wore stretched across his broad shoulders and chest. As he lifted his hand to push his hair back, he revealed a slice of skin between his low-hanging jeans and his shirt. Rock-hard abs peeked out.

I averted my gaze because that was the last thing I needed to be staring at. 'You're drunk.'

'Ah . . .' He swayed to the left like there was some kind of invisible gravitational pull I was unaware of. 'I wouldn't go as far as to say I am drunk. Maybe a little buzzing.'

I arched a brow as he wavered to the right. That's when I noticed the little pink box on the bench. 'Is that yours?'

He followed my gaze and then grinned. 'Shit. I forgot about it. Brought you a present.'

My brows shot up as he leaned over, nearly falling on his face before catching himself at the last moment, and picked up the box. 'What is it?'

He handed it over. 'Something as yummy as me.'

I snorted out a very attractive laugh as I looked down. Through the clear plastic top I could make out a huge, oversized cupcake. I glanced at Jase.

One shoulder went up in a shrug. 'Cupcakes are good. Thought I'd be good and share with you.'

'Thank you.' I pried open the box and dipped my pinkie in the icing. Tasting it, I nearly moaned at the sweet richness.

Jase swallowed as he looked away. 'I think I'll sit down. You should too . . . you know, because of your leg.'

Like I somehow forgot that.

Jase watched me as I eased down, finding my knee stiffer than normal. 'Is your leg bothering you?'

I opened my mouth, but he rushed on. 'I didn't even think about that. You probably shouldn't be on your leg so much and—'

'I'm okay.' I took a quick bite of the cupcake. It was like a sugary orgasm in my mouth. 'Want some?'

'Hells yeah.'

I broke the cupcake in half and handed him his half. Within five seconds, he'd devoured it. I finished mine off pretty quickly and after tossing the box in a nearby trash can, I took a deep breath. 'You didn't come here just to give me a cupcake, right?'

'Ah, no.'

'What . . . what are you doing here, Jase?'

He didn't answer immediately, but when his gray gaze settled on me, his eyes were surprisingly sharp. 'I want to talk to you.'

'That much I got, but I think you said everything you wanted to say already, and you showing up here is the last thing I expected.' I felt like a bitch for throwing it out there like that, but it was true. And he sort of deserved it. I was no one's doormat.

Jase looked away as his shoulders tensed, then he came forward and sat down beside me. The smell of alcohol was faint as he looked at me. Without saying a word, he reached over and plucked up my free hand. My eyes widened as he lifted my hand, turned it over, and placed a kiss against my palm.

Yep. He was drunk.

And my skin tingled from where his lips had met, like an electrical jolt. Speechless, I watched him lower my hand back to my lap.

'I'm a jackass,' he said.

31

I blinked slowly.

'I shouldn't have said the shit that I said to you earlier. It wasn't right and I *was* lying.' He took a deep breath, shifting his gaze to the empty bench across from us. 'I wasn't drunk that night. I was far from it.'

My heart had begun pounding from the moment he kissed my hand and went up a degree as he spoke, and my voice was barely above a whisper. 'I know.'

'And I really didn't think you'd assume it meant anything because you had a crush on me or whatever.' One side of his lips tipped up again, but he had been right on that aspect. The kiss had meant everything to me. 'I just . . . I shouldn't have kissed you that night—touched you. Not because it was gross or any of that shit, but because you're Cam's little sister. You're untouchable.'

As I stared at him, the butterfly moved from my chest to my stomach. Was that Jase's problem? He felt bad because Cam was his friend. Seriously? Part of me wanted to smack him upside the head. The other part of me wanted to crawl into his lap, because if that was his big hang-up, we could work with that. Couldn't we? Or did it matter?

But I just sat there, staring at him like I had all those times he'd come to visit Cam. If I started giggling, I was going to punch myself in the face.

'The moment . . . it had gotten away from me that night, Tess. You . . . you are a beautiful girl. Always have been and, goddamnit, that hasn't changed.'

He thought I was beautiful—wait. The moment had gotten away from him? Torn between being elated and insulted, I shook my head.

'Anyway, I just wanted to say I'm sorry.' He glanced over at me, half of his face shadowed. 'And if you think I'm the biggest jackass out there, I completely understand.'

What he had said earlier still stung like I'd kicked a nest

full of hornets, but what he was saying now soothed a little of the burn. 'I don't think that.'

Jase stilled for a moment and then he twisted toward me, his head cocking to the side again. Our eyes locked, and I found that I couldn't look away. 'You're still so . . . sweet.'

Sweet? I resisted the urge to spit on the ground. Of course Jase thought I was sweet and nice and as innocent and cuddly as an old, raggedy teddy bear. Not exactly how I wanted him to see me.

He broke eye contact first, and the air leaked out of my lungs. Wetting my lips, I ran the edge of my key card over the soft flannel of my jammie bottoms. 'So you decided to come over in the middle of the night to tell me this?'

'It's not exactly the middle of the night,' he said, smiling slightly. 'More like early late night.'

My brows rose. 'That doesn't make much sense.'

'If you drank half of an eighteen-pack, it just might.'

I pursed my lips, remembering he was more than just a little buzzed. 'Why didn't you just wait until, I don't know, you were sober and the sun was out to have this conversation?'

'I couldn't wait,' he said without a moment of hesitation, so quickly that there was no doubting how important it was to him. 'And the party sucked.'

'It did?' For some reason, I couldn't picture the big luau sucking that much.

Jase nodded and his brows lowered, furrowing together. 'This . . . this has been banging around in my head. Tried to drink it out. Didn't work. Decided I needed to tell you before I developed a mean case of alcohol poisoning.'

So the party hadn't really sucked, but more of a case of him feeling guilty enough to seek me out. I didn't know what to think about that or any of this. I'd obsessed over him and was convinced at one point that I was madly, deeply in love with him. And the night when he'd kissed me, I thought . . . well, I thought a lot of stupid things. That he would wake up the next morning and profess his undying love and devotion to me in front of baby Jesus and my entire family. And everyone would be thrilled by the prospect, even Cam. That somehow a relationship between a senior in high school and a college junior could work. Jase would visit me instead of my brother every weekend and he would come to my dance recitals and visit me in New York City when I left for the ballet school and . . .

And none of that happened.

Jase and Cam had left that next morning before I even woke up, and I hadn't seen him up until I started school at Shepherd. At some point during that last year, I'd thought I'd come to terms with Jase, chalked it up to stupid, naive fantasies, and even dated a time or two, but I'd been really off about all this. I hadn't come to terms. Obviously. And seeing Jase, being near him, made me remember everything that had drawn me to him—his kindness, humor, intelligence. And even if some of those qualities weren't so apparent now, I knew they were still there. The fact that it was after one in the morning and he hunted me down to apologize was proof of that.

He leaned back, stretching out his long legs. 'Tess . . . Tess . . . Tess . . .'

'What?' I forced my gaze back to him after staring at a square hedge for far too long.

Jase was watching me again, the look on his face completely unreadable. His eyes were so bright now, almost silver, as his gaze dipped. He made a sound deep in his throat, half curse and half groan. I didn't understand it. My attention followed his, and I drew in a shaky, surprised breath.

That was about when I realized I wasn't wearing a bra, and the cooler night air and thin tank top did nothing to hide what I had going on.

And right at that moment, I had a lot going on.

My nipples were hard, pressing against the material. Heat swamped my cheeks and I started to fold my arms, but then it struck me that Jase was looking, like *really* looking. And for someone who claimed that 'the moment' got away from him . . .

Wait. He *was* drunk right now.

I folded my arms over my chest. 'What?' I demanded again.

He dragged his burning gaze up, and I swore it had lingered over my lips. 'Why did you come here? To this place?'

The question caught me off guard, and so did the way he asked it, like he'd never in a million years expected me to be here, at the same college as him. 'I . . . my leg . . .' Couldn't I speak in complete sentences? A soft wind picked up, tossing my hair around. 'I didn't know what else to do.'

'You never planned on doing the college thing, right?'

'No. Not like this.'

'So what . . .' Jase paused, catching a piece of my hair. As he tucked it back, his fingers grazed my cheek, causing a fine shiver to work its way down my spine. His hand lingered for maybe a second, and then it fell into the space between us—a space that suddenly seemed much smaller. 'What are you studying?'

It took a moment for my brain to turn over the question. 'Elementary ed.'

The corner of his lip curled up once more as he draped his right arm over the back of the bench, still facing me. 'That takes a special kind of person.'

'How so?' The major had been a last-minute thing because I hadn't planned on having a normal career. I'd opened the registration manual and basically picked one. Teaching seemed like a good, stable idea. A plan B that I didn't plan on using.

'Kids are tough, Tess, especially at that age.'

'You'd know.' I smiled as I remembered how he was with his little brother. 'But I like kids.'

A sudden shadow passed over his face. 'Yeah, look, I better get going. It's late and you probably would like to go back to sleep.' He started to lean forward but stopped. 'We're friends, right? You and I? Like . . . like before?'

Like before he'd kissed me. I steeled myself against the sudden tumbling of my heart. This was it. Even if Jase thought I was beautiful and he was attracted to me, he wasn't going to act on it. Whether it was because of Cam or something else, whatever he felt for me wasn't going to be enough. And it didn't matter. I could be friends with him. It wasn't like I planned on being here for a long time. If I was cleared, I'd finish out the semester and then head back to the studio.

Jase . . . Jase would once more become a memory.

I forced a smile. 'Yes. We're friends.'

'Good. Perfect.' His smile spread, and it was that big smile, the one that didn't lessen his beauty whatsoever, that probably had panties dropping across the nation. He stood, and I watched him stumble to the left. Jase threw his hands out, balancing himself. 'Whoa.'

When he pulled his car keys out of his pocket, I pushed to my feet. There was no pain in my knee this time. 'You're not driving.'

He shot me a look and then laughed. 'I'm fine.'

'You are not fine. You can't even stand straight.'

'Well, it's a good thing that driving doesn't require standing straight.'

My eyes widened. 'Jase . . .'

He took another stumbling step, and I caught his arm, wrapping my hand around his forearm. My fingers didn't come anywhere close to meeting. He was startled by the contact and his gaze swung toward me. So was I. The feel of his warm skin branded mine, but I took advantage of the situation.

I swiped the keys from his hand and then let go, stepping back. 'You're not driving.'

Jase didn't make a grab for the keys. 'Then what do you expect me to do? Sleep out on this bench?'

I could've suggested that he call one of his friends, but that's not what I said. 'You can stay with me.'

His eyes widened, and then he barked out a short laugh. 'Stay with you?'

I scowled. 'Yeah, what's so funny about that?'

He started to respond, but then he seemed to rethink what he was about to say. Several seconds stretched out between us. 'Cam's gonna kill me.'

'Cam will kill me if I let you drive off. Besides, there's a couch in the suite. It's not like you're sharing my bed.'

In the light of the lamppost, his eyes glimmered. The look that suddenly filled his eyes had the tips of my ears burning.

'Suite or your bed,' he said finally. 'Your brother is still gonna kill me.'

There was a slight chance that Cam might, but he'd be more pissed if I let Jase drive off. And besides, it wasn't like either of us could call Cam to come get his drunk ass. How could we explain Jase being here? 'He doesn't have to know.'

Jase didn't look convinced, but when I turned to walk back toward the entrance, he stumbled into step beside me. He was quiet as he followed me up to my dorm and opened the door to the suite.

'Debbie's not back yet.' I flipped the floor lamp on. 'She might be spending it with—'

'Erik,' Jase interrupted, looking around the small sitting room. I so doubted this was the first time he'd been in one of these suites. 'They're still at the party. Who's in the other room?'

'Don't know.' I picked up the pillow from the floor and placed it on the couch, by the arm. 'I've never seen them. I think they're vampires or something.'

He chuckled as he brushed past me and then sat on the couch. The next second he was on his back, eyes closed and chest rising and falling evenly. Wow. It must be awesome to pass out that quickly.

Sighing, I went into my room and grabbed a quilt my mom had made from off the foot of my bed and then returned to the suite. He hadn't moved by the time I came to stand between the coffee table and his long legs, but his silvery eyes were open in thin slits.

'Friends?' he murmured.

The twinge of disappointment was lost in the lurch my heart gave as he smiled up at me. I was such an idiot. Draping the quilt over him, I started to back away.

Moving faster than I thought a drunk guy could move, he grabbed my wrist, holding me in place with a surprisingly gentle grip. 'Tess?' he said, eyes heavily hooded. 'Are we friends?'

My breath caught as his thumb moved in a slow, idle circle right under my palm. The slight touch did crazy things to my brain, completely shorting it out. 'Yes. We're friends.'

'Good,' he said, repeating what he'd spoken outside. 'Perfect.'

He didn't let go, but tugged me down until my hip was resting on the couch beside his. So many thoughts whirled

38

around, and I had no idea why I said what I did next. 'How did you know what dorm I was in?'

'I have my ways.' His hand slid up my arm, stopping just below my elbow, where his thumb moved over the sensitive skin there.

What was he doing? I was pretty sure friends didn't do this. I sure as hell didn't with my guy friends. But I really didn't have a lot of guy friends, just a few from the studio. And Jase didn't touch me like this before. Not even in the seconds before he'd kissed me. We'd been talking and I'd hugged him good night, but when I pulled back, he had held on and . . . the moment had gotten away from him. Was the moment going to get away from us again? He was drunk. It was quite possible and I knew I should pull away for a hundred different reasons, but I didn't.

And that made me a stupid girl.

I still didn't move away.

The smooth circling of his thumb sent little jolts of awareness through me. An ache filled my breasts and moved lower through my body. My lips parted of their own accord. God, I knew better. Honestly I did, but I had never, ever responded this way to a simple touch. I hadn't even known it was possible for my insides to twist up in such delicious knots from a thumb on the inside of my elbow.

'Friends,' he murmured again, and then he pulled me down.

Pulse pounding, I didn't resist. The very idea didn't even cross my mind as his head tilted up and his warm breath danced over my lips and then my cheek. I shivered when his chest rose, brushing mine.

A deep emotion sparked in my chest, and it tasted like panic. Self-control came out of nowhere. A will that surprised me was born, and I pulled away before I really did turn into a doormat that had WELCOME tattooed on my forehead.

Jase held on as I jerked up, rising into a sitting position. The combination of me being off balance, him being drunk, and poor leverage didn't mingle well with the quilt I had so nicely draped over him. Somehow he got his legs tangled in it. I stepped back and bumped into the coffee table. He kept moving as he pulled me down, half rolling, half sitting up. We tumbled right off the couch.

I hit the floor on my back and Jase's weight came down on me, pushing the air out of my lungs. A moment passed and then I blinked open my eyes. I was plastered to the carpet, unable to move my legs or my arms.

'Oh my God,' I managed to squeak out. 'Are you dead?'

He laughed deeply as he planted his hands on either side of my arms and lifted his upper body off mine. Air rushed into my lungs. 'No. Holy wow . . . are you okay?'

'Yeah. You?'

His thick, dark lashes lowered and he grinned. 'I don't know. I think I broke you.'

'I asked if you were okay,' I clarified in a voice that sounded strange in my ears. His weight and proximity had blood thundering through my veins. 'Breaking me has nothing to do with that.'

'I'm more concerned about you, but you did break my fall. How sweet of you, Tess.' He chuckled, and dear Lord, I knew he was three sheets to the wind and then some, and damnit, did he have to be an adorable albeit clumsy drunk? Wiggling to get my arms free, he shifted and our bodies ended up pressed together in all the ways that counted. I stilled when a raw, sexy sound rumbled up from his chest. My gaze lifted, meeting his. Neither of us moved. Neither of us spoke. His lips parted on a quick, shallow inhale. My chest rose against his in a deep, shaky breath. I felt him through my thin bottoms, right where he was hardening between my thighs. There was no mistaking it, no hiding his length and thickness.

A sweet and heady burn crawled over my body. Several points in my body throbbed acutely as he stared down at me. Entranced, I watched his eyes turn to a molten silver. Several shivers ran down my spine. The throbbing was intensifying in the very center of me, spreading through my limbs.

There was a slight, unfocused quality to his eyes, and I again told myself he was drunk, but that knowledge did nothing to dampen my arousal or the heat in his gaze.

'This . . . this is unexpected,' he said in a voice that stretched my nerve endings. 'Tess, I . . .' His eyes closed, and he let out a deep breath. 'You feel good under me, too good.'

My heart skipped a beat and then picked up. His words stirred up the kind of lust I had little experience with or understanding of. All I knew was that I wanted to wrap myself around him and hold on tight.

'Good isn't the right word. Maybe perfect?' He sounded almost like he was talking to himself. 'Fuck,' he growled, and then his hips rolled in a slow thrust, pressing against the part where I ached the most. My toes curled and I gasped. A tremble coursed through his large body. 'Do you believe in fate?'

The question came out of left field, but it didn't cut through the haze building in my head. 'I don't know,' I whispered. 'Do you?'

'I mean, do you believe that some things are just meant to happen?' he murmured as he dropped his head and his lips brushed my neck. Another strangled gasp parted my lips. 'Like no matter what you do, what you tell yourself,

41

things are just going to happen? Some things I don't think you can stop.'

My body overran my brain, losing what he was saying, and I wasn't even sure he knew what he was saying. My right arm was free and I lifted my hand slowly, resting my fingers against the cool, silky strands of his hair.

His lips grazed my skin again and then the tip of his tongue flicked over my pulse. I jerked, causing our lower halves to press together. He kissed the same spot, nipping at my skin gently enough that it would not bruise, but the sensation was a riot inside me.

'You never knew.' He shifted his weight onto one arm and his hand curved along my cheek, tilting my head back.

A thunder was in my veins, as dangerous as a summer storm. 'Never knew what?'

Jase shook his head as the rough pad of his thumb rubbed along my bottom lip. 'I didn't always . . . come up to see Cam. He wasn't the only reason why I made that trip every weekend.' As shock shot through me, he laughed and then closed his eyes. 'I came up to see you. Makes me a bastard, really. How old were you? Sixteen? Fuck me.'

Those words mixed with the feel of *him* were like an explosion, but there was little time to internalize and obsess over their meaning or to even question it. His head lowered and my body tensed. He was going to kiss me and I wasn't going to push him away. Not now. Not after what he'd just admitted. Not with the way my chest was swelling, erasing the horrible, wretched feeling from earlier.

His lips grazed the bridge of my nose, and then he pressed a kiss against my forehead as he rolled off me, onto his side. The hand that had been cupping my cheek slid down, between my breasts, stopping just above my belly button. That sweet kiss seized my chest, but I waited for those lips to move farther south.

But the lips never did.

I turned my head toward his and opened my eyes. My mouth dropped open as realization sunk in. Lying beside me on the floor, Jase was passed out cold.

Chapter 4

Forrest Gump had taken up residency in my head. The words *stupid is as stupid does* were on repeat. I should've ignored Jase's text. I should've agreed when he'd called himself a jackass. I should've called someone to come get his drunk ass. I shouldn't have yearned for more than a kiss on the forehead. And I really shouldn't have been lured in by anything he'd said last night, no matter how badly I wanted to believe him, because he'd been drunk.

A drunk man's words were a sober man's thoughts. That's what my dad always said, but I didn't think that was true. Not in the bright light of the morning.

I hadn't been able to get Jase onto the couch last night. So I had ended up shoving a pillow under his head and dropping the quilt over him. I'd sat on the couch afterward, fully intending on getting up and finding my own bed, but I had gotten a bit lost watching him sleep. Like I said, stupid is as stupid does. As I studied the softness in his features that were never present while he was awake, I'd fallen asleep.

When I'd woken up Sunday morning, the quilt that I'd placed over him had been tucked around me. And the pillow had replaced the armrest. Jase had already gone.

There was a huge part of me that wanted to believe that he'd spoken the truth last night and that it meant something, because that kiss . . . it had been so sweet. But he'd been hammered and he wasn't here now. I appreciated that he'd apologized. We could move forward from here and be friends, but I wanted to kick myself for rushing out in the middle of the night to talk to him like I was desperate and hoping that he'd kiss me.

On any other place except my forehead, but that had been so . . . so sweet.

'Ugh.' I dropped my head into my hands.

But I'd been so surprised by his text. Hell, I'd thought he'd purposely lost my number and . . . well, I was a girl. That was my excuse. *We're just friends.* I kept telling myself that over and over again. I needed to get that through my thick skull.

'You don't look like you had a good night.'

I lifted my head at the sound of Debbie's voice. She stood in the doorway with two cups of coffee in her hands. 'Ahh . . .'

Brown hair tucked up in a neon purple clip, she shoved a warm cup into my hands. 'Got a question.'

'Okay.' I sat down on my bed, crossing my legs. 'I might have an answer.'

Toeing off her sandals, she flashed a quick grin and then dropped down on the bed opposite me. 'So I got home this morning around . . . hmm, let's say—around four A.M. and I thought my eyes must be deceiving me, because there was one Jase Winstead passed out on our floor and you were asleep on the couch, all curled up like a little babe.'

A slow burn crept across my cheeks. 'Uh, yeah, well . . .'

Debbie giggled as I stumbled over my words. 'Now, when I see Jase in unexpected places, I expect him to be in a bed and not on a floor. Just saying, but come on, spill it. What

45

was he doing here? I saw him at the party and he didn't look like he wanted to be there—oh! Now it makes sense!' Her grin spread. 'There was somewhere else he wanted to be and that was here, with you.'

That was a huge leap of logic to take. 'It's not like that.' At her doubtful look, I took a sip of the sugary coffee and resisted the urge to ask what 'unexpected places' she had seen Jase in. 'I'm serious. We've known each other for a while. You know my brother is close friends with him, right?'

'I know who your brother is. Everyone does.' She smoothed a hand over her bangs. 'But I didn't know you were *good* friends with Jase.'

I shrugged. 'He was drunk, so I couldn't let him drive home. He crashed on the couch. That's about all. Not an exciting story to tell.'

One dark brow arched. 'And why was he here when he was drunk?'

Fuuuūuck. Good question. I bought time by taking a nice long drink of the coffee. 'He was seeing someone else or something. And he was drunk and texted me to say hi.'

She scrunched up her nose. 'Well, that is boring.'

I laughed. 'Sorry.'

'Damn, I was hoping I was going to get some dirty details and live vicariously through you.' She laughed when my eyes widened. 'Come on, Jase has this . . . I don't know, this *intensity* about him. Like he'd be the kind of guy who fucks you and changes your life.'

'Fucks you and changes your life?' I repeated dumbly. The few times I had sex hadn't been that impressive. 'That is some serious penis skills.'

Debbie laughed as she flopped onto her back, managing to hold on to her Styrofoam cup without spilling anything. 'Penis skills? Oh my God . . .'

I cracked a grin as I held the cup close. 'Erik wasn't with you, was he?'

'Nope.'

Tension eased out of my neck. If Erik had been, I was sure he would go back to Cam or one of the other frat brothers. 'Can I ask you a favor? Can you not tell Erik that Jase was here? I don't want people getting the wrong idea—'

'Like they obviously would,' she teased.

'Exactly. And I wouldn't want Cam to get ticked off for no apparent reason.'

She rolled onto her side, placing her cup on the nightstand. 'Cam the overprotective brother type?'

I snorted. 'You have no idea.'

'That's nice though, having someone looking out for you,' she said, stretching her legs. 'I bet he's a pain in the ass when it comes to boyfriends.'

I took another drink and figured it was time to change the conversation. 'Speaking of boyfriends, I'm surprised Erik didn't come back with you.'

She bit down on her lip. 'He wanted to go back to the party, so . . .'

So what Erik wanted, Erik got. Just like Jeremy. I glanced down at my cup, wanting to say something, but felt like I'd be overstepping a line. But to remain silent was killer. No one at school had asked questions when they saw Jeremy grab my arm or yell at me for the most insignificant infractions. Everyone had turned a blind eye. It was easier that way.

I squeezed my eyes shut as the feeling of helplessness returned like an old, needy friend you couldn't get rid of. I wasn't that girl anymore. I wasn't a victim.

When Debbie's phone went off, I opened my eyes to see her quickly pull it out of her pocket. 'Hey, babe, I was—' Her words were cut off suddenly, and I stiffened. 'I know—yes. Yes! I just left to get some coffee. You—' She twisted at the waist and swung her feet onto the floor. As she stood, her eyes met mine. A crimson stain swept across her cheeks. She looked away quickly as she hurried out of the room. 'Erik, babe, I'm sorry. I didn't know—'

She stopped at the door, bending to pick up the sandals she kicked off. Her cotton shorts rode up her thigh, revealing the skin just below her hip. I gasped, but the sound must've been lost in whatever Erik was saying to her.

Bruises in an array of yellow and blue marred her skin. Some old. Some so fresh, so vibrantly purple, that I knew they had to have been created within the last twenty-four hours.

Debbie straightened, sandals dangling from the tips of her fingers. 'I'm coming over now. I just need to get gas—I know you told me to get gas last night, but it was late . . .' She sucked in a breath. 'I'm sorry.'

Pressure clamped down on my chest as I watched her close the door behind her. I closed my eyes, but I couldn't erase what I saw or what it meant. All the bruises, a large cluster of blotches, were inflicted where they could not be normally seen.

They'd been hidden.

My shirt was already starting to cling to the middle of my back, and my right knee ached. The walk from history class in Whitehall all the way to music appreciation on west campus was truly a bitch in this heat. Even worse was the fact that if I wanted to eat anything, I would have to walk my happy ass back to east campus.

'You should've taken the bus,' Calla Fritz said, shifting her messenger-style book bag to the other shoulder. 'There's no reason for you to walk this far.'

'I'm okay.'

'My bullshit radar just went off.' Calla tugged her long, golden ponytail out from underneath the strap of her bag. I'd only met her last week when I started class. We shared history and music together, but in the short period of time, I discovered she was pretty blunt when she wanted to be.

Besides Debbie, she was probably my only friend. I didn't count Avery because she was my brother's girlfriend and had to like me. Mom had said right before I left for school that some of her longest-lasting friendships started her first year in college.

I didn't think that was going to happen for me.

Even my friendship with Sadi, and we'd been dancing together since we were five, hadn't lasted.

'You started limping by the time we reached the football field,' she added.

Sweat caused my sunglasses to slip on the bridge of my nose. Pushing them up, I smiled at her. Short and curvy, Calla Fritz reminded me of one of those '50s pinup girls. The kind of girls who'd dance burlesque and make a lot of money doing it.

But, like me, Calla was far from perfect.

A raised scar covered her left cheek, from the corner of her lips to her ear. With makeup, it was a faint mark. I didn't know how she got it and I didn't ask. I figured it would be something she'd volunteer.

'I always limp,' I told her. Hiding my gimp leg was impossible with the nice bright pink cut decorating my kneecap. I would've preferred to hide it, but I couldn't stand the heat of late August. 'And I need the exercise.'

She snorted. 'What the hell ever, my thighs need the exercise. You need a hamburger.'

'Have you seen my ass? It's known a lot of hamburgers up close and personal. And it's on speaking terms with french fries.'

'That's okay. My thighs make out with milkshakes.'

I laughed and then sighed as we entered the tunnel that connected the two sides of the campus. Since it was underground and lit by track lighting, it was a good twenty degrees cooler.

'I wonder if anyone would notice if I just lay down in the middle of this?' Calla asked.

'Probably, but I'd be right there with you.'

Calla spent the rest of our trip bitching about the fact that she—a nursing major—had to take music appreciation. I didn't blame her. It was an easy enough class, but not the most interesting. Our professor really didn't apply himself. After all, almost everyone in the classroom was there because they had to be.

College was so strange. It was like high school with little to no parental influence. We still had to take classes we didn't want to take, except we actually had to pay for them, which really kind of sucked ass.

The auditorium was half full, and we took our seats in the back. Sitting halfway down the aisle, I swallowed the groan of relief when I sat. My knee immediately thanked me. I popped my sunglasses up, cringing at the fine sheen of sweat dotting my forehead. Nothing like being a sweaty mess for class. I was so ready for fall.

'Wake me up about ten minutes till,' Calla said, sliding down in her seat. She kept her sunglasses on. 'Because then I'll feel like I attempted to pay attention.'

I grinned. 'Will do.'

As the class filed in, I started thumbing through my notebook, searching for the section I'd been taking notes in last week. I didn't realize anyone was heading for the unoccupied seat to my left until I heard the chair creak. I glanced over and my jaw dropped.

Jase Winstead was sprawled arrogantly in the seat beside

50

me, long legs bent and both arms draped lazily over the back of the seats. Dressed in faded jeans and a shirt, he looked like he had every right to be there, especially with his backpack resting against one of his legs.

Except I couldn't figure out why he was here.

A funny little half smile hitched up one corner of his lips. 'Hi.'

I glanced around, making sure I was in the right class. Beside me, Calla stared at Jase as she removed her sunglasses. I was in the right place. 'Hi.'

The smile spread about an inch. 'You look surprised.'

'I am,' I said, snapping out of my stupor. 'What are you doing here?'

He tapped a long finger off his notebook. 'Had a meeting with my adviser last week to make sure I had all my credits. Turned out I still needed music appreciation, and this was the only class that wasn't full. So I did a late add.'

Jase paused as his gaze slowly drifted over my face. His body was the epitome of relaxed, but there was an unnerving level of quiet intensity in his stare. 'I was actually sitting in front of you. You didn't see me, but I saw you.'

There was no way that Jase knew my schedule, and him being here had absolutely nothing to do with me or his late-night visit on Saturday. I totally knew that, but that knowledge did nothing to stop the bubbling of hope and excitement. 'Well, that's . . . um, that's cool.'

The other side of Jase's lips tipped up.

My cheeks heated as I hastily looked away. Okay. I could handle this. Jase and I had talked things over. We were cool. Everything was cool. We were *friends*. And the things he'd said and how he'd felt on top of me Saturday night didn't matter. He had been drunk. Another mistake. I clung to that, because considering anything else was sure to bring on a world of hurting.

I peeked at him, stealing a sideways glance. His gaze was still fixed on my face, but slowly moved down to my lap. My right leg was stretched out, and the way I held my notebook did nothing to hide the length of the scar covering my knee. I felt the burn in my face deepen as I shifted my notebook to my right leg.

'The class is really boring,' Calla announced, shoving her hand over and drawing his attention away. 'I'm Calla, by the way.'

He reached over with his left arm, shaking her hand as his gaze flickered across her face. His stare did not linger on her scar, and for that, he got bonus points when it came to compassion. 'I'm—'

'Jase Winstead,' she said, sitting back. 'I know you. Well, I don't *know* you. I've heard *of* you.'

A faint pink stained the tops of his broad cheeks. Was he blushing? 'You have?' he asked.

She nodded and a private, almost knowing smile formed on her lips. 'I think every female on this campus has heard of you.'

I rolled my eyes.

He chuckled. 'Ah, I see . . .'

'You do?' I arched a brow.

Focusing on the front of the auditorium as the professor strode in, Jase bit down on his lower lip. There was something boyish about the action, but in a strange way, also sensual. The muscles in my stomach tightened at the sudden image of him nipping down on *my* lower lip like he had on my neck. The skin there tingled as a reminder. An electric-like sensation shot through my veins at the memory of how he'd rocked his hips.

Good God, I needed to get laid or something.

'Some would say I'm quite popular . . .' he remarked finally.

'With the *ladies*?' I supplied as I pulled a pen out of my bag.

Thick lashes lowered as he sent me a sideways look. 'Maybe.'

'Definitely,' Calla murmured under her breath.

I grinned as Jase shifted in his seat. He was uncomfortable addressing his oh-so-stellar reputation?

Goodie gumdrops.

'So,' I said, unable to resist poking at him. My voice was low as the professor started to discuss the six elements of music. 'Would these ladies have good or bad things to say about you?'

He was silent as he scribbled the words *rhythm* and *melody* in his notebook. I didn't think he'd answer. 'Depends on who you ask.'

'What would it depend on?'

His grin spread on one side again. 'Several factors, but I can assure you that most of them would have many good things to say.' His light gray eyes sought mine out again as he bowed his head until his warm breath danced along my cheek. 'Actually, *great* things.'

My heart stumbled. Was he flirting with me? I swallowed. 'Like what kind of things?'

He didn't answer then, so I forced myself to focus on the lecture. I could feel Calla staring at me. She had no idea how I knew Jase and probably thought I was one of the girls who had many, many good things to say about him.

I wanted to say his comment was made out of arrogance and nothing else, but knowing how damn well he kissed, I was sure that he was just as skilled at everything else. The girls were probably boasting about his prowess on Internet message boards.

Jase shifted in the seat, and I stiffened as I felt his breath on my neck, just below my ear, teasing that sensitive spot that made me want to wiggle around—the same spot he'd nipped, licked, and then kissed. In a low whisper, he said, 'I think you know *exactly* what kind of things they'd say good things about.'

*

I didn't have a single clue about what was covered during music appreciation. The awareness of how close Jase sat was wholly distracting. Every time his leg or arm brushed mine, I was completely lost.

And I had an entire semester of this to look forward to.

There was a part of me that wanted to be grumpy about that, but I'd just be lying to myself. Knowing that I'd see Jase three times a week really increased my desire to attend this class.

After all, what was wrong with admiring a little eye candy?

Jase walked out with Calla and me, and it seemed like the temp had increased by ten degrees and the sun's strength amplified.

'Where are you guys heading?' Jase asked, running a hand through his mess of waves.

'I'm heading back to my dorm,' Calla answered as she adjusted her sunglasses. She glanced at me. 'Aren't you going back to east campus?'

Thinking about the torturous walk ahead, I nodded. 'Yeah, eventually. I have a class at one in Knutti. So I have an hour to make my way over there.'

'I can give you a ride over,' Jase offered, stopping at the edge of the pavilion surrounding the arts department. His gaze dipped briefly, but not quick enough that I didn't know he was checking out my leg. I stiffened. 'I can be your personal chauffeur,' he added with a grin that was nothing short of wicked.

For a moment, I got a little lost in that grin and the coils that formed in my tummy, but I managed to shake my head. 'Thanks, but you don't have to go out of your way.'

Jase waved at someone who called his name, but his attention was focused on me. 'I'll drive you. I'm parked over here anyway, in the back lot.'

'But—'

'It's not a big deal.' He squinted at the harsh glare off a passing car. 'I'm heading over there anyway.'

'That's really nice of you,' Calla said, sending me a look that said shut the hell up. 'Her knee is really bothering her.'

I flushed out of embarrassment. 'My leg isn't bothering me that much. And I need the exercise. Walking is a good—' I squealed as Jase hooked an arm around my waist and bent, lifting me over his shoulder like I weighed nothing more than a sack of sugar. My bag slipped off my arm, smacking the pavement. 'What are you doing?'

'Standing here discussing your ability to walk over to east campus in this heat makes me really impatient.'

I gripped the back of his shirt, unable to see through my hair. 'Then leave! What the hell does that have to do with picking me up like a caveman?'

'Because you're not walking over there.' He clamped his arm over the back of my thighs, dangerously close to getting hands-on with my ass. 'That's why.'

Calla laughed. 'Well, that's one way to settle the issue.'

Lifting my head, I glared at her through my hair. 'You're not helping.'

She smiled at me as she picked up my book bag and handed it over to Jase's waiting hand. 'See you later.'

'Traitor,' I muttered.

'Thanks.' Jase pivoted around, and I held on for dear life. He started walking down the road. 'How you doing up there?'

'How do you think?' I snapped.

As we passed a group of students, they burst into laughter. One of the guys shouted, 'So that's how Jase gets his girls!'

My entire body went rigid.

He turned suddenly, causing me to squeal. Walking backward, he chuckled. 'Some require a more hands-on approach.'

'I'd be down for a hands-on approach,' came a soft, feminine voice. 'When you're not so busy.'

I cursed.

Jase tsked as he spun. 'Language, Tess, *language*.'

Holding on with one hand, I jabbed him in the kidney with my other.

'Ouch!'

My lips split in a wide smile.

'If my other hand was free . . .'

I knew exactly what he was thinking. 'If you even consider for one second you think you can—*ompf*!' I gasped at the sudden extra hop in his step. 'You asshole.'

'I think you do need a spanking.'

My mouth opened for a blistering response, but he'd reached his car and for some reason being spanked didn't sound *that* bad. But he had to be teasing because there was no way he was going to put his hand on Cam's little sister's ass.

Jase dropped my bag and then opened the door. He moved his hand, and the rough calluses on his palms trailed along the back of my thighs. I shivered in spite of the heat, and mentally cursed my body's reaction to him.

He reached up, gripping my hips. 'You can let go of my shirt now.'

'Oh.' I released my grip.

His shoulders shook with a laugh, and then the front of my body slid down his. Air halted in my throat at the unexpected frisson. Awareness shimmered over certain parts of my body. My feet were on the pavement, but his hands lingered on my hips.

'There you go,' he said, his voice deeper than before as he dropped his hands. 'You can climb in, right?'

Pushing the hair out of my face, I took a deep breath. 'I'm not an invalid.'

'I didn't say you were.'

'I can walk, you know, and climb into Jeeps.'

He picked up my bag, dropping it in the backseat. 'I'm sure you can.'

When he raised an eyebrow, I realized that he was literally going to stand there until I got into the car. Sighing, I turned and climbed up. He flashed me a grin, closed the door, and then loped around the front.

He started the Jeep and warm air blasted out of the vents, stirring the hair around my face. His eyes were a clear, steely gray when they landed on me. 'Okay. Why didn't you want me to give you a ride?'

Seeing that all the humor had disappeared, I squirmed. 'It's not that I didn't want you to give me a ride.'

'Really?' He reached up, unhooking his sunglasses from the visor. Sliding them up his nose, he settled back against his seat. Locks of hair fell forward, brushing the rim of the aviators.

Goodness gracious, he looked damn good in sunglasses.

Even though his eyes were shielded, there was no escaping his stare. No one looked at you like Jase Winstead did. It was like he was seeing right through me, layer by exposing layer. 'Is it because of Saturday night? I was pretty inebriated. Shit, I don't remember anything from the moment I stepped into your dorm.'

The back of my neck prickled. 'Nothing?'

He shook his head. 'So God only knows what I said and did, and I must've said something, because you didn't want to get in this Jeep with me.'

Part of me wanted to punch him in the balls even though I knew beyond a doubt that he'd been drunk—drunk enough to have no recollection of telling me that I was a reason for why he'd visited Cam so much or our little interlude on the floor. It took a lot for me not to blast him over that, but what point would it serve? He'd been sloshed, and I had been the one who went out to meet him and then let him in my dorm. All this was temporary, and I couldn't let this make an already crappy situation worse.

I took a deep breath and let it out slowly. 'You didn't do or say anything to make me mad.'

He didn't respond for a moment. 'But I slept on your floor and you slept on the couch?'

'Yeah . . . uh, you sort of fell down and stayed there.' I shrugged a shoulder. 'I fell asleep on the couch.'

'Nice.' He coughed out a short laugh. Several seconds passed, and I considered making a mad dash out of the car. 'We're friends, right?'

My heart sunk in spite of my convictions on the state of him and me. 'Yes.'

'Correct me if I'm wrong, friends give friends rides, right?'

I nodded, knowing where this conversation was heading.

'So what's the big deal?'

Looking away, I blew out a long breath. Spending any amount of time in his presence didn't help my determination to put an end to this stupid crush, but there was another reason. 'I don't want people thinking . . .' Picking at the hem of my shorts, I shook my head. 'There're a lot of things I can't do right now—dance, work out, run, or even *jog* at a sedate pace. I can walk. That's about all I can do.'

I kind of felt stupid after saying that and I doubted he'd understand how hard it was for me to go from being so active to becoming a sloth. And not even the cute baby sloths.

'Ah, here I was thinking you were secretly hoping I'd pick you up.' He switched gears into reverse.

I laughed. 'Sorry to disappoint you.'

'You'd never be a disappointment.' Looking over his shoulder as he backed up, he smiled, and I wondered if he could see the way my pulse had jumped at his words. 'I get what you're saying. It's hard when you're used to doing something that was as common as breathing to you.'

'It is.' I tugged on the string dangling off my hem. 'I miss the rush of dancing and running. You know? The energy. It's calming and it's just me . . .' I wasn't sure I was making any sense. 'And I don't have that anymore.'

Shifting into drive, he relaxed his grip on the steering wheel. He was quiet as he navigated the parking lot. 'You know there are other things you could do.'

Like sex? I bet that was relaxing when it was all said and done.

'You know one of the most calming things I've found?' he asked, having no idea that my mind was happily playing in the gutter. 'Horseback riding.'

I blinked. 'Ah . . .'

He grinned. 'There really isn't anything like it. I'm telling you, Tess. You ever feel like you're flying when you're dancing?'

'Yeah,' I whispered, sort of stunned. I missed that most of all.

He nodded. 'That's how it feels to be on top of a horse. You should try it. I think you'd love it.'

I shifted, having no idea what to say to that. Was it an invitation to his parents' farm? Did it matter? Getting in a saddle was tantamount to playing chicken with a pissed-off T. rex to me.

'Hungry?' he asked, changing the subject before I could answer. 'I'm heading over to the Den. Cam and Avery are there. They've got to have better food than the dining hall.'

They did. I shrugged.

'Come on.' He reached over, nudging my arm. 'Come on and eat with us.'

My lips twitched as I glanced at him. This . . . this was the Jase I remembered. Teasing. Open. Fun. Someone I could talk to and be honest with. As stupid as it was, I found myself wishing that he'd remembered what had happened after he stepped into my dorm. Then again, it was probably better that he didn't. 'I don't want to come across as the little sister tagging along.'

'You're not.'

I shot him a dry as sand look. 'I've tagged along half of my life. I followed him to college.'

'You didn't follow him, Tess.' He paused as he slowed for the stop sign, glancing over at me. That half grin was back. 'And guess what?'

My lips responded, curving up at the corners. 'What?'

'He doesn't care if you did follow him here. He's happy that you're here,' he said. 'I don't care if you did follow him. And I'm happy that you did.'

Chapter 5

I stopped fighting Jase on the whole riding-versus-walking thing pretty quickly, especially as the leaves from the huge maple trees planted throughout the campus turned from bright green to a beautiful array of red, gold, and brown. September eased into October with a spell of rain that seemed to be never ending. Fall was well under way, and every morning and night, a chill rolled off the Potomac, warning that this could possibly be a very cold and a very wet winter.

And at least once a week, he'd stashed a cupcake in the Jeep, keeping it cool in a little cooler in the backseat. On the way to east campus, we'd share the tasty goodness. He was going to make me gain ten pounds this way, but so far I'd had a variety of cupcakes—Twix, Oreos, strawberry, white chocolate, Skittles—that was kind of gross—banana and chocolate, and a dark chocolate cupcake that was so decadent I felt like I had to go to church after eating it.

Today we shared a red velvet cupcake with some kind of cream cheese icing.

It was divine.

Wherever he got these cupcakes from deserved a gold medal in fucking awesome.

Thick, fat clouds crowded the sky by the time music class let out on Wednesday. It was going to rain. Again. With my knee, I had to be super-duper careful on the slick sidewalks. Busting my ass would be as embarrassing as it would be devastating.

I waved good-bye to Calla as I climbed into the Jeep. The second after Jase turned the ignition, the Elvis Presley channel on XM kicked on. Ugh. As he backed out, I leaned forward and turned it to the Octane channel.

Jase stopped—just completely stopped in the middle of the parking lot. 'Did you just do what I think you just did?'

'What?' I asked innocently.

Cars were pulling out behind us, but his Jeep blocked their path. The look on his face said he so did not care. 'You just turned off The Man for . . .' He glanced at the radio, grimacing. 'For Godsmack?'

'Hey. Don't you talk shit about Godsmack.'

'I have no problem with them.' A horn blew. He ignored it. 'Until it affects Elvis.'

'I cannot listen to Elvis.'

His mouth dropped as his brows winged up. 'We cannot be friends any longer.'

I giggled.

Jase narrowed his eyes as he finally—thank God—put the Jeep into drive. 'It's a good thing you're cute or I'd drop-kick you out of this car.'

I laughed outright as I settled back in the seat. 'I could say the same thing about you with your questionable tastes.' A wide smile pulled at my lips as he shot me a disgruntled look. 'Country music has got to go.'

'Oh, you don't know what good music is.' Jase hung a left. 'I'm gonna have to educate you.'

Warmth bubbled up in my chest, and I struggled to ignore it. We went back and forth on the music while he searched for parking. It took a bit of time since he passed up several open spaces farther out. I knew why. He didn't want me to walk, and while catering to my leg usually made my skin itchy and too tight, I didn't say anything as he circled the main drag a few times until a spot opened up between Sara Creed and the Den. It was nice of him, courteous even, and I couldn't let myself think that it meant anything else.

'How's Jack?' I asked when he started preaching the gospel of Johnny Cash.

A certain light filled his eyes, a look of pride, and I went all ooey gooey on the inside. 'He's doing great. Started kindergarten this year. His teacher—Mrs. Higgins—said he's the smartest kid in class.'

I smiled as I slid out of my seat. 'Are you sure he's your brother?'

'What do you mean?' He appeared in front of me and grabbed my bag out of the backseat before I could even move. There was an odd look to his gray eyes. 'Of course, he's my brother.'

'I was kidding.' I grabbed for my bag, but he slung it over his shoulder. 'You know, with him being the smartest kid in class, I wasn't sure how he could be related to you.'

The wariness vanished from his gaze and he smiled. 'Ha. Jack gets his intelligence, good looks, *and* charm from me.'

'Uh-huh.'

Chuckling deeply, he held my bag in one hand and draped his other arm over my shoulders. The weight was sudden and distracting, causing the nape of my neck to tingle, sending tiny shivers down my arm.

To Jase, this wasn't a big deal. Nor did he probably even notice the stares as we walked up the stairs to the Den, passing people who knew him—because *everyone* knew him. I easily remembered the first time he'd done something like this—the evening he'd arrived without any warning.

It had been the weekend after the . . . *incident* with Cam. My brother had holed himself up in the basement, having already drunk himself through the collection of scotch our father had stocked. Jase had apparently been talking to Cam through text and had grown concerned. He'd dropped everything and driven the several hours to see him.

I'd been dumbstruck when I saw Jase standing in the foyer, talking to Mom and Dad. He was the most handsome boy I'd ever seen—his hair shorter then, but no less wild, and his eyes a steely gray as they'd drifted and landed on where I'd been more or less hiding, peeking around the door to the family room.

Something had filled his gaze then, and I'd feared that all he saw in that moment was the cause of Cam's problem. It had been freezing that night, as the evenings were in early December, but the house had suddenly become suffocating and too hot.

I had hidden again, but this time outside, curled up on one of the wicker chairs on the patio, watching the stars twinkle in and out, wondering how exactly all this had come about.

And that was how Jase had found me. Instead of giving me the fourth degree about what happened with Jeremy and everything that Cam had done when he found out, he talked to me about Christmas, my dancing, what my favorite class was, and everything else that had nothing to do with what had almost ripped our family apart. To this day, he'd never asked me about Jeremy, never brought up the stuff with Cam. It just didn't exist between us.

By the time my fingers had turned to blocks of ice, Jase had dropped his arm around my shoulders and steered me back into the house, into the warmth, and it was probably that very second that I had fallen for him.

So this simple gesture was most likely nothing to him.

But to me, my insides were twisted into little, complicated knots. Made worse when his arm caught the edges of my ponytail, tugging my head back and sending a shiver of fire across my scalp. My breath caught as my gaze flicked up, unexpectedly meeting his as we stopped in front of the blue-and-gold double doors.

His eyes were silvery, a deep and brilliant gray that stood out in stark contrast against the darkness of his pupils. The look in his gaze was unreadable to me, but there was something hot to it, something so intense that it drew me in. My lips parted.

Jase's lashes swept down. His mouth worked around words, but the doors opened, and the cool air rushing out halted whatever he was about to say. That strange, secretive half smile appeared on his full lips as he looked away.

His arm slid off me as we entered the Den through the entrance where the food was ordered. Only then did he hand my bag over to me. Our fingers brushed as I took the strap, and heat flooded my cheeks.

He lowered his head, so dangerously close to grazing my cheek with his lips as he spoke. 'There's something about you that I've noticed.'

Standing as close as we were had my pulse pounding for two different reasons. My gaze immediately sought out the table where my brother usually sat. Fortunately, it was on the other side of the room, and I could see the top of Avery's coppery head. Their backs were to us.

'What?' I asked, a bit breathless.

Jase didn't respond immediately, and the fact that everything about this moment felt intimate and so public was nerve-racking. 'You blush a lot more now.'

65

And that made my cheeks burn brighter.

The lopsided grin grew. 'It really makes me curious about what you're thinking.'

I'd die a thousand deaths before I shared the interworking of *those* thoughts. 'I'm not thinking anything.'

'Uh-huh.' One finger trailed across my hot cheek as he drew back and straightened. Turning toward the line forming, he said, 'I don't know about you, but I'm starving.'

Nodding slowly, I followed him to the back of line. I *was* starving, but not for food—for him. For him to touch me again, to kiss me, to look at me with that half smile that had such a strange effect on me, and I shouldn't be thinking that way.

Especially when we were minutes from sitting down with my brother, who would not appreciate me drooling all over his best friend.

Using the time in line to get control of myself, I got a fried chicken salad, figuring the green stuff had to outweigh the crispy goodness. Jase ordered a basket of fries and the kind of hamburger that would go straight to my ass.

Plates in hand, we approached the table. Female heads turned and bowed together, whispering and giggling as we navigated the maze of white, square tables. I doubted he was unaware of it. Not when his lips curled up in a smug smirk.

My eyes narrowed on him.

'Hey!' Avery patted the empty seat to her left. Her face split into a wide, welcoming smile. The girl was gorgeous with her fiery hair and big eyes. 'We were wondering where you guys were.'

I ignored the heady rush hearing 'you guys' brought forth, like we came in a pair, as couples did. 'Hey.'

Cam made a face at me as he leaned back, tangling his fingers in Avery's hair. I was beginning to believe it was impossible for him to not be touching some part of her at any given time. 'What up?'

'Most likely not your IQ.' Jase sat across from the seat I was heading to, flashing my brother a quick grin.

He rolled his eyes. 'That was clever.'

'I like to think it was,' Jase replied.

Grinning, I sat beside Avery and gave a little wave at Brit and Jacob. I didn't know those two well. They were usually at the table when I was here, and Brit's penchant for mayo and fries turned my stomach. Today, thank God, the blonde was eating pizza. Beside her, Jacob was pouring over a thick textbook, his face scrunched up in confusion.

'Has it started raining yet?' Avery asked.

I shook my head as I unwrapped my plastic fork. 'Looks like it's going to happen soon.'

She sighed as she glanced over at Brit. 'It's going to pour the moment we have to walk over to west campus.'

'That's our luck.' Brit elbowed Jacob. 'Are you going to let me borrow your hat if it starts raining?'

He lifted his chin as he touched the top of his bowler hat. To me, he sort of looked like Bruno Mars. 'Yeah, I cannot let my hair get wet. Sorry for your luck.'

Brit shoved a finger into his narrow side. 'That is not gentlemanly at all.'

'Good thing I don't profess to be one, huh?' His dark eyes glinted with humor as he turned his attention to me. 'Honey, I really hope you pick better friends than this one beside me.'

'Hey!' Brit's mouth dropped open. 'What the hell? I am prime pickings for friendship. Just ask Avery.'

She nodded as her right hand disappeared under the table. 'It's true.'

I smiled as I stabbed a crispy slice of chicken. 'I think Brit is good people.'

'Thank you,' she said, smiling quite evilly at Jacob.

As I finished off the chicken in my salad, the conversation floated around the table, changing from Cam's training for the spring soccer tryouts with United to the upcoming party this weekend.

'I don't know if it's going to be a huge thing.' Jase had devoured the hamburger and now had moved on to the fries. 'I know Erik and Brandon are supposed to be running it. You're going, right?' he asked Cam.

Cam glanced at Avery first. Too cute. 'Are we?'

She bit her lip and nodded. 'I think so.'

I didn't know a whole ton about Avery, but I knew going to a party was a big deal. She didn't seem to be into those kinds of things.

Brit and Jacob planned on going, and I turned my attention to the salad, digging out the cucumbers. In high school, I didn't get to go to a lot of parties because of dance, so I really had no idea what to expect from a college one. Not that it looked like I was going to find out anytime soon.

'You're coming, right?' Jase asked, and I wondered who he was talking to. Then I felt his foot tap mine under the table, and I looked up. His brows rose. 'Tess, you're coming?'

I blinked tightly as surprise washed over me. 'Yeah,' I croaked, and then cleared my throat. 'Yes. I can go.'

'Wait. What?' Cam dropped his arm from Avery. Holy shit. Hold the presses. He wasn't touching her. He leaned forward, eyeing me with identical blue eyes. 'You are eighteen—'

'I'm almost nineteen,' I interrupted, deciding that made a big difference. After all, my birthday was November the second, and we were less than a month away.

'Yeah, still, you're not legal.' Cam glanced over at Jase. 'You seriously just invited her to a frat party?'

Oh my God, I was going to kill my brother.

'Awkward,' Jacob murmured, closing his textbook.

Jase popped a fry in his mouth. 'You're taking your *girlfriend* to a frat party.'

'That's different,' he replied.

I sighed. 'Cam, can you shut—'

'I don't like the idea of you hanging out at a frat house. Those guys there—'

'Like me,' Jase interrupted, winking at me.

My cheeks heated.

'Exactly,' Cam all but growled. 'Enough said.'

Brit giggled. 'Cam, when did you start going to frat parties?'

'And don't say it's different,' I jumped in, stabbing a piece of lettuce. 'Because you were partying when you were fifteen.'

Cam sat back, and that's when I saw that Avery's hand had been on his thigh this whole time. False alarm. They had *not* stopped touching. 'It is different,' he insisted. 'I'm a guy.'

'Holy shit, you serious?' Jase's eyes widened, and I grinned. 'Could've fooled me.'

'I'm not the one who needs a haircut.' Cam picked up his bottle of water. 'I'm half tempted to start braiding it.'

'I'd be down for that.' Jacob piped up, smiling. 'I'm really good with braiding.'

Jase sucked in his bottom lip. 'I think I'll pass on that, but thanks.'

He sighed. 'Story of my life.'

Avery tucked a strand of hair back behind her ear. 'You should really come and hang out with us. Cam—' She shot him a look that shut him up in a second. 'Cam *will* be okay with it. We'll actually give you a ride.'

My brother opened his mouth again, but this time it was Jase who swooped in. 'And if Cam doesn't want to give you a ride, I will. Either way, you're going. It's official.'

'Or I can,' Brit offered. 'Then again, I'm not the best driver, so—'

'I'll give her a ride.' Cam sighed. 'Whatever.'

My smile spread as Cam was universally defeated. Excitement swelled in me, and I felt sort of lame, but it was my first college party. My gaze drifted across from me. I needed to find something cute to wear. A sexy new shirt would be nice. Maybe I could convince Avery to go shopping with me.

Jacob shook his head as his gaze centered on something behind us. 'Man, there they go again.'

Cringing, Brit ducked her chin and smacked her hand over her eyes. 'I can't even watch. I'm serious. I get second-hand embarrassment.'

Twisting halfway in my seat, I immediately saw what they were talking about. My stomach sunk as I watched Debbie and Erik standing at the end of the tables, in front of the ram painted on the wall. Erik's mouth was running a mile a minute and her cheeks were pale.

'Isn't that your roommate?' Jase asked quietly.

I nodded, watching them over my shoulder. 'Yeah. Her boyfriend . . . he's . . .'

'He's a dick,' Jase replied, and I twisted back around in surprise. He picked up a fry. 'He's like a grade A fucking dick.'

'It's the truth.' Cam turned toward Avery, wrapping his arms around her waist. He rested his chin on her shoulder, closing his eyes. 'I mean, he can be cool, but he doesn't know how to act right.' Pausing, he kissed the side of her neck. 'I, on the other hand, do.'

Jase snorted.

'Don't hate,' Cam murmured.

My gaze met Jase's for a second, and I couldn't help myself. I glanced over my shoulder again. Erik had ahold of Debbie's arms, and now her lips were moving fast. Whatever they were saying was gaining the attention of the table in front of them.

I wanted to get up and rip Erik's hands away. Actually, I wanted to get up and kick him in the balls. As I forced myself to turn back around, words bubbled up in my throat—words that were suspicions.

Jacob shook his head as he raised his arms, stretching. 'Girls are stupid. No offense or anything.'

Brit made a face. 'Of course.'

'Care to explain?' Avery leaned back into Cam's embrace, and those two were the picture of what couples in love should look like.

'Come on, I don't care what he's packing in his jeans, how smart he is, or how cool.' Jacob sat back, eyeing where Debbie and Erik had moved to stand just outside the open doors, still arguing. Debbie looked close to tears. 'Any girl who puts up with that shit is fucking stupid.'

I stiffened, my fork halfway to my mouth. The piece of lettuce dangled there. Brit, like Jacob, was basically unaffected by the statement. Both of them had no idea that I had been one of those fucking stupid girls. And while I would never actively be that girl again, wouldn't I always be *that* girl?

Cold fingers drifted down my spine as I lowered my hand. My appetite was officially slaughtered. Avery had fallen silent; so had Jase and my brother. Of course, they knew. I hadn't told Avery, but I knew Cam had told her, because I had, in some ways, fucked up his life this many years later.

Because I didn't have the courage or the common sense or the whatever necessary to tell the truth, or to simply leave Jeremy, my silence had kick-started a chain of events that had almost destroyed my brother.

71

'I'm going to go ahead and head to class.' Picking up my backpack, I slung it over my shoulder as I stood. 'I don't want to get caught in the rain.'

'Teresa,' Cam said, his voice level. 'You—'

'I'll see you guys later.' I kept my gaze on my salad as I picked it up, not daring to look at anyone.

Dumping my food, I headed out the entrance we came in, purposefully avoiding the side where I'd seen Erik and Debbie. Thick, ominous clouds had rolled in and the scent of rain was strong, but it hadn't started yet.

A knot had crawled into my throat as I stepped onto the sidewalk. Jacob hadn't meant anything by what he said. I got that, but the truth in his words still stung. It was more than just the embarrassment. I didn't want to think about Jeremy—ever again. Except he kept popping up like a damn cold sore. If I could have my time with him scrubbed from my memory, I would.

Maybe you're not quite over what he did, whispered a snotty, annoying inner voice that I immediately told to shut up.

'Tess.'

Halfway up the hill, I stopped and turned as my heart did the same thing it did every time I heard *his* voice. It didn't matter that I'd just spent a good two hours with him, or the fact that my less than perfect past had just exploded all over our lunch table. I was hopeless.

There was a slight smile on his face as he came to me. Gently taking my arm, he steered me off the sidewalk, out of the path of the moving crowd. Coming to stand under a tree, I tightened my grip on my bag.

'You ran off quickly,' he said. 'I didn't get a chance to ask you something.'

He was still holding my arm, his hand warm and strong against my skin. 'What?'

Jase looked at me as if Jacob had never said anything,

and like I hadn't just run off with my tail between my legs. Instead, he smiled as he slid his hand down my arm, circling his long fingers around my wrist.

Dear God in heaven, if Cam stepped outside right now and saw this . . .

'What are you doing after class tomorrow?' he asked.

My eyes widened and holy moly, it was like a million run-on sentences invaded my brain all at once. Was he? Did he? Is he? I had to literally stop and force my head to work right. 'Um . . . I get out of class at one, but I don't have anything planned.'

'Good.'

I waited for more of an explanation, but there wasn't one. 'Good?'

'Yep.' He stepped in, so close his shoes brushed my toes. 'Because you have plans now.'

Chapter 6

Calla stood in the doorway, holding a Twizzler. 'So you have no idea what you're doing today?'

'No.' I tugged on the hem of my tank top. 'All Jase said was to dress to be outside. This is good enough, right?'

Her gaze swept over my jeans and sneakers. 'It's still a little warm outside, buddy. Might want to rethink the jeans.'

I gazed longingly at the tiny closet and the pair of lonely shorts that resided in there, but I really didn't want to spend whatever we were doing worrying about him staring at my scar. Not that I should care about that, but I obviously did. And it wasn't that warm, not like it had been a month ago. 'I'll keep the jeans.'

She studied me as she twisted the edge of her ponytail between her fingers. 'It's not that noticeable, you know. Just saying. Anyway,' she went on before I could say a word, 'where's Debbie?'

I glanced at the empty, unslept-in bed. 'I don't know.' I hadn't seen her since sometime yesterday, and she'd only been in the room for seconds before rushing off.

'And your suitemates?'

'Good question.' I dragged my gaze from the bed. 'I have yet to see them.'

'Weird,' she whispered, turning around. She crept toward their door. 'I want to knock.'

'Don't!'

'But—'

My phone chirped and my heart jumped. Snatching it off the bed, I quickly read the message. 'He's outside waiting for me.'

Calla grinned. 'Oh! Let's go then.'

Grabbing my purse, I dropped my phone in it after sending him a quick message. We headed out of the suite and past the open doors to rooms where people obviously had normal suitemates.

'So this is a date?' Calla asked as she went for the elevator, forcing me away from the stairs. 'Right?'

'No.'

She arched a brow at me as the doors slid shut. 'I think he likes you.'

For a moment, I entertained the thought that this might be a date and that he might like me. *I'm happy that you did.* A giggle bubbled its way up my chest. Okay, thinking this was a date was not a good thing. I shook my head. 'I've told you. I've known him for a while. He's best friends with—'

'Cam,' she interrupted. 'I know. But he's not with Cam. He's with you. And I doubt he's taking you out on this little outing because of your brother.'

I opened my mouth, but having not considered that he could be doing this because of his friendship with my brother, I snapped my jaw tight. What if that was the reason? I placed a hand against my belly. I didn't want his pity or whatever. Worse yet, what if he was doing this because he thought of me as a sister?

Well, I could probably rule out the sister thing.

'Ah, the look on your face is kind of scary.'

I worked at relaxing my expression.

She laughed as the elevator stopped and the doors eased open. 'Better.'

'Really?' When she nodded, I smoothed my hands through my hair and then dropped my arms as we stepped out. The lobby was crowded. Half of the people were sprawled across the couches and chairs. I stopped at the door, spying his Jeep idling in the no parking zone.

'Can I tell you something?' she asked as we stepped outside.

My heart was already pounding. 'Sure.'

A slow grin stretched across her pretty face, diminishing the faint line of the scar. 'I just have to say this, okay? That boy . . .'

'What?' I asked, stopping a few feet from the Jeep. Calla was from this area. She was younger than Jase, like me, but she might know things I didn't. Not that it mattered. It couldn't matter. We were friends.

And I was beginning to sound like a broken record.

Calla sighed as she started to back away from me. 'That boy is freaking unbelievably hot. That is all.'

A smile formed on my lips and I laughed, muscles tightening and then relaxing. 'Yeah, I'd have to agree with that.'

She glanced over at the Jeep and grinned as she wiggled her fingers. 'Have fun.'

Waving good-bye, I took a deep breath and made my way over to where he waited. He leaned over, opening the passenger door from the inside. Several locks of rich brown hair fell forward, brushing the tips of his lashes. Luke Bryan crooned from the radio.

'Hey there, pretty lady.'

'Hey.' I hoisted myself up and closed the door, overly pleased with his greeting. And I figured that wasn't very healthy. Reaching for the seat belt, I looked over at him again and tried not to gawk.

No shirt.

Jase possibly—and I was willing to bet money I didn't have on it—had the most perfectly formed body. Even sitting down, his abs were defined and appeared rock hard to touch. My gaze traveled over the ropy muscle of his forearm, visually tracing the intricate knotting of his tattoo.

'Got it?' he asked, giving me a lopsided grin.

Having no idea what he was talking about, I simply stared at him. He laughed softly as he reached over and took the seat belt from my hand. As he drew the strap across me, the back of his fingers brushed my chest.

I sucked in a soft gasp as raw sensation skittered through my veins.

The seat belt clicked into place as he lifted his chin. His eyes flashed silver. 'Good?'

I nodded.

Still grinning, he returned to his seat and picked up the pink box I only noticed then. God, I wasn't observant at all.

He handed it over to me. 'I already ate half. Couldn't wait.'

Smiling, I popped open the box and took a bite. I looked forward to the whole cupcake thing. There was something simply exciting about not knowing what I was about to taste.

One bite and I moaned. 'Oh my God, is that Reese's Pieces in this thing?'

He nodded. 'Yep. That's good shit right there, huh?'

'I want to marry it.'

Jase laughed deeply as he eased the Jeep away from the curb. I didn't trust myself to speak until I finished off the cupcake and the thrill of his brief, and most likely accidental, touch had stopped racing from my veins, and by that time, we were on the main road, heading toward Martinsburg.

'Where are we going?' I asked.

'It's a surprise.' He slid me a sideways glance. 'Though you might end up regretting the jeans. Weatherman was saying it was going to get up to the mideighties this afternoon.'

Which was unseasonably warm for early October, but whatever. 'I'm fine.'

That one-sided grin tipped up. 'That you are.'

Staring at him, a laugh burst free. 'Did you . . .? That was really . . .'

'Awesome?'

I shook my head, grinning like a complete fool. 'That was pretty bad.'

He chuckled as he reached over, flipping the station to a blues channel. 'I thought it was smooth.'

My mouth opened to ask why he was trying to be smooth, but luckily I stopped myself. That question would probably end up making me look like an idiot by the time it was answered.

Forcing my gaze to the window, I clasped my hands in my lap. 'So . . . how are your classes going?'

I cringed at how lame the question sounded, but Jase didn't appear to notice. 'They're going good. As long as I can get into the rest of my classes next semester, I'll be graduating in the spring.'

'That's great.' I smiled broadly, maybe a little too widely. I had no idea what Jase planned to do once he graduated, but I doubted he was going to stay around here. It shouldn't even be a concern of mine. 'Where are you going once you graduate?'

Jase shifted in the driver's seat, keeping one hand on the steering wheel and the other resting on his leg. 'Well, with a degree in environmental studies, I really could go anywhere, but I'll stay here or commute into D.C. if I can get on with the Department of Interior or WVU. You know they've got an agricultural research center outside of Kearneysville.'

'You're not leaving?' My question came fast.

'I can't,' he said, and added quickly, 'I mean, I like it here.'

I didn't miss the sudden tensing of his shoulders. Nibbling my lower lip, I peeked at him again. 'You can't?'

He didn't say anything as he reached forward, turning the station back to country music. Someone started singing about a tear in their beer, but I was hardly paying attention. What could he have meant by him not being able to leave? Nothing was holding him here. He seriously could go anywhere, especially if he did get in with the Department of Interior.

Running a hand through his messy mop of hair, he glanced over at me. 'What about you?'

'Me?' He was so trying to change the subject.

'Yeah. You. Are you going to stay around here?' The derision in his voice caused me to stiffen. 'Teaching?'

Indignation rose at his tone. 'What is that supposed to mean?'

He laughed, but for some reason, it sounded dry and harsh. 'Come on, Tess, teaching a bunch of elementary-school kids? Seriously?'

Twisting toward him, I crossed my arms. 'Okay. I don't get it. You acted like teaching was a good idea and I—'

'It is a good idea, but it's not . . .'

'What?' I demanded, getting all kinds of defensive. 'It's not what?'

'You.' He glanced at me as he turned right onto Queen Street. 'It's not you.'

I stared at him and then barked out a laugh. 'That's dumb. How do you know what's me and what's not?' Anger flared in me, and I didn't dare look too closely at why. 'You barely know me, Jase.'

'I know you.'

I scoffed. 'No, you don't.'

That infuriating half grin appeared. 'Oh, Tess . . .'

'Don't "oh, Tess" me. I want to know why you're so convinced that I'd make a horrible teacher.'

'I didn't say you'd make a horrible teacher.' Amusement danced over his face, and I wanted to know what the hell was so funny. 'You'd make a great teacher. Kids would probably love you and maybe you'll be happy with that, but that's not what you want.'

'In fact, I like being around kids. Back at the studio, I volunteered to help out with the younger classes.' Staring out the window, I watched the shopping centers and apartments quickly give way to trees and then open fields. 'So whatever.'

'Okay. You're not getting what I'm saying.'

'Obviously not,' I replied tartly.

He sighed. 'You'd make a great teacher, Tess, but you're a . . . you're a performer. That's what you've always wanted.'

I squeezed my eyes tight, as if doing so somehow blocked out the truth. 'That's not what I've always wanted to do.'

'No?'

'No.'

'I don't believe you,' he said. 'And here's why. You've been dancing since you could walk. You're just here until you can start dancing again, right? The whole teaching shit

80

is a backup plan just in case you *can't* dance. It's not what you really want to do. You already admitted that to me.'

My mouth opened and I planned on telling him he was wrong, but dear Lord that was not what came tumbling out of my mouth. 'A year ago I didn't think I'd be sitting here, enrolled in college. It hadn't even crossed my mind. And you're right. When Dr. Morgan tells me next month that I'm okay to start dancing in three months or whatever, that's what I will do, because that's what I loved to do. What's so wrong with that? I won't be *here*, where it feels like I don't understand anything.'

Jase was quiet for a few moments. 'Nothing is wrong with that.'

Feeling like I stripped bare and did a naked jig for no reason, I threw my hands up in frustration. 'Then what's the point of this conversation?'

He smiled and shrugged one shoulder. 'I don't know. You started it.'

'I did not!'

Jase retorted, 'Yes, you did. You asked me what I was planning on doing. I was just returning the favor.'

I rolled my eyes. 'I want to hit you.'

He chuckled.

'Even more now.' I shot him a look.

Slowing the Jeep down to turn onto a narrow road that looked vaguely familiar, he tilted his head to the side. A beat of silence passed. 'Well, if you do end up being around here and deciding to stick with teaching, you'll be wonderful at it. And if not, then that's good, too. I know how much dancing means to you.'

I didn't know what to say about that, but then I realized where we were. Sitting up straight, I peered at the sign dangling from the chain. 'We're at the farm?'

'Yep.'

Sudden nervousness hummed through my veins. 'Why?'

'It's just something I thought about.' He winked, and I bit back a groan as my stomach flopped in response. 'You'll see.'

I turned wide eyes forward as we traveled up the bumpy, uneven road. Beyond the cornstalks and the field where the cows grazed, I saw what I figured Jase was thinking about.

A fissure of fear ran down my spine as I remembered our conversation about dancing and riding horses. 'Oh no . . .'

Jase chuckled as he parked the Jeep in front of the barn. 'You don't even know what you're saying no to.'

Pulse picking up, I rubbed my sweaty palms over my jeans and swallowed hard. The last thing I wanted was to die a horrific death in front of the boy I harbored major feels for. 'Jase, I don't know about this. Horses are big and I've never been on one. I'm probably going to fa—'

He placed the blunt tip of his finger on my lips. Surprise jolted through me. 'Stop,' he said softly, his deep gray eyes locking on mine. 'You don't have to do anything you don't want to do. Okay? You've just got to trust me. And you trust me, right?'

Before I could respond, he moved his hand, smoothing the finger along my bottom lip. I shivered as his hand drifted over my chin and then disappeared.

'Tess?'

Drawing in a short breath, I nodded, but I'd probably agree to play inside a wood chipper if he touched my lips again. 'I trust you.'

'Good.' There was a flash of a quick smile and then he was out of the Jeep.

I tracked him with my eyes, feeling a little dizzy. It was

the truth. I did trust him and that was a big deal for me. I really hadn't trusted any guy since Jeremy, anyone except my brother.

But I had trusted Jase from the moment I had met him.

Chapter 7

I wasn't going to die today. At least that's what I kept telling myself as I climbed out into the sticky heat. Summer didn't want to loosen its hold on this area at all.

My hands trembled as Jase joined me. Unfortunately, he tugged a white shirt on over his head, covering up the feast for my eyes. That was a damn shame, because if I was going to end up breaking my neck today, at least I would do so staring at his chest and abs.

The barn door creaked open, and an older man stepped out. Having never seen him before, I still knew right off the bat he was Jase's father. It was like staring at Jase thirty years from now.

Hair the same rich, brown color, skin dark from either a life in the sun or long-forgotten ancestry, he was as tall and lean as his son. Steely gray eyes moved from Jase to me and then widened as they returned to his son.

He sat the metal bucket he was carrying down on the gravel as his dark brows furrowed. A small surprised smile appeared on his handsome face.

Jase grinned as he placed a hand on my lower back. 'Hey, Dad, this is Teresa. She's Cam's sister.'

Recognition flared. 'Cam's little sister? Ah, the dancer.'

I felt my cheeks flush. How in the world did this man know that? And if that piece of background news had come from my brother, God only knew what else Cam had told him.

'That's her,' Jase replied, moving the hand on my back up a notch.

'Hi,' I said, waving my hand as awkwardly as humanly possible.

His father's smile spread as he strode toward us, his head cocked to the side in a mannerism that reminded me of Jase. 'You cannot be related to Cam. There is no way a pretty girl like you shares DNA with that ugly mug.'

A surprised laugh broke free. I think I liked this guy.

'And there is also no way you're here with this one.' He nodded his head at Jase, who frowned. 'You must be lost.'

Okay. I *really* liked this guy. 'You're right. I don't even know who this person is.'

Jase's frown slipped into a scowl as he glanced down at me. 'What the hell?'

I grinned.

His father winked, and in that moment, I realized that Jase got not only his looks, but also his personality from his father. 'So what are ya'll doin' here?' He pulled a red handkerchief from his back pocket and wiped his hands as he eyed his son. 'Jack's with your mom, down at Betty's.'

'I know. He goes there every day after school.' Jase dropped his hand, and the spot along my back tingled. 'I'm showing Tess the horses.'

Mr. Winstead eyed his son. 'Well, I'm going to be out back if ya'll need anything.'

'We'll be fine, Dad.' Jase started to turn.

'Wasn't tellin' you.' He looked over at me, mischief in

his eyes. 'If this boy's improper with you, you let me know and I'll take care of him.'

'Oh God,' Jase groaned, rubbing a hand down his jaw. 'She's a friend, Dad.'

'Uh-huh.' His father backed up, picking up the bucket. 'Friends with a pretty gal like that, then you're doing something wrong, son.'

My smile reached my ears as I turned to Jase slowly.

'Don't even think it,' he warned. He looked like he wanted to strangle his dad as he reached down, wrapping his hand around mine. 'Come on, before I embarrass my father with a good ole-fashioned redneck thumping.'

His father chuckled as he gave our joined hands a pointed look. 'Friends?'

'Dad.' Jase sighed.

I giggled as he tugged me toward the fence and his father disappeared back into the barn. 'I like your dad.'

He snorted. 'I'm sure you do.'

'He acted like you don't bring . . . girls here a lot.'

'I don't.' Stopping, he let go of my hand and faced me as he stepped over a small retaining wall. 'Then again, you just met my dad, so I'm sure you can understand why.'

Part of me was flattered that he had brought me to his home, a place where no other girl had traveled. But I was his friend and the other girls probably weren't that.

'Here,' he said, placing his hands on my hips and lifting me up over the wall like it was nothing to him. 'There you go.'

'I could've done that,' I murmured.

He shrugged. 'I know.' Taking my hand again, he carefully led me through the high grass, toward the edges of the split-rail fence. 'Be careful. There's a damn groundhog or a family of them living on this farm. Holes everywhere.'

'Okay.' I wasn't thinking about farms or groundhogs. Focused on the weight and feel of his hand wrapped firmly around mine, I had little room in my mind to worry about holes in the ground.

He was quiet as he guided me toward the gate in the split rail. Letting go of my hand, he unhooked the lock. Hinges groaned as the metal gates swung open.

I hesitated. 'I don't know about this.'

An easy grin appeared as he swaggered up to where I stood. 'Tess, come on. You said you trust me.'

Shifting my weight from foot to foot, I stared over his shoulder. At the other end of the large pen, two horses grazed, their black tails flicking idly. 'I do trust you.'

'Then come with me.'

One of the horses, its coat a mixture of black and white, reared its massive head. It turned, angling its muzzle toward our side of the fence. Neither of the horses had saddles on.

'They're not going to trample you to death.' He took my hand again. 'And I don't even expect you to get on one.'

My chin jerked up. 'You don't?'

He smiled slightly as he caught a piece of hair that blew across my face, tucking it back. 'No. This is a horse meet and greet.'

'I've never done a horse meet and greet before.'

'You're going to love them.' He pulled me forward, and my lips twitched. 'They really are gentle. Jack's been on them a million times, and if I thought they were dangerous, he wouldn't be anywhere near them.'

That was a good point. 'Okay,' I said, taking a deep breath. 'Let's do this.'

He didn't give me a chance to second-guess myself. Within seconds we were inside the pen. Another steel bucket sat on the ground, full of grain. 'I'm going to call them over, okay? They're going to come flying. It's close to feeding time. So be ready.'

Throat tight, I nodded.

My fear seemed a little unreasonable up until Jase lifted two fingers to his perfectly formed mouth and let loose a high-pitched whistle. The horses' heads jerked up and then they took off, their hooves pounding on the beaten earth, racing straight for us.

Holy crap.

I took a step back, hitting an unmovable wall of muscle that was Jase and bouncing off. An arm wrapped around my waist from behind when I started to move away, keeping me firmly in place, his front pressed to my back.

'It's okay.' His breath was warm against my ear, and I was torn between being freaked out over the dinosaurs heading our way and freaked out over the fact I was in Jase's arms. 'You're doing great.'

I gripped his arm as I squeezed my eyes shut. My heart worked overtime, jumping around in my chest as the thunder of the hooves grew closer, shaking the ground. A sudden plume of dust filled the air and a warm, wet breeze caressed my face. I pressed back against Jase, straining away.

'You got a visitor, Tess.' He rested his chin atop my head, which caused my pulse to try to outrun my heart. 'Two of them to be exact.'

'Okay.'

There was a pause. 'Are your eyes closed?'

'No.'

His chin slid off my head and then his chest rumbled as he laughed. 'Your eyes are closed.' He laughed again. 'Open them up.'

Cursing under my breath, I pried one eye open and then jerked against him. His arm tightened. 'Oh wow . . .'

The black-and-white horse was the closest, standing mere feet away from me. The brown one wasn't too far, shaking its head and making soft snorts. My eyes were wide as they bounced between the two creatures. 'They're not carnivorous, right? Because at their size, they could eat me.'

Jase laughed deeply as his hand shifted up, resting in the center of my stomach, just below my breasts. 'Horses do not eat people, you little idiot.'

I started, eyes narrowing. 'There's always a first.'

The lips pulled back on the black-and-white horse as if it was smirking at me.

'This one right here? Mr. Friendly? Jack calls him Bubba One,' he said in a quiet, calming voice. But air hitched in my throat when his thumb moved in a slow circle over the thin material of my tank top, hitting against the wire in my bra. 'And the brown one is Bubba Two.'

Mouth dry, I wetted my lips. 'That's good for remembering names.'

He chuckled as his pinkie and forefinger started to move up and down, reaching my belly button and then sliding back up. It was almost as if he was unaware of what he was doing, or the electrifying response the tiny motions were dragging out of me. 'I think so too, but his real name is Lightning.'

Said horse shook his head, tossing the shaggy mane.

'Lightning seems to be a more suitable name,' I admitted, relaxing as the seconds passed. Maybe that was his intention. Distract me with the soft, *almost* innocent touches. It was working. 'What about Bubba Two?'

'Ah, the one who is staring at the pail like it's the holy mecca of grain?' His cheek grazed mine as I laughed. 'That's Thunder. And we're going to feed them. Together.'

The friction his fingers created with my shirt sent tiny shivers up and down my back. 'With our hands?'

His answering laugh tipped the corners of my lips up. 'Yes. With our hands.'

'After checking out the choppers on them, I'm not so sure about that.'

'You'll be okay.' He slid his hand off my stomach and wrapped it around my wrist. Slowly, he lifted my hand out in front of me. 'Hold still.'

My heart lurched. 'Jase—'

Lightning trotted forward and pressed his wet nose against my hand. I cringed, waiting for him to eat my poor fingers. The horse didn't. Nope. It nudged my hand as it whinnied softly.

He guided my hand up over Lightning's jaw, all the way to the pointy, twitchy ears. 'See?' he murmured. 'That's not too bad, is it?'

I shook my head as my fingers curled along the soft coat. Lightning seemed to anticipate the direction of the petting, pressing his long head against my hand as my fingers tangled in his mane. It wasn't bad at all.

Jase shifted behind me, and in an instant all thoughts of the horses evaporated. His hips lined up against my backside, and I bit down on my lower lip as I focused on the white splotch covering Lightning's muzzle.

I could *feel* him—feel Jase. And there was absolutely no doubt in my mind that he was affected by how close we were standing. That knowledge and the hard length of him left me dizzy, just like it had done that Saturday night. An all too warm flush spread down my neck. In the back of my head, I was rationalizing his physical reaction. He was a guy. Our bodies were pressed together. If a wind blew on a guy's private area, they got hard. So I should just ignore it, but my body was so not on board with my head. My body was operating on a different playing field. An ache centered low in my stomach. A sharp and sweet yearning raced through my veins.

'Not so scary, right?' His voice was deeper, richer. 'They're like dogs. Well, like a dog that can carry around two hundred pounds, if not more.' Hand sliding off mine, he stepped back, and the sudden emptiness of his body was like a cold shock. 'Trust me.'

Then he smacked my ass.

I yelped, eyes widening as I started to turn toward him, but Lightning, apparently annoyed with the lack of attention, nosed my arm. 'Uh . . .'

'It's okay. You were just petting him. And he didn't eat your hand.'

I considered that as Lightning stared at me with dark eyes. Scratching him behind the ear, I was still scared out of my mind. The size of the horses was astonishing up close, and I honestly couldn't ever picture myself sitting astride them, especially one named *Lightning*.

Jase returned to my side, sitting the bucket between us. Thunder followed, tail twitching in impatience. After kneeling and scooping up a handful of oats, Jase rose. The brown muzzle immediately went for his hand as Jase looked over at me. 'It's that easy.'

While letting a horse eat out of my hand wasn't something I imagined doing, I didn't complain when Jase dumped some oats in my open palm. Face scrunched, I offered my hand to Lightning.

'You should see yourself right now.' Jase laughed as he shook his head. 'It's cute.'

And probably a bit ridiculous. My cheeks warmed as Lightning nosed around the oats in my hand. 'Picky eater?'

Jase grinned as he rubbed Thunder's neck with his free hand. 'I think he's taking his time because he likes you.'

'Is that so?' I smiled as I slowly reached out with my other hand, caressing the elegant muzzle. Several moments passed as I considered how I ended up here. This was more than just a horse meet and greet for no reason. I got what Jase was trying to do. It all stemmed back to the conversation in his Jeep. Substituting the rush of adrenaline and pleasure dancing brought me with something else.

The fact that he even cared enough to do this, to take the time, moved me. More than a stolen kiss a year ago or brief touches now could. Emotion clogged my throat as Lightning nibbled at the oats, tickling my palm.

I didn't know why Jase was doing this for me. Yes, we were friends—friends for a while now. When he visited Cam, he'd also visited me, but this seemed like more than what a friend would do.

Then again, I wasn't an expert on friends.

As I stood there, the light breeze doing nothing to erase the fine sheen of humidity coating my skin, I realized with sudden clarity that I was really quite . . . friendless. Because if Sadi or any of my studio friends were true friends, we'd still be in contact even if we no longer shared a common goal. It wasn't just envy or bitterness that stood between us. Without dance, there just wasn't anything there.

I swallowed the burn in my throat. 'Is it really like flying?'

Jase glanced over at me and nodded. 'It is.'

Pushing the thickness down again, I returned my attention to Lightning, scooping up more oats once he'd finished with what I held. There was something peaceful about all this—the quiet of the farm, the simple act.

'This isn't bad,' I admitted quietly.

'I know. It will be better once you understand what *here* is to you.'

I bit my lip, remembering what I'd said in the Jeep. 'When did you get so wise sounding?'

'I've always been extremely wise. So much so, I consider it a curse.'

I laughed softly.

'Actually, it's experience. Things come along you don't expect all the time, Tess. Trust me. Things that change everything about your life—about what you thought you wanted, who you thought you were. Things that make you reevaluate everything and even if it doesn't sound like a good thing in the beginning?' He shrugged as he settled his gaze on Thunder. 'Sometimes they turn out better than you could've ever imagined.'

The way clarity rang in his voice, I had no doubt in my mind he had firsthand experience with the unexpected.

'You know something?' Jase asked after a couple of minutes passed. 'What Jacob said in the Den yesterday wasn't true.'

The swift change of the subject startled me. As Lightning ate out of my palm, I looked at Jase. 'What?'

Thunder, done eating, turned and trotted off as Jase wiped his hands along his jeans. He sauntered up to where I stood, idly scratching Lightning's ear since I dropped my free hand. 'You know what I'm talking about, Tess. And I know why you left immediately afterward.'

My first response was to deny, because denial was almost always easier than facing the truth. Especially when the truth was sort of humiliating. But Jase had intimate knowledge of said truth. Right now, denial would just make me look stupid.

'I don't want to talk about it.'

'Tess—'

'I could live happily ever after if I could never hear his name again or have to think about how he was or what it felt like to be with him and think—' My voice unexpectedly cracked, and I forced myself to take a deep, cleansing breath. 'I don't want to remember what all of that felt like.'

There was a moment of silence. 'But you know that you're never going to forget, and you need to understand what Jacob said wasn't true.'

Sighing, I watched Lightning go for the last of the oats. 'What he said was true.'

'No—'

'It is true. I was one of those "stupid girls" who let a guy beat on her.' I laughed, but the sound was grating on my ears. 'And I almost ruined my brother's life because I allowed the situation to get to that point. Trust me, I know.'

'You don't know shit, apparently.' Jase took my hand in his, brushing the dust from the oats off it. 'You did not almost ruin your brother's life. He made that decision to go after that punk ass. Not you. And I can't really blame him for doing so. If it had been me, I would've put that motherfucker into the ground.'

My gaze swung to him sharply, and all I saw was honesty in his gunmetal eyes. 'No. You wouldn't have, Jase.'

His brows rose. 'Uh, yeah, I would've. And you know what, that's wrong as shit, but that would've been *my* choice. Just like it was Cam's. It is *not* and *never* has been your fault. No matter what happened between you and that *dick*'—he spat the word—'what happened on Thanksgiving is not your fault.'

I stared into his eyes and—oh God—I wanted to believe him. The weight of that nasty guilt was worse than the weight of a future gone to shit. Some of the responsibility lessened, though. That much was true, but I ducked my gaze, following Lightning's retreat. With the lack of attention, the horse was off chasing Thunder.

Jase still held my hand, his fingers slipping around my wrist. 'And you weren't stupid.'

I bit out a laugh as I lifted my gaze. 'Okay. Why are you telling me all this? Why are you trying to make me feel better?'

'Because it's true.' His lips thinned as a troubled look settled into his striking features. 'You were how old when you started dating that guy?'

I shrugged a shoulder.

94

'How old, Tess?' Determination filled his tone.

Shaking my head, I tried to pull my hand free, but he held on. The whole conversation made me want to crawl under the thick and wide piles of hay behind us. 'I was fourteen when we started dating—the summer before my freshman year. Happy with that answer?'

He didn't look happy. 'You were young.'

My fingers curled helplessly inward. 'I was, but he . . .'

'He didn't hit you then?' Jase said it so bluntly that I flinched. The lines softened around his mouth. 'When did he first hit you?'

It was easy to remember. The memory was all too fresh in my mind. 'I'd just turned sixteen. I stepped on his new Nikes accidentally.'

Jase looked away. A muscle ticked along his jaw. Nearly ten months passed between the first time Jeremy hit me and the last time. Ten months of keeping it secret, of hiding the bruises, and of wondering what I had been doing to deserve it.

Ten months I never, ever wanted to relive.

'Even at sixteen, you were young. You're *still* young,' he said finally, his voice even, but tight. 'I can't even imagine what you were going through, but you were just a kid, Tess. You weren't stupid. You were scared.'

The knot came out of nowhere, filling my throat. My voice was hoarse when I spoke. 'I thought it was my fault.'

'It wasn't your fault.' His eyes flashed an intense silver. 'Please tell me you know it was not your fault.'

'I do now.' Blinking rapidly, I cleared my throat. 'What he did wasn't my fault, but my silence really didn't help my case.'

'Tess—'

'I get what you're saying, but I should've told someone. You can't argue that. Silence is not a fucking virtue. It's a

95

disease—a cancer that eats away at you and fucks with your head. I know that now. Not then and . . .' I trailed off, shaking my head as I drew in a stunted breath. I thought of Debbie in that moment. 'And, well, things are different now.'

'They are, but you weren't stupid and it wasn't your fault then. And because I say so, that's the way it is. End of discussion.'

I arched a brow. 'End of discussion?'

He nodded as his lips curled up on one corner. 'Yep. What I say goes.'

'Yeah. Sure.'

The grin grew as he tugged gently on my arm. His eyes lightened to a soft gray. 'Do not doubt my authority.'

I laughed and was surprised that I could do so after such a serious and sad conversation. 'You have absolutely no authority.'

He smirked. 'Oh, my authority is there. All the time. It's just stealth authority. You don't even know it's happening.'

I rolled my eyes, but as the initial burn of the awkward conversation faded, I recognized his words for what they were worth. Even if I had trouble accepting no fault in the mess, I knew that Jase firmly believed in what he said. And that did mean something. Heck, it meant a lot.

'So what did you think about the meet and greet?' he said, and it was like a thick cloud had passed. We were officially back in safe territory. 'Wasn't bad?'

'No.' I smiled up at him. 'It wasn't bad at all.'

'Then next time, maybe you'll ride one of them? Lightning?'

My stomach tumbled a bit. 'Ah . . .'

'I'll be with you,' he added, dipping his chin. 'The whole time.'

I pictured me practically sitting in his lap, his arm around my waist, holding me close, and . . . I felt hot. I needed to throw the brakes on the porn train before my mind veered into triple X land.

He chuckled, the sound deep and sexy, as he moved closer. His sneakers brushed mine, and I had to crane my neck to meet his eyes. 'I can tell you like that idea.'

'What?' I scowled, hopefully fiercely and not stupidly. 'No. I was thinking about music class tomorrow. Aren't we covering the baroque period? Stimulating stuff right there. I'm all kinds of excited.'

A smirk formed on his lips. 'I don't think that's what you are all excited about or what gets you excited.'

'It's not you.'

'Whatever.' The teasing glint grew in his gaze. 'You were thinking about me.'

I snorted. Like a pig. 'Yeah, I don't think so. I don't think about you at all.'

'You're a terrible liar.'

'And you have a terrible ego. Worse than my brother and that's saying something.'

'You can say whatever you want. I know better.' He dipped his head and his lips grazed my cheek, blazing a small fire across my cheeks. 'See? You're flushing and I haven't even done anything.'

'It's the sun,' I replied, straining back before I did something stupid. Like grabbing his face in a death grip and molesting him. 'I'm getting a heatstroke.'

He choked out a laugh. 'The sun isn't even out.'

I huffed. 'Like that makes a difference.'

'You know what?'

Cocking my head to the side, I waited.

That infuriating grin seemed permanently etched into his face. 'It's cute.'

'What is?' I hoped he wasn't thinking that about me because I'd like to be seen as more than 'cute' when it came to him.

97

'You.' He caught a piece of my hair in his other hand and tickled the edges along my neck while I fought the urge to stick my tongue out. 'This whole *act*—you pretending that you don't sit and think about me all the time. You probably sit in your dorm and write my name all over your dry-erase board.'

'Oh my God.' I laughed.

'And then you dream about me, right? You stay awake and—'

My laugh cut him off as I swung at him with my free hand, aiming for his chest. What he was saying was beyond ridiculous. Okay—maybe not the dreaming part. He did star in quite a few of them. My hand never landed though. He snatched it out of the air with his other hand with startling reflexes and hauled me against his chest in one quick, smooth move.

Impressive.

'Hitting is not nice,' he said, grinning. 'And neither is deluding yourself.'

My chest flush with his made this conversation all the more difficult. The tips of my breasts tingled sharply. 'You should listen to what you're saying. You said you regretted kissing me, so why would I sit around and think about you? I moved on, bud.'

The moment those words left my mouth and my gaze locked with his, I realized that I'd made a mistake. I don't know what he was thinking, but the intensity in his silvery eyes consumed me. Somehow we'd gone from harmless teasing and talking smack—because the stuff I'd been spouting off at him were some pretty bad lies—to this . . . and I didn't even know what this was.

The humor vanished from his striking face. 'I never said I regretted kissing you.'

'I'm pretty sure you did.'

His eyes burned like quicksilver. 'I'm pretty sure I *didn't*.'

Slowly, I shook my head. Confusion poured in and I didn't know what to say.

'And I don't regret kissing you.'

In my chest, my heart tripled its beats at those words. 'You don't?'

'No.' He looked away for a brief moment, jaw working, before his gaze latched onto mine again. 'I should. I wish I did.'

'I don't,' I whispered before I could stop myself. 'I don't regret it at all.'

He stared at me a moment as his hands on my wrists spasmed. His arms extended out, putting a few inches in between our bodies, and I should've kept my damn mouth shut.

'Fuck,' he said, voice hoarse, and dragged me back against him.

Jase lowered his head and his mouth was on mine before I even realized what was happening. My brain was way behind what was going on, but he kissed me—he was *kissing* me. His lips were on mine, and there was nothing soft and sweet about this kiss.

I was branded in seconds.

His mouth moved along as his hands moved to cup my cheeks, tilting my head back. I rose up onto the toes of my sneakers, placing my hands against his chest. Under my palm, his heart pounded as fast as mine. He shuddered as his fingers spread, and I think I stopped breathing.

Over three years of crushing on him, a year since the last time our lips met, and Jase . . . oh God, he was finally kissing me.

Mind reeling and senses spinning, I trembled as he nipped at my lower lip the same way he had at my neck before and then flicked the edge of his tongue over the seam of my lips, coaxing them open. He deepened the kiss, tasting me—owning me, and in the same instance, setting me free. This kiss was nothing like the one stolen a year ago. It blew it out of the water as a deep, nearly primitive rumble rose up from his chest.

He drank me in.

There was a brief second where I worried about his father finding us like this, and, well, that would just be awkward. The threat vanished as his hands slid down my throat, over my shoulders, to my hips. Being caught? Total nonissue.

My heart swelled until I thought it couldn't take any more as his hold on my hips tightened. He lifted me up without breaking the kiss. Instinct took over. I wrapped my legs around his waist as I looped my arms around his neck, thrusting my fingers through the soft edges of his hair.

He started walking, and I had no idea where he was heading, but I was in awe of his multitasking skills, the way his tongue tangled with mine, how his hands curved to the cheeks of my ass and never once stumbling.

A maddening rush of sensations shot through me as he went down on his knees and my back hit the hay. His powerful body hovered over mine, caging me in. The thin, itchy straws poked at my arms, but his lips seared mine and he stole my breath as he lowered his body onto mine. The hay drew in our combined weight, cradling us as one of Jase's hands drifted to my thigh, hooking my leg over his. This was nothing like the night he was drunk. We both knew he was fully aware of what he was doing. We both were *here*.

The pressure—the positioning of where he was the hardest and I was the softest—left little room for thought. I could feel him, and when his lower body rolled against mine, I whimpered at the sharp pleasure pounding through

100

me. I tilted my hips up, following his lead, and his answering groan was like thunder in my blood.

'Damn,' he growled against my swollen lips. 'Oh, fucking damn, Tess, I . . .'

His mouth melded to mine once more, but there was something deeper and slower about the kiss. Almost tender. I thought I felt his hand tremble against the curve of my waist as it slipped under my shirt. I knew for a fact that my hands shook as my fingers intertwined in his hair. The rough skin of his palm skimmed over my belly and I jerked against him, needing and wanting so very much more.

In that moment, where nothing seemed to exist outside of his kisses, of the way he tasted and how he felt, I would go all the way.

On a farm.

Near a barn.

In the hay.

His lips left mine, and I whimpered, immediately missing them. His smug chuckle sent darts of desire zinging through my veins and then his lips scorched a path to my neck. I threw my head back, giving him all the access he wanted.

And he took.

He kissed the sensitive spot under my jaw, nuzzling my neck. His lips soothed the burn of the fine stubble around his mouth. My entire body ached for him, for more—for everything that went beyond *this*.

As if in a tunnel, I heard the loud rumbling of a car. At first I thought it was my imagination—I prayed that it was. But as the seconds passed, the sound grew louder.

Jase sprang off me, onto his feet, and backed up. The rush of air felt cool in spite of the muggy day. In a daze, my gaze crawled down the length of him. Straw clung to his shirt and the fine hairs along his arms. My attention got snagged up below the hips before I looked down at myself.

My shirt was bunched up under my bra.

The car passed the bend in the road, and a flash of red appeared beyond the tall yellow and green cornstalks.

Processing skills had yet to catch up with the events. So when Jase came forward and towed me onto my feet, I was unprepared. I swayed to the right and tried to correct myself before I put my weight onto my bad leg. He caught me before I did, steadying me as I panted for breath like I'd just done a series of tricks on the stage.

'Shit, Tess,' he said, dragging his fingers along the hem of my tank top. He straightened my shirt while I stood there like an imbecile. 'That . . .'

The car had stopped beside Jase's Jeep and the passenger door creaked open and a tiny form stumbled out. A woman shouted.

'Jase!' shrieked a small voice. His little brother spun toward the pen. 'Jase!'

I was frozen in place, knowing that I was covered in hay and my skin was way too flushed, like a heatstroke was now a true possibility. My wild gaze swung toward Jase.

'I'm sorry. That shouldn't have happened,' Jase said, and then he turned and walked away.

Chapter 8

Jack threw himself into Jase's prepared arms. Lifting the little guy up, Jase spun him in a wide circle. Anyone standing nearby would've lost an eye if they'd been close. Jack shrieked happily, eyes screwed shut and mouth open.

My chest lurched at the sight of them together. Jase . . . he'd make a great father one day. Not that I'd obviously get firsthand experience with him as a dad, since I was one permanent, giant walking mistake according to him. Knowing that stung like I'd walked into a hornet's nest and started kicking it. I didn't know why it hurt so badly. The idea of having babies was so far off from what I planned on doing in the near future, but it didn't make the squeezing in my chest ease off.

Jack wiggled down and the moment his feet touched the ground, he sprinted toward me. Wrapping his little arms around my legs, he peered up at me, grinning in a way that melted my heart. The kid was adorable.

'Did you learn to ride the horsies?' he asked, surprising me with his memory.

I forced a smile. 'I fed them, but I didn't learn to ride

them.' And, apparently, I never would at the rate Jase and I were going.

'Why you not teached her?' Jack demanded as he craned his neck toward his brother.

'Teach,' Jase corrected absently. Walking up, he wrapped his fingers around Jack's upper arms. 'You're like a little amoeba.'

Jack's brows puckered as he held on to my legs. 'What's an ah-meeb-a?'

Jase chuckled as he tugged on him again. 'Something that has a tendency to attach itself to other things. You should let go.'

For a second, it didn't look like he would, but then he relinquished his surprisingly strong hold. Jase glanced up as he spun his brother away from me. Our gazes collided and then he hastily looked away.

Oh, joy. The trip back to the dorm was going to be fun.

But not as awkward as addressing his mother for the first time looking like I'd just gotten it on in the hay. Which I sort of just did.

Mrs. Winstead smiled warmly enough as I followed the two brothers over to the Jeep, but surprise was etched into her features. She was a pretty woman with fine lines around her mouth and eyes. Dressed in jeans and a worn shirt, she looked like she knew her way around the farm and hadn't been scared of getting hands-on.

Taking a deep breath, I held out my hand as Jase picked up his brother, draping him over his shoulders like a sack of potatoes. There weren't going to be any introductions. Not like with his father. Not after what happened, and I felt awkward, totally out of place, as if I didn't belong here. And I didn't. A burn crawled up my throat, deepening an ache in my chest.

My cheeks flushed. 'Hi. I'm Teresa.'

Jase glanced over sharply at the hoarse quality to my voice, and I cleared my throat, focusing on his mom. 'I'm Cam's sister.'

Recognition flared in her deep brown eyes. 'Ah, yes. How is that brother of yours doing?'

On safe, common ground, I started to relax a little. 'He's doing good. He's going to try out for D.C. United early next year.'

'Really? That's great to hear.' She glanced over at Jase, who now had his brother doing the Superman cape thing again. God, they were adorable together. Sigh. 'Did you know Jase used to play soccer?'

'Mom,' Jase groaned.

I nodded. 'Yeah, Cam's mentioned it a time or two, but he never said why he stopped.'

Mrs. Winstead opened her mouth, but Jase swung Jack around, putting him safely on the ground. 'We've got to run, Mom.' He barely looked at me. 'Come on, Tess.'

I folded my arms across my chest as I stepped back, biting my tongue. I was *not* a dog, and I did not respond to commands.

'I wanna go!' Jack immediately started toward the Jeep, but Jase caught up with him.

'Nah, little buddy, you have to sit this one out.'

His lower lip started to tremble. 'But I wanna go with you.'

'I know, but I've got to take Tess back, all right?'

Jack pouted, clearly seconds away from what would likely become an epic tantrum. Jase knelt in front of him, brows raised as he held the boy's shoulders. He got down on his level, so unlike most guys his age. 'I'll come back, okay? We'll go out for ice cream. How does that sound?'

Jack's eyes lit up, but the boys' mom frowned. 'Jase, you're going to ruin his dinner. Again.'

Jase stuck his tongue out. 'We aren't going to ruin anything, are we?'

He giggled. 'Nope!'

'Okay. Get your butt inside.' He rose, guiding Jack over to where Mrs. Winstead waited. 'I'll be back in a little while.' He turned to me, and I tensed.

Feeling as awkward as a dancer on a stage for the first time, I waved at Mrs. Winstead and Jack. 'It was nice meeting you.'

She smiled broadly as she glanced over at Jase and then back to me. 'I hope to see you again.'

Ah, well, shit just got more awkward.

I nodded, because what could I do? Jack tore away from Mrs. Winstead's hold and gave me one last hug. Squeezing him back, I knew it would be hard not to love the little boy.

Part of me wanted to stay behind and hitch a ride back to campus, but that would look weird, so after Jack ran off, I made my way over to the Jeep. Ever the gentleman when he wanted, Jase held open the door.

I didn't say thank you.

Jase climbed in, letting out a sigh that rivaled anything I could've produced, which pissed me off, because why was *he* feeling put out? Jaw locked down, he turned the car around and headed down the gravel road. He didn't speak until we neared the end of the long stretch of road.

'Tess—'

'Don't,' I said, cutting him off. 'There is really nothing you have to say right now that I'm probably going to want to hear. And if you tell me what just happened is a mistake again . . .' My voice cracked in an embarrassing way. 'I'm going to punch you in the throat. Seriously.'

His lips twitched as if he thought I was joking. 'I shouldn't have phrased it that way, but—'

'Nope,' I warned, sensing he was about to say something even worse. 'Just take me home.' I pressed my lips together to keep them from quivering like a pansy ass, and I could feel his eyes on me. 'I just want to go home.'

There was a beat of silence and then he said, '*Fuck*.'

Instead of pulling out, he shifted the gear into park. The Jeep idled as he twisted in his seat toward me. 'You don't understand, Tess.'

I rolled my eyes, about to make a smart-ass comment, but stopped when my throat closed up. 'You're right. I don't. You're attracted to me. You want me, but you keep pushing me away. Is it because of Cam? Because seriously, that's lame, Jase. He's my brother, not the holder of my chastity.'

Jase's face puckered as if he'd tasted something sour. 'Okay. That's an image I never wanted to picture.'

'Oh, shut up.'

His features smoothed out as he clenched the steering wheel. 'All right, it's not Cam. Maybe in the beginning it was, because hooking up with his little sister is crossing all kinds of lines, but I can get over that.'

'Obviously you did,' I muttered, turning my gaze to the passenger window. 'Or your cock got over it real quick like.'

Jase swallowed a strangled cough. 'Tess, I . . . it's just you don't want to be with me. You really don't want that.'

I barked out a short laugh. 'Wow. So this is a new attempt. You're not rejecting me, but it's more like I'm rejecting you? Smooth.'

'It's not like that,' he insisted. 'Trust me. There are things you don't know about me and if you did, you wouldn't be sitting here.'

Returning my gaze to him, I arched a brow. 'Did you kill someone? Cut up their body and feed it to hogs?'

'What?' His brows furrowed. 'No.'

'Have you beaten or raped a girl? Have a stash of kids locked in a basement somewhere? Or you're secretly a terrorist?'

His face contorted into disgust. 'Fuck. No.'

'Okaay,' I said slowly. 'I'm not sure exactly what you could've done that is so terrible then.'

He looked away, shaking his head. 'You don't get it, Tess. I *can't* have you.'

'But you do have me,' I whispered, and then clamped my mouth shut. Did I just say that? Horrified, I could only stare as his eyes widened.

Oh my God, I did just say that out loud.

But it was true. Jase had me whether he realized it or not, even if he wanted me or not. I couldn't change how I felt about him or what I wanted.

'I don't,' he said, shadows forming in his eyes. 'I don't want to hurt your feelings.'

But . . . there was an unspoken 'but' that sunk deep within me.

Closing my eyes, I sucked in a shrill breath as pressure in my chest formed and expanded. I put it out there for him, so pathetically, and that was all he could say? Embarrassed beyond belief, all I wanted was to get away. 'Please take me home.'

He remained still in the driver's seat. 'Tess—'

'Take me home!'

There was a heartbeat of silence as he dropped his hands into his lap. 'He's my son!' Jase shouted, startling him and me, and then he said lower, as if he couldn't believe he was actually saying it, 'Jack's my *son*.'

Chapter 9

I didn't think I heard him right at first. I had to have heard something other than what he said, because there was no way Jack was his son. Jack was his *brother*.

But as I stared at him and took in the paleness of his face and the clarity of his gray eyes, I knew that what he'd spoken was something so rare, so unknown to probably almost anyone, that it was the truth.

I shook my head, dumbfounded. 'Jack's your son?'

Jase held my gaze a moment longer and then focused ahead. Several seconds passed before he spoke. 'Shit. I . . . no one knows that, Tess. My parents do. Cam does, but he would never say anything. No one else knows.'

Unsurprised that Cam knew this about Jase, I was still a little shocked that he hadn't told me. Then again, it had never been my business.

I really didn't know how to process this as I stared at him. My thoughts raced. Jack and Jase did look an awful lot alike, but so did *brothers*. Jase was super-close with Jack, seeming to have a two-way bond with the boy, but so did a lot of *brothers*. Jase seemed to put Jack before a lot of things, but *brothers* did that.

But they weren't brothers.

They were father and son.

Holy shit.

Lots of things suddenly made sense. Besides how he acted around Jack, there was our conversation earlier. How he seemed to know firsthand that some of the best things in life weren't planned. And it probably explained why he no longer played soccer or had any plans of taking a job after college that would force him to move away. He wanted to be here with his son, no matter the status between them. It also explained why he didn't keep girls around, because he did have a kid, and even if he wasn't actively raising that child, he could be one day. And that was a lot to dump on a girl. I could get that. I was pretty shell-shocked.

Jase was a *dad*.

He was most definitely a FILF—a father I'd like to fuck.

I squeezed my eyes shut. Oh my God, I couldn't believe I just thought that. But he *was* a dad.

The air leaked out of me, and then I swallowed hard as he reached over, plucking something—a piece of hay—out of my hair. He twirled it between his fingers as I gawked at him. 'Does . . . does he know?'

Jase shook his head. 'No. He thinks his grandparents are his parents.'

'Why?' I asked the question before I could rethink how intrusive it was. God, that was rude of me. But I wanted to know. I needed to know how Jase, someone who clearly loved that little boy more than life, was letting someone else raise him.

'It's a mess,' he answered, leaning back in the seat. He rubbed his hand down his face and sighed. 'They've raised him since birth as their own. Even adopted him. That makes me sound like shit, doesn't it?' He tilted his head toward me, and pain filled his eyes, causing my chest to clench.

110

'I'm not even raising my own son. My fucking parents are and he doesn't even know. That makes me so attractive, doesn't it?'

I blinked rapidly, my mouth hung open, and I had no idea what to say to that.

He laughed harshly as he tipped his head back against the seat. Tension seeped out of his shoulders. 'I'm not raising my own kid,' he repeated, and I knew right off that was something he said to himself quite often. 'For five years, my parents have raised him. I want to change that, but I can't take back those years, and how do I change that now? Telling him could fucking destroy his world and I don't want to do that. It would also break my parents' hearts, because they think of him as their own.' His eyes closed. 'I'm a damn deadbeat dad.'

Jase laughed humorlessly again, and I sat up straighter. 'You are not a deadbeat.'

'Oh, come on.' A self-degrading smile appeared. 'I just told you I have a kid. I'm almost *twenty-two* years old and I have a *five*-year-old that my parents are raising. Do the math, Tess. I was sixteen when he was conceived. Sixteen. Still in high school. Obviously that's not something to be proud of.'

'Is it something you're ashamed of?'

His gaze sharpened on me and he seemed to toss around that question. 'No,' he said quietly. 'I'm not ashamed of Jack. I'll never be. But I am ashamed of the fact that I'm not owning up to my responsibility and being his father.'

I bit down on my lip, wanting to ask so many questions as a truck blew past the entrance road. 'So you were sixteen when he was conceived? You were just a kid, right? Just like I was a kid when I was with Jeremy.'

'That's different.' He closed his eyes. 'That doesn't excuse anything on my end.'

111

'How many sixteen-year-olds do you know that could be a parent?' I demanded.

'There are many who are.'

'So? That doesn't mean that every sixteen-year-old is equipped and ready for that. I sure as hell wouldn't have been. And my parents would've helped me out.' I paused, realizing like an idiot that it takes two people to make a baby the last time I checked. 'You also weren't the only person responsible. There had to have been a mom. Where is—?'

'I'm not talking about her,' he said sharply, and I flinched at his tone. '*None* of this has to do with her at all.'

Whoa. There was definitely some baby mama drama right there.

'And helping isn't the same thing as adopting.' His eyes opened into thin slits. 'When I told my parents what was going on, they were upset, but they wanted me to finish school, go to college and keep playing soccer. They didn't want me to give all that up.'

'I don't blame them,' I said softly. But what about the mother?

'So it was either that or give Jack up for adoption, because I wasn't ready. As fucked up as this sounds, I didn't want him at first. I didn't want anything to do with him; before he was even born or I even laid eyes on him, I gave him up in a way . . .' His voice grew thick and he cleared his throat. It was obvious that whoever the mom was, she was out of the picture the moment Jack was born, and I was *dying* to know why. 'So they filed for adoption and it was granted. Looking back, I realize how fucking selfish I was. I should've owned up then, but I didn't, and there is nothing I can do to change that right now.'

'But you are a part of his life, Jase. And I can tell that you wish you had done things differently and isn't that what matters most? That you love him nonetheless?'

Jase tipped his head back again and blew out a breath. 'I love him more than life, but it doesn't excuse the decisions I've made.'

Anger smoked its way through me, and I forgot about the mom thing. 'You just told me not too long ago that I was too young when I was sixteen—that I couldn't hold myself responsible for keeping quiet and not telling anyone about Jeremy. My age and general naïveté gives me a pass but not you?'

He opened his mouth.

'Does it? If so, that's not fair and is seriously subjective in all the wrong ways.' On a roll now, I wasn't shutting up anytime soon. 'You can't tell me that I need to let go of decisions and actions of the past when you refuse to do the very same!'

Jase drew back against the car seat, throat working as if he searched for the right thing to say but had trouble. 'Well, shit. You got me there.'

'Hells yeah, I do.'

His lips tipped up at the corner, but his eyes were somber. 'You . . . you don't need all of this.' He turned thundercloud eyes on me. 'You're young and you have all your life ahead of you.'

I raised my brows. 'What the hell does that have anything to do with anything? I care about you, Jase. A lot. Okay? And I want to be with you.' My cheeks burned, but I kept going. 'That's obvious, but you're making choices and getting things all twisted up in your head without even *asking* me or seeing how I feel about it.'

'And how do you feel about it, Tess?' The line of his jaw hardened as his eyes flashed a heated gray. 'You really want to be with me now? After knowing all that? And you think it's smart for you and me to get involved? What if we do? And what if you get close to Jack?'

I folded my hands against my chest. 'Why wouldn't you want me to get close to him? I thought you said I'd be—'

'You are planning on leaving, Tess. You aren't thinking about sticking around. And I'll be damned if that boy gets hurt just because you want to get laid.'

I jerked back, flinching. Tears crawled up my throat and burned behind my eyes. Was that what he really thought? After all I'd said? After everything he'd said and done for me? That he summed everything up in me wanting to get laid?

Knowing that's how he really thought of me stung worse than rejection.

'You know something, Jase?' My voice wavered, but I forged on. 'The fact you have a kid who is being raised by your parents or that you won't even breathe the mother's name isn't what would push me away or make me think differently of you. It's the way *you* act and how you make such fucked-up assumptions that does that.'

Chapter 10

Jase didn't show up for class on Friday.

Part of me wasn't surprised as the lecture started on the baroque music period and Jase was a no-show. The ride back to campus yesterday once he pulled out of his driveway had been filled with tense silence.

What I had said to him had been true. Yeah, I was mind blown by the fact that Jack was his kid. That had been the last thing I'd been expecting. Hindsight was twenty-twenty and holy crapola that was true in this case. But I didn't think of him differently. Not really. Okay. That wasn't completely true. Of course, I thought of him slightly differently. He was a dad for crying out loud. I didn't even know any dads close to my age, but it didn't make me think less of him, and it hadn't deterred how I felt about him. Granted, a relationship with him would be hard.

It would've been hard anyway.

But he had a little boy he might one day tell the truth to, and any girl in Jase's future would have to be okay with that and be ready. Who knows if I ever would be, but he hadn't given me the chance.

Like I'd said to him, it was how he viewed me that had

hurt. That he believed I would get involved with Jack's life without being aware of how a sudden departure could affect him.

Every so often, Jase's eyes had found mine on the drive back and then he'd look away quickly. The only thing he'd said to me was good-bye. That was it.

And that made my heart ache.

Jase hadn't called, and I refused to be the one to reach out like I did last time, only to be coldly ignored.

Jack's my son.

As stupid as it might've made me, my heart bled for him. In spite of his dickdom when it came to me, he loved that little boy and it was killing him, the choices that he'd made when he was just a kid.

Just like my choices haunted me.

And then there was the issue of the absentee mother that he absolutely refused to speak about. Where was she? Did she still live around here? And did the sharpness in his voice come from a broken heart?

A pang lit up my chest, and I wanted to punch myself. There was no way I could be jealous of a woman who was nameless to me, but there was something there—something big—and I had a feeling that his reluctance to get seriously involved with anyone had more to do with her than it did with Jack.

Did it matter?

He'd said I was a mistake, and although he'd admitted something so big and so honest with me, it didn't really change how he viewed me. Yeah, I got why he pushed me away, but it didn't alter the outcome.

I shouldn't have let him kiss me. Wasn't like I didn't know how it was going to end, but the ache in my chest throbbed as I glanced at the empty seat beside me. I'd barely slept last night, and when morning had come, the hurt had settled deep inside me. My feelings and thoughts had all twisted up into a messy ball.

But now?

Now I was pissed.

I hadn't kissed him—not this time or the first time. It wasn't me who had reasons to not be in a relationship. It was him, and he was the one who kept making moves, kept going from the kind of kisses that drugged the soul to shoving me away.

I didn't have a fountain of experience when it came to boys and sex and friends, but I knew enough to know that he'd been hot for me before he'd kissed me. His body had proved that the moment he'd put his arms around me while we fed Lightning. And I did get that lust and feelings were totally different things.

Hell, I fell in and out of lust about three times a week depending on who I saw.

And I understood that just because he had a son didn't mean he stopped wanting to get it on—and Jase *wanted* me. But was it more substantial?

It had to be more. He wanted to help me experience something other than dancing and what he said yesterday about what had happened with Cam not being my fault had meant a lot. That meant he had to care, right? Of course he cared somewhat because I was Cam's sister . . . damnit.

Irritation pricked my skin as I shifted in my seat, clutching the pen until the cap cracked. I stroked the flame until it turned into an orb of anger—anger was better than hurt.

God, what pissed me off even more was that I was sitting in music appreciation for God's sake and would probably fail my midterm because I had spent the last thirty minutes obsessing over that jackass.

'The baroque period saw the creation of tonality,' said Professor Gibson. 'Tonality is a language of music where a

117

specific hierarchical pitch is based on a key center—the tonic triad.'

Huh?

Phasing in halfway through the lecture, I had absolutely no clue what Gibson was talking about and as he continued, so did my confusion.

'The common, most well-known composers of the baroque period are Johann Sebastian Bach . . .'

I was going to *Sebastian Bach* Jase right in the face.

'You okay?' Calla asked as the lecture drew to a close.

I packed up my notebook and nodded. 'Yeah, I'm just tired.'

She didn't say anything as she stood. In history class, she had asked about yesterday and because I had no idea how to put any of what happened into words that didn't involve several fuck bombs, I'd told her everything had been great.

Despite it being sunny, the chill in the air when we left the arts building made me glad for once that I was wearing jeans. Poor Calla, in her red cotton shorts, looked like she was about to freeze her bum off.

'You know, when Gibson talks about Sebastian Bach, all I can think of is that rock singer in the eighties who was really hot. I doubt the real—'As we rounded the corner, she drew in a deep breath. 'Oh boy . . .'

Curious, I followed her gaze as I wrapped my arms around my waist. I squinted. A guy with close-cropped brown hair was heading across the packed parking lot. There was a line of cars heading in and out, and he cut between a Volkswagen and a van. Dressed in nylon dark blue pants and a gray Shepherd shirt that stretched over broad shoulders and a nice chest, he looked like he could've stepped out of any welcome-to-college advertisement.

I'd seen him a couple of times around Whitehall. He was hard to miss, with handsome angular features and wide, expressive lips. I glanced at Calla. 'Who's that?'

'You don't know him?' she asked, tugging on the hem of her shorts. 'That's Brandon Shriver.'

'Brandon Shriver?' I pulled my sunglasses out of my bag and slipped them on. 'I like the name.'

'So do I. But I'm surprised you don't know him. He's friends with Cam and Jase.'

I forced a grin. Jase. I was currently pretending that guy didn't exist. Wasn't working very well.

'He started last semester in the spring, but he's older than me.' The hollows of her cheeks flushed. Calla was twenty, so I tried to figure out how that worked. She answered before I could ask. 'He was deployed overseas for a couple of years. I think he's an education major, which is strange. He's too hot to become a teacher.'

'Hey,' I said, elbowing her. 'I'm going to be a teacher.'

'But I don't want to make beautiful babies with you. With him,' she said, and sighed dreamily. 'That's a different story—*oh*, here he comes.'

And he was. Hopping up on the curb, he crossed the pavilion. No more than a couple of feet from us, he glanced over to where we stood. Right off the bat, I noticed he had bright green eyes, something I hadn't been close enough to him to see before. That brilliant gaze moved over Calla, then to me before drifting back to the blonde.

Calla gave a short wave as her cheeks bloomed as red as her nail polish. 'Hey.'

'Hi.' His voice was nice and deep. He glanced over his shoulder and then cut over to where we stood. 'Traffic is a nightmare. I hope you aren't planning to leave campus anytime soon.'

A second passed, and then Calla shook her head. 'Not for the next couple of hours. Are you?'

She knew damn well I wasn't going anywhere, but I played along. 'No. I'm guessing I'm walking over to east campus.' Which already seemed weird after days of hitching a ride. Like the weather, everything changed in a heartbeat. I shook that thought out of my head.

Brandon nodded as he rapped the edge of his notebook off his thigh. 'You look familiar,' he said, eyes squinting until only a thin slit of emerald showed. 'Do we have classes together?'

If we did, I'd probably be more interested in that class. As the sun passed behind an endless stream of clouds, I popped my sunglasses up on my head, pushing the shorter strands of hair back.

'You know her brother,' Calla supplied.

'I do?' He returned his attention to her.

'Yes.' She angled her face in a way that only her profile—the unscarred cheek—was visible to him. 'She's Cameron Hamilton's sister.'

'No shit.' His lips formed a genuine smile, and I wondered if there was anywhere in the world where I wouldn't be recognized as Cam's sister. 'I see it—yeah, the eyes.'

I felt my cheeks heat.

'Anyway, he's a good guy.' Brandon shifted his weight. 'He's not a part of that one frat, right? The one with Jase Winstead?'

Goddamnit, I seriously could not escape that guy. 'No, but he's good friends with Jase and a couple of them and he goes to a lot of the parties.'

'Like the one this weekend?' he asked. When I nodded, he glanced at an abnormally silent Calla. 'Are you going?'

Calla cleared her throat. 'Nah, got to work.'

Interest flickered across his otherwise stoic expression. 'Where do you work?'

Man, this conversation was about as awkward as two monkeys trying to screw a football. But it was cute, the way Calla kept stealing looks at Brandon. As she answered his question, I looked over and took a startled step back. A way too familiar black-and-gray Jeep pulled around a truck, stopping at the curb. The window rolled down just as my mouth dropped open.

Jase was behind the wheel, a dark blue baseball cap on backward. Tufts of rich brown hair curled out from under the band.

Oh, I had a soft spot for guys in hats.

Apparently I had a soft spot for *guys* who were *dads* in hats.

His steel-colored gaze moved from me to Brandon. The dark look that crossed his face caused my chest to drop into my stomach. 'Hey, Shriver, what's up?'

Brandon grinned. 'Nothing, man; what are you up to?'

Good question.

'I'm here to pick up Tess.' A tight smile appeared on his face. 'You ready?'

What in the holy hell? My brows shot up. He was here to pick me up, after yesterday? After skipping music class? After kissing me and then apologizing for doing so and then dropping the daddy bomb and *then* insulting me? Did he live in an alternate universe where these things were acceptable?

'Tess?' he called, impatience ringing like a dinner bell in his tone.

Anger sunk its claws into me and I was more than tempted to turn and stalk off, but Brandon and Calla were staring at me with dual curious looks. Although I wanted to shove my middle finger so far in his face, the last thing I was going to do was cause a scene smack-dab in the middle of the quad. Pitching a fit would draw too much attention and the only kind of attention I'd ever been okay with had been when I was onstage. Probably had a lot to do with all the scenes Jeremy had caused in my past.

121

Squeezing the strap on my bag, I turned to Calla and Brandon. 'See you guys later.'

Brandon looked a little surprised as he waved good-bye. Calla grinned like I just said yes to a marriage proposal. Ugh. Skin stretching tight, I crossed the pavilion and yanked open the passenger door and slammed it shut behind me. A pink box rested in his lap and if he handed it over to me, I'd be likely to throw the cupcake in his face.

The hue of his eyes deepened as he watched me buckle myself in. A beat passed and then he said, 'Brandon Shriver?'

I pursed my lips as I leaned back against the seat. 'I think I'm missing the beginning part of this conversation because I have no idea why you're saying his name.'

His jaw tightened. 'You were talking to him.'

'Yeah,' I said slowly. 'So was Calla. I really don't even know him.'

Shifting the Jeep into drive, he focused ahead. 'Didn't seem that way to me. You do know he's older than I am, right? Too old for you—'

My spine straightened as I gaped at him. 'Are you fucking serious?'

He blinked once and then narrowed his eyes. 'You don't need to cuss.'

'I'll fucking cuss if I want to fucking cuss,' I snapped. 'Fucker.'

His lips twitched, and my anger swelled. 'But seriously, Brandon is . . . well, he's been through a lot and you don't need to get up close and personal with that kind of shit.'

'Well, thanks for the advice, *Dad*.' He shot me a look, and I returned it. 'But I didn't ask for any. And the last time I checked, I can talk to whoever I damn—*wait*.' The stupid yet necessary muscle in my chest turned over. 'Are you jealous?'

'What?' He snorted as he neared the parking lot in front of the dorms. 'I'm not jealous or anything. Honestly, emotion has nothing to do with what I'm telling you. Brandon's a good guy, but—'

'You are fucking unbelievable!' I bounced in my seat, causing my bag to slip out of my lap. 'Why are we even talking about Brandon?'

There was a pause. 'There was an accident on Route 45 and I was coming from the farm, so there was no way I was going to make it to class,' he said, as if that explained everything. 'Here's the cupcake. It's got Snickers in it—'

'Fuck the cupcake!' I stared at him and he stared back like I suggested we should kick a baby into a street. My thoughts raced. 'What in the hell does that have to do with any of this?'

'I didn't skip class on purpose. I don't want you to think that.' Which was exactly what I thought, but I sure as hell wasn't going to admit that now. He smoothed his hand over his cap, tugging it down farther. 'So that's why I wasn't there and that's why I'm here now. And it worked out, because you were waiting for me—'

'I was *not* waiting for you.'

He glanced at me, lashes lowered. 'Then you were talking to Brandon.'

'Oh my God.' I threw my hands up. 'This is a stupid conversation and not what we need to be talking about.'

'What do we need to be talking about, Tess?' he asked as he pulled out onto the road, coming to a complete stop. Traffic was backed up from the four-way stop.

'You know exactly what we need to be talking about. Yesterday—'

'Yesterday was yesterday.' He leaned back, rubbing a hand along his jaw. 'Things got out of hand. It happens.'

My brows flew up. 'It happens? Often? Do you just walk

around and *happen* to end up kissing girls? Do you slip and fall on girls' mouths? If so, that's got to be an awkward life to live.'

'Well . . .' The quirk to his lips was mischievous and teasing, but I was so not having it. He sighed. 'Tess, you're a beautiful girl and I'm a guy and—'

'Oh, shut up.'

His eyes widened.

'Don't even finish what will most likely be the lamest sentence in the history of lame sentences. You're attracted to me.'

'I haven't said that I wasn't.' Traffic hadn't moved an inch, but the muscle in his jaw was ticking like a speedometer.

'And that's the problem, right? You are attracted to me. You do want me, but you're going to deny it because of Jack?' Anger had my heart pounding and my mouth running, but the words that were forming deep inside me needed to be said. 'Oh, that's right. It's because I'm only interested in getting *laid*.'

He smacked both hands onto the steering wheel. Seething with frustration and about half a million other emotions, I unclicked my seat belt. He stiffened. 'Tess—'

'Be quiet. Seriously. This isn't cool. You don't kiss me and then apologize. Twice now. That's insulting. Nor do you get so drunk that you conveniently don't remember what you say to me. ' I bent over, grabbing my backpack. I needed to get away from him before I knocked him upside the head or cried. Both would be equally mortifying and oddly satisfying. 'You know I like you. You've known that for how long? Hell, you've even thrown that in my face. But you wanted to be friends and I get that you're not a normal dude. You have a kid.'

'I'm not raising him—'

124

'You're still a father!' I shouted and when he leaned back, I worked to cool my temper. 'Look, I'm trying to be cool with everything. But you can't kiss me if we're *friends*. You can't say shit when I talk to other guys if we're *friends*.'

Jase's chest rose in a heavy breath. 'You're right.'

A stupid burn encased my throat. His agreement was the wrong thing to say. I don't know why because it should've been right and it would be easier. Jase came with a crap load of baggage, but that burn was working its way up. I reached for the door handle. The thing called pride made it too hard to sit in that car and listen to what he had to say. 'See you later.'

'Tess!' He reached for me, but I was already out of the Jeep, in the middle of the congested street. 'Come on, don't do this. We need—'

'We don't need anything. Peace out.' I slammed the door shut and walked away. The heaviness in my chest threatened to move up my throat and, if it did, it would get messy. And ugly. Like watching-*The-Notebook* kind of ugly.

But I kept walking, hurrying between the lanes. When I heard him call out my name, I ignored it. The god-awful stone in my stomach weighed me down, but I gathered the shredded tatters of my dignity together.

Jase and his kisses and his horseback riding and his *everything* could go play in traffic. He was always the one walking away. It was now my turn.

Chapter 11

I cried like a fat, angry baby that night.

Thankfully, Debbie was out with Erik, so there was no witness to my sob fest. What I had said to Jase needed to be said. If we were going to attempt to at least be friends or social with each other, the kissing and all the other stuff had to stop, because while it might feel oh so right when it was happening, it wasn't when it was all said and done. Yes, he was physically attracted to me. Yes, he cared for me. Yes, I wanted him. Yes, he had a son and a baby mama somewhere out in the world. But whatever he felt for me, it wasn't enough to overcome any of the misgivings he had or this invisible line he'd drawn between us.

Knowing all this didn't change the fact that it cut deeply.

And truth be told, I doubted we really could be friends. I was honest enough with myself to admit that I couldn't separate his kindness from how I felt about him, and I'd always be attaching meanings where there were none. And he acted on his physical attraction at the drop of a hat. Hell, we hadn't been around each other that much, but the moment we were alone, something happened.

Something would always happen.

That made the hurt worse, because I knew if I just let it all go and rode the wave of hormones, I probably *would* get a piece of Jase. Eventually. But I wouldn't get enough and considering how I felt for him now, I didn't need that kind of hurting.

And it would only confirm what he thought I wanted from him.

My temples throbbed and it wasn't even nine in the morning when Debbie showed up with Erik right behind her.

'Hey.' Erik plopped down on my bed and stretched out his long legs. 'What's up?'

I stared at him a moment and then looked at Debbie. An apologetic look crossed her face. 'Nothing much. Just trying to get some studying done.' I nodded at my bio text. 'That's about it.'

Erik leaned back on his elbows. 'It's Saturday morning and you're studying?' He laughed, and I pictured myself kicking him off the bed. 'Wow. You must not have anything better to do.'

My eyes narrowed.

'Or she is just really dedicated,' said Debbie as she sat on the edge of her bed. She sent me a smile. 'It's biology, right? That class is pretty hard and—'

'Biology 101 isn't hard.' Erik laughed again as he shook his head. For once, I agreed with him, but I might not have found it hard because, oddly enough, science interested me. 'What Deb isn't telling you is that she failed bio her sophomore year and had to take it twice.'

Her cheeks flushed as she folded her arms. 'Thanks, Erik.'

He shrugged. 'Good thing you're hot.' He flashed a grin I bet he found charming, but was really just freaking sleazy. 'Because the whole intelligence thing? Well . . .'

I glanced over at her and I'd have to be blind and the

127

most unobservant person in the world to not see the hurt and embarrassment in her expression. Anger rose like a serpent about to strike, and my mouth opened before I could stop myself. 'You're a dick.'

Erik's head whipped toward me, his eyes widening as Debbie gasped. 'What?' he demanded.

Too late to take back those words, and I didn't want to. 'You heard me.' I picked up my textbook and notebook. Standing, I shoved them into my bag. 'That was a dickish thing to say. Therefore, you are a dick.'

Debbie was frozen on the bed, her mouth wide open. Two points on her cheeks turned pink. Erik's mouth worked like he had a truckload of nasty words he wanted to unleash on me but was filtering them out. And I bet that filter had a name.

Cam.

'I'm going to the library.' I smiled sweetly as I slung my backpack over my shoulder and turned to Debbie. 'Sorry.'

There was an odd, glassy look to her eyes that caused my stomach to pitch. The satisfaction faded quickly as I stalked out of the room. It wasn't until I was out in the hallway that I realized what that stare signified.

Fear.

An antsy, itchy feeling lingered while I spent several hours in the cool, silent library. I shouldn't have called Erik a dick. Not because he wasn't one, because he was, but the fear that had filled Debbie's eyes reminded me of myself.

No one had ever called Jeremy a dick. At least not to his face, but if they had, he would've blamed me, and I bet Erik blamed Debbie. And for that I felt terrible.

Realizing I had no idea what I read in the last chapter, I scrubbed my palms down my cheeks. Studying was pointless right now. The words had blurred together. The food chain and ecosystem breakdown made no sense when it should.

I snapped the text shut and glanced across the empty tables. There wasn't a single soul on the second floor. Sighing, I dug my cell out of my bag. No missed calls or texts. Of course not. Why had I even looked? Wasn't like I expected Jase to contact me or wanted him to.

I was such a terrible liar.

When I finally worked up the nerve to go back to my dorm, our suite was empty. Debbie's bed was tidy. Nothing was broken or out of place, but I wasn't surprised. Erik hadn't thrown a destructive temper tantrum yet. Jeremy never had.

It was eight before I decided to hop in the shower and get ready for the party. Part of me wanted to bail, but it was the first party I'd been invited to, and I was either going, facing the possibility of having to deal with Jase, or staying home and feeling sorry for myself.

I opted with leaving the pity party behind for the evening.

And going to the party was a good opportunity to prove to myself that I was done with Jase—that I could be around him without flailing.

After drying my hair, I tugged it up in a loose bun and pulled on a pair of black leggings. The cute shirt was out of the picture, so I settled on a long, loose polka-dotted blouse and my favorite, worn-way-too-much denim skirt. As I slid my feet into a pair of flats, my phone chirped.

Slipping my cell into my back pocket along with my key card, I took a deep breath and then headed out. Tonight will be fun. Tonight will be normal. I would be like any other almost nineteen-year-old heading out to a party. I would have fun.

Parked at the curb, Cam was behind the wheel of Avery's car. As I trotted up to the back door, Cam was pulling back from the passenger seat, where Avery sat with cheeks as pink as Valentine's Day cards.

I climbed in the back, grinning. 'I'll be amazed if you guys make it out of college without having procreated a soccer team's worth of kids.'

Avery's brown eyes widened. 'Oh, God, no . . .'

I laughed, buckling myself in as Cam's eyes appeared in the rearview mirror. I gave him a big smile. 'What? No kids?'

'Ah, not in the near future,' he replied.

'But that means you guys have thought about it?' I wondered if Jase had ever considered wanting kids with Jack's mother? Probably not when they were sixteen, but in the future.

Avery's cheeks were now red. 'Not really. I mean, that's really serious. Not that we're not serious.' She patted Cam's arm when he returned his gaze to her. She twisted around, grinning. 'Anyway, you look really cute. Love the shirt.'

'Thank you. So do you.' And she did, dressed in jeans and a pretty green shirt that complemented her coloring perfectly. 'How many people are going to be at the party?'

'Not many,' Cam answered, spinning the wheel. 'It's not one of their big ones. You're probably going to be bored.'

'She's not going to be bored.' Avery grinned. 'Jacob had to back out, but Brit is coming.'

I relaxed against the seat in spite of the twisty motion my stomach was doing. 'That's cool.'

'Is Ollie coming?' she asked Cam.

A smile crossed my lips. I'd met Ollie, Cam's old room-mate a few times. He'd graduated in the spring and while I hadn't known him well, I knew enough.

'I think he might be showing up later.' Cam reached over, finding Avery's hand without looking, and threading his fingers through hers.

130

I focused my gaze on the window, a little uncomfortable. Not because they were touchy-feely—and they were *always* touchy-feely—but because there was a little green-eyed bitch that lived in the pit of my stomach. I shouldn't be jealous of them.

Shaking my head, I cleared my throat. 'What is Ollie going to grad school for again?'

'Med school.'

My eyes widened. 'Are you serious? Holy crap. I didn't think he was . . .' Um, how did I say this nicely? 'I thought he smoked away most of his brain cells.'

Avery giggled. 'That's what I thought.'

'Ollie's smarter than most people realize,' replied Cam. He blew past the Sheetz, which made me yearn for a jalapeño cheese-stuffed pretzel. 'Hell, he's smarter than he realizes.'

Avery and Cam then fell into a conversation about how they both really believed something was up with Brit and Ollie, but neither of their friends was sharing. Clasping my hands together until my knuckles ached, I focused on the dark shadows outside the car. When Cam hung a right into a subdivision, passing several dark roads with no streetlamps, my breath hitched.

He came to a stop near the end of the street and pulled into an empty spot across from a large, three-story home that appeared to have every light on in the house. Stomach tumbling, I stepped out of the car and inhaled the cool night air. I considered pulling Cam aside and telling him that I knew about Jack, but it didn't feel right, like it wasn't my place.

Avery sidled up to my side, looping her arm through mine. 'Ready?'

I nodded. As the three of us crossed the street and headed toward the front door, all I could think about was how Jase would react when he saw me. Would he be upset I was there? Would he be happy? Mad?

Fudge on a fucker. It didn't matter. I was not here for Jase.

Cam held the door open, and Avery led me inside. I'd never been inside a frat house before, so I wasn't sure what to expect, but I was somehow still surprised.

The foyer was clean and smelled pretty good. A line of sneakers was near the doorway, and there weren't any holes in the walls. I wasn't sure why I expected to see holes.

'Yo!' Cam shouted, edging past us and into the living room. 'What's up?'

Avery rolled her eyes as she slipped her arm free. 'Wow. That wasn't loud.'

Several guys were in the living room, crowding around a couch and TV. My skin prickled when I recognized Erik. He looked up and then quickly refocused on the game. The way he sat was unnaturally straight. Beside him, Debbie appeared okay. She smiled and gave me a little wave.

I waved back, wanting to apologize for earlier, but I knew right now or when Erik was nearby wouldn't be a good thing.

Brandon Shriver was beside Erik, a game controller in one hand and a beer in the other. He nodded at me and then turned to Cam, holding up the controller. 'Want in?'

'Nah.' Cam slipped his baseball cap around backward. 'It's all yours.'

'Keg's outside, bro,' said a blond guy I'd never seen before. He was perched on the arm of a worn, old recliner. His dark gaze moved over Avery and then stopped on me. Taking a sip from his bottle, he grinned. 'And I think a game of beer pong is on.'

I smiled back. The guy was cute, even if he didn't have dark hair or gray eyes. Right then, I decided that was a good thing. My smile started to spread.

132

'Awesome.' Cam turned, dropping his arm over Avery's shoulder. 'And stop staring at my sister, jackass.'

My mouth dropped open.

The guy chuckled and winked. 'Yes, sir.'

'Cam.' Avery smacked his stomach as I turned away, my face burning. 'Stop,' she said, smacking him again.

He shrugged one shoulder as he walked toward the open door leading to the garage. 'Hey, I said she could come. I didn't say she wasn't going to regret it.'

Hurrying up, I squeezed past them and shoved my elbow into his side. Satisfaction rang throughout me as he grunted. 'Last time I checked, I didn't need your permission, ass wipe.'

'That is true,' Avery chimed in.

He made a face.

I shot him a look that warned if he opened his mouth again, I'd do bodily harm. Flicking the top of my bun, he dodged my swinging arm, bending and kissing Avery's cheek. 'Want to get in on the game of pong?'

She shook her head. 'I think I'll sit this one out. What about you?'

I had no idea how to play beer pong. 'Me too.'

'You okay then?' he asked Avery in a low voice, and when she nodded, he kissed her forehead again. 'I'll be right over there.'

My brows arched. Right over there was like, *right* in front of the empty lawn chairs. As he jogged over to the group of guys clustered around a Ping-Pong table, we headed to the keg and returned to the seats with plastic red cups full to the brim.

I watched my brother with the guys for a few moments as I took a drink of the bitterness. Then another. 'Not a lot of girls here.'

Avery leaned back, stretching out her legs. 'I don't come

to a lot of the parties, but I think these kinds are more like get-togethers. So it's usually just girlfriends.'

Wincing, I took another gulp. 'Then I'm kind of standing out?'

She smiled at me. 'Well . . . you want the truth or the make-you-feel-better truth?'

I laughed. 'Hit me with the make-me-cry truth.'

The skin around her eyes crinkled as her smile spread. 'Well, let's just say if you want to meet someone, you're definitely in the right place.'

Snorting, I gazed at the table. 'Like that will happen with Cam around.'

'True. The guy back in the living room?' She took a sip of her beer and then lowered her hands. 'His name's Eddie. I think he's actually a pretty nice guy, so . . .'

Looking over my shoulder, I couldn't see into the living room, but I could hear the sounds from the video game and laughter. 'Cam would probably pile drive the poor guy if I talked to him.'

Avery laughed. 'I'll distract him.'

Over the next hour we plotted, but that conversation drifted into the trip she and Cam were planning to take to the Poconos during fall break. 'That sounds really romantic.'

The apples of her cheeks almost matched her hair. 'It was his suggestion.'

'Aw.' I watched him, grinning. Who knew my brother was such a softie? 'I'm proud of him.'

She laughed. 'I'm so lucky.'

'More like he is.'

A ball zinged past us, smacking into the wall near the dartboard. Avery shook her head as one of the guys half ran, half stumbled after it. 'How's your knee doing?'

'It's doing okay. Only hurts off and on. I have an appointment the week before Thanksgiving.'

134

'Keeping my fingers crossed for you.' She glanced over at the table. Cam was doing what I think was a victory dance. Or he was having a seizure.

'You miss dancing?' I asked.

She nodded. 'Yeah. I really do.' There was a quick pause as she swallowed. 'What was your favorite recital?'

Her eyes lit up when I told her about the last recital—the one before I majorly screwed up. Although she hadn't danced for years, I could tell she was still passionate about it. I made a promise at that moment that at some point, I would get her to dance.

I stared into my empty cup, wanting to know where Jase was. I hadn't seen his Jeep out front, but I knew several of them parked along the back. I didn't ask because I wasn't here because of him.

Not at all.

But why did he live in this frat house instead of at the farm? Wouldn't he want to be closer to Jack? Or was it the opposite he *needed*?

I snuck another cup and then one more when Cam was busy making gooey eyes at Avery from the group of guys he stood among. Another girl had appeared at some point, but with the way one of the guys had his arm around her waist, I figured she was a girlfriend.

Brittany arrived, her short blond hair slicked back in a ponytail. Less than three minutes after she gave Avery and then me a hello hug, Ollie strode through the open garage doors, his hair hanging loosely, brushing his shoulders.

He raised his arms as practically everyone there shouted his name, a smile breaking out across his handsome face. 'Aw, you guys missed me!'

Brit rolled her eyes, but before she could say anything, Ollie sidled up behind her. 'Hello, Avery and Miss Teresa, how are you doing this fine evening?'

I giggled, shaking my head. 'We're doing good.'

'Great.' He captured Brit's tiny ponytail. 'I need to borrow you for a second, *sí*?'

Brit's eyes went heavenward, but her cheeks flushed a pretty shade of pink. 'I'll be right back. Señor Fucktard can't want me for that long.'

'It'll be awhile,' he corrected, and her flush deepened.

We watched the two of them head back out into the night, and then I turned to look at Avery.

'Interesting,' she murmured.

I glanced at her, grinning. 'I guess they are together.'

She raised her brows as she nodded. 'I'd say something is most definitely going on there.'

The combination of the Erik/Debbie situation and Jase's absence did not bode well for my good old liver, but it was doing great things for my mood. By the time I was halfway through my fourth cup, I didn't care that Jase wasn't around. Maybe later, when Avery coaxed Cam outside as planned, I'd go and find Ernest . . . or Edwin. Whatever his name was. And I would prove to myself that baggage-free guys could kiss just as well as Jase, if not better. That was my plan. But first, I needed the little girl's room before I died.

'I need to find the potty.' I stood just as a Ping-Pong ball flew across the garage and bounced off the dartboard once more. 'You need anything?'

Avery shook her head as she glanced at her barely touched cup of beer. 'You'd probably want to use the one upstairs, on the second floor,' she suggested, looking up with a smile. 'It's not as gross.'

'But still gross?'

She nodded. 'Pretty much.'

'Wish me luck then.'

Giggling, she scrunched up her face in distaste. 'You're going to need it.'

I headed for the door to the house at the same moment Cam darted away from the table and descended on Avery. It was like he'd been waiting for me to leave, to sneak in a kiss. And, boy, did he kiss her. Clasping her cheeks in his hands, his head lowered until there was no space between them.

A smile crossed my lips, but there was a pang in my chest—a throb of envy. And that was wrong. I shouldn't be envious of my brother's relationship. Both of them deserved the kind of love they shared, but I wanted to know what that felt like. To know firsthand the kind of love that healed instead of harmed.

Aaand I might be a tad bit tipsy.

In the living room, Erik's and Brandon's fingers were flying over their controllers. Both of their faces donned identical masks of concentration and determination. Debbie looked up from where she was perched on the arm of the couch beside her boyfriend, an extremely bored look marking her pretty face.

I sent her a sympathetic smile instead of asking her why she was sitting in here if she was so bored. I already knew the answer. Because Erik wanted her there, where he could see her. Control her. A bitter taste crawled up the back of my throat as I started up the stairs. I needed to get out of the room before I called him a dick again and threw a 'face' on the end of it.

Took a few moments to get up the steps. My depth perception appeared to be wonky at the moment. At the top of the landing, I stopped and stared down the hall. 'Oh . . .'

There were several doors on either side, most of them closed except for the one at the end of the hall, and that was clearly a bedroom where a hoarder of Mountain Dew bottles lived. Ew.

Having no other choice but to start opening doors, I

started with the closest one to my left. I knocked softly and when there was no answer, I tried the handle. The door was locked. Hopefully that wasn't the bathroom. The next room was an empty bedroom and the one after that was a laundry room with jeans and socks piled all over the floor.

Good God, they needed a house mom or something.

Closing that door before I started a load of laundry for the sad, sad creatures who lived here, I stepped around a pair of sneakers left in the middle of the hallway and went to the next door. I rapped my knuckles off the door and when there wasn't an answer, I reached down and twisted the handle. The door swung open easily, revealing not a bathroom, but a rather neat bedroom and—

Oh my God.

The room wasn't empty.

I knew what I was seeing and it only took seconds to take it all in, but my brain was slow to process everything. And that made it feel like forever.

Jase sat on a chair, his back to the organized desk. There was a pink box sitting there. I knew what was in it and for some reason that . . . that made what else I saw so much worse. His shirt was halfway unbuttoned, as if he'd grown tired with pushing the little buttons through their holes. His legs were spread wide, jaw locked and his arms hanging limply at his sides.

He wasn't alone.

Chapter 12

Standing before Jase was the kind of girl that could make me feel like last week's dried vomit on a good day. She was beautiful. Long, thick black hair shone like glass and a tan, tight body hinted at being soft in all the right places.

Her shirt was off.

She wore only a denim skirt and a lacy red bra that proved some breasts could defy gravity.

And I had a feeling those babies were natural.

I'd seen her a few times around campus, always with equally beautiful girls. I didn't know her name, but in that minute, I hated her like we were vying for the same spot during a performance. And I was staring. Maybe it was the beer. Maybe it was the boobs. I needed to stop staring.

Seconds had passed from the moment I opened the door until Jase and this girl looked over. Something flickered in his deep gunmetal gray eyes, and his mouth opened. I flashed hot and then cold as our gazes locked.

So this is where Jase had been.

I guess he didn't have a problem with getting laid with other girls.

A giggle bubbled up, escaping before I could stop it. I

clamped my mouth shut. The laugh sounded near hysterical. I shouldn't have drunk so much.

The girl's perfectly groomed eyebrows rose as she stared at me. Annoyance tightened the line of her pouty mouth. 'Excuse me?'

My stomach flipped over and over. For a moment, I couldn't move at all. A crushing feeling pressed down on me. Was he giving this girl cupcakes too? Oh God . . . I couldn't even bear the thought of that.

Then I started talking and walking. 'I'm sorry. I was looking for the bathroom.'

'This is obviously not the bathroom,' she replied tartly.

Heat swamped my cheeks as a knot moved into my throat. He'd kissed me. Less than forty-eight hours ago. Touched me. Told me the truth about Jack. Obviously, I'd taken those very small moments and made them into a very big deal.

'I'm sorry,' I said again, my gaze darting to Jase as he stood. 'I . . .' I stopped talking as the ball of emotion settled in the back of my throat. In such a haste to get away, I turned too quickly, knocking my left knee into the door. The hiss of sudden pain escaped my lips.

'Oh dear,' the girl murmured.

Face flaming like a red pepper, I spun around. I needed to get out of here.

'Tess,' Jase called. 'Hold on a sec—*Tess*!'

I didn't stop. Not when he called my name and then when the girl called out his. Forgetting why I even came upstairs, I hurried down the steps. My heart was pounding in a way that made me sick to my stomach. Torn between embarrassment and shock, I avoided the living room and went straight for the side door in the kitchen.

Common sense went right out the window, disappearing like that chick's shirt. I stepped out into the night air and I . . . I kept walking. I followed the cracked pavement overgrown with weeds and then slipped between two cars parked along the curb. I took a right and I kept walking.

There was a small voice in the back of my head telling me that I was being stupid and overreacting, but I was flying headfirst into drama llama land. All I knew was staying at that party was not in my stars. There was no way I could face Jase after what I so obviously interrupted, or face anyone, really.

My cell went off, the ring muffled, and I let it ring.

I wanted to go home.

Like my real home—not my dorm. I wanted to press rewind back to May and not take that stupid jump that destroyed *everything*. If I could, I wouldn't be here. I wouldn't be around Jase.

By the time I reached the last block before hitting the set of dark roads before the main one, I knew I should've asked Avery to take me home, but I didn't want to ruin their night. I could've asked Debbie, but Erik would've flipped out. I—

My cell phone vibrated once more in my back pocket and I ignored it again.

The beer dulled the ache in my knee. Or maybe it was the pressure in my chest that made everything else seem so freaking insignificant. And maybe it was the beer's fault for why I was seriously attempting to walk the mile plus back to campus in the middle of the night.

The last house in the subdivision was dark and silent, and a truck flew down the road so fast that it caused my pulse to spike. I stopped at the end of the road, lifting my hands and pulling the hair that had slipped free of my bun back from my face.

He'd kissed me. He'd touched me. He'd held me. He'd tried to make me find something other than dancing so I could fly again.

141

Stupid tears burned the back of my eyes, partly due to frustration and the other part—well, it was more stupid than me walking back home. I let go of my hair and the wind caught some of the strands, tossing them around.

What was I doing? Cam would freak when I didn't come back. He'd probably call search and rescue. And Jase? He probably thought I was completely psycho, but he said . . . and I thought . . . I had thought wrong.

I squeezed my eyes shut against the tears. Seeing Jase with another girl hurt like a kick to the face. It made me doubt what I harbored for him was just a stupid crush, because this—*this* was not how you reacted when you saw your crush with someone else.

I opened my eyes, hating the fact that my lashes felt damp. This was not me. I was not this kind of girl. I was not—

Two headlights lit up the road, quickly bearing down on me. I twisted halfway, and my heart plummeted. It was a Jeep, but it couldn't be.

No way.

Brakes squealed as the car screeched to a halt beside me, and I was suddenly staring at Jase's face through the open passenger window. His eyes were shadowed, but his lips were pressed into a tight, furious thin line. 'I've been calling you.'

I didn't have a response to that which didn't include fuck off.

Jase leaned half of his long body into the passenger seat, and now that I could see his eyes, they were a deep, stormy gray. 'Get in the car.'

'No.' The word came out, and fuck, if it didn't feel good saying it.

He glared at me. 'Get in the car, Tess.'

'I don't think so.'

He looked away, taking a deep breath before returning his attention to me. 'What are you doing all the way out here? It better not be what I think you're doing, because you cannot possibly be that stupid.'

And just like that, an emotional switch was thrown. Anger flooded my system. I skipped right out of drama llama land and straight into crazy bitch land. 'I'm not that stupid? The fact that you have to ask me what I'm doing is pretty stupid when it's damn obvious. I'm walking home.'

He stared at me like I'd just admitted to having a penis. 'You're walking home?'

'Did I stutter?' I snapped. Not my most clever of all comebacks, but I was rewarded when his expression clouded over.

'Are you fucking insane?' When I didn't respond, he cursed and then jerked the wheel to the curb. Leaving the engine running, he hopped out of the Jeep and was in front of me in an instant. With his height, he towered over me, but all I saw was that his shirt was still unbuttoned. 'First off, you are walking on a major *highway*. A car could come flying down too close to the shoulder and hit you! Kill you, Tess.'

As if to prove his point, a car flew down the road, music thumping from its speakers. Perfect timing. I folded my arms. 'I—'

'Or someone could stop.' He caught the edge of my chin, forcing me to hold his gaze when I started to look away. 'And not someone who's interested in just giving you a ride home. Do you understand me?'

I blanched. 'I do, but—'

'And then there's your knee. Did you even think about that?' Man, he was on a roll. He still had my chin, daring me to even blink. 'You think it's good for your injury to walk that far? And because of what?'

143

I opened my mouth to say something that was probably not going to make this situation any better, but that's not what came out of my mouth. 'Was the cupcake for her?'

Damn me straight to hell and back. I was never drinking again. Fuck beer and the keg it rode in on.

Jase's eyes held mine, and what felt like an eternity stretched out before he dropped his hand and cursed. 'Get in the car, Tess. And do not argue with me.' He started to turn, but then whipped back toward me. 'Fuck it.'

He didn't even give me a chance to follow him. Like the first day he joined music class, one second I was standing and the next second I was over his shoulder. The world tilted and my hair fell forward in a tangled mess.

'What the hell?' I shrieked, grabbing fistfuls of his shirt. 'Put me down!'

'Hell no. I'm not standing out here arguing with you.' He stalked over to the Jeep and yanked open the door. 'You and I are going to talk—'

'I don't want to talk to you!' I slammed my palm into his back. He didn't make a sound as he turned around, dropping me onto the front seat. 'You—'

'You move out of that seat, I swear to God, I will sit on you,' he warned.

'I don't—what? *Sit on me?* What are you? Two?'

Jase gripped the door. 'Stay there.'

'I'm not a dog.'

He leaned in, putting his face right in mine. Up close, his eyes were a stunning shade of silver. 'Stay here. If you get out, I will chase after you. Like a dog.'

I scrunched up my nose. 'That's an attractive mental image.'

'Focus on that image for a few seconds.' Backing up, he slammed the door shut.

There wasn't enough time to truly debate the whole running and him chasing me option. He was in the car and it was moving before my brain caught up with what was happening.

'That cupcake wasn't for *her*.'

I didn't believe him.

'It was for *you*. Shit, I can't believe you were going to walk home,' he said, shaking his head as he thrust his fingers through his hair. 'Why? Because of me?'

'No. Absolutely not. I just wanted to go home.'

'Yeah. You're a terrible liar.'

'You have terrible perception,' I snapped, folding my arms. The beer sloshed in my stomach. 'And why are you even here? Don't you have a half-naked chick waiting for you in your bedroom?'

'And that didn't have anything to do with why you left?'

I opened my mouth, but closed it. Crap. I stared out the window, pressing my lips together. 'I was obviously inter-rupting.'

'Actually, I was glad you interrupted.'

I barked out a laugh. 'Sure you were.'

There was a beat of silence as he hooked a right. 'That wasn't what you thought. What was going on in there? Nothing was going to happen.'

'I'm not stupid, Jase. And, honestly, do you even owe me an explanation? No. We're friends, remember? You can talk to or screw whoever. And I can talk to and screw whoever. After all, I just want to get—'

'I do owe you an explanation, damnit.' He gripped the steering wheel. 'And wait—screwing whoever? Who the fuck do you—'

My breath caught in a god-awful way, burning my eyes. 'I don't want to talk.'

'We need to talk,' he interrupted, voice hard. 'We needed to talk since yesterday.'

145

'And I have a phone.' I whipped toward him in the seat, planting my hand on the dashboard. 'You haven't called or anything.'

He sent me a side look. 'I figured I'd let you calm down. I would've talked to you tonight if Cam wasn't around.'

'Oh, but I guess you were too busy, huh?' God, I knew I sounded snide and snotty. I needed to shut up.

Jase took a deep breath. 'I didn't invite her up there, Tess. She came up on her own.'

'And I guess she just took her shirt off? Does that happen to you a lot without any warning?' I laughed harshly. 'What an interesting life you must lead. Falling on girls' mouths and having them whipping their shirts off.'

That half grin appeared. 'Well, I do live a charmed life . . .'

'Shut up.'

He sighed. 'Tess, I'm not lying to you. Okay? Her name is Steph. We've messed around a few times, but not recently. I didn't even know she was going to be here tonight. She came up and she took her shirt off.'

I snorted.

A muscle throbbed along his jaw. 'She wanted to do more. I'm not going to lie, I *briefly* considered it because I'm a guy, but I didn't, because she's not who I want. And nothing happened. Her shirt came off a minute before you walked in.'

I stared at him for a moment and then looked away. Believing him was equivalent to walking in front of a car. And damn, I wanted to believe him. The thumping in my chest was begging me to believe him.

'Shit, Tess, I even picked up that cupcake for you.' There was a pause. 'Do you really think I would've been screwing a girl knowing you were at the party?'

'You didn't know I was there.'

'I did,' he shot back.

Okay. Whatever. I shrugged.

'Damnit, Tess, you really think that?' He swore again. 'You think that?'

'You've kissed me and regretted it. You've said things you didn't remember when you were drunk, so—'

Jase hit the brakes and we stopped in the middle of the dark street. My eyes widened as I twisted toward him. 'What are you—'

'Nothing has happened between Steph and me for months, Tess. Nothing. And you know what? I've never kissed her.'

I blinked. 'What?'

'Never. And it's been years since I've actually kissed a girl, so don't sit there and think you know what happened. You don't.'

There was a good chance someone was going to come speeding down this road and plow into us. 'But you've kissed me.'

'I did. Shit, I did kiss you and . . .'

'How can I believe that?' Better yet, why should I believe that? Didn't matter. Not really.

Jase cursed again, and then his hand was wrapping around the back of my head. When he tugged me forward, my heart jumped. He kissed me. There was nothing slow about it. The kiss was fierce and hard. He kissed me like he was staking a claim or like he hadn't done so in a very long time. Blood turned to lava in my veins. He broke the kiss, and all I could do was stare at him, my heart pounding crazy fast.

I believed him.

I don't know why or how a kiss could prove what he said, but it did. To the day I died, I would believe what he said.

He returned to his seat, breathing heavy, and hit the gas.

The car started to moved again. 'That—*that* is what didn't happen between her and me. Not ever, Tess.'

Maybe it was the beer. The need to prove that I could be as sexy, daring, and alluring as the girl in his room without taking my shirt off or having her breasts. Or maybe it was the kiss. It could've been all the emotion rising in my chest and the lust that caused heat to pool between my thighs. Maybe it was all these things. It didn't matter. My brain had clicked off, and I was already moving before any rational thought could form or I could think about the consequences. Or about the fact that Jase had a lot going on. Or about hurt feelings.

I leaned over the center console, pressing my lips to the corner of his mouth. He didn't jerk away as I slipped my hand between his legs, cupping him. *Then* he jerked, but against my hand. He was hard, straining against the zipper.

'Jesus,' he groaned, and as I pulled my head back, I saw his hand farthest from me white knuckle the steering wheel. He cast me a quick sidelong glance with heavy hooded eyes. 'What are you doing?'

'Looks obvious, doesn't it?' I moved my hand up, following the rather impressive length.

He took a deep breath, shifting his gaze to the road. 'Nothing is obvious when it comes to you.' He could've removed my hand or told me stop. 'Nothing you do in this fucking world is obvious.'

The words mingled with the strange, warm haze invading my thoughts. My hands knew what to do. I'd done it before. Only a few times, but I imagined it was like riding a bicycle. You really couldn't forget or do it wrong.

Well, that was really an unsexy way to look at it.

I flicked open the button on his jeans, carefully tugging the zipper down. The tinny sound seemed louder than the air coming in from the partially rolled down windows.

Jase was breathing heavily as I reached in and wrapped my fingers around the warm, hard skin and eased him out. 'Tess,' he ground out. A shudder worked its way through him, and he jumped against my hand as I palmed him. The Jeep slowed.

His skin was red-hot, smooth as silk, and I was incredibly awed. There were a few seconds when I was mystified by the feel of him. I felt him from his base to the tip, and my stomach hollowed.

'Aw, God, this is going to drive me crazy.' His voice was thick. 'You really—'

I stretched as far as I could go and lowered my head. The salty taste of his skin danced over my tongue. I moved my hand down slowly as I kept exploring, bringing him deeper into my mouth.

'Tess,' he growled, his body flexing as I tasted him for the first time. As I moved up, I swirled my tongue along the head. 'Holy shit, where did you learn that? Fuck. Don't answer. I don't want to know. I prefer to think you were born with that talent.'

A laugh bubbled up and vibrated over him. He swore and his body tightened in response. Hmm. I had no idea a laugh in this position would do *that* to him. He was throbbing in my hand and in my mouth. Instinct seemed to take over as I matched my hand to my mouth.

'You're going to kill me—kill us.' His hips jerked, and I heard the engine roar. 'Fuck,' he growled as I picked up the pace. 'You're killing me.'

I smiled around him as I flicked my tongue along his head. Heat swamped me, moving down my body. I ached between my thighs. The few times I'd done this before I'd never been aroused. Not like this. It was like this was the first time I really wanted to do this, and that made me hot.

A murmur of triumph was muffled as his free hand

149

dropped to the back of my head. He threaded his fingers through my hair, loosening the bun as he placed the slightest weight on my head. He guided me for a few moments and then his hand slipped down, wrapping around my neck. His thumb found my pulse, gently massaging the skin until I was squeezing my thighs together.

'I'm not going to last. Ah fuck, I'm . . .' His hips powered up and he shook. He gripped the nape of my neck. 'Tess, you have to stop or I'm going to—'

I wasn't going anywhere. I don't know why. I never swallowed before. The idea of it wigged me out, but not with him. Apparently, it was my inner porn star. It took one more twist of my tongue, slide of my hand, and he shouted my name as he pulsed and spasmed.

When it was over, I pressed a kiss to him before I lifted my head, tucked him away, and zipped up his jeans. His hand trembled against the back of my neck as I returned to my seat, the pressure of his fingers carving a brand into my skin.

Jase stared straight ahead, lips parted and his chest rising and falling swiftly. Nothing was to be gained from his expression. I glanced out the window. The road was long and dark. I recognized nothing, so I knew it wasn't Route 45. I was surprised he hadn't wrecked.

My gaze swung back to him when he lowered his hand. His jaw was tight, and he was still breathing heavily. My heart skipped and then took a magnificent tumble. Oh my God. I shouldn't have done it. There was a thousand—no, a million—reasons as to why I shouldn't have done that. So many I could write an epic guide on how to do the wrong thing. Maybe you shouldn't give guys who had kids road head? How was I to know?

I immediately started working up excuses. I'd been drinking. And I was buzzing. I hadn't eaten much today.

Maybe I had diabetes and was prone to random acts of head. Oh yeah, that sounded believable. Must write that one down for later.

Without saying a word, Jase glanced over to me—no, to the side of the road. He cut over, slamming to a stop on the shoulder. I threw my arm out, catching myself before I face-planted on the dashboard.

Car idling, he was eerily silent as he opened the driver's door and got out. He got out of the car! The overhead light came on.

'Holy shit,' I murmured as I watched him step in front of the headlights, his striking profile cast in harsh, yellow lights.

Was he going to remove me from the car? Make me walk back from the middle of nowhere? That seemed like an excessive response. Right? After all, I think I gave him a pretty damn good orgasm. He should be thanking me—

Jase wretched open my door, and my gaze immediately dropped. The top of his jeans were still unbuttoned and clutch my pearls, that was hot.

I took a deep breath. 'Jase—'

He clasped the sides of my cheeks and his mouth was on mine. The kiss was like the one before I came up with the brilliant idea of a blow job. Demanding. Hungry. The kiss brokered no room for anything but tasting and sensation. His tongue parted my lips, capturing the gasp. His head slanted, deepening the kiss as his hands slid under my skirt, wrapping around my hips. Lifting his mouth, he kept his eyes riveted on mine as he turned me in the seat toward where he stood.

I squeaked as he tugged me forward to the edge of the seat. Reaching back, I slammed my hands down on the driver's seat, elbows bent. A fierce, raw tautness etched into his face as he lifted my butt off the seat and hooked his fingers into the band of my leggings.

There was a flash of understanding, and then he tugged them down, all the way to my ankles. Stunned, I flushed hot as my chest rose. Okay. He wasn't mad. He was most definitely not—

Jase lifted the edges of my shirt, and then kicked his head back. His throat worked. 'Holy fuck, no panties?'

No panties? What? Holy shit. I'd forgotten. My body burned twice as hot. 'I . . . I don't like to wear them with tights.'

He snapped forward, curving one hand around my neck. 'Perfect.' He kissed me again, thrusting his tongue in my mouth. 'That is fucking perfect.'

And then his mouth was off mine and he was staring at me, his large hands dark against the skin of my thighs. Out of habit, I kept myself practically bare down there from years of dancing in tights, leotards, and skimpy dresses. There was no way to hide. Absolutely no way as he parted my legs.

A deep, sexy sound rumbled up from him. 'You're beautiful, Tess. More beautiful than I could even imagine.'

My mouth dried as my body sizzled from the inside.

'Open up for me,' he murmured.

I fought the urge to close my legs. Anyone could drive by. I had no idea where we were, how close to the frat house or any house. Hell, the police could drive by, but I opened for him.

'More.'

Heart pounding, I spread my legs, stretching my leggings around my ankles. His hands drifted over my skin, resting against my hips. All of this was insanely surreal. It was like a dream with tingling skin and heightened senses. My heart was beating so fast I thought I'd surely have a heart attack.

Jase's quicksilver gaze held mine as he lowered his head. He went right for it, as bold and determined as I had been with him, but this . . . this was different. Intimate in an entirely unique way. I jerked when his warm breath neared and cried out when he kissed me between my legs—a sweet, heart-stopping kiss.

And then he devoured me.

His mouth was on me—hot, wet, and shattering. The strokes of his tongue were determined, teasing and shallow, and then relentless and deep. My head fell back as my thoughts spun. Panting heavily, my hips moved as raw sensations pounded me into the seat. My body was a tempest. I was out of control. My hands slipped over the vinyl and my head hit the driver's seat. I arched my back as he delved deep.

'Jase,' I moaned, my body coiling tight. Every part of me tensed. From the muscles in my fingers, all the way down to my toes. It was like being onstage, when the music started, and I glided into my first move—that moment when my body was locked up tight, ready to bloom and follow the call of the music.

'Keep saying my name.' His fingers bit into my skin, eliciting a hiss of pleasure from me. 'And I'll never stop. I swear to you.'

I'd die if he kept up. I was dying now. I cried out, completely lost as my body spiraled and liquefied. I couldn't breathe as release whipped through me, throbbing and pulsing. My legs trembled, my hands opened and closed, grasping air. There were these strange soft sounds echoing in the Jeep, and it took me a few seconds to realize they were coming from me.

Vaguely aware of him moving over me, I felt his lips on mine, tasting myself on his lips. I was in a daze as his hand smoothed over the skin of my thighs, and he whispered my name. Those calloused fingers drifted down my legs. He pulled my tights up, fixed my shirt, and helped me sit

153

up, putting my feet back in the Jeep. I'd lost a shoe in the process. He found it, slipping it on my foot.

I leaned my head back against the seat, dragging in breaths as he buckled me in. A shiver danced over me as he ran a hand up my arm, to my cheek. He turned my chin toward him. I blinked my eyes open.

'If you say we shouldn't have done that or if you apologize . . .' I yawned. Sexy. 'I will punch you in the balls.'

One side of Jase's glistening lips hitched up. 'I wasn't going to say either of those things.'

'Oh?'

'No.' His thumb smoothed over my lower lip. 'I was just going to tell you that was the best . . . the best goddamn drive down these roads I've ever had.'

Chapter 13

Jase stopped at McDonald's on the way back to my dorm, ordering us a sweet tea that we shared. I think we'd worked up quite a thirst. I felt like I had no bones or muscle and I was floating in my seat, tethered down by the seat belt. The euphoria seeped through me. It was like finishing a dance number at a competition and walking off that stage knowing I was going to take first place.

Actually, this was better. More tangible. If I closed my eyes, I could still feel his hands on my legs and his warm breath dancing over my most private place.

Tomorrow I'd probably bury my face under a rock, but right now, I didn't care. I didn't want to think about anything. I just wanted to ride this wave, because I hadn't felt this good in months.

Jase pulled into a parking spot near the entrance to the dorm. I forced my limbs to work as he hopped out and came around to the passenger side. He opened the door as I unbuckled my seat belt. My fingers felt detached.

When I slid out of the Jeep, I looked up into his eyes. A big smile stretched my lips as he reached between us, taking my hand in his. He closed the door and as I stepped forward, I stumbled way to the right.

He chuckled, tightening his hold on my hand. 'Easy there. You keep it up and I'll think I really swept you off your feet.'

I giggled, thinking that he'd most definitely been doing some sweeping. He led me to the sidewalk and my feet got tangled up a bit. I tripped and then laughed again.

Jase stopped, looking down at me. In the overhead lamps, and the way the shadows played across his face, I thought he looked like someone who stepped straight out of a dream. 'Did you drink at the party?'

'Maybe?'

The relaxed half smile faded. 'How much have you had to drink tonight?'

'Ah, three? Four? I don't know.' I paused. 'I don't really drink. With dancing, you know? Can't dance when I'm drunk. Well, I could, but it wouldn't be that good.'

'Shit.' He hung his head and took a stuttered breath. 'You're drunk?'

'God. You do sound like a dad,' I yakked.

He shot me a blank look.

'All right, I wouldn't say I was drunk.' I yawned as I turned toward the dorm and then glanced over my shoulder at him. He still held on to my hand, but our arms stretched out. 'I wish I could teleport myself into my dorm.'

His brows rose. 'Yeah, you're a bit drunk.'

Was I? I couldn't tell. The buzzy, happy feeling could be from the beer or the orgasm. 'I'm going to go with orgasm.'

'What?' He laughed deeply.

Tugging on his arm, I smiled when he started walking. 'I feel good—better than I've felt in months. And I'm going to say that it was the orgasm and not the beer that is making me feel this way.'

Another deep, alluring laugh rumbled from him. 'I'll take that as a compliment.'

'You should.' We were still horribly far away from the door, and Jase wasn't moving quickly enough. Maybe he would stay. I didn't think Debbie would be back for a long time. We'd have the place to ourselves. And we'd have a bed and—

'I didn't know you'd been drinking.'

Stopping at the somberness in his tone, I spun around and nearly lost my balance, which didn't help my case. His hands landed on my hips, steadying me. 'You regret it, don't you?' My happy bubble was about to burst. 'I'm not plastered. I know exactly what I was doing. I wanted to do it. Maybe it wasn't my smartest idea—'

'I fucking disagree with that,' he commented, eyes glimmering for a moment. 'It was brilliant, but . . .' His features softened as he placed his large hand against my cheek. 'If I'd known you'd been drinking, I would've stopped you.'

Tilting my head to the side, I tried to figure out what that meant. 'And if I wasn't drinking?'

'I think you know the answer to that.'

I guess I sort of did. 'But I'm not drunk. I wanted to do that to you. I wanted—'

Jase groaned. 'You have got to stop talking like that.'

'Like what?' My brows knitted.

'Telling me that you wanted to. Don't get me wrong. I'm glad to hear that, but it makes me want to let you do it again. And for me to do it again. But I wouldn't want to use just my tongue.' He pressed his forehead to mine, and I drew in a shaky breath at his closeness. 'I'd start with that, but I'd want to use my hands and I wouldn't stop there.'

His words scalded my cheeks, and maybe I was a bit more intoxicated than I realized, because a rush of boldness invaded me. 'I wouldn't stop you.'

He closed his eyes, and a deep sound came from the back of his throat. 'God, Tess . . .'

I swallowed hard, and then tilted my head, lining up our mouths. 'Jase?'

There was a moment of hesitation, and then he kissed me softly, a gentle sweep of his lips over mine. A barely there touch that somehow affected me more than any of the other kisses. 'I know you've been drinking. I don't want that hanging between us.'

'But—'

'We'll talk more later. Okay? Right now, let me just get your not-drunk-but-slightly-tipsy cute ass upstairs.'

'You think my ass is cute?'

He pulled away, laughing. 'Baby, your ass is like my own personal holy ground.'

'Oh my God . . .'

A grin appeared. 'Come on.'

'I can't believe you just said my ass was—ah!' I squealed as Jase slipped an arm around my waist and lifted me up, holding me to his chest. Stars cartwheeled for a few seconds. 'What are you doing?'

He looked down at me, eyebrow arched. 'Getting you to your room.'

'Carrying me is necessary?'

'Yep.' He strode across the pavilion. 'Card?'

Wiggling around, I dug it out from the back pocket of my skirt. He hefted me up and managed to grab it without dropping me. I didn't protest when he asked me to open the door and caught it with his foot. Resting my head against his chest, I closed my eyes. Seconds passed and the gentle bob of his steps swayed me back into that pleasant state. We needed to talk. About stuff. Serious stuff. And waiting until tomorrow was probably a bad idea, but I snuggled closer. Being in his arms, well . . .

Tomorrow could go screw itself with a rusty spork.

Much of the trip to my room was like being underwater, and opening my eyes required way too much effort. As usual, our suite was empty. He used his elbow to turn on the light.

'Are you sure you have roommates next door?' he asked, turning, somehow juggling me and the door.

'Uh-huh,' I murmured sleepily and opened my eyes long enough to confirm that my dorm room was also empty. 'I hear them every once in a while.'

'And you've never talked to them, right?' He crossed the small room.

'Nope.'

Jase laid me down on the bed, and as I opened my eyes, he'd already moved to the foot of my bed. 'Tell me something.'

'Something.'

He grinned as he peeked up through his lashes. The light from the suite cast enough glow that I could see only him. 'Did your brother know you were drinking?'

Cam was the last person I wanted to think about right now.

'Tess?' he persisted, tugging off one of my shoes. I wiggled my toes, and he captured my foot, holding it in his hand.

I let my eyes drift shut. 'No. He was too busy staring at Avery the entire time.'

'He should've been paying attention to you.' He removed my other shoe, dropping it somewhere on the floor.

A very attractive snort escaped me. 'Why? I'm not a child. I can drink if I want to.'

'Uh-huh.' He danced his fingers along the sole of my foot, causing me to giggle. I tried to pull my foot away, but I was too slow. He backed off, picking up the quilt. 'So are you going to be a weekly fixture at the parties now?'

Curling onto my side, I blinked my eyes open and smiled as he draped the quilt over me. 'I don't know. I didn't see a lot of girls there.'

He sat beside me, fixing the edge of the blanket so it covered my shoulder. 'There aren't usually. Except the regulars.'

'Regulars?'

'Girls who come around for the parties that aren't girl-friends.'

I didn't like the sound of that. 'Like the girl in your room?'

He ran a hand through his hair, messing it up. 'Yeah. Like her.'

'What was her name again?'

Jase shifted his weight and leaned back, resting on one elbow. 'Does it matter?'

Did it? Considering what had just happened between us? 'Yes.'

'She's a good girl.'

'Ah . . .'

His lips hitched back as he dipped his chin. 'I'm serious. She just likes to have fun and—'

'I don't want to hear about that kind of fun.'

He laughed, and I scowled. 'Cam used to hook up with her.'

'Ew.' I wrinkled up my nose. 'And so did you?'

'Not at the same time.'

'God, I hope not.' When he chuckled again, I nudged him with my knee. 'You do realize that means you've slept with Cam, right?'

'What? Fuck no.' In the dim light, he shrank back. 'I told you it wasn't—'

'He's been in there. So have you. So by association, you two have had sex.'

160

'That is disgusting.'

I grinned. 'What's disgusting is that you've both been up in there and—'

'Can we not talk about this?'

My smile went up a notch. There was a good chance tomorrow morning I wouldn't find any of this funny, but right now, I loved how he squirmed. 'Perhaps you'll think twice about doing what you aren't quite proud of.'

He arched a brow and then fixed his gaze on the empty bed across from us. 'I was telling the truth, Tess. I've known Steph for years, and, yeah, we've fooled around a couple of times, but nothing since the end of last semester. And I . . .' He tipped his head to the side and sighed. 'And I haven't ever kissed her. That was the truth, too. I hadn't kissed a girl since . . .'

My heart thumped heavily. 'Since when?'

Jase shook his head and then let out a short, dry laugh. 'Since a really long time.'

I watched him in silence. A change came over him. I wasn't sure what it was exactly, but a distant, almost sad look crept into his features, tightening the lines of his face that would drive an artist crazy to sketch.

I knew he was talking about Jack's mother, and he'd been hurt, nursing a broken heart for all these years.

God, maybe I was drunk, because I had no idea if he had even been in love with her. Jase was a dude. Dudes didn't harbor old love wounds. They either drank or screwed them away.

My eyes became too hard to keep open. 'I wish I had that cupcake now.'

He laughed as he slowly shook his head. 'You would have loved it. I got another Snickers one. I guess you're just not meant to eat that one.'

'I guess not.' A moment passed. 'You staying?'

161

There was a pause, and then I felt his finger drift over my cheek, scooping up a strand of hair and tucking it back. 'I'll stay until you fall asleep.'

'That won't be very long.' I willed my eyes open, but they wouldn't. 'And we need to talk . . .'

'Sleep, Tess. I promise'—the bed shifted and I felt his lips press against my forehead—'we'll talk tomorrow . . . if your brother doesn't kill me first.'

There was a small person living inside my head and it was banging on my skull with a sledgehammer. Moaning pitifully, I rolled onto my side and blinked my eyes open.

The small window by Debbie's bed let way too much light in and I winced, pressing the heel of my palm against my throbbing forehead.

'Ow,' I moaned, sitting up. The quilt slipped down to my waist, revealing the clothes I'd slept in last night.

A soft laugh floated through the room. 'I was wondering when you were going to wake up.'

My tortured gaze swung to the doorway. Debbie leaned against the frame, grinning. Mouth tasting like I made a series of bad decisions last night, I glanced at the clock. 'Holy crapola.'

It was almost one in the afternoon.

She laughed again. 'Did you overindulge last night?'

'Yeah,' I croaked.

Debbie pushed out of the doorway and headed to the small fridge. Digging out a small bottle of orange juice, she then grabbed another bottle off the desk. She walked them over to me and sat down on my bed.

My brain felt fuzzy, like it had grown tiny hairs during the night, as I watched her pop out two aspirins.

'Take them.' She handed over the OJ and aspirins. 'It will help.'

I would take a shotgun blast to the head if it helped. Swallowing the pills, I followed it up with a healthy gulp of OJ.

'You're officially a college student now,' she said, screwing the lid back on the aspirins.

'I am?' I officially felt like crap.

She nodded. 'You've got your first college hangover. It's a tradition.'

'It sucks.' I pressed my hand against my head. 'Big time.'

'Hey.' She patted my bent leg. 'At least you haven't vomited.'

I squeezed my eyes shut. 'True.'

'What happened to you last night?' Debbie asked, twisting around and sitting cross-legged. 'I saw you go upstairs, and then you never came back down. About an hour later, Cam came in looking for you.'

My eyes widened as last night came back in a rush. Cold doused my skin, and then heat.

Oh. My. God.

I had engaged in a bit of oral play with Jase.

Was this my life? A memory of his mouth and his tongue on me, *in* me, whipped through my brain. I flushed as my heart rate picked up. A different kind of ache filled my breasts, and then dipped much, much lower.

Yep. This was my life.

Turning swiftly, I ignored the fierce slice of pain between my temples and snatched my cell off the nightstand. I didn't remember putting it there. Jase must've gotten it out of my pocket. There were no missed calls from Cam. I assumed Jase had gone back to the frat house and told him that he'd taken me home. And left out a lot of detail.

God, I hoped he did.

As much as I wanted Jase—and I did want him—I didn't want to cause problems between him and my brother. Huh.

Which would make having a relationship in the open diffi-cult.

If we were even going to have a relationship.

There were also no missed calls or texts from Jase.

My stomach twisted, and I dropped the phone on the bed beside me. 'I came back to the dorm,' I said finally.

'That much I figured. Did something happen to cause you to leave?'

'No.' I forced a casual shrug and took another drink. 'I just wanted to come back.'

'Oh.' She bit down on her lip, and then she took a deep breath. 'Erik didn't say anything to you?'

'No.' I downed the rest of the juice. 'Why?' Once I asked the question, I thought it could be because I called him a dick. Guilt rose. 'Debbie, I'm sorry for calling him a dick. I just—'

'Don't apologize.' She waved her hand. 'He can be a dick. Anyway, he went to use the bathroom not too long after you'd gone upstairs, and I was worried he said something to you.'

A lock of brown hair slipped out of her hair clip and brushed her forehead. She knocked it away. My mind was whirling, centered on Jase and that wonderful, wicked tongue of his, but I thought of the bruises I'd seen on her legs, and the way Erik talked to her.

I needed to say something to her. Tell her that I knew what it was like. Someone needed to step up because I knew personally that when no one did, it only got worse. My skin burned. It was hard, though. Even now it was difficult telling someone I'd been in a relationship like that. It was more than the guilt and the embarrassment. It was that . . . that *fucking* fear that never really left, that festered like a rotten wound in the memories.

I averted my gaze to the empty bottle. 'Debbie, can I ask you a question?'

'Sure.' She smiled as she tossed the bottle of pills up, catching it. 'Ask away.'

Squaring my shoulders, I looked up. 'Does . . . does Erik hit you?'

A second or two passed and then she laughed. Too loudly. 'What? No. W-why would you even think that?'

I fiddled with the lid on the bottle. 'Because he isn't very nice and—'

'Just because he says ignorant stuff every once in a while doesn't make him an abuser.' She unfurled her long legs and shot off the bed. Folding her arms, she faced me. Her cheeks were molten. 'He doesn't hit me.'

Denial. God knows I tried that when Mom saw the bruises. Pushing the quilt off me, I swung my legs off the bed. Our gazes locked, and she looked away. I took a shallow breath. 'I saw the bruises on your legs.'

All the color drained from her face. 'Bruises?' She then glanced down at her jeans. 'What?'

'The other day. You were wearing shorts.'

Her brows furrowed as her mouth opened and then snapped shut. 'I walked into the side of the bed a few days ago. That's probably what you saw.'

Then she must've repeatedly walked into the bed several times over. I sat the bottle on the nightstand. 'Debbie—'

'Look, thank you for being concerned, but there's nothing to be concerned about.' She grabbed her phone off its charger and picked up a knit cap lying on her narrow bed. 'I've got things to do. I'll see you later.'

I pushed to my feet. 'I need to talk to you—'

'I don't have time for this.'

'Please. You don't understand. I'm not trying to upset you or be judgey. I just want you—'

The door slammed shut.

'To know that I know what it feels like,' I muttered to the empty room.

Well, that went over well. Sighing, I plopped back down on the bed. The ache in my temples had decreased, but I felt like a film of grossness was covering my skin. Which was sort of appropriate considering I now felt like a douche canoe after talking to Debbie.

But I knew my suspicions weren't off.

Gathering up my shower stuff, I headed to the bathroom. While I stood under the steady, hot stream, I replayed last night over in my head. The girl in his room. Me leaving like a lunatic. Jase in the Jeep. The taste of him in my mouth, and then him, his dark head bowed between my legs.

That image of him was forever seared into my brain.

I slid my hands down my face as I turned, letting the water hit my back. A flutter in my chest moved to my belly, and a smile peeked out from behind my fingers. The way I felt was . . . strange. Like I woke up with not only a possible hangover, but I also felt different somehow. As if I grew up a little overnight. I really didn't know what to make out of it. It was stupid because oral sex didn't change lives.

Well, it had been rather life-changing.

I giggled as I slid my hands through my wet hair.

As the foam from my body wash gathered on my toes, I bit down on my lip. Last night had really happened, and as I remembered, Jase hadn't pushed me away afterward. He'd stayed until I slept. He hadn't apologized or said that it shouldn't have happened.

I climbed out of the shower and quickly dried off. Slipping on a pair of comfy lounge pants and a shirt, I padded through the suite, stopping to glance at the door to the other dorm, ears tingling.

166

Holding my breath, I listened. The sound of footsteps neared the door and then faded away. I crept to the door, clutching my shower stuff to my chest. 'Hello?'

Silence.

I shook my head after waiting a few seconds and returned to my room. The first thing I did was check my phone. Nothing. A niggle of unease curled low in my stomach as I sat on my bed and grabbed my laptop.

If that conversation with Debbie hadn't been awkward enough, she returned in the late afternoon with Erik. By that point, I'd spoken to Avery and told her the same thing I'd told Debbie. There had been no mention of Jase.

I also hadn't heard from Jase.

But, right now, I wasn't really thinking about him.

Erik stood in front of the desk while Debbie packed up a small overnight bag. I sat my laptop on the pillow. She didn't look at me as she shoved a change of clothing into a small brown-and-pink bag. 'You're not staying here tonight?'

'No,' Erik answered, sending me a snotty look. 'She's staying with me.'

My temper snapped. 'I was asking her.'

'Do I look like I'm deaf?' He turned to me, brow raised, and I wanted to knock that cocky smile right off his face. 'Or stupid? I know you were talking to her, but—'

'Erik.' Debbie sighed. She zipped up her bag and turned around, her cheeks flushed. 'Can we not do this?'

Her boyfriend's pupils dilated as he turned his head slowly. 'Did you just interrupt me?'

The fine hairs on my body rose as I stood. The hardness and challenge in his voice threw me back several years. Muscles in my stomach twisted. I wanted to flee the room because in that moment I saw Jeremy standing there, face contorted in rage.

I don't know what happened next.

Erik grabbed for Debbie's bag, but she held on. Maybe she didn't know what he was trying to do, but it set something off. Redness swept over his face as his bicep flexed. He yanked the bag back, throwing Debbie off balance as the strap was ripped from her hand. Out of instinct, I shot forward, intent on grabbing her arm so she didn't fall. An angry retort burst from Erik as he swung the bag around. It smacked into my hip, knocking me back. I wasn't thinking as I stumbled back, arms flying out to catch myself, but fingers grasping air.

All I saw were Debbie's round eyes as I put my weight on my dominant leg—my *right* leg—without thinking.

My right leg immediately went out from underneath me as red-hot pain exploded in my knee. A strangled cry escaped me. I went down, landing on my ass as the air punched out of my lungs. The pain was vicious, like someone had taken a knife and shoved it through muscle and cartilage.

Debbie shouted, 'Teresa!'

Tears sprang to my eyes, and I squeezed them shut, refusing to look at my knee. I couldn't. Oh my God, I couldn't look at it.

'Is it your knee?' Debbie asked. 'Oh my God, is it your knee?'

Clenching my jaw tight, I nodded. The world outside—the door and the room—all constricted, closing in.

'I didn't mean to,' Erik said, voice pitched high. 'She was in the way. It was an accident. Tell her it was an accident!'

My hands curled into fists as my heart pumped erratically.

'Teresa,' whispered Debbie. I could feel her kneeling beside me. She placed a cold, trembling hand on my arm. 'Say something.'

Pressing my lips together, I shook my head. I couldn't speak. I couldn't look at my knee, because—oh God—I knew. *I knew*. The pain was too intense, too lasting. It wasn't just hurt.

My knee was blown.

Again.

Chapter 14

Erik bailed quickly, waiting for Debbie in the lobby below. He was lucky, because if I could walk like a normal person, I'd be kicking his ass across campus.

'I'm sorry,' Debbie said for the hundredth time as she helped me up on the bed. 'I'm so—'

'Stop,' I snapped, taking a deep breath as my leg jerked from a painful spasm. 'Stop apologizing. It wasn't your fault.'

She backed away, hands clasped together. 'He didn't mean to do it.'

My mouth opened, but I sucked in a sharp breath as a slice of pain traveled up my leg.

'Do you need some ice?' she asked.

Grinding my teeth, I nodded. By the time she returned with a pillowcase wrapped around ice, I'd managed to straighten out my knee and roll up my pant leg. The skin around my knee looked puffy. Not good. I hissed as I placed the ice on it.

'Teresa . . .'

Taking another shallow breath, I looked at her. 'He might not have really meant to do that, but he was pissed. He didn't stop to think when he swung that bag around. Or maybe he did, and he just didn't care.'

Tears pooled in her eyes. 'I know he didn't mean to.'

Falling silent, I adjusted the ice. My head was numb. Too many things were running through my thoughts.

She hesitated near the bed, shifting her weight from one foot to the other. Several moments passed before she spoke. 'Please . . . please don't tell anyone.'

My head swung toward her sharply. I couldn't believe she would ask that of me, and then my heart jumped. Hadn't I asked the same of my mom and then Cam? *Please don't tell anyone?* Because I had been afraid of how Jeremy would react.

The moment to confide in Debbie was here, but she rushed forward and hugged me around the arms and whispered, 'Please.'

I didn't say anything as she left because it was a promise I wasn't sure I could keep. Lowering my gaze, I slowly eased up the makeshift bag. My skin was red from the cold.

My ringer on my cell phone went off an hour or so later, but I didn't even look at it. Lying on my back, I'd shoved a pillow under my knee to keep it elevated. By the time I had to hobble down the hall for more ice, the pain had become a constant ache that spiked every so often, as if someone had placed a lit match against my skin.

My knee was swollen. The ice and elevation weren't helping. I hadn't heard a pop when I fell, but the swelling was bad news bears. And I knew I couldn't test my weight on it. Not yet.

There were two more calls that night. Out of the three, two of them were from Jase, but I couldn't bring myself to answer the phone. Last night . . . last night now felt like forever ago.

I stared at the phone, lip trembling as it signaled a message being left. As the screen blinked black, I reached for it, but drew up short. I couldn't talk to him yet. If I did, there was a good chance I'd lose it.

Because if my knee was blown again, everything changed. This wouldn't be temporary. There would be no going back to the studio. This . . . I looked around the dorm . . . this would truly be my life. This whole time I'd been *faking* it.

I pulled my hand back and rested my forehead against my palm. Another spasm rolled up my leg. I couldn't deal with this again—the pain, the surgery, the rehab. But this time . . . I shuddered. This time would be different because the worst possible thing you could do to a torn ACL was to reinjure it. Doing so increased the chances of permanent instability.

And I wouldn't be able to dance again.

When I finally slept, I don't think I dreamed, and when I woke, the swelling had increased until my knee looked twice its size. I didn't even consider getting more ice. I knew it wouldn't do any damn good. I had no crutches, so there was no way I was walking to class. I stayed in my bed as acid churned in my stomach.

My cell went off a few minutes after music class would've started. Thinking it was Calla or Debbie—who'd sent me two texts checking in that I hadn't responded to—I was surprised to see it was from Jase. I still hadn't checked his message.

Where r u?

Squeezing my eyes shut until they burned, I sat up a little. He deserved a response, even after all those times he ignored me. This wasn't about him. I sent him a quick message back.

Not feeling well.

His response was immediate.

R u ok?

Scrubbing my suddenly wet eyes, I texted back a quick *yes*, and then tossed the phone on the foot of the bed.

I knew I needed to call Dr. Morgan and Mom, but the mere thought of doing so caused my chest to seize. The pain and swelling—I already knew what it meant. My future and my dreams were over. I didn't need a doctor to tell me that.

Another shudder worked its way through me. Curling onto my side, I wrapped my arm around my pillow and shoved my face in it. The soft material quickly became damp. They weren't big tears. Just silent and unending. The hurt in the pit of my stomach was as strong as the pain in my knee.

It was a little after twelve thirty when there was a sharp rap on the door. I had no idea who it could be. Maybe my yet-to-be-seen suitemates? Frowning, I hastily wiped my cheeks as I sat up, and then cleared my throat. 'Come in.'

I tugged the quilt over my right leg. I don't know why I wanted to hide it. Maybe it was like if no one else saw it, then it wasn't true. Sort of a stupid mentality, but I was barely holding myself together. I was seconds away from throwing myself to the floor and flailing.

The door opened, and I blinked once and then twice, thinking I was seeing things, but the person before me didn't vanish.

Jase strolled into my room, like he'd done it a million times. He was dressed in jeans and a black, long-sleeve shirt, and a plastic bag dangled from his long fingertips. He drew up short when he spotted me.

Concern filled his gray eyes. 'Wow. You do look rough.'

I cringed. Must've been the puffy eyes. 'Thanks.'

A small smile crossed his lips as he came forward. 'You

don't look *that* bad.' He sat on the edge of the bed, placing the bag on the floor between his feet. 'Should I be worried?'

My brows rose. I was still too stunned by seeing him to understand where he was going with that statement.

'Is whatever you have contagious?' he clarified.

'Oh. No.' I paused, peeking up at him through damp lashes. 'Why are you here?'

'Why?' He coughed out a laugh. 'Seems pretty obvious.' Bending over, he picked up the bag and pulled out a plastic container. 'Chicken noodle soup. Not for the soul. But for your hopefully not contagious disease.'

That damn fluttering feeling was back with a vengeance. I took the warm container and plastic spoon. A ginger ale bottle appeared next, and he placed that on the nightstand, then a pink box. A cupcake. I wanted to cry. 'If you are so worried about getting sick, why did you come?'

One side of his lips curved up again. 'Well, considering what we did Saturday night, I think that concern is beside the point.'

'Yeah,' I murmured, flushing at the reminder.

'And I figured you were worth the risk,' he added, rolling the bag up and tossing it in the wastebasket by the desk. 'Knowing that should make you already feel better.'

I laughed, but the smile slipped off my face as I peeled the lid off the soup. What he'd done had rocked me straight to the center of my chest. I wasn't sick, but there was no way I was going to deny this feeling. In spite of the dull ache in my leg and what it meant, warmth bubbled up my chest.

'Thank you,' I said, my voice hoarse. 'This . . . this was really nice of you.'

He shrugged. 'It's not a big deal.'

Dipping the spoon into the noodle heavy soup, I took a healthy swallow to help ease the lump in my throat. What he'd done was a big deal. Tears burned my eyes again. I was turning into a big crybaby, but these tears were different. I wanted to tackle-hug him. I wanted to rain kisses all over his beautiful face. I wanted to be able to get up and do those things without hobbling through it. Him being here wasn't the equivalent of him professing his undying love for me, but it meant something—something more than stolen kisses.

When I looked at him, he was studying me closely—too closely. I averted my attention to the soup.

'I was worried last night,' he admitted quietly. 'When you didn't answer, I thought . . . well, I thought you were ignoring me.'

Holding the container close, I gathered up some noodles. 'I wasn't.'

'I wouldn't blame you if you had, especially when I've done the same to you.' He thrust his fingers through his hair, and as soon as he dropped his hand, his hair flopped back over his forehead. 'I don't think I ever apologized for that.'

My heart rate picked up. Where was all this coming from? And why right now, when it felt like my kneecap was about to jump out of my leg totally alien-monster style.

'So I'm sorry about that. And when I made the comment about you just wanting to get laid. I know that's not what you want. You're better than that and you deserve more than that. I know that doesn't mean a lot, but it wasn't the right way, and in the end, it was fucking pointless because here you are and I can't stay away from you.' He twisted toward me, leaning his upper body over my legs. 'You know about Jack, but—'

His hip pressed into my knee, and I jerked. My body jackknifed as the slicing pain traveled up my leg. His hand snatched out lightning quick, catching the container of

175

soup before it spilled all over me. Blood drained from my face as I slammed my hands into the bed, clutching the sheets.

'Jesus! What happened?' He jumped up like the bed had bitten his ass. 'Are you okay?'

Reeling from the sharpness, I could only nod. Breathe in. Breathe out. Slowly, after several moments, the pain dulled back to a throb. My fingers eased off the sheets, and I forced my gaze up.

Jase stared at me. He glanced at my leg, and then my face. 'You aren't sick, are you? You've been crying. That's why you look that way.' Before I could respond, he snatched the quilt and flipped it over. 'Shit, Tess, your knee. Fuck. I didn't know. I'm—'

'Don't,' I said, voice hoarse. 'You didn't know. It's okay.'

He raised wide eyes to mine. 'How did this happen?'

'I came down on it wrong Sunday night.' The lie came out easier than the truth. Guilt immediately settled like a stone in my stomach. Hand shaking, I brushed my hair out of my face. 'I think I've really messed it up.'

'You think?' He put the container of soup on the nightstand. 'How much pain are you in?'

I watched him gingerly sit on the edge of the bed. 'It comes and goes.'

'Me sitting on it didn't help, huh?'

A weak smile appeared on my lips. 'It's okay.'

Jase reached over, catching the strand of hair that kept falling in my face. He tucked it back. 'Have you told Cam? Your mom?'

I shook my head. 'I didn't want them to worry.'

'Want more soup?' When I nodded, he handed it off. I hadn't eaten since yesterday afternoon, so this was doing my tummy good. 'But sitting here with your leg like this isn't helping anyone, Tess.'

'I know,' I whispered, ducking my gaze. I focused on his jaw as I scooped up noodles. Nice area to stare at. There was a thin blanket of stubble covering his lower cheek, giving him a rough, sexy look.

Jase ran a hand through his hair. 'Then I'm guessing you haven't called your doctor?'

Swallowing a mouthful of chicken noodle soup, I shook my head again.

'Okay. Then that's the first thing we need—hold up.' He reached over, sweeping his thumb along my chin, catching the broth and causing me to flush. 'We need to call your doctor. And don't give me any shit. We need to do that. And we need to do that now.'

He let me finish my soup before he retrieved my cell from the foot of the bed. Handing it over, he waited, arms crossed, until I found my doctor's contact. I had to leave a message, but the call was returned quickly. An appointment was set up for tomorrow morning, and my heart was already pounding with the ugliness of it all.

'I'll take you,' Jase announced after returning from the hall, where he'd disposed of the soup container.

'What?' I pushed myself up against the headboard.

He was matter-of-fact. 'I'll take you tomorrow. He's at WVU, right?'

'Around there, but—'

'But you haven't even told Cam yet or your mom, so how do you expect to get there? Hitch a ride?' His grin was full of arrogance. 'I can miss my classes tomorrow. It won't be a big deal. And if I didn't want to do it, I wouldn't offer. So don't argue with me.'

'I know,' I said. 'But why would you want to do that? Sitting in class is better than leaving at butt crack in the morning and driving for hours. I mean, I'd rather sit through music class.'

He laughed as he sat back down, placing one hand on the other side of my hip. 'You must really hate the drive and the doctor to prefer sitting in that class. You missed it today. Your friend Calla's head fell all the way back. She snored.'

I laughed. 'She doesn't snore. And I know because she sleeps through that class almost every time.'

His thick lashes lowered, shielding his startling eyes. 'I want to be there for you. Let me.'

My mouth opened and the proverbial why formed on the tip of my tongue. Did the why matter? The way things were between Jase and me at this moment confused the ever-loving crap out of me. Something had changed Saturday night, shifted. He was doing the exact opposite of pushing me away and running. Was I that good at giving head? I almost laughed because that was just stupid.

'Okay,' I said finally.

Jase smiled, and suddenly, it felt like I'd agreed to much more than a ride.

I hated the whole atmosphere of doctors' offices—the white paint, the tacky decorations, and the smell of disinfectant. It didn't matter what kind of doctor you were seeing; the offices were all the same.

An x-ray had been done before I even saw the middle-aged doctor. My butt had been planted in the dreaded wheelchair, and I'd been rolled away, leaving Jase in the main waiting room. Once I was deposited in the room where the doctor would see me, I hobbled out of the chair and sat on one of the plastic ones. I was glaring at the wheelchair when the door opened, and one of the blushing front desk nurses ushered Jase inside.

'We thought you could use the company,' she said, smoothing a hand over her blond head.

178

Jase winked as he sauntered in. 'She was probably beside herself without me.'

I snorted.

The nurse giggled and then hastily backed out of the room. I arched a brow at him. 'How did you manage to get yourself back here considering you're not family?'

He hopped up on the table I should've been sitting on. From there, he swung his long legs like a mischievous boy. 'I have considerable charm, Tess.'

'That's true.' I cracked a grin.

'And with said charm comes great responsibility to use it wisely,' he continued, eyes dancing. 'I only break it out when necessary.'

'Good to hear.' I shifted my weight on the uncomfortable plastic. Having him back here was good because my nerves were stretched tight. 'Thank you again. I really appreciate it.'

'No problem. Just remember your promise.'

I laughed as I shook my head. 'How can I forget?'

'You're going to love it.' He dipped his chin, and messy waves tumbled forward. 'And you have nothing to fear. I'll be right there with you.'

My stomach still lurched at the thought of being on a horse. Jase had spent the drive to the doctor's convincing me to agree to doing a little more than a horsey meet and greet. As in getting on top of one. Jase would be with me, and I agreed because I trusted him. And because it gave me something other than my leg to fret over.

'Cam texted me earlier,' Jase announced.

I jerked my gaze to him. His expression was unreadable. 'Did you tell him that you were with me?'

'Did you tell him?'

'No. He still thinks I'm sick.' I wrapped the edge of my ponytail around my fingers. 'Did you?'

He shook his head. 'I figured he'd ask why I was with you and not him. And then that would lead to other questions, and well, I figured they'd best be answered not over the phone.'

'You think answering some of the questions would be best face-to-face?' Doubt colored my tone. Considering what Jase would tell him, I easily foresaw that conversation ending with a fist to a face.

Jase laughed. 'I'd have to deploy my charm again.'

'I don't think that kind of charm will work on my brother.'

'Ye of little faith,' he said, and his lips hitched up on one side. The devilish look caused my heart to skip a beat.

I pressed my lips together, wondering what would even be said to Cam. Less would be better I supposed, no matter what happened between Jase and me going forward. My gaze glided over the near perfect contours of his face and then down, over his broad shoulders. When I looked up, he caught my gaze and he smiled reassuringly.

My breath caught on the realization that I could easily fall in love with him.

That was if I hadn't already.

'What are you thinking about?' he asked, biting down on that delicious lower lip.

Tension coiled low in my stomach. Oh, I was so screwed. I looked away, feeling my cheeks flood with color. 'Yeah, I'm not caring and sharing that.'

A deep, husky chuckle came from him. 'That's no fun.'

'Sorry.'

Thank God, the door opened and Dr. Morgan stepped into the room. At the moment, I'd rather focus on my knee than pay too much attention to what was going on inside my heart and head.

White lab coat swinging about his knees, Dr. Morgan had close-cut curls that were sprinkled with gray. He smiled as he walked in, eyeing where I was and where Jase was. 'Do I have a new patient today?'

Trying not to get too hopeful over the smile, I cleared my throat. 'That's Jase. He's, um . . . he's my friend. He came with me.'

'Nice to meet you.' The good doc walked over and shook his hand. When Jase started to get up, Dr. Morgan waved him off. 'No need to move. We're all good this way.' Sitting in one of the rolling chairs, he dropped the file with my x-rays on the counter. He toed his way to me, grabbed ahold of another chair, and slid it around. Gently, he lifted my leg up and placed it on the chair. 'Let's get a look at this.'

I rolled up the hem of my jeans, wincing as it revealed my oversized knee. Sexy.

He drew in a low whistle. 'You know the drill.'

I did. Closing my eyes, I clapped my hands together and pressed them against my stomach. Dr. Morgan's fingers were cool as they pressed against my knee. The touch didn't hurt. Not yet. He applied a little more pressure, checking the stabilization. Pain flared, and I gritted my teeth.

'Pain on a one to ten scale?' he asked quietly.

'Um.' I sucked at these things. Like who knew the pain scale? I needed one of those funny stick people pictures to use as a guide. 'Six?'

'Okay.' He pushed a little harder, and I jumped. 'How about now?'

'Seven?' I squeaked.

He continued to torture me, and my eyes snapped open when I felt a hand wrap around mine. I hadn't even heard him move. Jase was kneeling beside me, and the moment my eyes locked with his gray ones, I couldn't look away.

'And this?' Dr. Morgan asked. At the sound of my harsh hiss, he removed his hands. 'No need to answer.' He smiled

181

gently as he rolled my pants leg down. 'Okay. You iced and elevated?'

I nodded, still looking at Jase. 'Yeah.'

'But it didn't help?'

'No.' I wet my lips, and Jase smiled. Tearing my gaze away from him so I didn't look like too much of a doofus, I faced the doctor. As I spoke, Jase managed to ease my hands apart and thread his fingers through my left hand. 'It's not as painful as the first time, and I didn't hear any pops, but I'm afraid I really screwed it up.'

'I need to know exactly what you were doing when you hurt your knee Sunday,' he said, dropping his hands on his knees. 'Were you walking? Did you lose your balance?'

My gaze dropped to the doctor's long fingers. They were slender, but the knuckles were surprisingly big and round. My throat closed off.

'She said she just lost her balance,' Jase said, and my free hand closed into a fist.

'Were you walking when it happened? Getting out of bed or off a chair?' Dr. Morgan paused. 'It's really important to know exactly what you were doing.'

Blood pounded in my ears as I slowly lifted my gaze. The truth. Damnit, the truth was always a pesky, nosy bitch. I shook my head as I bit down on my lip. 'I . . . I was in my dorm room and my roommate's boyfriend had a bag in his hand. Like a weekender bag. Anyway, I was standing too close when he swung it around. It hit my hip and I stumbled back, putting my weight on my right leg.'

Jase's fingers tightened until I could feel the bones in my hand starting to grind, and then he eased off, slipping his hand free. I couldn't look at him, but I could feel him staring.

'So it was an unplanned action. Not a major misstep. That gives me a really clear picture of what's going on.' Dr.

182

Morgan reached for my file, flipping it open. 'Well, bad or good news first?'

My heart jumped, and I glanced at Jase. His eyes were sharp, expression stony. 'Good? I guess?'

'The good news is that the x-rays do not show any additional tears,' he said, and my shoulders immediately relaxed. 'I know that was your biggest fear. The original tear is healing.'

I took a deep breath. 'So what's the bad news?'

Dr. Morgan smiled tightly. 'What this injury shows is a destabilization of the ACL. And with the kind of tear you suffered, there was a forty to sixty percent chance of re-injury. Now, like I said, the tear doesn't appear to be reinjured. So no surgery, and I really do think this will heal if you go back to the brace and use the crutches over the next couple of days.'

Instead of feeling better, the walls started to close in around me. 'But?'

'But . . .' He smiled, but I tensed. The smile didn't reach his dark eyes. It was the kind of smile doctors made when they were about to deliver a death blow. 'This injury shows that there is a destabilization there and that is what concerns me, Teresa. When you first injured your ACL, we talked about the possibility—although slim at that time—of continuous destabilization and . . .'

My brain cut him off right there, but I nodded and I stared at him, barely aware of the way Jase was stiffening with every word spoken. I even smiled when Dr. Morgan patted my hand and told me it was going to be okay. I agreed. Everything would be fucking perfect. And then I said nothing when the nurse came in, and the dreaded blue brace was returned to my knee. I took the crutches with grace. And I kept breathing. In. Out. In. Out.

Somehow I ended up outside, in Jase's Jeep, staring out the windshield.

'Tess . . .'

I looked over at him, and he shook his head as our gazes locked. His face was pale. 'I'm so fucking sorry.'

Drawing in a deep breath, I shuddered as it got stuck. The destabilization was a bad, bad thing. It was worse than having surgery because it meant one thing. My knee would always be wicked weak. I would always have problems with it, even after the tear was completely healed. The chance of getting arthritis in the knee earlier than most had nearly doubled.

Professional dancing was out of the picture. No more. Done. There was no returning to the studio, no more lessons or recitals or competitions. I'd be stupid to even attempt it. And my instructors wouldn't allow it. Neither would the Joffrey School.

College was no longer temporary. Teaching was no longer plan B. It was the only plan.

Oh my God.

I shook my head, opened my mouth, but there were no words.

Jase cursed, and I . . . I cracked wide open. Like a well deep inside me had burst.

The tears came, spilling down my cheeks, and once they started, there was no stopping them. The interior blurred— Jase disappeared in the haze.

A deep sound came from him, and then his arms were around me. One second I was sitting there by myself, my world crumbling apart, and the next moment, he was holding me against him—holding me together.

Chapter 15

I cried so hard and for so long that it was worse than having a hangover, and the entire front of Jase's shirt was drenched.

It was not a pretty sight.

Why he didn't untangle my arms and push me away was beyond my understanding, but he held on. Cupping one hand to the back of my head, he held me to his chest as best he could with the gear shift between us, running his other hand up and down my spine. The whole time he whispered soothing, nonsensical words until he finally made me laugh.

'I always knew I'd make an excellent human tissue.' He dipped his head so that his chin rested atop my head. 'Thank you for letting me achieve that dream.'

He was one durable tissue.

When I finally pulled myself together, we left Morgantown. I needed to call my mom, but I couldn't bring myself to do that yet. She'd support me no matter what I did with my life, but she'd loved watching me dance and compete. In a way, it had been her dream, too.

When we neared Martinsburg, I glanced over at Jase. 'Do we have to go back yet?'

'No. We can do whatever you want.'

Going back to that dorm meant going back and facing the future. Like all the classes I needed to take more seriously. 'I mean, you probably have—'

'I'm where I want to be,' Jase said, sending me a look that shut me up. 'You don't want to go back yet. Fine. I got the perfect place we can go.'

'You do?' My voice sounded stuffy, and while I was curious to what level of a hot mess I looked, I didn't dare peek in the mirror.

'Yep.' He winked.

The corners of my lips tipped up as I tugged the band out of my hair. Silence descended between us as we took the road that led to his parents' farm, but he veered off halfway, turning between two thick oaks.

I clutched the oh-shit handle, my eyes widening. 'Is this a road?'

He grinned. 'Yes. No.'

A narrow strip of ground was beaten down to where only a few patches of grass peeked through the packed soil. 'If this is a road, it's the kind those kids took in *Wrong Turn*.'

Tipping his head back, Jase laughed deeply. 'Trust me. Where we're going is much better than where they were heading.'

'That's not saying much.' With my hand clamped on the handle, I swallowed hard as the Jeep bumped along. Jase gripped the steering wheel hard, and the grin on his face as he winged around trees and rocks was contagious. The motion didn't hurt my leg, not with the brace on, and before I knew it, I was laughing as I hopped in the seat. In those precious moments, I forgot everything.

'Hold on,' Jase warned.

The Jeep dipped into a gully, and I hooted as we bounced back up. The trees cleared away, revealing a grassy field blanketed with tiny, white flowers. Several yards ahead, the field eased into a body of water. There was a wooden dock that looked rather lonely.

He slowed down, coming to a stop a few feet away from the dock. 'Welcome to the Winstead Lake,' he said, turning off the car.

'That's what it's called?'

He laughed. 'No. It's really just a pond. But it's deep enough to go swimming in the summer, and there's a lot of fish in there. It's where Jack caught his first fish actually. He did it the first time I brought him out here.'

I smiled, picturing the two of them sitting on the edge of the dock, fishing poles in hand, and one of them much, much smaller. 'How old was he?'

'Three,' he said, a proud smile forming on his lips. 'He's got fishing in his blood.'

'And horseback riding?' I unbuckled my seat belt.

'Yep. And he rocks at drawing stick figures, too.' He flashed a quick grin when I laughed, and I was happy that he'd still talk about Jack so easily knowing that I was privy to the truth. 'Stay put, okay?'

My hands froze near the door handle. 'All right?'

Jase hopped out and headed around the back of the Jeep. The hatch opened and then shut. A few seconds later, he reappeared a few feet away. Leaning back in the seat, I reached down and picked at the brace through my jeans as he spread a dark blue blanket over the dainty flowers.

Emotion clogged my throat, and I struggled to get it to go away. God, sometimes when I was with Jase, it was like all my girlie fantasies were coming true, but even my imagination wouldn't have created a scene like this.

Was any of this real?

My fingers trailed along the edge of the brace. It was real. The good and the bad.

When he returned to the Jeep, he opened the door and then stopped, looking concerned. 'You okay? The ride didn't hurt your knee, did it?'

'I'm fine.' I smiled as I blinked. I needed meds or something. 'Can I move now?'

'Nope.'

'No?'

A lopsided grin appeared as he reached in and gently maneuvered me so that my legs dangled out of the Jeep. Our eyes met as he slipped an arm under my knees and the other around my back. 'Hold on.'

My heart did a backflip. A perfect one. 'You do not need to carry me.'

'I know,' he replied. 'Now hold on.'

I folded my arms around his neck. My fingers fisted the shirt along his shoulders. 'I could use my crutches.'

'And I'm using my brawny, spectacular muscles.'

'They are quite spectacular,' I admitted.

He grinned. 'Damn straight they are. Ready?'

I nodded, and he lifted me up smoothly. I felt kind of stupid as he carried me over to the blanket, but the ground was uneven and the crutches would've been a real bitch. When he sat me down, I reluctantly loosened my hold on him. 'Using crutches on campus is going to suck butt.'

'It is.' He sat beside me, facing the pond. 'But from what the doc said, it didn't sound like you'd need them for long.'

I stretched my legs out on the blanket and reached down, adjusting the brace through my jeans. It had taken me forever to get used to it the first time. At the thought of having to wear this for weeks, if not months, my mood plummeted as if I swan dived off the top of the Empire State Building.

Tucking the loose hairs back behind my ears, I let out a breath I didn't realize I was holding. With the exception of the chirps from the trees around us, there was no other sound. The place was tranquil. A place I wondered if Jase visited when he needed to think or get away. 'Does this place get a lot of traffic?'

'We're at least two miles from the farm, where Mom and Dad are, but this is still our property,' he explained. 'No one comes out here except us, and they aren't going to be coming anywhere near here, so we can stay as long as you want.'

I dropped my hands into my lap. 'Thank you for bringing me out here.'

'No problem.' He nudged my arm with his. 'You sure you don't want to pick up those pain meds the doc gave you a prescription for?'

The script was burning a hole in my pocket. 'No. I mean, it would be nice to take them and just not care, because that's how they make me feel, but I need to deal with this. You know?'

'I get that, but you shouldn't be in pain.'

'I'm not in a lot of pain.' And that much was true. It hurt, but it was manageable. Beside me, Jase lay back, folding his arms under his head. For a few moments, I got a little lost staring at the straight line of his nose and the way his lashes fanned to an indecent length. 'Can I ask you something?'

'Something.'

I smiled, remembering my drunken response from Saturday night. 'Why don't you live at the farm? You love being around Jack. I'm surprised you're not living there. I mean, can I ask you that?'

'Yeah,' he said immediately, frowning slightly. 'I want to. You know, I'd be able to spend more time with him, but I don't think it's a good idea. It makes it . . . harder, especially when Mom and Dad do the parent thing with him. I want to step in and that would just confuse him.'

'Understandable.' I wet my lips. 'I'm sorry.'

'For what?'

I gave a lopsided shrug. 'It's just, what you face with Jack is hard. You're trying to do the right thing, but what's really the right thing? No one knows. It's got to be hard.'

'It is. That's why I'm not sure if telling him the truth will ever be the right thing,' he admitted, and I was relieved that he was talking to me about this, because this was more important than my stupid leg. 'On the flip side, shouldn't he know? And what if he finds out by accident when he's older? That kind of shit keeps me up at night.'

Reaching over, I squeezed his hand. 'I think you'll figure it out.'

He didn't say anything, but there was something about the way he looked at me that forced the words beyond my lips.

'I don't know what I'm going to do,' I whispered, switching my gaze to the still waters. That's how I felt. Too still. As if my life was stuck on the pause button. 'I thought . . . I always thought I'd be able to go back. That I would dance again. That's what I always thought I'd do and now . . .' I trailed off, shaking my head.

'Everything has changed,' he added quietly.

I nodded as I blew out a breath.

'I said it before and I'll say it again. Sometimes some really good things come from something unexpected.' His lashes lifted, and the intensity in his gaze was unnerving, as if his words meant more than what he was saying. 'I know that's not easy to swallow right now and doesn't help you, but I'm speaking the truth.'

I nodded again. 'You're talking about Jack?'

'I am.'

I looked over my shoulder at him again. His gaze was trained on the cloudless, deep blue sky. One side of his lips curled up. 'You know, you'll make a great teacher, Tess.'

A strangled-sounding laugh escaped me. 'You said I'd be unhappy being a teacher.'

'No. I said that you'd be happy doing it, but it's not what you want.'

'How's that any different?'

He slid me a sideways look. 'It's very different. Teaching could become something you want and something you love to do. You just need time.'

Time was a funny and fickle thing. Sometimes there was never enough of it, and other times it stretched out endlessly.

'I really believe that,' he said quietly.

Pressure clamped down on my chest. Maybe he was right. Maybe tomorrow or next week or next month, all of this wouldn't seem like such a death sentence. But right now, I felt like I was free-falling, my arms flailing and there wasn't anything to grab onto to stop my fall.

'I don't want to talk about this,' I said, voice hoarse as I squeezed my eyes shut.

'What do you want?'

'I . . . I don't want to think about this. Maybe that makes me weak.'

'It doesn't,' he said, and I felt him roll onto his side.

'And I don't want to feel this right now—this emptiness and uncertainty and confusion.' The next breath I took was shaky. 'I just don't want to feel *this*.'

Maybe I should've gotten the prescription filled.

There was a moment, perhaps no more than a heartbeat, and then his hand wrapped around the curve of my elbow. My eyes snapped open when he tugged me onto my back. Air hitched in my throat as his lean body hovered over mine as he rose up on his elbow.

'I have an idea,' he said with a small grin. The teasing

look didn't reach his eyes. Something else burned there. A powerful intensity that caused the muscles in my stomach to quiver. 'And I think this idea will definitely have you feeling something else.'

'You do?' My heart rate picked up.

'Uh-huh.' He placed the tips of his fingers on my cheek and very slowly dragged them over my parted lips and then down my throat. 'I have a degree in art.'

My brows rose. 'What?'

'You didn't know?' His hand moved farther south, over the hem of my shirt and then he stopped, his palm resting against the swells of my breasts. 'I have a degree in the art of distraction.'

I laughed. 'That's so lame.'

'But it's working, right?' He grinned as he lowered his head. His lips brushed the curve of my cheek, exactly where his fingers had been. 'You know what else?'

'What?' I shivered as his hand moved again, sliding between my breasts and resting just below my belly button.

'There's something else I have a degree in.' His lips grazed the corner of mine, and a rush of tingles shot over my skin. 'You're going to say it's lame, but I'll know the truth. You're secretly amazed by my skill.'

'God only knows what it is.' I moved my lower lip, to bite down on it, but Jase beat me to it. His teeth caught my lip in a gentle nip. I gasped at the unexpected sensation, and he took that as an invitation. Covering my lips with his, he slipped his tongue in, twirling it over mine and then flicking along the roof of my mouth.

Heat surged through my body, coiling low in my stomach. A sharp pulse shot to every limb as he explored my mouth with his, kissing as if time was truly a luxury we both had. When he lifted his head, my lips felt pleasantly swollen.

I placed a hand against his chest, delighted to find his heart was pounding as fast as mine, and he was the one doing the kissing. 'You have a degree in kissing?'

'That . . .' The firm glide of his lips over mine deepened as his hand moved down. He deftly undid the button on my jeans. 'And in taking girls' clothes off.'

I laughed and he caught the sound, turning it into a soft moan I couldn't hold back. He answered with a deep sound that vibrated against my chest. My mouth dried as a thrumming hum of desire buzzed through me. In the back of my mind, uncertainty lingered—not the same as earlier, but a concern for Jase and me—for us. There were no labels between us, or definitions of what we were to each other, and I desperately wanted to place a label there. I wanted that security of tomorrow with him, the promise of another kiss. And I wanted more than that.

But then his hand slipped under my panties and the feel of his fingers nearing the very center of me scattered all thoughts and concerns. He really did have a degree in distraction, because my whole being became focused on what he was up to with his hand.

His lips scorched a path down my neck, nuzzling the skin as one long finger skimmed through the wetness between my thighs. I jerked at the intimate touch. He hadn't touched me with his hands last time, so the whisper of his skin against mine was new and different and just as intoxicating.

Jase pressed a trail of hot, wet kisses up to the sensitive spot under my ear as he made another teasing pass with his finger. My entire body vibrated.

His hand stilled as he lifted his head. Our gazes locked. His eyes were a startling quicksilver. 'I can't forget the taste of you,' he said, and my entire body flushed. 'And I've been dying to know how you feel.'

God knows I was not a blushing virgin on a good day, but his bold words absolutely scandalized me . . . in a totally good, wicked way. The fact that we were lying out in the open might also have something to do with that.

He kissed me again, resting most of his weight on the arm beside my head. The pressure of his finger below increased, and the knot in my lower stomach tightened. My body jerked on reflex, and another deep, grumbling sound came from him.

'You're so wet,' he said in a husky voice, and I burned at those words. 'I love it. You were probably like this before I even got my hand down there.'

Oh dear . . .

I swallowed hard, and he chuckled. 'Am I embarrassing you?' he asked.

'No.' His words made me feel something entirely different.

'Good.'

Jase lowered his head, claiming my mouth in a kiss that shook me inside and out at the same moment he thrust one finger inside me. The sound that rose from me was muffled by his lips. I gripped his shoulders as my hips tipped up, seeking more. And I got more.

He pressed his palm against my most sensitive area, and lightning struck my veins. My toes curled in my flip-flops and both my legs jerked. A lick of pain encased my knee, but the other sensations racing through my system over-whelmed everything else. Desire clouded me. Jase was dangerous in all the right ways.

'God,' he groaned, tugging on my lower lip as his finger moved in and out. He added another finger, stretching me as he broke the kiss, resting his forehead against mine.

A tremble rocked his body as my hips followed his hand. The way his self-control stretched to its breaking point was my undoing. The tension unraveled, whipping through my body. Seeking his kiss, I came with his tongue tangled with mine, and the tremors seemed to go on forever.

Jase eased his hand away, but he stayed there, above me for a bit, his cheek pressed against mine as I dragged in deep breaths. It took me a few seconds to realize that he was breathing just as hard. When he rolled onto his side, I missed the weight of him, the warmth and closeness.

He pressed up against me. The pleasant numbness had sunk deep into my bones, but I could feel his hardness. I wanted to see him. It had been dark Saturday night, but what I could see and feel had been rather impressive. I also wanted to give him what he'd given me. I started to reach for him, but he caught my hand and brought it to his lips. He dropped a kiss to each of my knuckles. 'I told you. This was for you.'

I didn't know what to say to that as my eyes fluttered shut. A thank-you was definitely in order, but that seemed widely inappropriate. Not that I was turned off by doing inappropriate things obviously. Hell, my jeans were still unbuttoned, and I knew if I looked down, my polka-dotted undies would be peeking through, and I didn't care enough to zip up my pants.

He kissed my temple then, and my heart did another crazy jump. And then it did a series of leaps that spelled L. O. V. E. The rush that came after that was so intense it was almost as frightening as it was consuming.

God, I wasn't falling in love with Jase.

I was *in* love with him.

Probably had been since that night he showed up at my parents' house, nearly three years ago, and that hadn't lessened learning that he had a son, and one day that could turn into a very tricky situation, especially if momma ever reappeared, but we were here, together . . . but not.

'Hey,' Jase murmured, placing two fingers under my chin. He turned my head to his. 'Where'd you go?'

195

Straight into crazy land. That's where I went. Suddenly, I had to go there—go there with him, because my heart was already there, making itself comfy and happy, and I needed to be careful. I needed . . .

I needed that *label*.

Or I needed the truth of what we were to each other, and I needed that now.

Chapter 16

'What are we doing?' I asked, and I thought I'd be afraid of that question once asked. Because if I didn't ask, this relationship—whatever it was—could keep going, but it wasn't enough.

'Relaxing.'

Tipping my head back, I bit back a sigh as his lips brushed mine, threatening to tug me back into the sensual haze. I so needed to focus. 'You know what I mean. Us. What are we doing?'

He trailed his fingers down my throat, causing me to shiver as if a chill had danced over my bones. 'Are you sure you want to talk about that right now?'

Unease exploded in my belly, chasing away the pleasant hum. 'I think we need to, especially after *that*. And this weekend. And hell, the hay—'

'Hey, I didn't mean it like that.' He rose up again, onto his elbow. 'It's just a lot has happened in the last couple of days. With your knee and—'

'What happened with my knee hasn't anything to do with this.' Feeling like I needed to be sitting for this conversation, I rose and gathered up my courage. This conversation could end badly and it would hurt—oh God, it would hurt—but I needed to know. 'Jase, I've had feelings for you since you came to my parents' house—that very first night. And I know that sounds stupid and childish, but you . . . well, you were like a hero to me.'

He blinked and opened his mouth.

'Wait.' I placed a finger on his lips, silencing him. 'Like I said, I know that sounds stupid, but it was how I felt. That night you kissed me, well, all it did was cement the way I felt. And when I didn't hear from you or see you until I showed up here, I did see other people.'

His brows lowered as he tugged my hand away from his lips. 'I'm not sure I like the sound of that.'

'But none of them compared to you. And I did compare *everyone* to you. I couldn't help it. They . . . they just weren't you.' My cheeks burned. 'They were never you.'

'That sounds better.'

I narrowed my eyes at him. '*Anywho*, what I want has nothing to do with my knee or dancing. I've always wanted you, regardless of the time we didn't see each other or because you have a son. That hasn't changed how I feel.'

Jase stared at me a moment and then gave a little shake of his head. My heart stopped and then skipped a beat. He sat up and said, 'When I saw you for the first time, I thought you were absolutely beautiful.'

Not expecting that as a response, but sure as hell not unhappy with it, I sucked in a shallow breath.

Two spots on his cheeks flushed. 'Man, I felt like a dirtbag. You were my best friend's little sister. You were only sixteen and you had just gotten out of a terrible situation.'

'Not exactly relationship material, huh?' I teased.

He chuckled. 'And I . . . well, I always knew you deserved someone better than me.' When I opened my mouth, he went on. 'It's the truth, Tess. And I haven't met a single guy who deserves you.' He thrust his hand through the messy, russet-colored waves and looked up, his gaze meeting mine. 'You know, I've tried staying away from you. I've tried ignoring how I feel about you, which isn't how I *should* feel. But it's like fighting a losing battle. And I don't want to fight it anymore. I don't want to ignore this.

'And I'm going to be honest, baby, things won't be easy with me. There's going to be a lot of bridges we're going to have to cross when we get to them. And I really don't know what "this" is.' He planted his hands on either side of my legs and leaned in, so close that his warm breath danced over my lips. 'I gave up a long time ago when it comes to figuring out why we do the things we do. Or why we want the things we want. Truth is, we've known each other for years, but we don't really know each other. Not like that. But I need to know you.'

This declaration of feelings wasn't the most romantic I could've imagined, but there was an honesty behind those words. And Jase was right. We might've been lusting and wanting each other for three years and we shared quite a few intimate moments since we were united, but there was so much I didn't know about him. Who knew if a relationship would even work between us, but what I did know about him I liked and I wanted to try.

A different kind of smile appeared on his lips, one I've never seen before. It was unsure, almost boyish in the way it was lopsided. 'I want you to be with me.'

At first I didn't think I was hearing him right. Maybe the orgasm had blown some of my brain cells. For three years I had wanted this moment, to hear that he'd struggled with the same thing I did, that he wanted me just as badly and that he wanted to be with me, and now that he was saying this I was torn.

Torn between wanting to jump up and do a little jig, and

tackling him and knocking him on his back. I couldn't do either. My knee wouldn't be happy about that and I'd probably ruin this nearly perfect moment.

Strange that this huge thing that was so good was happening after something so bad.

'So I want this,' he said, gliding his fingers along my cheeks. 'With you. I wanted it from the first time you ran down those stairs back at your home and hugged me, even though I knew it was wrong. For a fuck ton of reasons, but I want this.'

My gaze lifted, meeting his. I was almost too afraid to speak for a moment. 'You want me?'

One side of his lips kicked up as he tilted his head, lining up his mouth with mine. His kiss was infinitely tender and sweet. He took his time, and the kiss went on forever. 'I think that's obvious, but yes.'

Good Lord, I was seconds from combusting. 'As your girlfriend?'

'Yes.'

Trying to maintain a scrap of dignity and not break into a fit of squeals, I managed to keep my voice even. 'So you're not going to ask me to be your girlfriend?'

He curved his hand around my waist as he grinned. 'Not like you're gonna say no.'

My mouth dropped open and I smacked his chest. 'Geez. Arrogant, much?'

'No.' He kissed the corner of my lips. 'Just extremely confident when it comes to how you feel about me.'

'Wow. Is there a difference?'

'Am I wrong?'

Unable to stop myself, I grinned like someone had just handed me a plate of freshly baked sugar cookies. 'No.'

'So there you go.'

I laughed. 'But how do you feel about me?'

'You should be as confident as I am about it.'

My mouth opened, but I closed it. I wanted to be as confident, but I wasn't. Considering everything that had happened, my mind was still reeling.

The hue of his eyes was a bright silver. 'Close your eyes.'

Swallowing the need to ask why, I obeyed. Several seconds passed and then he tugged me onto my back. His hands came down on either side of my head.

'Keep them closed,' he urged.

I had no idea how this would make me more confident, and it took everything in me not to open my eyes when I felt the warmth of his body hovering over mine. I held my breath.

Jase kissed the tip of my nose.

My eyelids flew open, and I giggled as he pulled back. The skin around his eyes crinkled as he smiled down at me. 'Now here comes the scary part,' he said, taking a deep breath. 'We need to tell your brother.'

And that would be terrifying. For Jase. But I smiled. 'Maybe I'll just update my Facebook to "in a relationship" and tag you?'

Jase snickered and then dropped another kiss on my forehead. 'That should go over well.'

Sadness filled Avery's gaze as she handed me a glass of sweet tea. After one sip, I knew Cam had made it. The overabundant amount of sugar was a dead giveaway. I took another drink as I peeked over at Jase. He sat beside me on Avery's couch, with a respectable three or so inches between us.

When we'd left the farm, I'd texted Cam and asked him where he was. Surprise. Surprise. He was over at Avery's. My stomach had been in knots as I hobbled up the stairs to her apartment, but the reason for us coming here had taken the backseat the moment Cam saw me with the crutches.

Cam stood in the corner of the living room, beside a moon chair. His arms were crossed on his chest, expression clouded. 'Why didn't you call and let me know that you were hurt?'

I opened my mouth, but he wasn't done.

'I would've come and gotten you, Teresa. You didn't need to call Jase.'

I snapped my mouth shut.

'And I would've taken you up to Dr. Morgan,' he continued, and I held back a sigh. 'You know that, right? Have you even called Mom and Dad?'

'She called them,' Jase answered, throwing his arm over the back of the couch. Mom had cried. It had been a terrible, hard call. 'And I texted her yesterday because she wasn't in class. She didn't call me.'

'So you lied and told me you were sick when you weren't?' Cam demanded.

'I think you know the answer to that,' I said.

The look on his face would've sent most people running and he turned it on Jase. 'And you didn't call me? Man, that's fucked up.'

'It's not fucked up,' I jumped in, holding the glass of tea tight. 'He's not required to tell you. I am. And I am telling you. I just didn't want you to worry needlessly. You've got a lot on your plate right now. I wanted to be sure of what was wrong with my knee before I said anything.'

'Still,' Cam said, staring at Jase. 'You should've told me.'

Jase held my brother's gaze with his own steady one. 'I *could* have, but she wanted to go to the doc first before she got anyone upset. I respected that decision.'

'I can understand that,' Avery said diplomatically, plopping into the moon chair. 'Jase was being a good friend.'

'I was being a *great* friend,' replied Jase, and I almost choked on my tea when I felt his fingers tangle in my hair. From our positions, Avery and Cam couldn't see what he was doing.

Cam only looked placated when Avery wrapped her arm around his knee. 'How did it happen anyway?'

I sat the tea on the coffee table. 'It was just an accident. I was standing up. Got hit in the hip with a bag and I tried to step out of the way and I came down on my knee wrong.'

Saying it like that sounded innocent enough. Even I could believe it when it was thrown out like that.

Cam smoothed his hand over his baseball cap, tugging the bill down. 'Shit, Teresa . . .'

As I sat back, Jase's fingers slipped under my hair and spread out. My eyes widened as he started to move his hand up and down.

'The doctor really thinks you won't be able to dance anymore?' asked Avery. She rested her head against Cam's leg, her eyes wide with sympathy.

Taking a breath that got stuck in my throat, I nodded and then told them what Dr. Morgan had explained. By the time I was done with the sad story, Avery was close to tears and Cam was kneeling beside her, his chin lowered and gaze fixed to the carpet. 'So that's . . . that's it,' I said, wincing when I heard my voice catch. 'I can't dance anymore.'

Speaking the words cut with a swipe of a hot knife.

'I really am sorry,' she said.

I shifted my weight, wishing the coffee table was high enough to shove my leg under it. 'Thanks.'

Twenty kinds of awkward silence descended in the room. This was probably the worst part of it all. No one knew what to say because there wasn't anything to say.

Jase slid his hand off my back and leaned forward.

'Anyone hungry? I'm starving and I'd do some terrible, nasty things for some Aussie cheese fries.'

Avery laughed. 'Do we even want to know?'

He opened his mouth.

'No,' Cam answered immediately, standing straight. 'You do not want to know what Jase has already probably done for cheese fries.'

'All I have to say is desperate hookers ain't got nothing on me,' Jase said, and he winked when Avery flushed the color of the throw pillow I was leaning against.

I laughed. 'Wow. That's . . . well, that's disgusting.'

His grin turned mischievous.

The muscles in my back eased as Cam glanced over at Avery. 'What about you?' he asked, and I whispered a little prayer of thanks that the conversation had switched gears. 'Want to go grab something to eat?'

She nodded as she tugged her coppery hair around her shoulder. 'I'd love some fries. And ahi tuna.'

'Mmm,' I said, stomach rumbling.

'Then let's go.' Cam took Avery's hands and hauled her up. 'Outback trip for the win.'

Jase was up and had my crutches by the time I stood. Our eyes met as he handed them over, and I felt my cheeks burn. I looked away quickly, catching Avery watching us closely. I forced a casual smile. She grinned back at me as we headed out to the landing.

I grabbed Jase's arm, stopping him as Cam and Avery walked down the stairs, planning on bringing her car around to the front. I kept my voice low. 'Maybe we should wait until he's in a better mood.'

Jase nodded absently. 'Was it an accident?'

'Huh?'

A muscle popped along his jaw. 'Erik and the bag?'

I was confused to how we'd gotten back to that. Erik

was the last person I wanted to think about. Not after breaking my bum leg news to Cam and the fact that the four of us were going out on our first double date . . . that the other two didn't realize they were on. A stupid, silly grin loomed as my mind took a rapid detour back to the lake and our conversation.

We were together.

'Tess?' he queried quietly.

I shrugged as I gripped the handles on my crutches. 'Probably.'

'Are you guys coming?' Cam's voice floated up the stairwell. 'Or is Jase doing some of those hooker acts of desperation for cheese fries?'

I cocked my head to the side. 'What exactly will you do for extra cheese and bacon?'

'I'd get on my knees and get right up between your pretty thighs and eat you out like you can only dream of,' he whispered, causing my mouth to drop open. Holy hotness, I felt warm all over as he shouted, 'Yeah. We're having problems with the crutches!'

I made a face.

He ignored it and asked in a much lower voice, 'What do you mean by probably?'

'He was pissed at Debbie and he was pushing her. I got in the way.' I shrugged again. 'And he swung the bag around. End of story.' I paused as concern trickled through me. 'Don't tell Cam. He will fly off the handle. You know he will. He doesn't need to know that. Okay? Promise me.'

Jase's eyes turned a hard, stormy gray as he took a deep breath. 'I won't say a thing to Cam.'

Chapter 17

Dinner with Cam and Avery made me feel like a voyeur who was watching a couple who were only minutes away from getting it on like two rabbits who'd been forced into celibacy. During dinner, I counted five kisses on the cheek or temple. Four kisses on the lips. At least ten times when Cam's hand seemed to disappear under the table and half of that when Avery's arm moved far to the right of her.

By the time dinner was over, they were too caught up in playing grabby hands to question why I crutched my way over to Jase's Jeep instead of catching a ride with them. Spending all this time with Jase wouldn't go unnoticed for too long, but it wasn't a conversation we could have in the parking lot between Outback and a Christian bookstore.

Although Cam and Avery had no problem with fusing their mouths together in said parking lot.

The ride back to my dorm was quiet. The radio was turned to the '90s channel, volume low. It was still early in the night, but I had to keep covering my mouth with my hand. So much had happened today. So much had changed in the last three days. There was a bone-deep weariness in my core. I glanced over at Jase, his striking profile dark. Extreme giddiness swept through me when I realized that Jase and I . . . well, we were together. He was my boyfriend. There was a label, and I felt like I was seconds from breaking into a fit of giggles like I was thirteen.

Sadness snapped at the heels of the happiness, and I returned my gaze to the passenger window. I closed my eyes against the sudden burn. I couldn't dance anymore. The loss of something that had been so important to me was like a dark shadow creeping over everything else. It had been this way during dinner. I'd feel happy. I'd smile and laugh and then I'd remember what I lost today.

All my plans. My goals. My hopes. My future. All gone.

I didn't want to focus on the crap part of my life, but pushing it out of my head was hard, and those thoughts lingered in the recesses of my mind.

Jase rode the elevator up with me at the dorm, took my key card, and opened the door to my suite. He stepped inside, flipping on the light so I didn't slam my crutches into anything. As usual, the door to our suitemates' room was closed. On the dry-erase board by the desk, there was a note from Debbie with today's date, saying she was spending the night at Erik's.

'Do you want to stay?' I blushed because it sounded like an invite for some bow-chicka-bow-wow. Not that I was entirely against that, but standing there with crutches didn't make me feel sexy. 'I mean, you're welcome to hang out.'

Welcome to hang out? God, I sounded like an idiot.

Jase grinned as he sauntered in. 'There's really no other place I'd rather be.'

My lips split into a wide smile, and I turned before he could see how obviously happy that made me. 'Be right back.'

Leaving the crutches in the corner, I carefully gathered up my nightclothes and bath stuff. I changed into a pair of cotton sleep pants and a shirt, forgoing the bra. The shirt was black, so it didn't show much. I left the brace on and quickly washed my face. After pulling down my ponytail, I ran a brush through my hair and then returned to my room.

Jase had made himself comfortable on my narrow bed. Stretched out on his back, the remote control to the TV that sat on our dresser rested on his flat stomach. He'd even kicked his shoes off. Seeing him there caused a flutter deep in my belly, which only increased when he patted the spot next to him.

'Should you be walking around without the crutches?' he asked.

Ignoring the ache in my knee, I slowly made my way over to him and sat. 'It's not that big of a distance. Besides, these rooms are too small to use crutches.'

He settled on the ID channel and then rolled onto his side, dropping the remote onto the nightstand. He cupped his hand around my elbow and tugged as he peered up at me through thick, dark lashes. 'Lie down with me?'

How in the world could I resist that request? With him on his side, I was able to lie on my back beside him. The moment my head touched the pillow, he smiled in a way that made my toes curl.

'How you doing?'

'I don't know,' I answered honestly.

'Understandable.' He scooped up the strands of my hair, brushing them back from my face. 'You've had a lot going on today—the last couple of days.'

'Yeah. My head is going in different directions.' My chest rose sharply as he traced the outline of my lower lip with his thumb. 'Everything feels different now.'

'Does it?'

I nodded and then stilled as his hand drifted down the valley between my breasts and then stopped just below them. Sharp tingles followed his hand, and the tips of my breasts tightened. I knew he noticed because his gaze dipped, and he sucked his bottom lip between his teeth. His lashes swept up, and our gazes locked.

He curved his hand around my ribs. 'You talking about us or . . .?'

'Both,' I whispered.

His gaze traveled over my face, lingering on my lips. Heat moved from my belly and seemed to pool between my thighs. There was a moment where the only sound was my pounding heart and the low hum from the TV. 'It's going to be okay.'

I smiled as I placed my hand over his. 'I know.'

'About us. The difference? Good or bad?'

'Good. Very good.'

He tipped his head down and brushed his lips over my forehead. A shiver coursed over my skin. 'We're going to have to do better than good.'

'We are?'

'Uh-huh,' he murmured, and then he kissed me.

There was something different about this kiss. Maybe it was because it was taking place in my bed or it was our first real kiss after our conversation. Or maybe it was something else. Either way, he sipped from my lips, drank from my mouth. The kiss went on forever as he tasted and explored. I never knew it was possible for a kiss to be so powerful, but it was.

'How about that?' he asked, a slight tremble running up his arm as his lips brushed mine.

My body seemed to sink through the mattress. In that moment, with my lips still tingling with the touch of his, I didn't—couldn't—think about all the things that were wrong. 'That was better than good. That was great.'

He kissed me again, but this time with a slow, sweet

sweep of his lips. It was those soft, dragging kisses that affected me beyond the physical that caused the swelling warmth in my chest that spoke of love and forever and other tender, silly things I didn't want to admit out loud.

But it still got me on a physical level. Even with the constant ache in my knee, the ache in other parts of my body hadn't diminished. I wanted Jase on an almost painful level. The very idea of nothing between our bodies, of him inside me, nearly drove me crazy with the desire to explore.

Jase lifted his mouth from mine, breathing raggedly as he settled on his side beside me. I expected him to touch me. My breasts felt swollen and full with his hand so close, but he did nothing.

I turned my head toward him. His eyes were a fierce silver as he groaned deeply. 'You keep looking at me like that, I'm going to strip the clothes off you and get so far deep inside you that I'll never get out.'

Everything in my body tightened, and the muscles in my lower stomach spasmed in response to his words. 'I don't see anything wrong with that.'

He made that deep, sexy rumble again, and I burned partly due to my own boldness. 'You make this so hard.'

'I do?' I reached for him, and as my fingers brushed the visible line in his jeans, he caught my wrist in a gentle grasp. In confusion, I raised my gaze to his.

His eyes squeezed closed. 'Yeah, you make me hard. All the fucking time. I'm a constant walking erection around you, but I . . . I want to do this the right way.'

My fingers curled in as he held my hand near his chest. 'The right way?'

When his eyes reopened, a slight pink flush stained his cheeks. 'The right way. You know. Us not being just all about sex.'

My lips parted, but I didn't say anything. I was stunned by the fact Jase was blushing and from what he'd said.

The hue in his cheeks deepened. 'As hard as it is to go slow with this, because damn, baby, I want you in every way imaginable.' He lowered my hand and pressed his erection against my palm, proving his next words. 'I want you so badly right now it's killing me, but every girl I've been with since . . . since a really long time has only ever been about sex. Getting in. Getting off. Then getting out.'

'Like Steph?' I blurted out before I could stop myself.

He cringed. 'Yeah, like Steph. And that was okay with her—with them. Because as much of a dick as this makes me sound like, I didn't care about them. Not like I care about you, Tess. I want this—I want us to be different. I want us to mean more than sex. I need us to mean more than that. Okay?'

As I stared at him, a knot climbed up and got lodged in my throat. Tears filled my eyes.

His pupils dilated as he dropped my hand and cupped my cheeks. 'Baby, why are you about to cry? Did I—'

'You didn't do anything wrong,' I said quickly, my voice cracking. 'You did everything perfectly.'

Confusion marked his expression. 'I don't understand.'

I laughed hoarsely. 'It's okay.' Leaning over, I kissed him. Whoever Jack's mom was, was truly missing out. 'It's perfect.'

'You sure? Fuck what I think is right and wrong. Because I can get naked in like two seconds flat and be inside you quicker than that.'

I nodded and laughed again.

Jase rested his forehead against mine and closed his eyes. His warm breath danced over my lips. 'I want to take you out on a date. I want to take you horseback riding. I want to tell your brother. I want to take you home to my parents and introduce you as my girlfriend. I want to prove this means more to me. I want to do this the right way.'

My chest squeezed under the pressure of what I felt for him in that moment. If I hadn't already tumbled head over heels in love with him, I would've tonight, but I was already lost in him. Those three little words formed on my tongue, but I kept them to myself as I snuggled closer, closed my eyes, and allowed myself to just enjoy his closeness and his almost desperate want to do this the right way.

In spite of all the stuff running through my head, I slept like the dead after Jase left, waking up oddly refreshed. I'd thought Wednesday morning would be hard to face, waking up to a future I hadn't planned, but if anything, what I really felt was an odd sense of anticipation.

As I got ready for classes, I received a text from Jase. He wouldn't be in music but would be there to pick me up afterward. When I asked if everything was okay, he'd replied with a quick text saying everything was cool.

Excitement was palpable in the halls of Whitehall. Somehow I'd forgotten that we didn't have classes Thursday or Friday. Fall break—a four-day weekend. History wasn't nearly as crowded, but maneuvering with crutches was still damn inconveniencing.

Sympathy clouded Calla's face when she got an eyeful of me and my crutches. 'What happened?'

As I sat awkwardly in the chair, I told her I'd lost my balance on Sunday. I didn't mention anything about Erik or Debbie. Not because I cared what people thought about the asshole, but I didn't want Debbie to have to deal with it. Somewhere between yesterday morning and today, I decided Deb and I were going to have a nice long chat the next time she was in the dorm. I was going to tell her the truth—of what happened to me. It might not make a difference, but maybe it would.

'What about dancing?' Calla asked, and I winced.

'My knee is too unstable and it will most likely stay that way.' My stomach dipped at those words, as if saying them made it somehow more real. 'It shouldn't have given out on me Sunday, so . . .'

She leaned forward, lowering her voice. 'So no dancing?'

Unable to say those words, I shook my head.

Her face fell. 'I'm so sorry.'

'Thanks,' I croaked out.

I wasn't very talkative after that. The whole 'refreshed' mood evaporated when we missed the bus to west campus and I had to hoof it over. My armpits were killing me by the time we hit the arts center, and they still ached when I hobbled out at the end of class.

God knows how long I had to worry with these crutches. My lips slipped into a scowl as I tried to balance myself and pull down the back of my shirt. It would be so much easier if I didn't have classes on both sides of the campus. I could drop music. Or if I dropped history, then I only had to go from my dorm to music then to east campus—

I cut those thoughts off. Dropping classes was like quitting. Giving up. I would not do that. No matter how much of a pain in my ass this would become.

'There's your man,' Calla said, causing me to almost topple over as I stood on the pavilion.

I almost asked her how she knew, but then I realized that she was just teasing me. I wanted to tell Calla about us, but I needed to tell Cam first. Strangely, it didn't seem real until then. Like if I couldn't announce it on Facebook, then it hadn't happened yet.

I rolled my eyes at that and turned to her. 'I'll see you later.'

She waved good-bye as I painstakingly made my way to

213

where he was idling in the no parking zone. Jase got out and jogged around to my side. Brown hair curled out from under the gray knit skullcap he wore. I decided it was a good look for him.

He opened my door and then took my crutches, placing them in the back, and when he turned to me, he started to lower his head, as if he were going to kiss me hello. My insides tensed. He stopped short, let out a deep breath, and then cupped my elbow.

'Up you go,' he said, and I shivered at the deepness in his voice.

Once he was in the Jeep, I glanced over at him. 'Did you get everything taken care of this morning?'

'Yeah.' His gaze flicked to the rearview mirror. A campus police cruiser was coming around the bend. With a quick, satisfied grin, he pulled out before they could get him for where he was parked. 'Mom called me early this morning. Jack was sick all night. Throwing up.'

'Oh no, is he okay?'

He nodded. 'He's got a bug. Doc said he just needed to drink lots of fluids and rest. He'll be out of school the rest of the week. He was pretty upset about that.'

'Really?'

'Yeah, he loves his teacher and going to school.' He paused, rubbing his chin. 'Hopefully he stays like that.'

I leaned toward him. 'Did you like going to school when you were little?'

'Yes.'

'Did it stay that way?'

He laughed. 'Hell no. I skipped more than I went to class—Jack's different, though. He will be different.'

I smiled at that, silently wishing him luck.

'If he's feeling better this weekend, I thought we could . . . I don't know, take him out to lunch or something?'

That was huge. I nodded eagerly, a little nervous. What if Jack woke up one morning and decided he hated me? Kids were fickle like that.

'Good,' he said, relaxing.

Since a lot of students had already bailed for the four-day weekend, we didn't have any problem finding a parking spot near the Den, and the place was practically empty as I walked in. Jase carried my bag and slowed his long-legged steps to match mine.

Only Cam and Avery were at the table, sharing a slice of pizza. I opted for a hot dog and fries—breaking up the monotony of greasy hamburgers—and Jase, I think, got an entire pizza judging by the stacks of slices on his plate.

Sitting down across from the lovebirds, I stretched out my right leg. 'I'm surprised you guys are here. I thought you were heading up to Pennsylvania?'

'We are.' Cam swiped a handful of fries off my plate and didn't even bother to look guilty. 'We're leaving tonight.'

'Excited?' I asked Avery.

She nodded rapidly, causing her high ponytail to bounce. 'I've never been there, so I can't wait.'

'What are you guys planning to do there?' Jase dropped an elbow on the table, and as he leaned forward, he picked up the second slice of pizza and lowered his other hand under the table. 'I mean, what do you do in the Poconos? Stare at trees?'

Cam snorted. 'No. There's hiking, indoor saunas, wine, fishing—I'm taking Avery fishing. She's never done it . . .'

As my brother went on . . . and on, Jase shifted closer, pressing his right leg against my left one. A second later, his hand landed just above my knee. My eyes widened as I stilled, hot dog halfway to my mouth.

'And we're renting a boat on Saturday,' Cam continued,

215

sending Jase a meaningful look that made me drop my hot dog.

Did he see what Jase was doing? Oh God . . .

Cam frowned at me. 'You okay over there?'

'Yeah,' I squeaked, and grabbed my hot dog as Jase's hand crept up my leg. 'So, um, a boat?'

My brother said something that made the skin around Avery's eyes crinkle as she laughed, but I was too focused on Jase's hand curving over my upper thigh. I took a deep breath when he leaned over, plucking up a few fries, using the closeness to his advantage.

His hand slipped between my thighs.

Oh my God . . .

Heat flooded my face as I ducked my chin, but the warmth also went way south, traveling to one point, right where his hand was heading. He wouldn't do it.

'What kind of boat is it?' Jase asked, and dear God, he sounded completely at ease.

Whatever boat Cam was renting totally wasn't even on my radar. Jase's hand inched closer, the tips of his fingers brushing the band covering the zipper of my jeans.

I drew in a deep breath as my hand tightened around the hot dog. Pieces of the bun crumbled. He wouldn't go any farther. No way.

'So what are you doing?' Avery asked, resting her chin in her hands.

'Nothing really, I'm going—' Words were cut off when those long fingers slipped down the band and pressed in. Sensation flared. A sharp pulse shot through me. I don't know how I didn't jump.

Cam tilted his head to the side. 'Yeah, what?'

'I'm going to . . .' I placed my bun on the plate as he slid his finger down and then up, tugging on the jeans. The motion increased the intensity, creating an ache deep inside me.

'Going to . . .?' Jase asked innocently.

What a beastly bastard.

'Going to stay here,' I finished.

'You need to get a car,' Cam said. 'Then you could at least go home and visit Mom and Dad.'

Jase's hand moved to my thigh, and I wasn't sure if I should be relieved or disappointed. My body throbbed, but my head cleared a little. 'Well, I'll buy the car with my imaginary money from my imaginary job.'

He made a face. 'I know damn well Mom and Dad are giving you money.'

'Yeah, like to buy food. Not a car,' I replied.

'You're leaving your truck here, right?' Avery picked up her water. 'Maybe she could—'

'Oh, hell no to that.' Cam looked at Avery like she was crazy. 'She is not driving my truck.'

Jase kept his hand on my thigh, and by the time lunch was done, I was torn between wanting to punch Jase and climb up on him, rip his pants open, and—

'Hey,' Cam said, interrupting my really inappropriate thoughts. 'I need to talk to you for a second. You done with lunch?'

My stomach tumbled like a baby rolling down the hill. 'Sure,' I said as I peeked at Jase. He didn't look worried. Not that he should be worried. Cam wouldn't hurt him too badly once he found out, especially since Jase had confided in me.

I said good-bye to Avery and followed Cam outside on my crutches. We didn't go too far, stopping under one of the large maples that had turned dizzying shades of golds and reds. As Cam flipped his baseball hat around backward, I tugged my cardigan close. The chill in the air wasn't too bad, but it had a decent bite to it.

'What's up?' I asked, feeling like I was about to hurl up what little I'd eaten.

Cam smiled, but it faded as he took a deep breath. Unease unfurled in my belly as he looked at me. Oh God, it was about Jase and me. He knew. We should've told him. Granted, it only happened yesterday, but we should've—

'I'm proposing to Avery this weekend,' he blurted out.

'Wait.' I almost dropped my crutches. 'What?'

'I'm proposing to Avery this weekend—on the boat. It's just going to be her and me. Going to have the boat loaded with flowers and chocolate. The ring . . . isn't too big. Only two carats.'

'*Only* two carats?'

'Yeah, and I'm going to put it on one of the roses.' The hollows of his cheeks flushed. 'Anyway, I just wanted to let—'

I snapped out of it. Happiness bubbled up like champagne inside me. In my haste, I almost toppled over as I awkwardly maintained my grip on the crutches and got one arm around him. 'Oh my God!' I squealed. 'Cam, you're going to get married!'

'Well, hopefully.' He hugged me back, and when he drew away, he was smiling broadly. 'If she says yes.'

'Of course she's going to say yes.' I was grinning so hard my face hurt. 'Oh, I'm so happy for you two! She's such a sweet girl and I love her and I love you!'

Cam laughed deeply and hugged me again. 'She's . . . she's perfect.'

I nodded. 'When are you doing it? Saturday?' When he nodded, I was exceptionally glad I hadn't said anything to him about Jase. Not when he was about to do this. He needed to be completely focused on Avery and his plans. 'Call me or text me when she says yes. You have to promise me.'

'I promise.'

I squealed again, earning a few strange looks from people passing on the sidewalk. I gave him one more epically awkward hug, and then I saw Jase exiting the double doors, carrying my bag.

'Here comes your little helper.' Cam smirked as he kissed my cheek. 'I'm gonna get back to Avery.'

'Good luck, but you don't need it.'

The usual cockiness was gone when he glanced back at me. 'You really don't think so?'

I blinked back tears—happy tears. 'No. Not at all.'

'Thank you,' he replied. 'Love ya, sis.'

'Love you.'

Watching Cam pass Jase and sock him in the arm, I took several deep breaths. My eyes were all watery, and there was a good chance I'd start hugging random people. Even the townies.

'So I'm thinking the big-ass grin on your face doesn't mean that Cam questioned you about us.' Jase slung my bright pink bag over his shoulder. 'Have I told you how much I like your smiles?'

My smile grew to epic proportions and I couldn't contain it. 'Cam's proposing to Avery!'

'He's done lost his damn mind.'

'What!' Holding on to my crutches, I smacked him on the chest. 'He hasn't lost his mind. He's found it.'

Jase laughed. 'I'm kidding. And I already knew.'

'What?' I shrieked and slapped his chest again. 'What do you mean you already knew?'

'Ouch.' He rubbed the spot. 'Does it disturb you that I'm kind of getting turned on right now?'

I shook my head. 'Seriously?'

'Maybe?' he murmured, dipping his head and causing the ends sticking out from under the skullcap to sway. 'I'm pretty erect right now to be honest.'

'Oh my God . . .' I rubbed my hand over my hot cheek. 'Okay. Back to the proposal. When did he tell you?'

'About a month ago. Want to smack me again? You could try my ass. I'll probably like that.'

I stared at him.

He chuckled. 'I went with him to pick out the ring. I'm pretty sure the jeweler thought we were getting married.'

'You could've told me.' I huffed.

'Hey, he asked me to keep it a secret. He doesn't want Avery to find out.' When I opened my mouth to argue, he folded his arms. 'It's like when I took you to the doc, Tess. You didn't want him to know . . .'

I nodded. 'You got me.'

'I know.'

Too happy over the recent development to be any bit irritated, I broke out in a huge grin. 'I'm so thrilled for them. They really are perfect for each other. You know, like once-in-a-life kind of thing. I know you think that's pretty stupid, but I believe it.'

'I don't think it's stupid at all. I know . . . exactly what you mean.' He unfolded his arms.

His words were laced with a heavy meaning, but my attention was snagged by something else. Since his hands had been mostly occupied during lunch, I hadn't noticed them until then. The flesh around his knuckles was an angry red, the skin roughed up and swollen. I frowned as I took his hand carefully in one of mine. 'What happened to your knuckles?'

He pulled his hand free, glancing down at them with a frown. 'I don't know. Must've scraped them on something at the farm.'

'You don't know?'

Jase shook his head. 'Let's get your pretty butt to class. Come on, hopalong.'

Though a teasing grin had appeared, a dark look had crossed his face. I glanced at his knuckles again, and for some reason, I thought of Cam's hands after he'd confronted Jeremy. I pushed that thought away because that was . . . that was too weird. Jase said he scraped them at the farm and that's what had to have happened because there was no other reason to how it could have happened.

None whatsoever.

Chapter 18

Late morning on the first day of fall break, I stood in front of Lightning, gripping my crutches until my knuckles ached. 'No.'

'You promised,' Jase reminded me gently, as if he was speaking to Jack.

'I don't care.'

'That's wrong.'

I glared at Jase, and he grinned. 'I can't get up there with my knee.'

'I'll make sure you get up there just fine.'

My lower lip jutted out in a way that would've made Jack proud, who was currently quarantined to his bedroom and had thrown a Godzilla-sized fit when Jase said he couldn't come out with us. Jase's mom was in the shower when we showed up and his dad was somewhere on the farm. I wasn't sure if he was going to make good on his promise to introduce me as his girlfriend today, but I was nervous for some reason. Maybe it was because that was such a huge step.

But I still felt bad for the little dude. 'Can we see Jack before we leave?' I asked.

Jase blinked once and then twice. 'Yeah.'

'I feel bad for him,' I explained, shifting my weight on the crutches. 'He really wanted to come outside.'

A soft look crept into his eyes. 'We can most definitely see him before we leave. He'd like that.' He leaned in, brushing his nose across mine. 'I'd like that.'

I smiled.

'But changing the subject isn't going to distract me. You're getting up on this horse. End of discussion.'

'I wasn't trying to change the subject.' Even I recognized the whine in my voice as I looked at Lightning. The horse sniffed and turned his head in the other direction, obviously done with me.

'Stand still.' He pried the crutches from my hands and propped them against the split-rail fence. Giving Lightning one more pat on the nose, Jase picked up the reins as he walked around to the other side. In the bright sunlight, strands of red and gold shone in his hair.

He leaped up on the horse with the grace of someone who'd grown up doing just that. Once on top of the beast, he appeared bigger and larger than life.

And strangely hot sitting astride a horse.

'Lift your arms,' he said.

That was the last thing I wanted to do, but I gathered up my courage and lifted my arms. The muscles in his thighs tensed against the horse as he leaned over, fitting his hands to my ribs. Our eyes met, he winked, and then he lifted me right off my feet and up in the air. I didn't have time to panic because it seemed like in a heartbeat I was sitting sideways on the horse.

'Bring your left leg over,' he said, his hands slipping to my hips and holding tight. 'I'm not going to let you fall.'

Gripping his arms, I twisted, keeping my injured leg

stationary as I brought my left leg over the wide back of the horse. I bit down on my lip and my heart tripped up as Lightning moved sideways, but Jase didn't let me fall. I slipped back in the saddle, resting between Jase's legs.

'Good girl,' he said, his breath warm against the back of my neck, causing me to shiver. 'See? That wasn't too bad.'

My mouth was dry. 'I guess not.'

His answering chuckle rumbled through me. He secured his arms around my waist, holding the reins in one hand. 'You ready?'

I shook my head and added, 'No,' just in case he was confused.

Jase laughed again. 'You're going to enjoy it. I promise.' Dipping his head, he pressed a kiss to the back of my neck, sending a race of tingles up and down my back. 'I'm not going to let anything happen to you.'

With the slight movement of his heels, Lightning moved into a slow canter, following the worn-down track that circled the split rail. It took a bit to get used to the bouncing. Jase kept me tucked close as he told me about the first time he'd ridden a horse. He'd been six and had slipped right off the animal, breaking his arm.

'Did you get right back on?' I asked as we made another pass. 'Or were you scared.'

'I was scared.' His thumb moved in a slow circle across my belly. 'But Dad knew I needed to get back up on there. And I did. I didn't fall again.'

An image of a young Jase filled my head. I bet he looked a lot like Jack and was just as adorable, but probably more of a handful. It took a good twenty minutes before I relaxed enough that I released my death grip on Jase's arm. When I eased off, my fingernails had left little indentations in his skin.

'Sorry,' I said hoarsely, staring at the trees.

'It's okay. It's only skin.' He kissed the back of my neck again, a quick movement that was most likely undetectable, but then he pressed his lips to the space below my ear.

Our conversation from last night moved to the forefront. A lump formed in my throat. His words still got me all choked up. He wanted to take things slowly. He wanted me to be different from all the other girls—which sounded like an extremely long list, but I would not think of them. He wanted our relationship to start off not being about sex.

Jase nipped at my ear.

A bolt of liquid pleasure zinged through my blood, immediately sparking an ache deep inside my body that throbbed whenever he was around.

The muscles in my back tensed and then relaxed. I felt him then, pressing against my lower back. A smug sort of smile formed at the knowledge he was just as affected as I was. Tipping my head back against his chest, I closed my eyes and smiled as the wind glided over my cheeks. My grip loosened once more, and under my legs, Lightning's powerful muscles bunched as he picked up speed.

A trickle of fear inked down my spine as we went faster, but another emotion rose, overshadowing the tendrils of panic. Muscles in my core tensed. Not of anxiety but in anticipation, like those precious moments I'd lost, the ones that came seconds after I stepped onstage.

'I can feel it,' I whispered. I was awed because I could feel it.

His rough chin grazed my cheek as his arm tightened. 'Would it make me a bastard to say I told you so?'

Opening my eyes, I laughed as I straightened in the saddle, gaining confidence that I wouldn't fall and break my neck. Glancing over my shoulder, I met his smile with my own. The crushing disappointment of my recent reinjury eased a little. 'Can we go faster?'

We went faster.

Back on the ground, with crutches under my arms, I admitted that horseback riding was pretty damn cool. I didn't see myself riding one alone in the near future, but Jase had been right. Riding was like dancing in a way. It wouldn't completely replace the gap in my life, but it was a start.

And it wasn't the only thing I had.

I smiled as Jase strolled past me, leading Lightning back to the stable. My heart did a cabriole—a complicated, big jump I'd never be able to do again in reality, but my heart was doing it.

When Jase returned, his father was prowling behind him. Seeing them together again was disconcerting. Same height. Same dark hair. Their long-legged pace was even identical. Mr. Winstead grinned as they stopped in front of me. 'Never seen a prettier gal on crutches before.'

Warmth cascaded over my cheeks. 'Thank you.'

'Good to see ya back, but not in those things.' He pulled out a red rag, wiping his hands. 'Ain't too serious?'

I shook my head, thinking getting into the story was probably not something anyone wanted to hear.

'She was just riding Lightning,' Jase said, grinning. 'Did damn good for her first time.'

His father's brows rose. 'Ya got up on the horse in yer condition?'

'That she did,' Jase replied, and pleasure hummed through me at the sight of his proud smile. Mom and Dad used to smile like that after my recitals and competitions.

Mr. Winstead cocked his head to the side. 'Well, darn, if I was about twenty years younger and there wasn't your mom . . .'

Jase's head whipped toward his father. 'Come on, Dad, that's my girlfriend you're trying to hit on.'

Yep. There was my heart again, doing an escaping step, and damn if I didn't feel as weightless as a dancer looked when she executed the jump perfectly.

'Girlfriend?' Surprise filled his father's voice as he looked between us.

Jase grinned shamelessly, and both my knees felt weak. 'Girlfriend.'

'Well . . .' He drew in a breath and shook his head, as if he didn't know what to say. If I doubted what Jase had said about the other girls last night, I didn't anymore. It was obvious he didn't bring girls home, and the fact he'd brought me home was a big deal.

'That's good to hear,' he finally finished, and then smiled, causing those stunningly familiar eyes to light to a beautiful silver. He looked at his son and nodded in a way I felt meant more than I could understand. 'That's really great.'

Jase said nothing, but shifted his gaze back to me.

'Why don't you two kids come inside for a few minutes?' his father said, stuffing the hanky back into his pocket. 'Yer momma just made fresh tea.'

His eyes lit up, and I giggled.

'We'll be up in a second.' Jase turned to me as his dad ambled off. 'You okay with how I broke the news? Guess I could've done it better, but really, how do you announce you have a girlfriend without sounding lame.'

'No. It was fine.' I paused as he sauntered up to me. 'So I'm the first girl you've brought home?'

He tucked a loose strand of hair back. 'Since high school.'

That was forever ago it seemed, and I bet it was Jack's mom. One of these days I was going to get him to talk about her. 'That's . . . wow. I'm . . .'

'Honored?'

I snorted. So ladylike. 'That sounds a bit extreme.'

Jase laughed as he sidled up to my side. 'Well, a guy only takes a girl home to his parents that he's really serious or cares about.'

It was late when we returned to my dorm, and when Jase pulled around, I could see that the light was on in my dorm room. Deb must be back.

Jase followed my gaze. 'We still on for dinner tomorrow?'

I glanced back at him. 'I thought we were having lunch at Betty's?'

He grinned. 'Doesn't mean we can't have dinner.'

'True,' I laughed, but the sound died off as he pulled up to the sidewalk. I was reluctant to leave him. Today . . . today had been a great day. Jeep idling, he reached for the door handle. 'You don't have to walk me up.'

'But—'

I silenced him with a kiss. If he came up, I wouldn't want him to leave, and I needed to talk to Deb. 'You don't have to do it. I'll call you tomorrow.'

He took his hand off the door. 'Text me before you go to bed.'

My lips split into a wide grin. 'Okay.'

Before I could pull away, he wrapped his hand around the nape of my neck and kissed me. At once, my mouth opened to his. He tasted me in a way that made it even harder to leave. 'Night, Tess.'

I closed my eyes as I pulled back. 'Night.'

Jase waited until I was inside before pulling away and I hopped along on my crutches, taking the elevator. Like I suspected, Deb was in the dorm.

She was sitting on the bed, cross-legged, hair pulled back and wearing an oversized hoodie. When she looked up, she smacked her hand over her mouth. 'Oh my God.'

I stilled in the door, confused. 'What?'

'Crutches!' She unfurled her legs but didn't make it far. 'I knew you would be on crutches, but I just . . . I don't know.' She pressed her hand to her chest. 'I'm so sorry.'

Placing the crutches against the wall, I carefully walked to my bed and sat down. I didn't know how to start this conversation, but I knew I was going to tell her about my past. It just wasn't easy to say, by the way, I dated a fucking loser who beat me. 'Debbie—'

'I broke up with Erik.'

I blinked, thinking I hadn't heard her right. And then hope sprang within me. 'What?'

She got up and sat beside me. 'I broke up with Erik earlier today.'

'That's . . .' What did I say? Great? Fantastic? That seemed inappropriate because I think Deb really cared about him.

'It needed to be done. It had to be because . . .' She ducked her chin, hiding her gaze. 'Because you were right on Sunday. Erik . . . he can be a really good guy, but . . .'

'But he hits you,' I said quietly, and for some damn reason, my chest began to squeeze.

She nodded slowly. 'He didn't hit me often. You know, it wasn't all the time. Sometimes he would just grab me or yell at me. He always—*always*—seemed to regret it afterward. Or at least his apologies seemed believable, and I always forgave him.' She paused, drawing in a deep breath. 'No one has ever said anything. Not until you did. I think it was partly because he's been—uh, losing his cool a lot more lately, but everyone just looked away.'

'It's hard to say something,' I said, tucking my left leg against my chest. 'I didn't want to make you mad.' Or embarrass her because that was the main emotion I had felt when my family discovered what I'd been hiding.

'I wasn't mad. I was ashamed,' she said, confirming my

229

thoughts. 'Because why would I stay with him when it's so obvious he doesn't treat me right?'

'Because sometimes he treats you like a queen?' I fiddled with the frayed hem of my jeans. 'And you hang on to those moments because you know he's capable of being a good guy.'

I could feel her eyes on me. 'You've been . . .?'

Without saying anything, I nodded.

She let out a low breath. 'And you broke up with him?'

'Not really.' I barked out a short laugh. 'My mom and Cam saw the bruises and I finally told them the truth. I wanted to leave him before then, but I was scared and . . .'

'And you loved him?' she asked in a quiet voice that was laced with pain.

Tugging the little white strings on my jeans, I swallowed hard. 'He was my first—first of everything. I thought I was in love with him. Looking back now, I know it was more about being afraid of being—'

'Alone?' she said, and I nodded. 'We're pretty stupid, huh? Being afraid of being single outweighs the fear of being hit.'

'You're not stupid anymore,' I pointed out. 'You broke up with him.'

'I did.' Her eyes filled with tears, and she blinked tightly.

The squeezing pressure moved up my throat. I was happy for her—thrilled to be exact, but I knew this had to be hard for her. The first night things were over between Jeremy and me had been the hardest. Because like with Erik, Jeremy had this almost magical ability of making me forget the bad moments. He excelled at that, so much so that it was also one of the reasons why I hadn't left him. Now that I was older, I realized that was a hallmark of an abuser. They could be as charming as sin when required, and that made them as dangerous as a rattlesnake.

'How did Erik take it?' I asked.

A wobbly smile appeared. 'Not very good.'

My stomach tumbled a little. 'He didn't—'

'No! He didn't. It was the opposite.' She wiped at her eyes with the back of her hands. I put a hand on her arm and squeezed. 'He apologized and cried and begged . . .' She shook her head. 'He got angry at the end, but I left before it could go any further.'

'Good.'

She looked up, meeting my eyes. 'I'm sorry that I didn't listen to you on Sunday and for what happened when I came back with Erik. I do think it was accident, but it shouldn't have happened because when he gets angry, he doesn't think.'

'Is that what made you break up with him?'

'Yes. And no.' She cleared her throat. 'When Jase confronted him Wednesday morning and I found out that your knee was completely blown—'

'Jase confronted him?' I cut in, feeling my eyes widen as I stared at her.

She nodded. 'He showed up right before we were leaving for classes. I didn't know he'd hurt you that badly.'

I waved that off, feeling my pulse pick up. 'What did Jase say to him?'

'Not much really. Jase told him that if you ever ended up hurt again, that he'd pretty much put him in a grave. Erik was in a mood.' Reaching up, she tugged her ponytail down. 'He mouthed off and called you . . . called you a nosy bitch who needed to stay away from me.'

I didn't give two shits what Erik said about me, but my stomach fell out of my butt.

'Jase didn't take to that well,' she continued. 'Neither did Erik's face when it was all said and done.'

Squeezing my eyes shut, I fought for breath as I flashed

hot and cold. Images of Jase's knuckles rushed through my head. He'd gone after Erik. Just like Cam had gone after Jeremy. In a way, history had totally repeated itself. Anger and disappointment and something else I didn't want to acknowledge crashed together inside me.

'You okay?' Deb asked.

'Yeah, I'm fine. Things are going to be so much better now for you.' My voice was hoarse as I focused on what was important right now, which was Debbie, and not what Jase had done. 'I really do mean that.'

'I know.' She hugged me tightly, and when she pulled away, the tears had dried. 'My life starts over now, and I only have good things to look forward to.'

Chapter 19

Debbie and I had stayed up late talking. At first it had been hard to hear about how Jase had confronted Jeremy the morning I believed he'd been with Jack. Maybe he'd done both. Not that it mattered, because it didn't change anything. But eventually I told Debbie everything about Jeremy. I watered down Cam's reaction, but it still felt so, so damn good to get it off my shoulders. To share what it had been like with someone who could truly understand. And Deb told me about the good times, the bad times, and the downright horrifying moments. There were moments when I could sense that Deb was having doubts and that was natural. They'd been together for years and sometimes it was hard to let someone go, even if he was a sociopath. People who hadn't been in a situation like we'd been in just wouldn't understand. They'd think we were stupid and weak, but the smartest and strongest girl could fall prey to a poison-tongued charmer.

And there had been tears—cleansing tears. The kind that renewed instead of hurt.

I ended up sleeping late on Friday; when I was up, Deb told me she was going to visit her parents and break the news. I wished her luck—luck that I needed.

I'd ended up canceling the lunch date, Debbie had left the dorm, and Jase was now minutes away from picking me up for dinner—for our first real honest-to-goodness date—and all I could think about as I waited outside, holding my crutches, was that he'd done nearly the same thing my brother had done.

I still hadn't worked out how I felt about what he did, if I should be as angry as I felt or if I should be angrier? Jase knew the kind of guilt I carried around because of what Cam had done.

When Jase pulled up to the curb, he hopped out and came around the front of the Jeep. He was wearing jeans and a dark V-neck sweater that somehow made me feel underdressed in my jeans and cardigan. No matter what he wore, he looked damn good, like he was ready to step off the pages of *GQ*. Not like every other guy around; they all looked like they belonged in a Sears catalog.

He helped me in, taking the crutches and then holding my arm as I climbed up. Waiting for me on the dashboard was a square pink box. I picked it up and glanced at him.

'For dessert,' he said, grinning.

I didn't want to pop the lid, but the light brown frosting looked tasty. 'What flavor?'

'Guess?'

'Chocolate?'

'Boring,' he said, easing away from the curb. 'It's peanut butter icing and filling.'

'Oh.' Momentarily distracted by the awesomeness that was peanut butter and chocolate, I was tempted to crack the bad boy open and devour it.

'You're more than welcome to eat it now. Fuck dinner rules, right? Dessert can come first.'

Another small smile appeared. I don't know what it was about the cupcakes that seemed to affect me. Besides the fact that they tasted delicious ninety-nine percent of the time, they'd become something I looked forward to.

'Where do you get them?' I said, surprised that this was the first time I even thought to ask. 'At the bakery in town?'

'Nope.'

My gaze dropped to his knuckles as I waited for a more detailed explanation. The skin wasn't nearly as raw, but still pink and ruddy. My stomach tightened.

'My mom's sister—her daughter Jen makes them.'

'Wow. These taste like something you'd get in a gourmet bakery. She should really start her own business.'

'That's what we've been telling her.' He glanced over at me and a lopsided grin appeared. 'Jen's been asking about the girl she keeps making extra special cupcakes for. I told her I was going to have to bring her over one day.'

My stare started to wander to his hands, but I jerked my gaze to him. 'I'd . . . I'd like that.'

'Me too.' He reached over and threaded his fingers through mine and squeezed.

There was a soft flutter in my chest that moved into my belly as I ended up studying his knuckles. His skin had split Erik's. He'd gone after the boy for something that may or may not have been an accident. This was the perfect chance for me to bring everything up, but I wasn't ready.

'Does Jen know about Jack?' I asked, changing the subject.

He nodded. 'Family knows. No one talks about it though. It's kind of like the worst well-kept secret.'

After that, I fell silent. My mind was occupied. The ride to Frederick didn't take very long and the food was served quickly at Bonefish Grill. I could've eaten an entire meal of bang bang shrimp. Jase kept the conversation going, talking about Jack and then moving on to my brother.

'So tomorrow's the big deal, right?' he said, spearing a scallop on my plate and stealing it. 'You think he's going to go through with it?'

I hadn't considered that he wouldn't. 'You don't think he'll do it?'

'He's really nervous.' Jase laughed as he settled back in the booth. 'Hell, I've never seen your brother like that.'

'Me neither. I hope he does do it. They're perfect together.'

Jase ran his finger along the rim of his glass as he watched me from beneath lowered lashes. 'We need to tell Cam as soon as he gets back.'

My breath caught and I nodded. 'We do.'

The waitress appeared with the check and as Jase leaned forward to pull out his wallet, he pressed a quick kiss against the corner of my lips. The silvery light in his eyes as he pulled back caused my chest to lurch.

'Debbie broke up with Erik,' I blurted out.

He paused for just a second and then pulled cash out of his wallet. 'That's good news, right? I mean, he's always been a dick to the girl. No one could figure out why she stayed with him.'

I watched him as he laid the money near the check. My heart beat faster. 'He . . . hit her.'

Jase froze again, but this time he'd been in the process of leaning back. His thick lashes lifted. 'What?'

Nothing about his expression told me he was hiding something from me, but I knew he was. 'He hit her. Like Jeremy had hit me.'

The line of his jaw tightened, and then he pursed his lips, letting out a low whistle as he looked away. 'I don't know what to say, Tess.'

'Maybe that you're now double glad that you beat him up?'

His eyes locked with mine, the color a startling shade of

236

silver. He opened his mouth and then seemed to rethink what he was about to say. His broad shoulders tensed.

'I know,' I whispered. 'Deb told me last night.'

'Last night,' he repeated dumbly. 'And you're just now saying something?' He laughed as a muscle thumped in his jaw. 'You know, I knew something was up with you. You've been too quiet. You didn't eat the cupcake immediately. I thought maybe your knee was bothering you.'

I tucked my hair back behind my ears. 'You didn't tell me.'

He drew in a deep breath and then slid out of the booth, rising as he grabbed my crutches. 'Let's take this conversation outside.'

Since it wasn't a dinner type of conversation, I waited until we were in the Jeep before pushing the subject. 'You went after him.'

'I didn't go after him, Tess. It wasn't like with Cam. I know that's what you're getting at. That wasn't my intention. I ran into him at the frat house when I came back from my parents' place. He was sitting on the couch like he hadn't a fucking care in the world.'

Holding my breath, I watched him as he leaned forward and turned the key. The engine roared to life and he didn't speak again until he was out on the main road, cruising toward Interstate 70. 'And all I could think was that he fucking ended your dreams. He took that from you and I didn't give a fuck if it was an accident or not. He did that.'

Erik had. 'Jase—'

'After everything you've been through, I had to say something. I had to,' he went on, his profile stark in the shadows of the car's interior. 'I told him that he needed to stay away from you and no more accidents better happen. That's it. That's all I wanted to say to him, and, yeah, I might not have said it that nicely, but I wanted to get my point across.'

237

What he was saying was the same as Deb had said, so his next words didn't surprise me.

'But then he said some shit, Tess. Stuff that no one should ever say about you, and I made sure he didn't say anything else.'

There wasn't pride in his voice. Maybe the smugness of a man who knew he'd put another man—and I used the term man for Erik loosely—in his place. 'You hit him.'

He glanced at me, expression hard. 'I did.'

'And that's all you have to say about that?'

Turning his gaze back to the dark road, he ran one hand through his messy hair. 'I don't regret it.'

I sucked in a sharp breath. 'Neither did Cam.'

'This isn't the same. I didn't beat the shit out of Erik. I didn't end up in jail or put a boy in a hospital,' he spat out, and I flinched. 'Shit, Tess. That's not what I mean—'

'You know how I feel about what Cam did and how guilty it made me feel. Cam nearly ruined his life because of my—'

'And that wasn't your fault! What he did wasn't your fault. What I did wasn't your fault. Erik ran his mouth and I hit him. Okay. I hit him two times.'

Blood pounded through my veins as I struggled to make sense of what I was feeling. Most of the confusion came from the fact that there was a little, teeny tiny part of me that was *glad* he'd given Erik a taste of his own medicine. And I'd felt that way when I first heard what Cam had done.

And I didn't know what that said about me.

I stared at the dark blurs of the trees lining the interstate. 'Why didn't you tell me?'

'I . . .' He swore again. 'I knew you'd get upset. I was hoping Debbie wouldn't say anything.'

My hands curled in my lap. 'Did you really think she wouldn't?'

238

'Would you want people to know your boyfriend got owned? No. I thought she wouldn't say anything. I know that's wrong. I'm sorry. But I would rather you hadn't known.'

The unapologetic nature of his response made his apology hard to swallow. It wasn't that he was being a jerk about it, just that he hadn't regretted it. 'You promised me you wouldn't say anything.'

'I promised to not say anything to Cam, which I haven't. And trust me. Eric isn't going to say shit to him, because then he'd have to tell your brother why I gave him a black eye, which is all I did.' The hand with the busted knuckles curled around the steering wheel. 'Shit, you didn't enjoy yourself tonight, did you? This is supposed to be our first—I don't know. Fuck. Our first date and this whole time you were pissed off.'

I sat in silence, rigidly still. Tonight was our first real date, except it hadn't felt like that. Not because I didn't want to be with him, but because of what had been lingering over my head and his.

'I should've told you Wednesday. I shouldn't have tried to keep it from you. That's where I fucked up.' There was a beat of silence. 'Tess, say something.'

Squeezing my eyes shut, I slowly unclenched my hands. What could I say? It wasn't just him who'd ruined this night—ruined what was supposed to be this monumental step in our current closet relationship. I could've said something the moment I saw him. Or when he'd texted me earlier in the day or when I sent him a text before I went to bed. And I didn't. We could've cleared the air and then enjoyed ourselves. Hopefully.

'I don't know what to say,' I admitted finally.

Jase didn't respond, and that was that for the thirty minutes or so the car ride back to my dorm took. Maybe

I was overreacting. He hadn't done what Cam had done, but he still had lied, and in the end, he took things to a physical level in retribution.

But Erik had provoked Jase.

My brain hurt by the time the Jeep idled up to the curb. Like the night before, he went to turn off the engine, but I stopped him. I needed to get my head straight.

'I'll call you tomorrow,' I said.

He stared at me for a moment and then nodded. 'Let me get your crutches at least.'

'Okay.'

Easing out of the Jeep, I put my weight down on my good leg and waited until he pulled my crutches out of the backseat and handed them to me. I had the distinct feeling that as I met his steely gaze, he was more upset with this than I probably understood.

I started to invite him up, but he cupped my cheeks gently, leaned down, pressed his lips to mine, and kissed me so softly I was acutely reminded of the inherent tenderness inside of Jase. 'Are we okay?' he asked, and I felt the ground drop out from under my feet.

The idea of us not being good before we even had a chance to do something with this relationship was a cold smack in the face. The words burst from me, surprising me. 'It's not just that it reminded me of what Cam did. It reminded me of *him*—of *everything* I felt while I was with him and *everything* I felt afterward.'

Jase closed his eyes briefly. 'I'm sorry. I didn't think.'

'It's okay,' I whispered.

He didn't look like he believed me. 'You sure?'

I nodded because I was unable to speak. His fingers slipped away, and he jerked his chin toward the entrance.

'I'll wait until you get inside.'

Emotion clogged my throat. 'Good night, Jase.'

'Night,' he murmured.

It was when I was in the brightly lit lobby that I realized I'd left my cupcake and my heart out there. I twisted at the waist, burning to hobble outside and to just forget about everything, but like Jase had promised, he'd waited until I made it inside.

The Jeep was gone.

Swallowing the lump in my throat, I headed to the elevator. Regret burned like food that didn't set right in the stomach, but him leaving was probably a good thing. I needed to sort my head out.

I still didn't know what to think or how to feel, but how could I stay mad? And should I? All I wanted to do was sleep. Tomorrow I would know what to say to him.

When I flipped on the light, it flickered once and then went out, pitching the room back into darkness.

'Fudge pucker,' I muttered as I hobbled around the coffee table, knocking the edges of the crutches into it. I found the little lamp and flipped it on. The energy-saving bulb only cast enough light that I wouldn't break my neck getting around the room. I propped my crutches in the corner and turned.

I groaned. 'Are you fucking kidding me?'

A pink scarf dangled from the cracked open door. Deb had broken up with the jerk! And they were in there screwing? Anger whirled through me, spitting fire into my blood. I was going to beat both of them with my crutches. And that would be great, because then I couldn't be mad at Jase for hitting Erik. At least knocking them upside their heads would solve one of my problems.

I limped toward the door. Pain flared up my leg as I felt my knee start to slide in the brace, but I stormed forward and pushed the door open. The room was pitch-black and surprisingly quiet. No grunts or moans or

241

bedsprings squeaking as someone tried to cover themselves.

Tiny hairs on the back of my neck rose. 'Debbie?' My eyes hadn't adjusted to the darkness as I reached for the light switch. 'Are you . . .?'

The light didn't turn on.

I tried it again, hearing the switch flick, but there was nothing . . . nothing but a strange creaking sound. Almost like a loose floorboard.

A chill snaked down my spine as I swallowed hard. 'Deb?'

There was no response. Just the creak . . . creak . . . creak.

Instinct screamed for me to turn and run away. Fear sunk its icy claws deep inside me as I stepped farther into the room, blinking my eyes. I tried calling her name out again, but no words formed. They were frozen inside me.

The darkness started to loosen its grip on the room. Shadows took on deeper forms, more solid, more substance—

I bounced into something, something that shouldn't be there in the middle of the room, shouldn't be swaying back and forth, making that creaking sound.

Air hitched in my throat as I lifted my head, my sight slowly returning to me.

Two bare legs—pale, bare legs.

A dark sleep shirt.

Two arms hanging limply at the sides.

The air punched out of my lungs as realization set in, but—oh God—I didn't want to believe it. I couldn't. There was no way. A cry worked its way up.

It wasn't her.

It wasn't her brown hair shielding half of her face. It wasn't her mouth gaping open. It wasn't Debbie hanging from the light fixture in our dorm room. It couldn't be her.

A terrible sound filled the suite, hurting my ears. The sound didn't stop, but kept coming and coming. There were voices in the background, shouts of alarm, hands gripped my shoulders as my legs went out from underneath me, but the screams were louder than everything.

It was me screaming, I realized dumbly. I couldn't stop. I'd never stop.

Debbie had hung herself.

Chapter 20

Things happened in a continuous blur that I was detached from. Eventually I stopped screaming, only because my voice gave out. The hands that had tried to stop me from falling belonged to the most unlikely person ever. Our suitemate.

And our suitemate turned out to be the half-naked chick from Jase's room—Steph. Any other time I would've laughed at the irony. That the MIA suitemate was her of all people. I almost did laugh, but I stopped it before it could bubble up, because I knew if I started laughing, I'd never stop.

Beautiful Steph, with her raven-colored hair pulled in a high ponytail and wearing sleep shorts that were shorter than the chicks at Hooters wore, had tried to talk to me once I was in the too-bright lobby, sitting on one of the uncomfortable chairs with its hard cushions. She'd given up when all I could do was stare at her blankly.

Debbie was dead.

A shudder rocked through me, followed by a series of less powerful shivers.

The lobby was full of people huddled in corners, some whispering and others crying. People were hugging one another. Others looked shell-shocked by the knowledge that a few floors above us, someone was dead.

Steph returned to my side with a blanket and draped it over my shoulders. I murmured a barely audible 'Thank you.' She nodded as she sat beside me. Another girl, someone I knew I recognized but couldn't place, approached us.

'Not now,' Steph snapped, causing me to jump.

The girl stopped, her bare toes curling on the lobby floor. 'But—'

'But I don't care,' she interrupted. 'Leave her alone.'

I blinked dumbly as the girl wheeled around and disappeared back into a huddle. A few minutes later a guy started toward us, and Steph sent him off, too. She was like a watchdog.

Red and blue lights from outside the dorm cast strange flashes across the lobby, and I squeezed my eyes shut.

Debbie had hung herself.

I couldn't wrap my head around it. I couldn't even begin to understand why she had done it. Last night she had made such a big decision and this morning she'd been okay as she talked about going to her parents and now . . .

She was dead.

The campus police finally came down to talk to me; one of the younger officers crouched down and in low, even tones, asked me to recount how I came to find her. When they asked if Debbie had been acting strange in the last couple of days, I sucked in a shuddering breath.

'No. But she broke up with her boyfriend,' I said, my voice hoarse and flat. 'She was in a good mood when I last talked to her. I thought she'd left to tell her folks about the breakup.'

The police exchanged looks, like the fact that Deb had broken up with her boyfriend explained everything, but it didn't. If anything, it made this whole situation even more confusing. Why would she do it when she said she had so much to look forward to?

Once I was done talking to the campus police, the county and state officials showed up, asking the same questions.

'She's already answered those questions,' Steph spat when a deputy asked what I was doing before I returned to the apartment.

The deputy nodded. 'I understand, but—'

'But don't you think she's, like, I don't know, a bit traumatized by everything right now? That you could give her some breathing room? Maybe a few minutes to deal with everything?'

The deputy's eyes widened a bit, but before he could respond, Steph stood suddenly and stepped around the deputy. 'Thank God, you're here. It took you long enough.'

I didn't get a chance to look up to see who she was talking to. The deputy sidestepped as a tall shadow fell over me, and the next second, arms went around my shoulders. I inhaled deeply, recognizing the faint trace of cologne that belonged to *him*—to Jase. Shuddering, I turned into his embrace, burying my face against his chest.

'I was back at the farm when you called,' he said to Steph. She called him? What the what? 'I came as fast as I could.' His hand slid up my back, tangling in my hair. 'Oh, baby, I am so sorry.'

I couldn't speak as I burrowed closer and gripped his sides until I was bunching up the same sweater he'd worn on our date earlier. I wasn't close enough. I was so cold that I wanted to get inside him.

'I wish I'd come inside with you. Damnit, I wish you didn't have to see that.' He dropped his head to mine as he tightened his hold, keeping the blanket from slipping away. 'I'm so sorry, baby.'

246

The deputy must've given up, because he wasn't asking questions I didn't want to think about anymore. God, I didn't want to think at all.

'Thank you,' I heard Jase say, and then there were the soft footsteps of Steph walking away from us.

I wanted to tell Jase how she'd stayed by my side, but my lips were pressed together too tightly. He held me, whispering words in my ear that didn't make much sense to me, but somehow had this calming effect.

A sudden hush descended on the lobby, and Jase's body tensed against mine. Suddenly, someone cried out and some residents' sobbing grew louder. A sickening feeling pooled in my stomach and I started to pull free, to look because I had to look.

'No.' His hand clamped down on the back of my head, holding me in place. 'You do not need to look right now, baby. I'm not going to let you see this.'

I gripped his sweater until my knuckles ached. I knew without looking what was happening. They were taking Debbie out. Another shudder coursed through me.

Minutes ticked by, and then we were approached again by the police. They wanted to take a formal statement.

'Can this wait?' Jase asked. 'Please? I can bring her to the office tomorrow, but I really just want to get her out of here for right now.'

There was a pause and then the officer relented. 'We have enough information for tonight, but here's my card. She needs to come by the office tomorrow.'

Jase shifted as he took the card. 'Thank you.'

The officer cleared his throat. 'I'm sorry for this, Miss Hamilton. Try to get some rest and we'll see you tomorrow.'

Try to get some rest? I almost laughed.

'We're going to get out of here, but I need to get your crutches, okay?' Jase said as he pulled back, cupping my face. My eyes locked with his. Concern tightened the lines around his mouth, thinning his lips. He looked as pale as I felt. 'You going to be okay while I go get them?'

I hadn't realized that I'd come down here without them. Closing my eyes, I took several deep breaths as I tried to pull myself together. 'Okay. I'll . . . I'll be fine.'

'You sure?'

When I nodded, he started to get up, but I gripped his wrists. 'Where are we going?'

'We can go back to the house up here or my parents—'

I didn't want to be around people and I especially didn't want to run into Erik. 'I have a key to Cam's apartment. It's . . . it's in my purse. Can we go there?'

'Yeah, baby, we can go anywhere you want.' He glanced over my shoulder. 'I'll be—'

My grip on his wrists tightened. 'Don't tell Cam. Please. If you do, he'll come home and it will ruin the trip. Please don't tell him.'

'I won't tell him,' he promised, kissing my cheek. 'And don't worry about that. Okay? Just don't worry about anything.'

Relieved that this wouldn't interfere with Cam's plans, I relaxed a little. Jase left to find one of the officers so he could go upstairs and get my stuff. As I waited for him, I kept my gaze trained on the scuffed tile. I could feel the stares on me, and I wanted to shrink into the blanket and disappear.

When Jase returned, it wasn't soon enough. Holding my purse, he helped me up and guided me outside. I barely felt the cool air as we made our way past the police cruisers that were parked along the curb and into the parking lot.

The ride to University Heights was silent. Jase held my hand, but I barely felt his grip. I was numb inside and out, and I wondered when I'd start feeling things again.

Immediately after I'd injured my knee the first time, it had been like this. Empty. In a daze. The out-of-it feeling had lasted for days, but this was on such a deep, different level.

Cam's apartment was dark when we stepped inside. Jase stepped around me, easily finding the switch to the overhead light. I imagined the apartment was like a third home to him.

He stopped a few feet from me and turned, thrusting both of his hands through his hair. 'Tess, baby . . .' He shook his head, as if he had no idea what to say. And what does one say in a situation like this?

I took a deep breath, feeling weak in my knees. 'I've . . . I've never seen a dead person before.'

He closed his eyes briefly.

'And she was dead.' I stopped, swallowing. That was a stupid, unnecessary clarification, but I needed to say it out loud. 'She killed herself. Why would she do that?'

'I don't know.' He started toward me, a look of pain clouding his eyes.

The back of my throat burned. 'She told me last night that she was happy that she broke up with Erik. That she had her whole life to look forward to.' I drew in a breath that got caught. 'She was *okay* today. I don't understand.'

'I know.' He stopped in front of me, and when he spoke again, his voice was low. 'You may never understand.'

I didn't want to believe that. Something had to have happened to make her do what she did, because I didn't want this to be something I never understood and had to live with. I wasn't moving, but somehow I stumbled. The crutches fell to the floor, thudding softly off the carpet. Jase caught my elbow and led me over to the couch.

'You doing okay?' He sat beside me, placing a warm hand against my cool cheek.

I nodded as I closed my eyes, leaning into his touch. The

249

words—they sort of just came out of me. 'Maybe I should've said something earlier to her about Erik—about what I'd been through with Jeremy. I could've helped her. Maybe paid more attention—'

'Stop,' he said, cupping my cheeks with both hands as he pressed his forehead against mine. 'There was absolutely nothing you could've done to have made any of this different. Do you understand that?'

I wasn't sure. I had been silent from the start with her and Erik, and Debbie had stayed silent over what had happened. Silence, no matter which way you look at it, destroyed lives.

He made a deep, torn sound. 'If she wanted to kill herself, she would've done it no matter what anyone did or said, Tess.'

Kill herself.

Something didn't ring true about that, made it hard to believe that she would've actually hung herself. Denial was riding me pretty strongly, but there was something in the back of my head that screamed she wouldn't have done this.

'I wonder if they've found a suicide note,' I mused out loud, feeling a heaviness settle in my stomach and chest. 'Do you think they did?'

He pulled back, dropping his hands to my legs as he shook his head. 'I don't know. They might tell you tomorrow when I take you to the office.'

That was the last thing I wanted to think about having to do. I scrubbed the heels of my palms down my face. So many thoughts raced through my head that I blurted out one of them. 'Did you know Steph lived there? I mean, that she was my suitemate?'

'No. I've never been to her dorm. Never asked, either.'

I chose to believe him in that moment, because it was stupid to care about that right now. 'She called you?'

250

'She did and I . . . she said you were really upset—screaming—and she called me.'

I shuddered as those horrible moments after finding Debbie came back. 'How did she know?'

He looked at me, confused. 'The night at the party—she pretty much guessed that you meant something to me and that something was going on between us.'

Made sense. I turned a little and focused on taking several deep breaths.

'I'm going to see if Cam has something to drink.'

'Make it strong,' I mumbled.

'You sure?' He kissed my cheek after I nodded. 'I'm sure he has something.'

Lifting my gaze, I found myself staring at where the crutches had landed on Cam's beige carpet. A few days ago I'd thought my life was ruined. Not completely, because good things happened at the same time that something so terrible had. I got Jase. Finally, after years of pining for the boy, I had him. Earlier tonight, when I'd been upset with Jase over hitting Erik, seemed so irrelevant. As did my bum knee. Those issues paled in comparison to what had just happened to Debbie and her family. My problems were nothing, because Deb . . . she was gone.

Jase returned with a small glass of amber-colored liquor. 'Scotch,' he said, handing it over. 'It should help.'

I took a sip and winced as it burned my throat. 'Whoa.'

'The second drink will be easier.' He held the entire bottle and took a swig, obviously a pro at drinking the fancy stuff.

He'd been right. The second drink was easier and the third even more so. When I finished, I placed the glass on the coffee table.

'Did it help?' he asked, placing the bottle beside my glass.

Did it? I turned to him. 'I want . . . want to sleep.'

His expression softened. 'That's probably a good idea.'

Yes. That did sound like a magnificent idea. 'Will you stay with me tonight? I don't want to be alone.'

'Of course I'll stay with you. There's no way I'm letting you be by yourself tonight.'

I scooted toward him and looped my arms around his neck. 'Thank you so much for coming.'

He returned the embrace. 'You don't have to thank me for this.'

'But I do. I don't know what I would be doing if you weren't here. Probably losing my mind. I just . . .' I didn't finish. Gratitude swelled in me. 'Thank you.'

Jase dropped a kiss to the top of my head, and I found it hard to disentangle my arms from him. I found an old, oversize shirt of Cam's to wear to bed while Jase investigated the extra bedroom.

'Sorry. I can't sleep in Cam's bed. Too weird.'

I limped into the extra room and eyed the full-size bed that had a blue comforter neatly tucked in. 'Isn't this Ollie's old room?'

Jase glanced over his shoulder. His gaze was quick, but I didn't miss that he was taking in all the exposed flesh. Cam's shirt slipped off one shoulder and the material ended midthigh. If I bent over, someone would be getting an eyeful of my undies.

He looked away as he widened his stance by the bed. 'Cam actually replaced the bed and stuff because the old one belonged to Ollie. Sometimes I stay here.'

'You sure?'

Jase chuckled. 'I would not sleep in the same bed as Ollie unless it's been disinfected.'

My lips twitched. 'That's mean.'

'Uh, you didn't want to sleep in his bed either,' he pointed out as he faced me. 'That boy has been around. His bed has had more action than a subway train.'

I cracked a grin.

His eyes lightened. 'There they are.'

'What?'

'The dimples.'

I smiled.

'Even better.' He swooped down, kissing the one on my left side and then the right. 'I love them.'

In spite of everything, my chest warmed and I knew it had nothing to do with the liquor. The warmth lasted until I climbed into the bed that smelled like fresh linen and Jase disappeared back into the apartment, checking the door and grabbing some water for himself.

Shivering again, I tugged the comforter up onto my shoulder and curled onto my side, my back to the door. When I closed my eyes, I saw a set of pale legs and limp arms.

Why did she do it? Nothing, no matter what it was, was worth ending a life over. Tears pricked at my eyes and spilled over. Debbie and I weren't extremely close, but that didn't seem to matter. My heart hurt for her anyway.

I heard the door shut softly and quickly wiped at my cheeks. The light beside the bed turned off and there was the sound of clothing rustling and falling to the floor. My heart stuttered. The bed dipped and Jase rose up behind me. Somehow, in the darkness of the room that smelled like coconut and vanilla, his fingers found the tears on my cheeks, brushing them away. He said nothing as he curled his body around mine, securing his arm around my waist.

The warmth of his bare chest pressed along my back and down my legs, but it was like half of my body was in a pile of snow while the other half was cozied up to a fire. I tried closing my eyes once more, but the image of Debbie appeared again and I shuddered.

'Don't think about it.' He tightened his arm.

'I can't stop seeing her,' I admitted after a few moments. 'When I close my eyes, I see her hanging there—' I cut myself off. I didn't want to think about this or feel anything. He shifted behind me, and I focused on the way he felt, tucked so close, his body so warm and hard. I could lose myself in him. Once the idea formed, it seemed like another brilliant idea. Jase could make me forget, even if it was for only a little while.

I wiggled my hips, and I felt him tense. 'Jase?'

'Yeah?' His voice was deep and gruff.

My cheeks burned when I spoke again. 'Make me forget.'

His chest rose sharply against my back. 'What are you asking for?'

'You,' I whispered.

He took another deep, dragging breath. 'Tess . . .'

'I feel so cold.' I rolled onto my back and turned my head toward him. Our faces were inches apart. 'I don't want to feel that way. Please, Jase, I want to feel warm. I don't want to think. I don't want to see her hanging there. Please. Take it away. Even if it's just for right now.'

I moved, rolling until I was half on him. My right leg, brace and all, slipped between his legs, and I folded my hands against his hard chest. Before he could tell me no, I placed my mouth to his, kissing him. At first, he didn't respond, like I had shocked him with my boldness. I tried to remember if I had ever been the one to initiate a kiss before; other than the night after the party, I didn't think I had been. And even that night, I hadn't kissed him.

I'd kissed something else.

To be the one initiating something now after such a tragic event left a bad taste in my mouth, but I pushed that feeling away, shoving it among the other bad feelings I didn't want to experience.

His lips were firm and warm under mine, absolutely perfect. And then they moved, gently following my lead. I moaned as our tongues met and the kiss deepened, spreading warmth down the front of my body. Tiny flames of desire curled low in my belly.

Jase gripped my upper arms and anticipation swelled, about to burst as I felt him harden against my hip. I expected him to pull me closer, to smash our bodies together, but . . . he lifted me off him.

My eyelids snapped open. 'Why?'

His features came together in the shadows, taut and harsh. 'Not like this, Tess.'

That's not what I wanted to hear. I pressed my weight down, causing him to groan in a way that made me ache between my thighs. He shuddered as I dipped my head, catching his bottom lip. I sucked and nipped at the flesh until his hips punched up, grinding against me. A fire moved through my veins and this—*yes, this*—was what I needed right now. To forget. To be warm. To live.

Jase shifted and without any warning, I was on my back and he was on top of me, his thickness pressing between my legs. Shards of pleasure darted through my veins. My back arched as I lifted my left knee, settling him deeper.

'Jesus Christ, Tess . . .' He caught my wrists, pinning them down. His chest was rising and falling rapidly. 'We are not going to do this.'

I rocked my hips, and he pulsed against me. 'I think *he* disagrees.'

He choked on a laugh.

When I moved against him again, his grip on my wrists tightened. 'Don't you want me?'

'Fuck,' he ground out. 'I always want you. I've wanted you for years. I want you in every position known to man.' Pausing, he dropped his forehead against mine. 'But our

255

first time isn't going to be after something like that, when you just want to forget what you saw and what you're feeling.'

Heart pounding, I stared up into his eyes. 'Our first time?' I repeated dumbly, as if it just occurred to me that we hadn't done the deed yet.

'I want you to only be thinking about me. I want you to be focused on me because you want to be and not because you are trying to escape something,' he said, and slowly loosened his grip. 'I don't want what will happen between us to ever be overshadowed by something else.'

I was aching in so many ways, but his words slowly filtered through the haze. He watched me as it all clicked together. What was I thinking? My face started to crumble. 'I'm—'

'Don't apologize, baby.' He dropped a sweet, quick kiss on my forehead and then eased on his side. 'Not allowing this is the fucking hardest thing I've ever done.'

I willed myself to pull it together, but my eyes stung and then filled with tears. When they spilled over, it didn't have anything to do with Jase putting the brakes on my little sexual escapades. I was feeling what I needed to feel right then and there—sorrow, pain, confusion, and hurt. It all whirled together, forming a maelstrom of violent emotion.

Jase swept his arms around me, pulling me to his chest, his hand cradling the back of my head. He seemed to know why the tears came, and he held me to him until I tired myself out and slipped into the sweet oblivion that was nothingness.

We had to have slept for hours, maybe even sleeping half of the day away, because when I opened my eyes, faint sunlight streamed in from the window behind the bed.

And we weren't alone.

What the . . .?

The cobwebs of sleep cluttered my head as the rest of the room came into view. My brother stood at the foot of the bed, his mouth hanging open. The top of Avery's red head appeared, and her wide brown eyes peeked over his shoulder. I blinked slowly. What were they doing here? Was I dreaming? Or having a nightmare?

A muscle popped in Cam's jaw as his gaze moved down the bed. I looked down and my eyes widened. The comforter had been tangled around our legs in the middle of the night. My left leg was outside the blanket and was snuggly fit between Jase's thighs. While I knew he had his boxers on, it didn't look that way. Hell, we looked naked. My borrowed shirt had slipped completely off my shoulder and with the way I'd hogged all the blankets, it didn't look like I was wearing anything and Jase's chest was exposed.

Worse yet, I was half on top of Jase.

Holy shit.

I stiffened, my gaze meeting Cam's. His blue eyes were on fire as he snapped his mouth shut. Avery popped out from behind my brother, looking like she was fighting a grin as she clamped her hands under her chin.

Jase's arm flexed around my waist, tugging me closer. He turned his head, nuzzling my neck. He yawned, a deep rousing sound that echoed through the room. 'What's wrong, baby?'

I was speechless.

Every line in my brother's body tensed in a way that spelled big, mothertrucker kind of trouble. '*Baby?*'

Jase stilled, but he didn't remove his arm as he pulled his face out of my neck. He looked toward the foot of the bed and exhaled slowly.

There was a beat of silence and then Cam said, 'What the *fuck*?'

257

Chapter 21

Things could not possibly get any more awkward.

'What in the fuck are you doing in bed with my sister?' Cam demanded.

Jase reached down casually and flipped the blanket so my legs were covered. 'Well, we were sleeping.'

Cam's jaw worked. 'Naked?'

Whelp, this just got more awkward. Face burning, I started to sit up, but Jase's arm was like a band of steel. 'We're not naked.'

'That's good to know.'

Avery looked away, pressing her lips together.

'And we weren't doing anything,' I said, and it sounded lame even to my own ears.

Jase glanced at me. 'Now, that is a lie.' My heart stopped in disbelief as he sat up, making sure I still stayed covered, which was a good thing. I was pretty sure my shirt was twisted up around my breasts. 'We weren't doing anything right this moment and maybe not exactly last night, but we have done things. Things I'm sure you don't want to hear about.'

Oh. My. God.

'Actually, I do want to hear exactly what things *my* best friend has been doing to *my* sister when I busted my ass to get back here after hearing what happened to Debbie.'

Avery placed her hand on Cam's arm. 'I don't think this thing with Jase is any of our business.'

'No,' Jase said. 'It is your business and we were going to tell you, but it didn't happen.'

'Tell me what exactly?' Cam demanded, his hands opening and closing at his sides.

This was so not how I pictured telling my brother about Jase and me. Not while I was in bed with his best friend or when Avery stood in the corner, now looking like she would rather be standing on her head while getting a bikini wax.

'We're together.' I cleared my throat. Couldn't I have at least had time to brush my teeth before having this conversation? 'Jase and I are together.'

My brother stared at me like I'd told him I was now dating his pet turtle. 'Bull. Shit.'

'Excuse me?' I said.

'You are not with Jase,' he said, ignoring Avery when she reached for his arm. It was then that I noticed her left hand—her ring finger did not have a big old rock on it. 'No girl is with Jase—not longer than a night or a hookup here or there.'

Jase stilled. 'It's not like that with Tess.'

My brother cut him a dark look. 'That's my fucking sister, Jase. This isn't some fucking random girl. Don't forget that I know—I know shit and you're not getting my sister—'

'Whoa!' I shouted. 'I'm not "some fucking random girl," and it's different between us.'

Cam snorted. 'Fucking Christ, Teresa, are you stupid?'

It literally was a nanosecond. One moment Jase was beside me, and the next he was off that bed, standing in front of my brother. Might make me a bad, bad girl, but I got a bit hung up on seeing Jase in his half-naked glory. The tight, black undies hugged the muscular curve of his ass like a glove. His thighs were perfectly formed, wide but not too much. The cords of the muscles in his back rippled and tensed, causing the knots of his tattoos that reached along his side and shaded into his back to move.

'Now, you can be pissed off at me all you want, Cam, but don't get in her face. Not after what—'

'Don't fucking step to me.' Cam got up in Jase's face, and my stomach plummeted. I scrambled out from under the covers, tugging the shirt down as my brother's face reddened. 'That's my little sister—'

'I'm not a kid, Cam! And you know Jase is a good guy, so stop being such an ass. We were going to tell you, but—' I gasped as I put my weight down hard on my right leg and my knee started to turn.

Jase whirled and started toward me. 'Tess—'

'I'm fine.' I bent over slightly, placing my hand over my knee.

Cam cursed. 'Look at what you did.'

'He didn't do anything,' Avery said, her eyes wide. 'Cam, I think we need to step out for a few and give everyone time to cool off.'

'I agree.' Jase gently pushed me down until I was sitting, which put me at eye level of his crotch, and this whole situation just got fucked up on a multitude of levels. 'I think we both need to calm down.'

'Like I give a fuck,' Cam spat back, running a hand through his hair. He turned halfway, shook his head, and faced us. 'How long? How long has this been going on?'

Jase straightened as he turned to my brother. 'The first time I kissed her was a year ago—'

That was all he got out.

Like a speeding bullet, Cam shot forward. Avery shouted in alarm, and I lurched from the bed, but it was too late.

Cam's fist connected with Jase's jaw, spinning him back. He hit the wall with a loud curse and slid down, clutching his jaw. 'Fuck,' Jase grunted.

I cried out, dropping onto the floor next to him. My leg screamed in pain, but I ignored it. Grabbing Jase's arm, I glared at my brother. 'What the fuck is wrong with you?'

He was breathing heavily as he lowered his hands, blinking rapidly. Avery kept a hold on his straining upper arms. 'He shouldn't—'

'He shouldn't what? Be there for me? Treat me like I should be? Be with me? Because he's doing all those things. So too fucking bad, because he is and I love him. So you can go fuck . . .' I trailed off as tingles swirled down the back of my neck. Slowly I turned to look at Jase. Blood drained from my face so fast that I thought I might pass out. What did I just say? 'Oh God . . .'

The right side of his jaw was red, but he stared up at me, his eyes a bright silver. 'What?' he whispered.

I loved Jase. I knew that. I'd fully accepted that, but I hadn't been ready to tell him and especially not in front of my brother after he'd just *hit* him.

This was so unromantic.

'Come on, Cam, let's give them some space.' Avery tugged on his arm, and for fuck's sake, my brother finally listened. He stumbled around, letting her lead him out of the room like he was in a daze.

I watched the door close and debated on running out of the apartment. Maybe Avery's was unlocked and I could go hide in her closet. For like a week. I did not just admit that I loved him. Please God, let him think I said something else—anything else. Like maybe I dove you. That was better.

The tips of Jase's fingers pressed into my cheeks, and he

261

turned my head toward him. The look on his face, a mixture of wildness and stark vulnerability tripped up my heart. I opened my mouth to blurt out something else that probably didn't need to be said.

Jase's mouth captured mine, and there was nothing calm or gentle about the kiss. Our lips and teeth mashed together as his tongue thrust in. He slanted his head, spreading his hands as he devoured me. The kiss was rough, intense and sensual, overwhelmingly powerful. Shivers raced through me.

'Wait,' I gasped out, breaking the kiss. 'Your jaw . . .'

'I don't give a fuck about my jaw right now.' He slid his hands down my sides and grasped my hips. Lifting me up, he sat me in his lap so that I straddled him. The position was awkward on my right leg, but it was lost in the sensation of him pressing against my core. The thin layer of clothing between us down there left little to the imagination.

I had no idea how he'd gotten so hard so quickly.

Gripping my hips, he rocked up and raw sensation spiraled through me. His lips were on mine, silencing the needy moan building in my throat. His hands slid down to my thighs and then up under the hem of the shirt, skating over the skin of my sides. I jerked as his fingers brushed the underside of my bare breasts.

'Jase,' I whispered, breathing raggedly. A heavy ache filled my breasts, their tips tightening until I wanted to scream. 'My brother is right out there.'

'Fuck your brother.' His hands moved up, closing over my breasts. *Finally*. 'Fuck everything outside of this room.'

My senses spiraled as his thumbs brushed over my nipples and he rocked his hips up again. I moaned his name against his mouth as he gently squeezed my breasts, molding his hands around them. Pleasure streaked through me. I never was very impressed with my breasts before, but I was then, knowing they seemed to fit his palms perfectly.

Jase shuddered as he shifted, leaving my breasts and wrapping an arm around my waist. It seemed in one moment he was leaning against the wall and we were sitting and then he was standing, lifting me with him as he explored my mouth, and the next second my back was against the soft mattress.

He hovered over me, his eyes a burning quicksilver. A bruise was forming on his jaw, a harsh reminder of what lay outside the doors, but oh my word, I didn't care. I wanted him. My body throbbed I wanted him so badly.

Our gazes found each other, and up until that moment I didn't realize how much control Jase had been exercising every time we'd been together. That control was gone now, lost in a storm of lust and need and something far deeper.

His biceps bulged as he lowered himself between my legs. He rocked slowly as he took my mouth and drew his hand down to my thigh, hooking my left leg over his hip. I heard him moan as I matched his movements, our bodies mimicking what we both wanted. His lips blazed a path down my throat, over the skin of my shoulder, and then back across my collarbone.

My fingers threaded through his soft hair as his mouth worked its way dangerously close to my breast. My breath caught as his mouth closed over the tip of my left breast, sucking the hardened point through the thin cloth. I arched clear off the bed, grinding my teeth together to keep from crying out. His hand closed around my right breast, catching the nipple between skillful, artful fingers. My hands knotted in his hair as his teeth closed on my nipple through the shirt.

A low cry escaped me as a riot of sensation pelted me and I shivered, wanting him closer, inside me. 'Please.'

Jase rose up over me, his lips swollen and moist. 'You're so fucking beautiful like this.' His hips rolled forward, causing my toes to curl.

Warmth spread through me. I tugged on his hair, urging him down to my lips, and he came, his kiss seeking and sucking. His fingers hooked around the band of my panties, and I knew what was coming if he took them off. He'd be on me and in me, and that's what I wanted desperately.

He shot me a look that scorched. 'I wanted to make this perfect. I wanted to wait, but I can't now.'

My heart and pulse pounded, my core already rippling. I lifted my behind, pleased when the growl of approval rumbled through him. 'I want you,' I said passionately. 'I've wanted you for so long. I lo—'

A soft knock on the bedroom door intruded. 'Teresa? Jase? I have a bag of ice for you.'

It was like that bag of ice had pressed between both of our legs. We stopped, breathing heavily.

'Teresa?' Avery called softly.

He dropped his forehead on mine and swore swiftly under his breath. A hard shudder rocked him, and he rolled off onto his back. 'I can't go to the door.'

My gaze dropped to his pelvis and his arousal was so visible it made me want to weep in more than one way. Cursing her timing, I reined in my hormones and cleared my throat. 'Coming.'

Jase snorted. 'Almost.'

I smacked him on the chest, and he laughed, curling up his knees, and once he started, he didn't stop. The skin around his eyes crinkled and his hair was a rich, russet mess of waves, and in that second, I was reminded of why I loved him so much.

Chapter 22

Avery had handed over a bag of ice, promising that Cam was almost under control. Us being under control was a totally different story. I knew when Avery saw me at the door that she had a good idea what had been going on in the room between Jase and me. My hair was a ratty messy, lips swollen and cheeks flushed. She didn't say anything, but as she turned, I swore I saw her grin.

They were in Cam's bedroom, and we were in the other. Both Jase and I were back in the clothes we'd worn yesterday, which at least made me feel more appropriate, while I held the ice to his jaw. It hadn't begun to swell, but it was an angry shade of red.

He eyed me over the bag. 'That didn't go as planned.'

I laughed in spite of everything. 'No shit.'

A smile turned up his lips and he groaned, pulling back. 'Ow.'

'Don't smile,' I ordered. I pressed the bag back to his jaw. A couple of moments passed. 'Some of it wasn't bad.'

'Wasn't bad?' His eyes had been a smoldering silver since he'd rolled off me, and they now burned even brighter. Slipping an arm around my waist, he tugged me forward

265

and down, so I was sitting on his bent legs. 'Some of it was stuff wet dreams are made of.'

I made a face. 'That's romantic.'

He curled his fingers around my wrist, pulling my hand with the ice down as his gaze swept over my face. 'I didn't mean to lose control like that.'

'I didn't mind.' My cheeks heated. 'Wish we could've finished.'

A deep sound rolled out from him as he wrapped his hand around the nape of my neck, guiding my head down. His lips sealed over mine in a slow, languid kiss that stroked the unspent flames of desire. The kiss deepened as his tongue met mine, twisted and spiraled and, damn, this boy could kiss—

The bedroom door burst open and Cam barreled in. 'For shit's sake, do I need to hit you again, Jase?'

'Damnit,' I moaned, breaking away and casting Cam a dirty look. 'Do you know how to knock? It isn't that hard.'

He looked unrepentant as he glared at Jase. 'I came in here to try to talk this out and I walk in, and she's in your lap and you're fucking her with your tongue.'

Jase's mouth opened and I had a god-awful feeling he was going to explain that he wasn't fucking me with his mouth at *this* moment.

'Cam,' I started, shifting the ice in my hand. 'You really need to chill.'

'And you will need to get out of his lap.'

Avery's eyes rolled.

'She's where she wants to be,' Jase replied, voice surprisingly calm. 'And I'm going to tell you this. I'm not pissed that you hit me. I deserved it. I should've told you the first time we kissed, which was a year ago.'

Cam tensed.

266

'Let me finish,' Jase went on, keeping his arm secured around my waist. 'We kissed that night before we left early during fall break. Nothing happened again until this fall. I tried to fight it.'

'Yeah, looks like you tried *really* hard.'

Irritation pricked my skin as I stared up at my brother. 'He did try, Cam. And it wasn't like we've been hiding this forever. We planned to tell you on Wednesday, but you had *other* things going on.' I waited until recognition flared in his gaze. 'And then this with Debbie—' My throat closed up, and Jase's arm tightened around me. 'Anyway, it wasn't like we were trying to hide it from you. There just wasn't a good moment for it.'

'And they're telling you now,' Avery said. Apparently she'd become the voice of reason when it came to my brother. 'I think this is a good thing.'

'I think it makes me doubt Teresa's ability to tell the difference between common sense and her hormones,' he muttered, running a hand through his hair.

My mouth snapped shut as I sent him a look that should've shriveled his balls right up. Jase, who'd been rather calm during round two, had a totally different reaction. Picking me up out of his lap, he deposited me on the edge of the bed and stood.

A muscle thrummed along his jaw. 'Look, I'm not going to hold you hitting me against you, but if you talk to your sister like that again or say shit about her intelligence or, in general, insult or embarrass her, we're going to have a problem. A big motherfucking problem. I care about her,' Jase said, meeting Cam's glare when those words apparently didn't do anything to make him feel better. 'I care about her . . . just as much as I care about Jack.'

Cam took a step back and paled like Jase had punched him in the throat. Avery didn't catch the meaning, but my brother did. He glanced at me, and I raised my brows, signaling that I knew the truth.

My brother looked like he was about to pass out, and I suddenly had the wild urge to laugh. He slowly shook his head and then said, 'For real?'

Jase nodded. 'For real.'

'Well . . .' He backed off, appearing startled. 'I guess I'm . . .'

'Happy for us?' I suggested, tossing the bag of ice up and catching it. 'Because I could really focus on the happy stuff right about now.'

Cam looked at me, his features softening, even as Jase returned to the bed and placed a hand on my thigh, squeezing gently. 'Shit, Teresa, sorry. I'm just—'

'Overprotective,' Avery suggested, smiling when he looked at her. 'And a bit of a douche canoe sometimes?'

I grinned. 'Sounds about right.'

'Yeah, okay, I might've overreacted, but it's just because I care about you. You're my sister and I'm supposed to act like a douche when it comes to guys you're with.'

'You got that part down to a science,' Jase muttered.

Cam flipped him off, and the tension in my muscles started to ease. If they were flipping the bird to each other, they were back to normal.

'Anyway, the reason why we're back so early is because we started receiving texts this morning about Debbie,' Avery explained, veering the topic into a less-happy subject, but a necessary one. 'We needed to come home.'

'I wish you hadn't,' I murmured, thinking of Cam's plans.

'There was no way we wouldn't,' my brother replied, crouching down in front of me. 'Please tell me the rumors aren't true. That you didn't find her like that.'

I wrapped my arms around my chest, as if I could ward off the memory of her. 'It's true.'

268

Cam swore.

'Oh, my God . . .' Avery pressed her hand to her mouth. 'That's horrible.'

It was, but not as horrific as what Debbie had done. As Jase explained that I needed to go to the police today to give a statement, I tried to figure out why she would've done it. She'd been upset the night before, but she'd also been so full of hope. I didn't know her extremely well, but there were no signs that she was that depressed or that she would consider doing something so final.

'You can't stay in that dorm,' Cam decided as he stood. 'You can stay here.'

Jase dropped his arm over my shoulders. 'I agree with this idea.'

Part of me jumped at the idea, because there was no way I could go back to the dorm, but it was asking a lot. 'I don't want to be a pain in the ass.'

'Cam pretty much lives in my apartment as it is,' Avery interjected. 'You'd probably have this place to yourself for the most part.'

'But—'

'And it's a great offer,' Jase said, drawing my attention. 'I don't want you back in that dorm. So it's either staying here or you're coming to live in the frat house with me.'

The idea of being under the same roof as Erik turned my stomach. 'I want to pay rent or something. I'll get a job once my leg gets better.'

Cam waved me off. 'If that's what you want to do, have at it. No rush. Rent's paid up till summer.'

Once the decision was made for me to stay at Cam's, a lot of the dread faded like smoke in the wind. I'd sleep on the streets before I slept in that dorm room. Some people might think it was weird, but I wasn't sure I could even step foot in the dorm again. Bad enough, I doubted I'd ever get rid of the memory of her . . . of her hanging from the ceiling light.

'Cam and I will go get most of your stuff,' Jase announced. 'Tell me what you want and I'll get it.'

I glanced between the two, a bit concerned about them spending an immediate one-on-one time together. Jase caught my look and winked.

'We'll be fine,' he said.

Cam smiled tightly as he cracked his knuckles. 'Yeah, we'll be just perfect.'

Sitting beside me on the couch, Avery cringed as she glanced at the wall clock. 'They've been gone an awful long time.'

I nodded slowly. 'Yep.'

Calla had returned from visiting family that morning. Upon hearing the news, she'd texted and made her way over from the dorms not too long after the boys left. She sat in the recliner, brows knitted. 'Why are you guys worried about how long it's taking?'

'Well, there's a good chance they might kill each other. Cam is not happy about me and Jase being together—'

'Wait. What?' She sat forward, eyes popping wide. 'You and Jase are together? When in the holy hell did this happen?'

I picked up the glass of sweet tea. 'Uh, it happened last week.'

'But I saw you on Wednesday! Did you not think about telling me?'

Cheeks burning, I glanced at Avery. She focused on the wall. Totally unhelpful. 'It just didn't come up and it had just happened, so I was still feeling the, uh, freshness.'

'Freshness?' Avery murmured.

'Wow.' Calla curled her legs up. 'Way to go, Teresa. He's a hottie-Mc-hotters.'

I laughed. 'Yes, he is.'

'I love your brother with all my heart,' Avery said, twisting the ends of her hair around her slender fingers. Her cheeks flushed, blending the freckles. 'But Jase is . . . he's something else. I mean, I've always been a little intimidated by him.'

'Really?'

She let go of her hair. 'Yep. He just always looks so intense, like . . .'

'Like one night with him would change your life?' Calla suggested with a grin. 'I'm pretty sure I've said the same thing about him.'

I wouldn't know since I hadn't made it that far with him, but what I had experienced with him really backed what Calla was saying. I turned my gaze to the tea, oddly proud that I could sit there and call him mine, which was weird. I never felt that way before about someone.

In the silence that followed, I knew what everyone was thinking about. Debbie. Even though we all could talk about other things and laugh, what had happened lingered at the edge of every thought.

'I don't know why she did it,' I said, only realizing I said it out loud when both girls looked at me. 'I don't understand.'

'Sometimes you never understand,' Calla said, stretching out her legs. A pinched, sad look crossed her face. 'More often than not, it's not just one thing that sends a person over the edge. It's several things.'

Avery nodded as she fiddled with the bracelet on her wrist. 'It's true. A lot of stuff builds up and while it might be one thing that topples the person over, it's really a lot of things, big and small.'

'I get that, but Debbie was a happy girl. Except for breaking up with Erik, she was okay.'

'But how happy could she be if she stayed with him so long?' Avery asked. 'And I don't mean she was bad for being with him, but that's how many years of being treated like that?'

She had a good point.

'We don't know what other issues she might have had.' Calla paused, casting her attention to her hands she folded in her lap. 'My mom killed herself.'

I pressed the heel of my hand to my chest as I exchanged a look with Avery. 'What?'

Calla ducked her chin as she nibbled on her lower lip. 'Well, not like Debbie. She didn't do it just one night. She did it over the course of several years.'

'I'm really sorry to hear that, Cal.' Setting the tea aside, I picked up a pillow and pressed it against my tummy. 'How?'

'She drank and drugged herself to death. It wasn't an accident,' she said, looking up. 'My mom didn't want to live. She just chose the passive way out. Anyway, no one really knew she was like that. She had everyone fooled. I'm not saying Debbie wanted out for a long time, but you just don't know.'

I wanted to ask her more questions, but her stiffness told me she was done sharing for now. 'I just don't know. Something doesn't feel right.'

'When does something like this ever feel right?' Avery asked softly.

Again, good point, but as I trekked through my memories of that night, I knew I was missing something—something forced out of my head by the trauma of it, and that had been pretty damn traumatizing.

Then it hit me as I lifted my gaze and met Calla's. I started to rise as my heart pounded in my chest. 'Oh my God.'

'What?' Calla stood too, even though she looked confused. She looked at Avery, who was also starting to rise. 'What?' she said. 'What the hell, Teresa?'

I shook my head as it sunk in. How had I forgotten this? 'Pink scarf.'

'Huh.' She looked at Avery again.

'There was a pink scarf on the dorm door!' My legs gave out, and I plopped back on the couch. 'Holy crap . . .'

'Are you okay?' Avery grasped my arm, her fingers cool. 'Should I call Jase? Cam?'

'No! But I need to go give my statement! I need to do it now.' I felt sick. 'I need to go to the police.'

'All right.' Calla grabbed her keys. 'We can take you, but you have to tell us what the hell is going on.'

'The pink scarf—Debbie always hung a pink scarf on the door whenever Erik was there and they wanted privacy,' I explained in a rush, my hands shaking. 'She hung that damn pink scarf when she didn't want to be interrupted.'

'Okaaay.' Avery drew the word out.

'You don't understand.' I took a shallow breath. 'There was a pink scarf on the door when I got there. I thought she was in there with Erik and they'd gotten back together. That pink scarf means Erik *was* there earlier!'

Chapter 23

Avery and Calla got what I was saying to them, that Debbie hadn't been alone at some point during the evening, but it didn't seem to register on the importance scale for them.

But it did for me.

My brain was not willing to accept the idea that Debbie committed suicide. It wasn't that I was naive and didn't believe that it was possible, but Erik had been there and to me, it made more sense that the fucker lost his temper and—and really hurt her.

They took me to the police to give my statement and while I'd stressed the importance of the pink scarf and that it had meant that Debbie hadn't been alone, they didn't appear too overly concerned.

'We plan on talking to her ex-boyfriend later today,' the officer said, guiding me out of the office, to where Calla and Avery waited. He smiled, but it was tight and fake, and I felt like one of those nosy little old ladies who ran the neighborhood watch and always reported things incorrectly.

'So what did they say?' Avery asked once we were back in Calla's car.

I sighed. 'I told them what I saw and what I knew. That her and Erik had broken up and that he . . .' I bit down on my lip, realizing I'd never told them how Debbie's relationship was. It felt wrong somehow, even though she had never asked me to not tell anyone, but I'd been so embarrassed—still was—and I knew she probably never wanted anyone to know. I'd told the police and they'd written down what I'd seen—the bruises and what Debbie had told me, but I could tell that they really thought Debbie had killed herself. And without anyone there to file charges against Erik, there'd be nothing they could do.

Avery peeked over the passenger seat, her brown eyes wide. 'He hit her, didn't he?'

Wondering if she could read minds, I glanced at the rearview mirror, finding Calla's gaze darting from the road to it. 'Yeah, he . . . he hit her. I asked her about it once and she denied it, but then she told me the truth after, well . . .' Cam still didn't know about that and I wanted to keep it that way. 'Well, she told me the night before she died.'

'Jesus,' Calla muttered.

My gaze met Avery's, and she smiled sympathetically. 'Anyway, I told them what I knew and how the pink scarf had to have meant that Erik had been there. They said they were planning on talking to him today.'

She nibbled on her lower lip. 'Do you think he really did it to her and then . . . hung her up?'

I shuddered at the prospect. 'I don't know how anyone could do that to someone, but there are really messed-up people in this world.'

Calla nodded. 'So very true.'

'And he's lost his temper with her before. Maybe it wasn't on purpose,' I wondered out loud. 'And then he panicked and made it look like a suicide.'

'It sounds a little out there, but people have done crazier

stuff.' Avery turned in her seat and looked out the window. 'I've learned to never underestimate people.'

'Yeah,' I breathed, sitting back.

It seemed crazy to sit here and consider that a college-age guy might've killed his ex-girlfriend—accident or not—and then staged it as a suicide, but like Calla and Avery both said, people had committed crazier acts.

Cam and Jase were already back at the apartment and the moment we stepped through the doors, they started bombarding us with questions about what went down at the police.

Neither boy looked like they had done each other any bodily harm, and I spied two pink boxes sitting on the kitchen counter. I couldn't help but grin as I sat beside Jase on the couch. Him and his cupcakes. It was contagious, spreading to Cam.

'We didn't get everything, but we got enough that you'll be fine for a while.' Jase reached over, tucking my hair back. 'Everything is in your bedroom.'

'Thank you so much.' I looked between the boys. 'Both of you.'

'No problem.' Cam wrapped his arms around Avery, tucking her back against his chest. 'Just don't burn down my apartment.'

Everyone laughed while I shot him a dirty look. Calla was the first to bow out, having to head into work for a short shift, and then Avery and Cam got that googly-eyed look about them. They soon made an exit.

Jase reached for me, tugging me back so I rested curled against his chest. As much as I wanted to shut my brain down and simply enjoy being in his arms, I couldn't.

'You think I'm jumping to conclusions, don't you?' I asked, thinking back to what I told him about my visit to the police and my suspicions.

He brushed my hair back and pressed a kiss to my temple. 'I wouldn't say you were jumping. Maybe hopping, but you're right. Erik has one hell of a temper, and it wouldn't be the first time someone lost control and did something like that.'

At least he wasn't saying I was crazy. 'Do you think the police will do an autopsy?'

'I don't know.' His hold on me was secure. 'You'd think they would just in case.'

I prayed that they did. If my suspicions were correct, then wouldn't it show in the exam? I hated even thinking about Debbie in terms of autopsies and cause of death, like that was what she'd been reduced to.

'You know what it makes me wonder about?' I said, closing my eyes. 'What if Jeremy had gotten to that point? He could've easily been Erik, if that's what he did.'

Jase stiffened and he didn't say anything for a long moment. 'Then thank God Cam beat the ever-living shit out of him. Sorry. I know how that makes you feel, but thank God is all I can say.'

'Yeah,' I whispered, my stomach soured by the idea that Erik had murdered Debbie, but the more I thought about it, the more I feared that it was the truth.

'I want you to promise me something, okay?' he said, tipping my chin up with his fingers, until I could see his eyes. 'I don't want you being anywhere near Erik, especially alone.'

'That won't be a problem,' I said dryly.

One side of his lips hitched up. 'And unless you're talking to the police or one of us, I don't want you to voice your suspicions.'

Ready to argue that fine point, I opened my mouth, but he shook his head. 'Not because I think you should be silent, but if Erik did do this, I don't want you in danger because he thinks you know the truth. That's all I'm saying.'

I smiled a little. 'Okay. I can do that.'

We stayed like that for a little while, watching the natural light fade out of the living room. Wind picked up outside, rolling across the sides of the building. A long night yawned ahead and I didn't want to face it alone.

'Stay the night with me?' I asked, knowing it was asking a lot. He probably wanted to swing by the farm or go to the frat.

'Already ahead of you.' He grinned, jerking his chin at a backpack sitting next to the recliner. I hadn't even noticed it. 'I picked up a change of clothing when we were out. Just need a shower.'

'Thank you.' I stretched up, kissing his cheek. 'Thank you for everything.'

He tipped his forehead against mine. 'Why don't you order some Chinese? The place down the street delivers, and I'll hop into the shower.'

Sounded like a good plan. I placed the order while he dipped into the bathroom. The moment the water came on, I found myself staring at the door, heart pounding.

What would he do if I just joined him?

I bit down on my lip as I entertained the image of me stripping, sans crutches and knee brace, and sexily slinking into the shower. Picking up the soap . . .

Sigh.

Turning my attention to hobbling into my new bedroom, I unpacked what I could until I heard the shower turn off. I made my way back into the hall as the bathroom door opened. 'I ordered chicken—whoa.'

Jase stood in the doorway, his hair wet and curling around his chiseled cheekbones. The fine sprinkling of hair on his chest was damp. The jeans he'd thrown on hung low on his hips, revealing those V-shaped muscles on either side of his hips.

278

'Is chicken whoa a new plate?' he teased, dragging a white towel down those rippled abs.

'It's a kind of plate I want to eat.'

His eyes flashed silver and he started toward me, a look of stark hunger carved into his face. Just as his fingers brushed my cheeks, the doorbell rang.

He groaned as he backed off. 'I'll get it.'

Mouth dry, I watched him go to the door. The delivery-man got an eyeful of Jase's half nakedness, but I doubted it was the oddest thing the teenager had ever seen. We ate dinner on the couch, watching TV.

He remained there while I headed into the shower, washing away the funk of the day. I wished the water sluicing over my skin could rid me of what I saw when I closed my eyes or how my thoughts kept going back to that pink scarf and Erik.

Could he've really done it? From what I'd seen and from what Debbie had told me, he had the temper. When he'd swung that bag around, he'd been on the verge of losing control, but swinging a bag violently didn't mean he was capable of murder.

The water had started to go lukewarm when I stepped out and wrapped a fluffy green towel around me. Getting the brace on proved difficult with wet skin and I nearly broke a sweat by the time I finished.

Jase wasn't in the living room when I stepped out of the steamed-up bathroom. Holding on to the tightly wrapped towel, I quietly made my way into the bedroom.

He was hanging up my clothes, humming a song under his breath. He didn't hear me as I stopped in the doorway. My throat closed up as he slipped a sweater onto a hanger he must've found in the closet or snatched from the dorm. When he turned to my bed and picked up the stack of jeans—folded jeans—all my clothes were put away.

'You're a keeper.'

He backed out of the closet, looking toward the door. A single pair of jeans were in his hands, forgotten as his silvery gaze traveled from the top of my head down to my curled toes. 'Damn.'

I flushed to the roots of my hair. 'Thank you for putting my clothes away.'

'Uh-huh.' He dropped my jeans on the floor and stalked toward me. The look in his gaze made me want to back up *and* run toward him. He placed just the tips of his fingers on my arms, his gaze burning into mine. 'I'm going to make this crazy suggestion, okay?'

'Okay.'

One side of his lips tipped up. 'I think you should walk around like this at least twice a day when I'm around. Once in the morning. Once at night.'

I laughed. 'You just want me to prance around in a towel then?'

'Prance. Walk. Sit. Stand. Breathe.' He brushed his lips across my cheekbone, causing me to shiver. 'I'll be okay with any of those things.'

Turning my head just the slightest, our lips glided together. The kiss started off sweet as he drew his fingertips up to my cheek. My grasp on my towel loosened as his tongue flicked over my lips, coaxing my mouth open.

I loved the way he kissed, how he tasted me and could practically bring me to the tips of my toes with his lips and tongue. My breath quickened as he shifted closer and there was only an inch or so separating us.

Need rose swiftly, and I was so hot for him. The desire for him ran deeper than the physical. I wanted nothing to be in between us.

He moaned against my lips. 'I want you.'

Molten lava flowed through my veins. 'You are what I want.'

His hands skimmed down my sides, reaching the edge of my towel as he growled deep in his throat. I swayed into him. 'I'm yours,' I whispered.

He kissed me again, dragging his tongue over mine. When he pulled back, he nipped at my lip, causing me to gasp. My eyes fluttered open, and I got snared in his silvery gaze.

Jase had been right to stop things the night before. I didn't want our first time to have shadows clinging to it. Like him, I wanted it to be perfect. I wanted to look back on this moment and have absolutely no regrets.

But I knew it couldn't be perfectly planned. It was all about both of us wanting the same thing, and while him wanting to do everything the right way melted me inside, he didn't realize that he'd already done things in the right way.

Taking a deep breath and drawing on my courage, I loosened the knot holding my towel closed. It was like stepping out on the stage and knowing all eyes were on me, but this was different—more potent. Because only his eyes mattered, and right now I was his entire world.

I tugged the knot free and let the towel drop.

'Christ,' he groaned, lips parting on a sharp inhale.

Completely bare with the exception of my very sexy blue knee brace, I was more vulnerable to him than I'd been with anyone in my life.

I wasn't just offering him my body, I was truly offering him my heart.

Jase took a step back, his hands following to his sides. He opened and closed his fists. 'Do you know how beautiful you are? How it affects me?' A pleasant haze invaded my system as my body and heart responded to his words. He slowly shook his head. 'I don't think you really understand, because if you did, I don't think you could just stand there.

God, Tess, there isn't a part of you that's not perfect in my eyes.'

There was a lot of me that wasn't perfect. Without dancing, I'd lost the lithe figure about fifty cheeseburgers ago. My hips were more rounded, my thighs not as lean as before. Instead of the perfectly flat stomach I used to rock, it was now convex and my breasts were larger. Not a bad thing, but so was my ass.

But in his eyes, I felt more beautiful then I ever did before.

I'd never felt such anticipation before. His stare was doing crazy things to me. I was flushed, excited, and I knew I was making the right decision.

'I've never . . . been this bold before,' I said, voice shaky. 'But this is the right moment for us. I want you, Jase. Do you want me?'

'Yes.' His voice was gruff as he dragged his gaze up, lingering on my chest until I ached and throbbed there for his touch. 'I want you.'

Jase touched me then, his hands closing around my upper arms as he dipped his head. Strands of his soft, still damp hair brushed my cheeks. 'Are you sure this is what you want?'

'Surer than anything,' I breathed.

His bare chest rose, brushing mine. The sensation rocketed through me. He made another deep sound in the back of his throat. 'Stay right here. Don't move. Okay?'

'Okay.'

He kissed me quickly, sucking deeply before he broke off and left the bedroom. He returned a few seconds later with several foil packets in his hand. I arched a brow as I started to grin. 'You came prepared, huh?'

A cocky grin appeared. 'I wanted to be prepared with you.' He tossed them on the bed behind me, and I moved until the back of my legs hit the mattress. 'Watch me?'

'I'm not looking anywhere else.'

My breath caught as a full smile appeared, but then I held my breath as he reached down, thumbing out the button on his jeans. The zipper came next, and then his jeans slid down. They were gone in a second and his boxers were next.

I gasped at the sight of him, and he chuckled. He was utterly magnificent. That deeply tanned skin of his rippled in all the right places.

Jase was . . . well, he was endowed. And then some.

Two fingers pressed against my chin, lifting my gaze. 'You like what you see?'

I shivered. 'Oh yes.'

'Good.' He kissed me, and the very air in the room became laden with sexual tension. 'You have no idea how long I've wanted this,' he murmured against my lips as he wrapped an arm around my waist, lifting me until I was flush against him. The next kiss ignited a fire. 'Or how many times I lay awake at night, thinking of you like this with me.'

'As many times as I dreamed of this,' I said as he lowered me to the bed, so I was lying down the middle. 'I don't want to wait any longer.'

'Neither do I.' He grabbed a condom, ripped the foil open, and slid it on.

He lowered himself, trailing his lips over my flushed face and then down, blazing a path across my chest, suckling and nipping until my hips moved restlessly against him. The moment my hips pushed into his, he shuddered. His hands were everywhere, caressing me as if he sought to etch the lines of my body into his memory.

My body arched into his, aching and tense as I ran my hands down his chest. Desire flooded me, like a dam bursting after a long storm.

'I want to take my time.' He reached down between us, finding me and slipping a finger inside as he nudged my thighs apart. 'I want to kiss and taste every part of your body, because that's what you deserve, but I don't think I can wait, baby. I really don't.'

And he was shaking as he spoke those words. He slowly withdrew his fingers as his gaze fixed on mine. I almost came apart at the first touch of him pressing into me.

'God, you're so . . .' He faded off, as if he was incapable of words.

Halfway in, the pressure and fullness was unbelievable. I lifted my hips, wrapping my legs around his waist. Our mutual groans filled the room as he rolled his hips, driving in until he was completely inside.

Keeping still inside me, he panted with the control to hold himself immobile. 'Are you okay?'

There was a bit of stinging since it had been so long, but I was okay. I was better than okay. 'Yes.'

His lips brushed mine in a sweet kiss as he cupped my cheek. 'Nothing is better than the feeling of you holding me tight.'

'I can say the same.' I curled my fingers around his hair, tipping my hips against his, and whatever restraint he had up to that point, it broke.

He thrust in me, moving deeper with each long, powerful stroke. My body tensed around him as he cradled my hips in his hands, rocking me up against him. The increasing intensity turned into a feverish pace that tore open a floodgate of pleasure. Bliss built inside me and he moved faster, grinding against me as his hands moved, exploring my body, heightening the pleasure until a tightly sprung coil deep inside me started to unravel, to whip through me.

Jase kissed me deeply, and I broke apart, shuddering around him. Spasms racked my body, and he followed quickly, shouting his release, burying his head in the crook of my neck. As one last aftershock jolted my body, my hands slipped lazily down his back as his body still twitched.

Minutes passed before he lifted himself onto his forearms. 'Tess, baby . . .'

Opening my eyes to a beautiful silver pair, I fell in love all over again. 'That . . . that was wonderful.'

We stayed joined together for what felt like forever, before he pulled out from me, quickly moving from the bed and getting rid of the condom in the nearby bin. Seconds later he was stretched out beside me. We lay there, him on his side, me on my back, staring at each other long after our breathing returned to normal.

A lopsided grin appeared. 'You know, that . . . it felt like the first time.' A laugh burst from him as he ducked his head, kissing my shoulder. 'That sounds stupid, doesn't it?'

'No. Not at all.'

'It really did feel like that. I can't even say my first time felt that good, and I thought I'd discovered the key to life then.'

I laughed as I rolled so I was facing him and my breast pressed against his chest. His eyes flared quicksilver as he rested a hand on my bare hip. Closing my eyes, I anticipated a kiss. I didn't have to wait long. He nipped at my bottom lip, and I sighed. 'It sounds perfect.'

'You know what else sounds great?' He shifted closer, and I felt him against my belly. My eyes widened, and a wicked gleam appeared in his eyes as his body slid against mine. The fine coarse hair teased my skin, adding to the sensualness of nothing being between us.

My breath caught. 'Already.'

'I told you I'm always ready when it comes to you.'

'Yeah, but . . . oh!' His hand had wiggled in between my thighs, cupping me.

The grin on his face was pure appeal. 'What about you?'

It was like he controlled a switch to my sex drive. It was wonderfully ridiculous. My hips jerked as he snaked a finger inside. 'What do you think?'

'I think that catch of your breath means yes.' He kissed my damp temple. 'I want you. Again.' His lips then skated over my flushed cheek, capturing my mouth in a deep, searing kiss. 'I want in you. Deep.' Withdrawing his hand, he reached behind him, smacked around until he found a condom in the mess of sheets. A moment later he grasped my hips, lifting me into his lap as he rolled onto his back. The deep growl that rumbled through him sent a flood of heat to my core as his tip pressed into me. 'I want to go so deep you can never get me out. You want that?'

My lashes drifted down as I whispered, 'Yes.'

'Look at me.' His demand was guttural and dangerously seductive. I obeyed without hesitation. His eyes were liquid silver. 'God, you're beautiful like this.' Reaching up, he brushed my hair back over one shoulder and then drew his fingers down to my breast. He cupped me, smoothing a thumb over the hardened tip. 'I don't think I can get enough of this.'

I gripped his shoulders as my toes curled. Inch by slow inch, he guided me down until he'd done just as he'd promised. One thing led to another, and like the first time, it didn't take much to get either of us to the point we were hovering on the edge of release. Even straddling him didn't seem to affect my knee; I was too concentrated on the pressure building in my core as I rocked up and down. We plunged into each other, our bodies straining and reaching together until we both shattered into a million pieces, our names a hoarse shout on each other's lips.

Wrapping his arms around me, Jase drew me tightly to his chest, burying me against him as he jerked against me, running his hand idly up and down my back, tangling in my hair.

I didn't want to ever move. Not when he turned my head gently and his lips were a hot brand against my neck as he whispered the most powerful words I'd ever known. 'I love you.'

Chapter 24

He loved me.

Those whispered words pounded throughout my body, playing over and over again. *He loved me*. It was like a dream come true, a happily every after in romance novels. The boy I crushed on for years, the one I loved, loved *me* in return. And it was the good kind of love, the kind that nurtured and flourished, not hurt and destroyed. The kind of love I saw between my brother and Avery. I no longer had a reason to be envious, because I had that epic love, the Hallmark Channel movie ending.

Hands shaking, I ran them down his sides as the long, lean muscles slowly relaxed and his breathing returned to normal. 'I love you too,' I whispered against the side of his neck, smiling into his damp skin.

The arms around my lower back tensed, and then his hands slid to my hips. He lifted me, gently placing me next to him. He kissed my temple. 'I'll be right back.'

Closing my eyes, I sighed as I curled onto my side. Jase disappeared into the bathroom and then on his way back, he turned off the bedroom light. Climbing into the bed behind me, he wrapped his arms around me.

He didn't speak, and I was okay with that, because he'd said everything that I ever needed to hear from him.

Insides warm and cozy, I drifted off to sleep with what must've been a 'cat ate an entire cage worth of canaries' type of grin. Jase's arms and the way his body was tucked around mine provided a lulling warmth that temporarily held the darkness of the weekend at bay.

I don't know how long I slept and I was sure I didn't dream, but the warmth that had curled along my back was absent and that was what had pulled me out the contented haze of sleep.

As I blinked my eyes open, my vision slowly adjusted. A pale blue light crept into the shadows crowding the bedroom. I reached over, finding that the spot where Jase had been was empty. Still lethargic, I rolled onto my back.

Jase sat at the corner of the bed, elbows resting against his bent knees. His head was propped between his hands, his bare back hunched.

Concern chased away the lingering sleep. I sat up. 'Are you okay?'

He jerked his head up, as if startled out of deep thought. In the low light, his eyes were dark and shadowed. 'Yeah, I just . . . there's something that I forgot to do.'

A little confused, I watched him stand and grab his jeans off the floor. He pulled them up and zipped them, leaving the button open as he turned to me. 'I got to run to the frat. There's some stuff I left there I need for class.'

'Okay.' My brows puckered. 'We can leave early if you want and run by there, so you don't—'

'It's okay.' He bent quickly, swiping his lips across my cheek, and then he pulled back. 'I'll lock the door behind me so you don't have to get up. You still have a couple of hours yet to sleep. I'll pick you up around eight thirty.'

I nodded, feeling suddenly cold inside. 'Sure.'

Jase backed away to the door, turned, and then stopped, glancing back at me. I could barely make out his features. 'Tess . . .'

Air caught in my throat.

He seemed to lower his chin, and I heard the deep breath he took next. 'Thank you for last night.'

Thank you for last night?

I was knocked so speechless that I'd heard the front door open and close before I was even able to open my mouth. He thanked me? Not that there was anything wrong with him thanking me, I guessed, but it seemed like a weird thing to say, especially when hours before he'd said he loved me.

My stomach dipped and then knotted itself right up.

Minutes turned into hours as I sat there in bed, until the pale blue light spread across the floor, chasing away the remnants of night. It's okay, I told myself. I didn't need to read anything into his abrupt departure. He said there was stuff he needed for class and that was all.

But he hadn't said he loved me as he left.

I squeezed my eyes shut, desperately trying to ignore the hollow feeling opening up in my chest, quickly filling with insecurities and doubts.

Everything was okay after what we'd shared last night. I couldn't allow myself to think anything else, because . . . I shook my head fiercely, sending a sharp pain down my neck.

Everything *had* to be okay.

Jase was quiet when he picked me up for classes a few hours later. So was I. I hadn't fallen back asleep and had worked myself into a nervous mess by the time I got into his Jeep. He'd dropped me off in front of Whitehall, and I think we might've spoken about five words to each other.

290

Something was wrong.

But my worry over what was going on with Jase fell to the side by the time I stepped into Whitehall. People were staring. Not because I was on crutches. Groups of two or three would turn to one another. Some whispered. Some didn't.

'She's the one who found her.'

I heard that same statement about four times by the time I made it to history class an hour later.

Calla frowned as she saw me. 'You look like crap.'

'Thanks,' I muttered.

Tucking a strand of blond hair back behind her ear, her frown deepened. 'Sorry. That was a bitchy greeting. Are you okay?'

No. I wasn't okay. For a fuck load of reasons. 'Everyone is staring at me.'

She glanced around the room. A few students up front had been glancing over their shoulders from the moment I sat down. 'No one is looking at you.'

I sent her a dry look, and she cringed. 'Thanks for trying to make me feel better, but everyone is looking at me like I'm some kind of morbid fascination.'

Her eyes narrowed on the boys up front. Both hastily turned back away. 'Ignore them,' she said. 'And they'll stop staring. Or you'll stop caring. Trust me, I know.'

I nodded and put all my effort into ignoring the curious stares of classmates. One would think there'd be nothing exciting about what I had experienced, but it was like people who rubbernecked when they came upon a crash scene.

'So how's the delish Jase doing today?' she asked as we headed out of history, branching into another subject I wasn't wanting to delve into.

'I don't know,' I admitted, adjusting my grips on the

291

crutches. I wanted to toss these mothafuckas into oncoming traffic. 'He was kind of moody and silent today.'

She rolled her eyes. 'So typical of boys. They accuse us of PMSing, but they have more mood swings than a pregnant woman.'

We made it to the connecting spot where the bus would take us to west campus. I glanced around the crowded corner. No one was paying attention to us and I probably shouldn't say anything, but I needed to tell someone. I kept my voice low. 'But we had sex last night.'

Her lips formed a perfect O.

'It was our first time,' I added, feeling my cheeks burn. 'And before you ask, yes, it was great. It was freaking outstanding, but I woke up this morning and he was just sitting there on the bed. He left after that, saying he had something he needed to get from his house and when I saw him this morning, he barely spoke to me.'

She snapped her mouth shut. 'Okay. Did you guys get into an argument or anything?'

'No. Nothing like that.'

'Maybe he really just had to go get something from his house and he's just tired this morning. Or just plain moody,' she said after a few moments. 'Either way, just ask him if he's okay. That's better than standing here stressing yourself out about it. You have enough to be worrying about.'

She was right, but there was nothing about her words that looked like she even convinced herself, and my stomach twisted even further. I just needed to ask him. And I would the first chance I had. I'd ask him if he was okay and he'd tell me everything was fine and I'd just feel stupid afterward for making a big deal out of nothing.

Jase's mood hadn't improved much when he arrived to music. He'd said hi to Calla, smiled at me, and then stared

292

straight ahead, like he was engrossed in what our professor was droning on about. Which was such BS, because I didn't think one person in the entire class had any idea what was going on.

And that smile of his—it had been so tight and never reached his steely gaze. The smile was all wrong. It was fake. It reminded me of Dr. Morgan's smile. It reminded me of the police officers' as they'd ushered me out of their offices.

My palms were sweaty, causing the grip on my pen to slip. I'd scribbled maybe two or three lines during the entire class. After saying good-bye to Calla, I crutched my way to where Jase had parked. He'd taken my bag as usual, putting it on the floor by my feet to make it easier for me to grab.

Not seeing a familiar pink box, I bit down on my lip as I watched him make his way around the front of the Jeep. With the gray toboggan hat pulled low, only the ends of his hair peeked out from underneath it. He hoisted himself up, closing the door behind him. The hard set of his jaw caused my stomach to flop.

My mouth was dry as he backed out and hit the main road leading to east campus. Riddled with anxiety and uncertainty, I used the entire time while he searched for a parking spot near the Byrd Center to work up the nerve to speak.

Hands clasped tightly together, I swallowed hard. 'Is everything okay?'

Jase turned off the engine and pulled the keys out. Sitting back, he lifted his free hand and smoothed it over the toboggan. My muscles seized up as the seconds ticked by in tense silence.

'No,' he said finally, voice so low I thought I heard him incorrectly. 'Everything is not okay.'

I opened my mouth, but anything I was about to say died

on the tip of my tongue when he looked at me. Oh, this was going to be bad. Very bad. I seized up, muscles rigid.

'I don't know how to say this.' He pressed his lips together while a burn picked up in the back of my throat. 'I'm sorry.'

'Sorry for what?' I croaked out. Because he couldn't be sorry for what happened between us. Absolutely no way.

He looked away, tilting his head to the side. 'This is just too much.'

I blinked slowly, feeling like I missed the beginning half of this conversation. 'What is?'

'This,' he stated with force, raising his hands. 'All of this is too much—you and me.'

My nails were leaving little indents in my palms from how tightly I was clenching my hands. 'I . . . I don't understand.' Those words sounded weak and pathetic to my own ears, and the blood drained from my face. 'What's going on?'

'It's too much.' He closed his eyes, features pinched and strained. 'It's too much too soon.'

'What? Us? We're moving too fast?' He thought so because we'd had sex? That seemed wildly out of character for someone with his reputation. I got that he wanted to do things right, and last night had been *right*. 'We can slow down if that's what you think we need—'

'I can't do this,' he interrupted, opening his eyes. 'It's too serious and I thought I was ready for that, but I'm not.'

He thought he wasn't ready? What in the hell was holding him back? I knew about Jack and how it would impact a future with—it occurred to me then as I took my next breath. This wasn't about Jack or us. This was about Jack's *mother*.

'This is about her, isn't it? You're—'

'I'm not talking about her,' he snapped, and something cracked in my chest, a deep fissure that spread throughout, cleaving me in two as he spoke. 'I don't want anything serious. Not with Jack being so young, and I need to focus on graduating, getting a job, and helping raise Jack.'

'And none of that includes me?'

His clouded gaze met mine for an instant. 'It doesn't. It can't. Because I can't go through . . .' His jaw locked down as he gave a quick jerk of his head. 'I'm sorry. Please know I never meant to hurt you. That's the last thing I ever wanted. You have to believe that.'

My chest rose sharply, and it felt like he'd reached inside me and crushed my lungs into a crumbled-up wad of paper. The burn in my chest increased, building behind my eyes. I tried to calm down, but that hurting was raw and real.

'And I know I've hurt you and I'm so fucking sorry for that.' He glanced at me quickly, and he tensed. The crack deepened. 'I'll still pick you up for school and get you to your classes,' he rushed on as I stared at him. 'So I don't want you to worry about that.'

I reared back, pressing against the door as what he was saying finally sunk through the shock. The seat—the floor—dropped out from underneath me. I blinked back hot, stinging tears. 'Just to make sure I understand this. You don't want to be my boyfriend, but you want to be my chauffeur?'

Jase's brows furrowed together. 'I want to be your friend, Tess. Not your chauffeur.'

Sucking in a shallow breath, I turned my attention to the front of the car. My thoughts raced as my stomach continued to do gymnastics. My skin tingled and felt tight.

'I'm sorry—'

'Stop saying that!' A tear rolled down my cheek, and I roughly wiped it away. 'Just stop apologizing, because that makes this so much worse.'

He said nothing as he nodded his acquiescence.

My hands shook as I reached for my bag. Numbly, I

picked up my bag and reached for the door. He didn't try to stop me as I slid out awkwardly, but he looked like he was about to get out to hand over the crutches.

'Don't,' I said, voice hoarse. 'I don't want your help.'

Jase stilled in his seat, nostrils flared. 'But I want to help you, Tess. I want us to—'

'To be friends?' I choked on my laugh. 'Are you serious?'

He looked completely serious.

And that made this so much more screwed up to even think about, and it summed up just how shallow the depth of his feelings was for me. 'We can't be friends. *I* can't be friends with you, because I *love* you, and you've *hurt* me.'

He flinched, and I got no satisfaction out of it. I tugged my crutches free, the motion unsettling me and I stumbled back, dropping my book bag.

'Tess!' He opened the door. 'Goddamnit, let me help you.'

Cursing under my breath and through a sheen of tears, I picked it up and slugged it over my shoulder. He was standing in front of me by then, holding my crutches.

I snatched them away from him, shaking. 'I wish you had decided that this was too much for you *before* we told my brother we were together.' My voice gave out to a strangled sob as I backed away. 'I wish you would've figured this out *before* we made love.'

Jase jerked back, his lips parted.

I turned from him and without looking back, I started away from the Jeep. Not toward the Den, because I couldn't face Cam and Avery. Slamming the crutches into the ground, I focused on a bench near Knutti. I needed to keep it together and I needed to keep calm. Losing it in public would just add to my humiliation.

Oh God, Cam was going to flip out. He was going to—the rubber end of the left crutch snapped off, nearly sending me to the sidewalk.

Frustrated and feeling a thousand other emotions, I evened out my weight on my legs and took the crutches, shoving them into a nearby trash bin. They stuck out like legs, and a couple of people walking by passed me weird looks as I limped across the street, toward an empty bench.

My knee was already throbbing as I sat down, but I didn't care, because it was nothing compared to the feeling inside me. I dug my elbows into my thighs, resting my head against my palms, and squeezed my eyes shut against the rush of blinding tears.

What happened?

Jase had been so perfect this weekend and last night . . . last night had been one of the most amazing experiences of my life. We hadn't screwed. We hadn't fucked. We'd made love. It had been the perfect, the right moment, but . . .

Oh God, was I such a fool that I initiated it? That I had taken words uttered in the moment of heat and passion as being the real thing.

I'd never felt more young or stupid than I did in that moment. In two weeks I'd be nineteen, but I suddenly felt too young and too old.

A cold wind whipped up through the walkway, stirring my hair around me. I shivered, but I barely felt the chilly October air. I curled my fingers in, tangling them with my hair. Tears soaked my lashes and my arms trembled.

I don't know how long I sat there, but I was losing my hold on myself. There was no way I was going to make it through my afternoon classes. Digging out my cell, I sent a text to Calla, begging her to pick me up and take me to my dorm. When she responded that she was on her way, I told her where I was and slipped the cell back into my bag.

Taking a deep breath, I let it out slowly as I let my teary

297

gaze drift over the lawn. I stiffened when I saw Erik standing under the small, bare tree near the sidewalk.

He was staring right back at me.

A fine shiver skated down my spine as he pushed away from the tree, crossing the distance between us with long-legged paces. He was the last person I wanted to deal with, especially considering what I suspected.

As he grew closer, I could see he looked just as bad as I did but for very different reasons. His usually styled hair was a mess, and his face was pale. 'You told the police that I was with Debbie before she . . . before she died.'

Blinking several times, I leaned back and tried to sort out my thoughts enough to hold a conversation I so didn't want to have. 'I told them about the pink scarf and—'

'I wasn't there. She broke up with me as I'm sure you know and were fucking thrilled about.' He bent at the waist, getting right up in my face. So close that I could see the fine lines around the corners of his eyes. 'And you told them that I hit her. You know that's not true.'

Disbelief rocketed through me. Shit on a bull, I knew that was true!

'So if you know what's good for you,' he said, 'keep your fucking mouth shut.'

Chapter 25

'What a dick!' Calla clutched a carton of ice cream we'd found in the fridge. 'Fuck guys. Seriously. Fuck them and not in a good way.'

My eyes were blurry and puffy as I watched her pace. There was a lot about Jase that Calla didn't know and I wouldn't tell her out of respect for his privacy. As much as he hurt me, I wasn't about to announce to the world that he had a son and was most likely still very much in love with the mother of his child.

Because wasn't that what this was really about? He hadn't been ready for something serious, and I knew so very little about this girl, where she lived, if she was in some way still in the picture, or how long the two had been split. Knowing that his heart quite likely belonged to someone else made me feel all the more foolish. The first time he'd refused to talk about her should've been warning enough, and yet, I ignored it.

'Yeah, fuck 'em,' I whispered.

She stopped in front of me, holding out the ice cream. 'More?'

I shook my head, clutching the pillow to my too full stomach.

Sighing, she plopped down next to me. 'I'm so sorry, Teresa. This is the last thing you need right now—your knee, Debbie, and crazy-pants Erik.'

'I guess it could be worse,' I murmured, thinking about how I was never going to be able to sleep in that bed again. I knew it would still carry his scent and I couldn't bear that. Run out of my dorm and my bed, I was about to become close friends with this couch.

Calla gave me a quizzical look. 'I'm pretty sure you've eaten a shit sandwich this last week or so.'

That much was true, but Debbie still had it worse than me. At least I was alive. Closing my eyes, I rubbed my aching brow. 'I don't think I'm ever going to have sex again.'

'Join the club.' She sighed heavily. 'I've sworn off guys.'

I peeked at her. 'Completely?'

She nodded. 'Yep. Life's easier that way.'

'Do you like girls?'

'I wish.' She laughed. 'I just think sex makes things complicated and messy. I mean, yeah, I talk about how hot guys are and make a ton of sexual innuendoes to the point someone probably thinks something's wrong with me, but I've never had sex.'

'What?' I said in a disbelieving voice. 'You're a virgin?'

She laughed again. 'Is it really that shocking? I can't be the only twenty-one-year-old who hasn't had sex.'

'You're not,' I said immediately.

Straightening, she switched the carton of ice cream to her other hand. 'And look at me, Teresa. I don't look like you or Avery. I'm not thin, and I sort of look like the Joker.' She gestured at her scarred face.

My mouth dropped open. 'First off, you're not fat.'

She arched a brow.

I rolled my eyes. 'And you do not look like the Joker, you dumbass. You're really pretty.' And that part was true.

300

Scar or not, Calla was really pretty. 'I can't believe you said that.'

Shrugging, she stood. 'Enough about me and my lack of sex and whatnot; is what you told me all that Erik said to you?'

The change of subject threw me for a loop. 'Yeah, that's pretty much it.'

'Are you going to the police?'

I shook my head. 'He didn't do anything I can report. What he said really wasn't a threat—what he said was what anyone would probably say if someone cast suspicion on them.'

'Yeah, but I don't like what he said to you.'

'Neither do I.' I rubbed my hands across my face again.

Calla left for the kitchen, tossing the ice cream in the garbage. When she returned, she curled up beside me, remote in hand. 'Let's watch some bad TV. I'm pretty sure that cures all.'

Bad TV might cure a lot of things, but I knew it wouldn't fix what was ailing me. I wasn't sure what could. I'd given my body and my heart to Jase and he had handed them back.

A few things became clear by the end of the week. If the police suspected that Erik was guilty of anything other than being a shitty human being, it didn't show. I saw him around campus and he didn't look like a guy who had the police breathing down his neck or was about to be arrested for murder at any given second.

Maybe my suspicions were totally off the mark, but I avoided Erik at all costs, even if it meant crossing the street when I didn't have to or turning and walking in the other direction. Even if he hadn't hurt Debbie this time, he had in the past.

The other thing was that there was no keeping the fact that Jase and I were not together from Cam and Avery. By Friday, when I guessed neither of us showed up for lunch in the Den for the third time, they suspected something was up.

Cam cornered me when he'd come over to grab some extra clothes. I was sitting on the couch watching a marathon of *Dance Moms*, an open bag of Cheetos on the coffee table and two empty soda cans keeping me company.

He sat beside me, dropping his hands between his knees. 'So . . .?'

I exhaled loudly.

'Yeaah,' he said slowly. 'So what the hell is up with you and Jase? You two haven't been coming to the Den. At first I thought ya'll just wanted some privacy, which, by the way, irked me, but I haven't seen his Jeep here since Sunday morning.'

Debating if I should draw this out or just get it over with, I tugged the quilt our grandmother had made for Cam a few years back up to my chin. 'We're not together,' I said, like ripping a Band-Aid off. I laughed then, the sound dry. 'I don't even think the couple of days we were together really counts as being in a relationship. I'm pretty sure Britney Spears and Kim Kardashian have been married longer than we were together.'

I thought that last bit was pretty damn funny, but Cam looked like someone just died in front of us. 'I knew it. That son of a—'

'I really don't want to hear that right now.' I turned to him, and whatever he saw in my face caused him to shut up. 'Whatever happened between us shouldn't affect your friendship.'

'How can it not? Look at you!' He glanced around the room, gaze landing on the bag of junk food and soda cans.

He sent a pointed glare at the TV, right when a small girl burst into tears. 'You're my baby sister and you're obviously sitting here heartbroken. I knew he would fuck this up and he had to have known it too.'

'How did you know, Cam?'

He opened his mouth and he closed it.

My smile was weak. 'I know—I know about Jack. Everything.'

Shock flickered across his face as he sat back. 'He told you everything?'

I nodded. 'Yeah, he told me. Is that why you knew he'd fuck up? Because he has a kid or because he's still in love with Jack's mother?' I was just throwing the last part out there. I didn't really know for a hundred percent that he was in love with her still, but it seemed that way. By the way Cam's eyes widened even more, I feared I hit it right on the nail.

'He told you about Kari?'

'Her name's Kari?' I asked.

Cam stared at me a moment then looked away. Several seconds passed. 'So he didn't tell you about her? I guessed as much as he told you about Jack, but he didn't say anything about her?'

'No.' I swallowed, lowering the quilt by an inch. 'When he told me about Jack, he wouldn't talk about her and when he . . . when he said we couldn't be together, he said it was because he wasn't ready for something serious.' I was so leaving out the sex part, because as far as Cam knew, our relationship hadn't progressed to that part. If Cam knew it had and that Jase had called things off the day afterward, he would do more than punch him. 'I asked if it was about her, but he still wouldn't talk about her. I think . . . I think he's still in love with her.'

Cam ran his hand through his hair, causing several

303

strands to stick straight up. 'Shit, Teresa, I don't know what to say.'

A ball of ice formed in my stomach. 'Yeah, you do, but you just don't want to say it. You know about her, and he's still in love with her, isn't he? That's why you didn't want us to be together. She is—'

'Was,' he correctly quietly. 'Her name was Kari and I'm sure Jase loved her, loved her in a way that any sixteen-or-so-year-old guy could love his girlfriend.'

My brain got hung up on the past tense. Not the loved part being in the past but the reference to her. 'What do you mean by "was," Cam?'

He blew out a long breath. 'I've never told another soul any of this, Teresa. I don't know if Jase even realizes that he told me all about her. We were drunk one night and got to talking, you know, back when I was on house arrest. He never brought her up again. He'll talk to me about Jack, but not her.'

The ball of ice was starting to spread for a different reason. 'Cam . . .'

'She's dead, sis. She died shortly after Jack was born, in a car accident.'

I smacked my hand over my throat as I stared at my brother. 'Oh, my God . . .'

'I don't know a lot about her parents, but I think they were kind of like Avery's—very concerned about perception and shit. I got the impression that they sent her away when she got pregnant and had wanted her to give Jack up, but Jase's parents stepped in. I know Jase and Kari were together since they were thirteen or so. And I do know that he cared very deeply for her and as long as I've known Jase, he's never been serious about another girl.'

My chest ached as it all started to click together. The girl . . . Jack's mother was dead? That had never crossed my

304

mind. At all. But it made sense. Holy crap, what was worse than having someone break your heart? Having your heart broken because someone died.

'The fact that Jase even told you about Jack blows my mind. No one but his family knows the truth, and I don't think her family lives around here anymore,' he explained. 'Once I realized he'd told you, I backed off, because I knew he was for real if he told you. At least, I hoped he was, but . . .'

'But he hasn't gotten over her, has he?' I said, hurting for him, because I could not imagine what it must be like to lose someone I loved to something so final. 'That's why. Oh, my God . . .'

'I don't know, Teresa. I'm not sure he's still in love with her. I mean, I'm sure he does in a way, but I think . . . God, he'll kill me for this, but I think he's scared of caring for someone else and then losing them.'

'Really?' Doubt colored my tone.

'Look at it this way. He didn't have a normal situation. They were young and she got pregnant. Her parents sent her away and then his folks step in and adopt the kid. So both of them—Jase and Kari—saw Jack afterward, knowing that's their son, but no one else does. It was their secret and who knows what they planned for the future.'

I knew what Jase had said about not wanting Jack at first, but that had changed afterward. And it could've changed while Kari was still around.

'And then she dies, completely unexpectedly and *young*. Those kinds of situations, wrapped all together, have got to mess with someone. So I don't think he's still in love with her. I think he's scared of loving someone else.'

'Then that would have to mean that he loves me, and I don't think that's the case.'

He smiled a little. 'He risked my wrath to get with you

and he told you about Jack. I'm telling you what, Teresa. He has to have—'

'It doesn't matter,' I cut him off, because I didn't need to hear that Jase potentially loved me. It would just fill my head with fairy tales and my chest with hope. What Jase had said to me after having sex was nothing more than a product of an orgasm. 'I can't compete with Kari. No one can.'

'Teresa—'

'I don't want you saying anything to him,' I insisted. 'I'm serious, Cam. I know you want to thump him upside the head or something, but please let it go, because . . .' Because I truly felt bad for him. Knowing about Kari made this different. Didn't mean I wasn't upset with him, because he had hurt me, but he had been hurt in one of the worst ways. 'Because it doesn't matter and I'm okay.'

His brows rose. 'You don't look okay.'

I glanced down at the tentlike quilt. 'Thanks.'

'I didn't mean it like that.' He patted in the general vicinity of my good knee. 'I'm just worried about you. You've been through a lot.'

'I'm okay, but you've got to promise you won't say anything to him. Just leave it alone. Please, Cam.'

He sighed. 'Okay. I won't say anything. You were right earlier when you said it's not any of my business, but seeing how upset you are and not slamming my—'

'I get it,' I said, smiling slightly. 'You can't always take care of things for me, you know?'

Cam laughed. 'Says who?'

Shaking my head, I settled back. Having a little more background on what made Jase tick helped, but it didn't make the heartache any better. Kind of made it all the more sad.

At the sound of a knock on the door, Cam rose. 'That's probably going to be Avery. You up for some girl time?'

'Girl time?'

He made a face. 'Whatever. You want her in?'

'Sure.' Hanging out with someone was better than sitting here alone feeling sorry for myself.

If Avery knew what was going on, she wisely chatted about everything and anything else while she coaxed me off the couch and helped me straighten the apartment. The place was a mess. Partly not my fault. Cam had vacuumed and dusted around the time the president was last inaugurated.

'I've heard that Debbie's funeral is next Tuesday,' she said, tying her coppery hair up in a messy ponytail. 'Are you okay?'

I nodded as I tossed the rag I'd used to dust off the nightstand into the little waste bin. 'Calla's dropping me off, and she's gonna pick me up when it's done. She doesn't do funerals.'

'Neither do I.' She bent over, picking up a bag resting on the closet floor. 'I don't think Cam's going, but if you want him there, I'm sure he'll go.'

I knew he would, but I wasn't going to force him to go to a funeral he wasn't planning on attending.

Avery suddenly stood ramrod straight as she opened up the department store bag. Over her shoulder I saw it was full of shoes I hadn't gotten around to unloading yet, which reminded me there was still a lot of stuff I needed to get out of the dorm.

Curious about what she was staring at, I hobbled around her. 'What's up?'

Wordlessly, she reached inside and pulled out my old pair of ballet shoes. 'I haven't held a pair of these in forever.'

Seeing them sent a pang through me. I turned and sat on the bed. 'Well, we're about the same shoe size. Probably

307

have roughly the same fit. You can have them if you want.'

'Don't you want to keep them?'

I shrugged. 'I don't know. You can borrow them. How about that?'

She glanced down at the satiny slippers and sighed a little. A wistful look crossed her face and my curiosity grew. 'Why don't you dance anymore, Avery?'

Her gaze lifted and her cheeks reddened. 'It's just a long story that's not really important right now. It doesn't matter. I probably couldn't even lift my leg now, let alone do a simple ballet move.'

'I bet you could,' I said instead of pushing her for more details.

She laughed it off, but her eyes lit up with something akin to excitement, like maybe she wanted to try. 'I'd probably pull a muscle.'

'No you won't.' My knee started to stiffen so I gingerly stretched it out. 'Try it.'

The slippers dangled from her fingertips. 'I'll look like an idiot.'

'It's only me here and I haven't even showered today. Also, I can't walk without a limp, so I'm pretty sure you don't have to worry about impressing me.'

She hesitated and then crossed the room, placing the slippers on the bed beside me. 'If you laugh, I might cry.'

'I won't laugh!' But I did smile. 'Come on. Just do it.'

Stepping back, Avery looked around the room, checking out the space as she toed off her shoes. She took a deep breath as she kicked a leg up. Closing her eyes, she planted her sock-clad foot on the inside of her thigh and twirled once and then twice, extending her leg out elegantly. Even on carpet, in jeans and out of commission for years, the girl had a natural-born talent that every studio-taught dancer envied.

308

When she completed the turn, I clapped loudly. 'That was perfect!'

Her face was flushed as she straightened out her shirt. 'It wasn't. My leg—'

'Oh my God, you haven't danced in years and you did the turn better than most of the people who haven't stopped.' I picked up the ballet shoes. 'You have to get on a stage. Even if it's just with me at the Learning Arts Center. Just once.'

'I don't know—'

'You have to!' I wiggled the shoes, and her gaze followed them like I was dangling something shiny in her face. I don't know how I knew this, but I did know that getting her to dance again was important. 'You need to. So I can live vicariously through you. Just once before spring semester. Please.'

Avery took a deep breath as she eyed me. 'What's in it for me?'

'What do you want?'

Her lips pursed. 'I want two things. First being you help me find a gift for Cam for Christmas, because I suck at that kind of stuff.'

I chuckled. 'All right, that's totally doable. What's the second thing?'

'You have to babysit Michelangelo and Raphael this weekend.'

'The turtles?'

She grinned as she nodded. 'We're getting this one large habitat, so, you know, they can . . . I don't know, head bob at each other and Cam wanted to go to this movie, but I'm afraid they're going to kill each other.'

'So you want me to be like a turtle bouncer? Break them up if one of them gets out of hand?'

Avery giggled. 'Exactly.'

I laughed. 'Okay. Deal.' I wiggled the shoes at her.

She snatched them up. 'Oh, and I'm pretty sure Michelangelo is a girl, so try to stop them if they happen to look like they're getting it on. Cam and I aren't ready to be parents to a bunch of baby turtles.'

Groaning, I flopped on my back. 'Oh God . . .'

Chapter 26

The sun was out, shining brightly, but it didn't chase away the chill in the air the morning of Debbie's funeral.

As Calla had promised, she'd dropped me at the start of the service, and once the graveside part was done, I'd text her. She'd taken me to class last week, but Cam started taking me to class this week and hadn't taken no for an answer.

I really needed to get a car.

It helped as I stood back from the gravesite to focus on stupid, mundane things. I'd never been good at funerals. When my grandpappy passed away, I'd been too wigged out to get near the coffin. Not much had changed. The coffin hadn't been opened, but I'd sat at the back of the packed church at the cemetery grounds.

My knee ached from the walk to the gravesite, but whatever pain was worth it. I felt like I needed to be here for Debbie, and if I hadn't been, I would've regretted it.

Her parents looked like they were in a daze, huddled together along with a younger boy who looked like he'd just entered high school. I couldn't imagine what they were going through or what they could be thinking.

Off to their right was Erik Dobbs, and he was surrounded by what appeared to be every member of his fraternity. I didn't know if Jase was among them; the crowd of guys dressed in wrinkled suits was too thick.

It wasn't hard to tell apart the students from the family members. We were the ones dressed in something—anything—black. I'd pulled on leggings this morning and a dark blue sweater dress. It didn't seem like the best thing to wear to a funeral, but it was all I had handy.

As the graveside service drew to a close, I was surprised to find my lashes damp. I'd been doing so well, keeping my face relatively dry through the whole service, even when they played that one country song that was always played during sad moments. I hastily wiped at my cheeks with chilled hands as I turned.

A hand clamped down on my shoulder, spinning me around. I almost put my weight on my bad leg, but corrected myself at the last minute. Heart pounding in surprise, I lifted my gaze.

Erik stood there, his dark eyes fastened on mine. 'What are you doing here?'

I shook his grip off my shoulder or at least tried to. His hand tightened for a second and then he let go, but he didn't back up. 'Don't touch me ever again,' I said, voice low.

Something dark and ugly flashed across his face. 'You shouldn't be here. She's dead and in that coffin because of you.'

Gaping, I jerked back from him. 'Excuse me?'

'She's dead because you filled her head with bullshit.' His voice rose, drawing the attention of those standing nearby. 'If you had just minded your own business instead of trying to stir up drama, she'd be alive right now.'

Blood drained from my face as I stared into his. Was he crazy? My stomach rolled as I noticed that more people were staring—fellow students. 'I wasn't stirring up drama and you know that.'

Erik shook his head. 'It's your fault.'

'Hey man,' one of his friends said, stepping forward. 'I think we need to get you home.'

'I think she needs to leave,' he sneered. 'She of all people shouldn't—'

Erik was spun away from me in the same manner he'd turned me around. I had no idea where Jase came from, but he was suddenly standing there, his hand clamped down on Erik's shoulders, his face inches from his.

'I know you got a lot on your mind,' Jase said, voice low and dangerously calm. 'But I suggest you walk away from her right now before you say anything you're going to regret.'

He opened his mouth, but Jase shook his head. 'Walk away, brother.'

For a second I didn't think Erik was going to, but he nodded curtly. Shaking off Jase's hand, he spun away without looking back at me, pushing through the crowd of his frat brothers. None of them went after him that I could see. If anything, they looked disgusted with his behavior.

Jase cupped my elbow as he lowered his head toward mine. 'Where are your crutches?' he demanded.

I shot him a pissy look, which he ignored. 'Not that it's any of your business, but I tossed them in the garbage.'

He stared at me. 'You threw them in the garbage?'

'Yeah, I did.' A little slow on the uptake, anger from what Erik had said to me flooded my system. Unfortunately for Jase, he was the one there. 'And I don't need you getting involved there. I had it under control.'

'Totally looked that way.' He started walking, and with his hand firmly around my arm, it left me little choice but to walk with him. 'I'm taking you home.'

'Calla is going to take me home.'

'Text her and tell her you have a ride.' When I didn't respond, he shot me a look. His eyes were a deep, thunderous shade of gray. 'Please don't argue with me, Tess. I just want to get you home. Okay? I just want to make sure you're not standing around alone waiting for Calla to come get you.'

Part of me wanted to dig my heels in, but I was being stupid. The last thing I wanted to do was stand out in the cold waiting for her while Erik was slinking around, ready to point a finger at me for something I had absolutely nothing to do with.

'Okay,' I said finally, pulling out my cell. 'You don't need to hold my arm, though.'

His eyes flared in color. 'What if I want to?'

I stopped, forcing him to come to a standstill. Our gazes locked. 'You don't have the right to touch me, Jase.'

He dropped his hand immediately. 'Sorry.'

As we started to his Jeep, I sent Calla a quick text letting her know I had a ride. When we got inside his car, he asked again about the crutches.

'What?' I yanked the seat belt with all my power and clicked myself in. 'I don't need them forever.'

'The doctor said—'

'I needed them for a few days or a week, depending on if I was relying on them.' I hated remembering that he'd been there that day—had been there for me only to crush my heart a few days later, no matter how tragic the why behind his reasoning was. 'I don't need them.'

'You *limped* the whole way to the gravesite and to the car.'

'You were watching me?'

'Yeah, I was.' His gaze flicked over my face and then settled straight ahead. 'I kept an eye on you almost the whole time. You didn't seem to notice.'

I didn't know what to think about that. 'I didn't see you.'

'I was standing in the back, by the door. I bowed out before people started walking out,' he explained. 'Anyway, did Erik hurt you? He turned you around pretty quickly.'

I shook my head and then realized he wasn't looking at me. 'No.'

'I would've gotten there quicker, so I'm sorry about that.' He finally turned the engine on and cool air blasted out of the vent. Neither of us spoke until we were on Route 45 heading back to Shepherdstown. 'He needs to stay away from you. I'm going to make sure he does—hey, I'm not going to beat on him or anything crazy, okay? He just needs to not pull any shit like that again.' He cut me a sharp look. 'That was the first time he said anything to you?'

'Why?' I asked. 'Why do you even care, Jase, what he says to me?'

Another razor-edged look was cast in my direction. 'That's a stupid question.'

'No, it's not. We aren't friends. We were two people who were a little more than friends for a very short period of time and we had sex.' My heart turned over from my own words. 'That's all we were.'

Jase clenched the steering wheel. 'Is that what you think of us?'

'Isn't that what you want?'

He didn't answer immediately, and when he did, it was so low I wasn't sure I heard him right. 'No.'

I sucked in a sharp breath. 'No?'

'That's not what I wanted from us. God, Tess, not at all.' He propped his left arm on the driver's window and pressed his cheek into his fist. 'But I'm just . . . I told you before you didn't want to get with me.'

A burn encompassed my chest and throat as I stared at

his profile. 'I know,' I whispered, and I hoped he didn't get too upset with Cam. 'I know about Kari.'

His jaw clamped down so fast and hard I wouldn't have been surprised if he cracked his molars. A mile passed before he spoke. 'I don't even have to ask how you know.'

'Please don't be mad at him. He thought I already knew, because I knew about Jack. You can't get mad at him.'

'I'm not.' He sighed heavily. 'So you know the whole sordid tale then.'

'I . . . I didn't think it was sordid.' I bit my lip. I knew what Jase had said about not wanting Jack at first and now his guilt made even more sense, because what if Kari had wanted Jack down the road? 'It was just sad.'

'Oh, I must not have told him everything.' He coughed out a laugh. 'When Kari got pregnant, I wasn't there for her when she told her parents. I should've been. I knew they would be hard on her and when they said they were going to send her to her grandparents down in southern West Virginia, I was kind of relieved, because it was like if she wasn't there, I didn't have to think about the fact that she was pregnant.'

He laughed again, but it was such a sad sound. 'I was never there for her. You know, I was just a kid, but still . . .'

'But you were—what? Sixteen?'

He nodded. 'When my parents stepped in and adopted Jack, and Kari came back, she talked about a future with all three of us. Scared the shit out of me. We got into an argument. She drove off and she died. End of story right there.'

Oh my God . . .

'You don't blame yourself. Please tell me you don't.'

'I did for a long time, but I know I didn't cause the accident. We'd sort of made out before she left, but you

316

know, the last conversation you have with someone, you don't want it filled with shit like that.'

'I'm sorry,' I whispered. 'I know that's not a lot, but I'm sorry.'

Jase didn't say anything again until we reached the apartment buildings. 'I haven't even visited her grave.'

I pulled myself out of my own thoughts. 'Not once?'

He shook his head. 'I just . . . I don't know. I've moved on, but . . .'

'You haven't moved on, Jase. If you haven't been able to visit her grave, you haven't moved on.'

We pulled into a parking spot in the middle of the lot. He turned off the engine and looked at me. His gaze dropped to my lips, and he seemed unable to drag his attention from them. The hand on the steering wheel tightened.

'Do you still love her?' I whispered.

Jase didn't answer for a long moment. 'I will always love Kari. She was a great person. I don't know where we'd be right now if she had lived, but I will always care for her.' His chest rose slowly. He looked like he was about to say more, but changed his mind.

I recalled what Cam had said about him being scared. Maybe that really was it. Maybe he did love me, but it wouldn't be enough. Some wounds, festered by silence, ran too deep. And there would be nothing I could do to change him and how he saw relationships. He had to find that in himself and he had to *want* to. And I hoped he did. Not just for my sake, but because, even though the wound he'd left on my heart was fresh and bleeding, he was a good man.

He just needed to sort himself out.

As I watched him work through what to say, I did what was probably the most mature thing I'd ever done in my almost nineteen years. Like earn-a-medal-or-a-box-of-cookies type of mature, because I was still hurting so badly when it came to him.

I leaned across the seat and pressed my lips against his cool cheek. Jase sucked in a sharp breath and turned a wild gaze on me as I pulled back. 'I'm sorry for everything you've had to go through and I . . . I still love you, so I hope one day you're able to move on, because you deserve that, Jase Winstead.'

Chapter 27

Living in Cam's apartment should've made life better. It did in a lot of ways. Staying there made it easier to avoid fixating on Debbie's death or living somewhere that creeped the bejesus out of me. It helped with steering clear of crazy-sauce Erik. I caught rides to campus with either Avery or my brother, and since my knee rarely hurt as badly as it did in the beginning, the trek from music over to east campus wasn't a big deal.

Not that I was eating lunch with Cam and everyone anymore. I didn't know if Jase was. I doubted it since I was sure my brother had gone off on his friend once he realized we weren't together any longer. But I couldn't deal with it and pretend everything was dandy if Jase was there, so I stayed far away from the Den.

It was bad enough seeing him three times a week in music and then every so often around campus. He never spoke to me. Never once approached me to see how I was doing after the funeral. And it was stupid and pointless to allow this ache to fester and spread. Kari was a ghost. She was in the past, but Jase had loved her. They had brought a child into this world and ghost or not, I could not rid myself of the pain.

319

But it was more than just Jase. It seemed like it finally had sunk in—that my dream of being a professional dancer was truly over and that school was my future, which meant I had a lot of catching up on the taking-school-seriously thing, which stressed me out.

I was drained like an overeager blood donor by the time finals rolled around.

Dark shadows had bloomed under my eyes. Some days they were swollen, because late at night, when I'd wake up and there was nothing but silence, the tears would come. It was embarrassing knowing that Cam and Avery knew I'd been crying. I looked like crap. Wasn't like I could hide it.

Over Thanksgiving, when Cam and Avery left to visit our parents, I'd gone with them to just get away. The trip had been good for me and Mom had loaded us up with baked goodies—the first apple pie of the season, two pumpkin rolls, and fresh bread. Cam had looked like he'd won the lottery, and I had checked out my ever-expanding ass and sighed. But when it had come time to return to Shepherdstown, the reprieve ended.

I hadn't wanted to go back, because it felt like there was nothing there but sadness for me now.

Right before we'd left, I'd gone upstairs to my bedroom to grab a couple of sweaters I hadn't taken with me in August. I'd gotten lost in staring at all the trophies lining my bookshelves, the ribbons hanging from the walls, and the sparkling crowns that had been given out during some competitions.

I'd picked up almost every trophy and tried to remember what it had felt like when my name had been called for first place or best overall, but the emotions had seemed cut off from me—a well I couldn't access.

'You okay?'

I'd put a trophy back in its place and turned at the sound of Mom's voice. I nodded as I wiped the tears off my cheeks with the back of my hands. When I'd started crying, I didn't know.

A sad, sympathetic smile appeared on her lips as she'd crossed the room. Her bright blue eyes were shining in a way that made me want to cry harder. Cupping my cheeks, she'd brushed away a few tears that had lingered. 'It will get easier, baby. I promise you.'

'Which part?' I'd mumbled. She'd known about Debbie, of course, and I'd told her about Jase—*everything* about Jase. We'd decided to keep that part from Dad if Jase ever decided to visit home with Cam. That wasn't likely, but if Dad had known that his little princess's heart was broken, he probably would've taken Jase out for hunting and had an 'accident' during it.

'Everything—it will get better. I know that's hard to believe now,' she'd said. 'But eventually you'll find something else to be passionate about and you'll find someone who will love you like you deserve.'

'Jase deserves to love me. I mean, he's not a bad guy,' I'd said, sniffling. 'At least, I thought he did.'

Mom had pulled me into her arms and she'd smelled of pumpkin and spice, making it even harder to leave. I wanted to be that little girl again, the one who didn't have to pull up her big girl panties and deal with the shit sandwich that was life.

'The young man has a lot on his plate.' She'd squeezed me the way I loved. 'He reminds me of this guy I knew in med school. He'd been involved with this girl for years and she'd died unexpectedly over summer break. I think it was a heart issue.' Mom had pulled back, grasping my cold hands. 'But it's been how long? Decades? I still see him every so often and he's never married and I don't think he's ever been in a long-term relationship. And Jase . . . well, he had a child with this girl. It's even more difficult for us to really understand.

Hearing that really didn't make me feel any better. Even if Jase didn't want me, I still wanted him to move on, to find love again and to have a life that he shared with someone. I didn't want to think of him like Mom's friend, spending years alone with nothing more than casual relationships and not letting anyone close.

Jase deserved better than that, because deep down, he was a good guy who was just . . . messed up in a way I couldn't fathom.

I'd forced myself to go to sleep early the Sunday we returned, but it was like every night recently. I'd only be asleep for a few hours before I'd start to dream. Some nights I dreamed of Debbie in the dorm, of her . . . *hanging* in the dorm. There were nights where I was back at the funeral again and instead of Erik yelling at me, he'd push me into the open grave.

And other times, I dreamed of Jase. Of him loving me and telling me that he'd always be there for me. Those dreams weren't bad until I woke up and realized that that's what they were. Just dreams. Then there were dreams where we were stuck in a strange house and I'd call out his name, but he never seemed to hear as he walked through doors and I could never catch him.

Every morning I'd wake up feeling like I hadn't slept at all and I went through the semester's last classes in a fog. Still, I'd breezed through most of my finals. Considering I'd had a crap ton of free time on my hands, I'd done a lot of studying while I was alone in the apartment. And eating. But the studying had me more than prepared, which was great, because this was my future. Maybe not the one I'd planned, but the one I needed to accept. And teaching wouldn't be bad. I'd enjoy it. So passing my finals was a big deal.

My muscles tensed as Calla and I entered music and took our seats. Her cheeks were ruddy from the cold, making the scar stand out. Rubbing her hands together, she huddled down in her seat.

'I can't deal with this cold,' she said, shivering. 'When I finish college, I am so moving to Florida.'

'A few months ago you were saying you couldn't deal with the heat.' I pulled out a pen, ready to be done with this class. Like for real. 'You should probably find a place that has the same kind of lukewarm temp all year-round.'

Her lips puckered up. 'That's a good idea. Now just finding a place like that. What about you?'

Graduation was so far off I couldn't even think about it. I shrugged. 'Probably stay around here, I guess.'

She sighed as she reached over, tugging on the hem of my hoodie. It was then when I realized I'd worn the same Old Navy hoodie the last three days. Wait. Did I even shower this morning? I didn't think so. I did brush my hair before I pulled it up in a messy pony.

Nice.

'Come over to my dorm tonight?' she asked, like she'd been asking for the last two weeks. 'We can get a bunch of junk food—make a run to Sheetz. You know my love of their nachos.'

I started to tell her no, but stopped myself. I needed to pull my head out of my ass. At least for a few hours. 'Okay, but can you pick me up? It's too cold to walk over the field at night.'

'Of course!' A wide smile broke out over her face—a

323

breathtaking smile. 'Yay! And I'll get beer, because nothing like supporting underage drinking. Or I can get some of those girlie hard lemonades. Bitch, I'm gonna get you so drunk you don't . . .' She trailed off, lips thinning.

'You're gonna take advantage of me?' I joked, and when she didn't laugh, I sighed. But then I felt eyes on me and I looked over. The air froze in my lungs.

Jase stood at the end of the aisle, dressed in a hoodie and worn jeans. He had that damn gray toboggan on, the one I loved so much. I wanted to rip it off his head and do something crazy, like stash it under my pillow or something.

I cringed inwardly.

Good thing I only had insanity-sauce thoughts and didn't actually act on them.

Seeing him, just like every time I saw him, was so fucking hard. Even before we got together it had been bad, but it was so much worse now knowing what it was like to be in his arms, to feel his skin against mine, and to know his kisses. Harder yet was trying to reconcile his kindness, good humor, and protectiveness with this Jase—the same one who'd dropped me after our very first kiss.

I got that he had baggage, but I wouldn't have run from dealing with it. I would've *helped* him once I wrapped my head around it all. I would've loved him nonetheless.

The pen slipped out of my fingers and rolled onto my lap. A knot formed in my chest as he shifted his weight. He looked like he wanted to say something, but I couldn't imagine what it would be since he'd been avoiding me like I was a bad case of herpes.

'Tess,' he said. My entire body tensed at the sound of his deep voice, and I closed my eyes.

Hearing him say my name . . . I forced the tears welling up in my eyes to dry when I reopened them. It hurt, because the boy . . . the boy broke my heart.

Calla stiffened, and I knew she was seconds from going mama bear all over his ass.

And he must've sensed it too, because his thundercloud-colored eyes shifted to her and then back to me. Whatever he was about to say was lost to the forever and never going to happen. He gave his head a quick shake and then pivoted on his heel and walked several rows down, taking a seat.

My gaze was fixed on the back of his head, on the way the ends of his hair curled up over the edges of the toboggan.

'Forget him,' Calla said.

But I couldn't. I couldn't ever *just* forget him.

'I mean it, Teresa. You deserve a guy that doesn't bail on you and ignore you for weeks.'

'I know,' I whispered, studying the back of his head, easily recalling what it felt like to let his hair sift through my fingers. 'Doesn't make it any easier.'

Calla didn't say anything, because what I said was the truth.

Heart heavy and chest aching so badly I wanted to just throw myself down and cry under the chairs, I turned my attention to my music final, determined not to fail because of Jase.

And to not shed another tear because of him.

After my last final, I trekked over to West Woods. Since I wasn't planning on hanging around in Cam's apartment during winter break all by myself like a total loser—instead I was going home to mommy and daddy like a total loser—there were still a few things I needed to get out of my dorm since I was planning on staying in Cam's apartment next semester.

Even though Cam said he had no problem with me staying there, I needed to get a jobbie job and contribute something to the rent. And a job would help keep me distracted. Between not being able to dance, Deb's death and Erik, and now Jase, I needed something to focus on bad until my brain and heart moved on.

That didn't seem like it would happen anytime soon.

Cold wind chilled my cheeks, and the scent of snow was in the air as I crossed the lawn leading up to the dorms. My knee ached a little by the time I reached the lobby of Yost. With most kids already on their way home, the main room was pretty quiet with the exception of a few people lounging on the couches.

Digging out the key card from my backpack while I waited for the elevator, I tried to ignore the tightness between my shoulder blades. I hadn't been back to the dorm since that horrible night. I didn't want to go in our room, but I needed to get my stuff out and Cam would be over in an hour to load up his truck.

And I needed to act like a grown adult. There was nothing wrong with the dorm, and I seriously doubted the room was haunted. Bad vibes were expected, but I could spend the next however many minutes necessary to grab my remaining stuff.

Emboldened by my pep talk, I stepped into the elevator and rode it up to my floor. As I made it out to the hallway, my phone chirped, signaling that I had received a text. Thinking it was Calla or Cam, I pulled it out of the front pocket on my bag and nearly tripped.

Coming w/ Cam to help. Need to talk to u.

That was all the text from Jase said, but my heart was pounding and my stomach dipping as if the text had said much more than that. Like the text had read: I'm a fucking turd and I made a big mistake and I'll love you a long time.

Except the text hadn't said all that, but he *was* coming to help Cam. And that had to mean he'd gotten my brother's permission and that *also* meant he had to have said something that made Cam agree. Which would've been hard considering I'd been a hot mess and that was partly his doing.

I stopped in front of my dorm suite, my pulse skyrocketing from the buzz of elation. *Don't read into it,* I told myself. Just because he was coming over to help and he wanted to talk didn't mean anything. And I also shouldn't be as excited as I was. I reeked of desperation. Should I even tell him he could help? Part of me wanted to tell him no, but then I'd spend the rest of the night punching myself in the face. We did need to talk . . . and I wanted to talk to him.

My hand shook as I sent back a completely calm and unenthused *Ok.*

His response was almost immediate, tripping up my heart. *See u soon.*

Forcing out a breath I wasn't holding, I slipped my phone back into my bag. With Cam present, this was sure to make the awkward hall of fame list, but there was no denying the jubilation building despite that pesky thing called common sense.

I swiped my keycard and pushed thoughts of the upcoming visit from Jase out of my head as I opened the door to the suite and stepped inside, letting the door slide shut behind me.

My gaze crawled over the suite. Nothing looked different. One pillow was on the couch, the other was on the floor, under the coffee table. A musky smell lingered, a residue of the humid summer. The door to the suitemates' room—to Steph—was most likely locked. Although she'd helped me out the night of Deb's death, I hadn't really seen her around, and I didn't want to think of her, because when I did, I thought about how she used to hook up with Jase.

And that made me wonder if they were hooking up now.

A knot twisted in my stomach at that thought, and I cursed under my breath. I was literally my own worst enemy.

Dropping my bag on the couch, I swiped my card again and opened the bedroom door. I blinked as I sucked in a sharp breath. My heart kicked into overdrive. At first I thought the lack of sleep and stress was causing me to hallucinate. I didn't believe what I was seeing. I blinked again, but nothing changed.

Erik sat on Debbie's bed.

Chapter 28

Tingles skipped between my shoulder blades and then raced down my spine. Erik was in here. What was he doing in here? In his lap, he was holding something—a sweater. Understanding burgeoned. It was one of Debbie's sweaters.

Gone was the stylish coifed hair and clothing. Everything about Erik was messy and wrinkled. Dark bruises sunk his eyes in. Lines appeared around his lips like thin cracks in marble. Scruff covered his cheeks, telling me he hadn't seen a razor in days.

Our eyes met and locked, sending a series of chills down my back. Something in his gaze punched a hole through my chest.

'What are you doing here?' he asked, voice flat.

I was too dumbfounded to question why he was asking me that. 'I . . . I needed to get the rest of my things from my room.'

Erik looked around the dorm room slowly. All Debbie's stuff had been removed. The bed was made, blankets folded over, but the pillow was flat, as if someone had been lying on it. The closet door was open, revealing what was left of my clothes and my books.

'You couldn't stay in here?'

The accusation in his voice snapped me out of my stupor. My eyes swung back to his sharply. 'No. I couldn't. Could you?'

A muscle tensed in his jaw and a moment passed. 'I couldn't.' He slowly set her sweater beside him, his hand lingering on the wool before going to his knee. 'But I'm here. So are you.'

My mouth and throat were dry as he continued to stare at me. Deep down I never believed that Debbie's death was a simple suicide that no one would ever understand and I always believed that Erik had something to do with it. Either he'd pushed her to it or he'd done something to her and made it look like she'd killed herself. No one could ever explain the pink scarf and how it got on the door, especially since Erik claimed to not have been there.

In his stare, I could tell he knew exactly what I was thinking.

Breath catching, I took an uneasy step back. 'Cam and Jase are coming over to help me. They'll be here any minute.'

'I overheard your brother earlier. He's got a final right now.' He took a slow, measured step forward. 'Why would you say that when it's not true?'

My heart thudded as my thoughts raced. 'I thought he was coming over sooner than that. I got the time—'

He laughed a short, dark sound as he looked away, running a hand through his hair. 'You didn't get shit messed up.'

I drew in a deep breath as I took another step back, close to the open door. Screw getting my stuff. I didn't want to be in the room with him a second longer. 'I'll just come back another—'

Erik shot forward so fast I didn't see him move. One second he was standing by Deb's bed and the next he was in front of me. A scream built in my throat, but it never escaped. He was on me before I could make a sound.

Smacking his hand down on my mouth, he twisted his arm, spinning me back from the door. A metallic taste filled my mouth as my lips smashed into my teeth. Off balance, my right leg gave out as he slammed his hand in the center of my back. I went down on my left side, catching myself with my hands at the same point I heard the door slam shut and lock.

I was stunned for a moment as I slowly lifted my head up. Strands of hair fell forward, obscuring my vision. The inside of my lips burned, and my brain had a hard time catching up with what just happened, but when it did, fear roared through me, coating my skin in ice and freezing my breath.

He wrapped his fingers around my ponytail, wrenching my head back. I yelped as heat spiked down my spine. 'It was your fault.'

I grasped his hand, trying to leverage my weight as fire spread across my scalp. 'What are—?'

'Don't act like you have no idea.' He dragged me until I was perched on my knees. I shifted my weight onto my left, but the position *hurt*. 'Debbie's dead because of you.'

'You're crazy.' The words were out of my mouth before I could stop myself. 'You're fucking crazy. You killed—'

Erik let go of me so quickly that I fell back. His hand snaked out, striking me across the face and spinning my thoughts. I fell to the side, jaw stinging, and the room seemed to shift floor to ceiling. Tears of pain filled my eyes as I dragged in air. A burn raced across my face as I slowly opened my jaw. My brain couldn't process any of this. How did I go from taking finals to this?

This couldn't be real—could not be happening.

Every part of me froze up. It was too familiar. The way

331

my lip ached, how numb my skin felt, the buzzing inside my head. I'd been here before, on the floor, head spinning from a hit I hadn't seen coming.

Suddenly, it was like being sixteen all over again, cowering on the floor as Jeremy went into one of his rages over something so simple, so stupid. Helpless. Scared. Confused. Body and hands shaking.

'I'm not crazy, and it's not my fault that Deb died.' Anger edged his voice, making it razor-sharp. 'If you hadn't said anything to her and minded your own goddamn business, she wouldn't have broken up with me.'

'What?' Blood leaked out of the corner of my mouth. I wiped it away with a trembling hand and found myself staring at the horrifying smear of red.

Too familiar.

'When you asked her about the bruises! And then that fucking Sunday. You had to get involved.' He started toward me. 'You just had to be standing there and get hurt. Like it was my fucking fault. It wasn't! It was yours!'

Fury snapped at the heels of the rising fear, and I did something I'd never done with Jeremy, no matter how bad it got.

I wasn't a victim anymore. I would never be the victim again.

'So typical.' I spat the words out. 'You hit someone and it's always *their* fault. Never yours.'

'Oh, shut up, you stupid gimpy bitch.'

Planting my hands on the floor, I ignored the dizziness that assaulted me. 'I guess your fists just slip and fall on people's faces?'

'Only those who deserve it.'

'Did Debbie deserve it?'

He cursed. 'Don't you dare talk about her. You don't know shit.'

332

I lurched to my feet and staggered back, bumping into the bed. Lifting my head, I saw Erik advance through a haze of tears. I spun, reaching for the closest weapon. I grabbed the bedside lamp, ripping it from its plug, more than prepared to knock him upside the head so hard that it kicked him into the next dorm.

He swung at me, and I jumped back. The momentary loss of balance gave him a second to gain the upper hand. He snatched the lamp from my hand and tossed it across the room. It hit my clothes and then thudded off the wall. My heart stopped, and then I whirled toward the door.

Pain exploded along the back of my head, doubling me over. The walls tilted again, and I blinked to clear my vision, but it felt like it took hours to reopen my eyes. The next thing I knew I was on the floor, on my back in between the beds, staring dumbly at the ceiling.

Erik was pacing, his sneakers crunching over my hair. How had my hair come loose? My entire body throbbed like I was giant bruise. I drew in a deep breath, and it hurt my ribs and back.

'You're awake.' He stood over me, sneering. 'I didn't even hit you that hard.'

My head was full of cobwebs. I must've fallen and passed out, which meant I probably had a concussion.

And concussions were bad news, right?

Feeling like I'd been abruptly woken up, I slowly rose onto my elbows. For a second, I felt like I was swimming through mud.

'I wasted so much time. I should've . . .' He stopped, pressing his palms against his temples and then he started pacing again. 'I didn't mean to do it.'

What was he talking about? Forcing myself into a sitting position, I leaned against the bed, winded. He didn't mean to do what?

333

'It just . . . it just happened. I came over to talk to her, to prove to her that she made a mistake and that we needed to get back together, but she told me to leave.' His hands dropped to his sides, closing into sizable fists.

I winced as I pushed back against the bed, trying to gather my spinning thoughts.

'She wouldn't listen to me. All she needed to do was listen to me!' His voice rose and then dropped. 'She made me mad and I—and I pushed her. It was an accident.'

Erik dropped down suddenly and gripped my chin. I cried out as his fingers dug into my chin, bruising. 'It was an accident! She fell backward, and I don't even understand how it happened. Her neck hit the corner of the bed and I heard the snap. Oh God . . .' He pushed away from me, wrenching my head to the side as he stood. Clutching his hair, he backed up. 'Her neck just snapped.'

I squeezed my eyes shut against the images pouring in.

'I knew no one would believe it was an accident. They'd blame me when it wasn't my fault! Debbie just—' He cut himself off as he sat on the edge of her bed. 'She just wouldn't listen.'

Horror seized me. I'd suspected the truth all along, but to hear him put it out there sickened and shocked me. 'You killed her.' My jaw and mouth ached—it hurt to talk.

'It was an accident.' He stood again, walking the length of the small room. 'It wouldn't have happened if you had just kept your mouth shut. It's your fault.'

Erik had deep psychological problems. That much was official.

As he made another pass around the room, my head began to clear, but a low-level pounding ache throbbed along the back of my head. I turned, wincing as pain shot down my neck. My face felt swollen and my ribs bruised, but I knew the longer I was in here with him, the worse these injuries would get, if not—I cut off that line of thought. No need to feed anxiety.

'This is on your conscience. It's your fault. Debbie would still be here if you hadn't said anything, if you hadn't gotten in the way,' he ranted, hands clenching and unclenching, and I knew he wanted to put those hands on me, and not in a happy way. 'You've ruined everything.'

I heard my cell phone go off in the next room and hope surged. Had an hour passed already? Maybe—just maybe—Cam was out of his final early. Or Jase had decided to go ahead and come over. Oh, please God, let it be one of them.

Erik didn't seem to notice. He continued to pace the small room, grabbing fistfuls of hair. He stopped by the foot of Debbie's bed and pounded his fists off the sides of his head. 'You've ruined everything, and now look what's happened. I have no choice.'

My cell went off again.

Please. Please. Please.

Drawing my legs to my chest, my muscles tensed in anticipation of bum-rushing the door. 'You won't get away with this.'

He lowered his hands, piercing me with a crazed glare. 'Get away with what?'

'This.' I placed my palms on the carpet, ready. 'Whatever this is, you won't get away with it.'

Once more, my cell phone went off, and this time, he noticed. Erik glanced at the door, brows furrowing. 'I'm not planning to get away with anything.'

I let out a breath. Maybe he wasn't completely crazy. I'd be happy with just half crazy. 'You're not? Because we can forget this ever happened.' That was such a lie, because I was totally not forgetting that this happened. 'We can walk out of here—'

He shook his head. 'I'm not planning to get away,' he said casually, like we were talking about finals. 'I'm not planning to walk away from this.'

Whatever tiny smidgen of relief that had blossomed from his statement crashed and burned in a race car kind of crash. *Not planning to walk away from this.* 'You sound like you're never leaving this room.'

'I'm not.' He barked out a laugh as he turned to me. 'Not unless it's in a body bag.'

Horror exploded in my gut like a buckshot. Fuck the waiting for a good moment to go for the door. Instinct kicked back in and I lumbered to my feet, cursing my bad leg as I pushed off. I used to be light on my feet and fast. Not anymore.

He crashed into me, knocking me to the floor and pushing a scream out of my throat. Out in the suite, something smashed off the wall as Erik's fingers dug into my shoulders, flipping me onto my back roughly.

As my wide eyes stared into Erik's, time seemed to stop for a second. A horrible sinking feeling tried to drag me down through the carpet with the truth of what he was about to do.

Erik's head jerked at the sound of someone banging on the bedroom door, and a wild look filled his eyes. Taking advantage of the momentary distraction, I swung my arm off the floor. My fist connected with the corner of his mouth, snapping his head to the side.

He reared back, grunting as blood and spit flew from his busted lip. He grip loosened on my arms, and I twisted to my side and opened my mouth to call out.

'Fucking bitch,' he ground out, slamming his fist into my lower back. A perfect kidney punch that immobilized me.

'Tess!'

Jase—it was *Jase*!

The door groaned as he beat it. 'Are you in there? Are you okay?'

I reached out toward the door, my fingers digging into the carpet. 'Jase—' His name ended in a grunt.

Erik rolled me over, and I was suddenly staring into the eyes of someone who'd come unhinged. Eyes that I was sure Debbie had stared into countless times and were quite possibly the last thing she'd seen.

Terror caught me in an unbreakable grip and a scream tore through me, piercing the air and then cutting off abruptly as Erik's hand circled around my neck, closing in.

The door rattled on its hinges. 'Tess! What the fuck? Tess!'

Panic dug in deep with its sharp, icy claws. His grip was bruising, cutting into my windpipe. I opened my mouth to scream again, but there was no sound—no air! Heart pounding, I slapped him and then caught his chin with my fist. He yelped, but his hold remained.

'Tess!' called Jase. The door rocked, sounding like he'd rammed it with his shoulder. 'Goddamnit!'

Stars burst behind my eyes, and I couldn't—I couldn't drag in enough air. I clawed at Erik's hands, feeling his skin tear under my nails. The door shuddered again, but it wasn't going to give in time.

'Stop it!' Erik lifted me up and then slammed my head back down. 'Just stop!'

Darkness crept upon the corners of my vision, crowding my sight. A fiery burn flamed deep in my chest, spreading rapidly into my throat. I needed to breathe!

'Teresa! Baby,' shouted Jase, and the sound of his voice shot a bolt of desperate strength through me. The door shook and groaned. 'Come on . . .'

Using everything in me, I beat on Erik's chest—his face and shoulders. I rolled my hips, trying to throw him, but he pushed down and down, and it felt like I was floating through the floor, slowly disappearing into the waiting abyss. I knew I shouldn't let go, that I must not, but my hands slipped down, arms falling to my sides.

In the background, something shattered. Maybe it was the last of my oxygen-deprived cells. I didn't know what, but Erik's dark eyes latched onto mine, and I was sure that this was it. My lashes drifted shut. He was going to be the last thing I saw, just like Debbie. And it wasn't fair. I hadn't even begun to live life, to embrace this new future or to get Jase, because if I'd survived this, I wouldn't let him walk away. Not anymore. But . . . but it didn't matter now. My hearing dwindled until there was only a fine point, a roaring of blood.

Suddenly the unbearable pressure was off my throat and air rushed in as a pained grunt filled the room. Something broke—snapped like old, dry twigs and it sounded far away, like it was outside.

Hands pressed against my cheeks and then arms lifted me. My head felt too heavy, floppy. Like there was something wrong with my neck. 'Oh God, open your eyes. Come on baby, open your eyes.' There was a pause, and his large body shuddered. 'I'm sorry: Fuck. Open your eyes. *Please.*'

It felt like my lids had been glued shut, but I pried them open. All I saw was Jase's deep gray eyes, darker than I'd ever seen them.

'There you are,' he said, cradling me closer. 'Stay with me. Tess! Oh God, don't leave me. Please. I . . .'

His lips were moving, but the words didn't make sense, and I couldn't keep my eyes open. There was nothing but darkness.

Chapter 29

The steady sound of beeping slowly, insistently drilled through the layers of haze and sleep until I felt my chest rise with a deep, shuddering breath.

'Teresa.' What I was lying on shifted as weight settled beside me. A hand pressed against my cheek, cool and comforting. 'Are you there?'

Was I? I thought so. My surroundings slowly came into play. I was in a stiff bed, and it was my brother's voice I was hearing. My head felt weighted down, though, like I was glued to the mattress.

I slowly blinked my eyes open and winced at the bright overhead lights. Once my vision cleared, it was obvious I was in a hospital room. The white walls, mounted TV, and pea green curtain were a dead giveaway.

'Hey,' Cam said gently. 'How are you feeling?'

Turning my head to him slightly, I ran my tongue over the roof of my mouth. 'I feel . . . strange.' My voice was hoarse, and my jaw *ached* from speaking those three words.

'You've been sleeping for a little while, long enough for the parents to get down here and then some.' Cam smiled wearily as he reached for a pitcher and poured water into a small, plastic cup. 'Mom and Dad are down the hall talking to the police.'

The police? I stared at him dumbly as he played Mr. Nurse, carefully reaching around to the back of my neck and helping me take a drink. The cool water was like jumping into a pool on a hot, sweltering day.

He placed the cup on the bedside table. A sudden look of understanding crept across his face. 'You don't remember, do you?'

I shook my head and then grimaced as a sharp pain arced between my temples. Cam glanced at the door as if he wanted to run out and get someone, but he placed his hand over mine, drawing my gaze to my knuckles.

They were red, scratched, and swollen.

I jerked up halfway, muscles and skin protesting the unexpected movement as the fog cleared from my head. 'Oh my God . . .'

Concern flared in Cam's eyes 'You remember?'

'Erik. He—'

'I know. We all know. You don't have to worry about him anymore,' Cam said, gently pressing his hand down on my shoulder so I was lying down. 'You need to stay still. You have a concussion—a minor one but you can't be moving around a lot. Okay?'

My heart was pounding as I took in the IV hooked to the center of my arm, pumping clear fluids in. That horrible snapping sound came back to me, reminding me of bones breaking. 'Is he dead?'

'Fuck. I wish.' Anger stormed across his face. 'Jase broke his jaw and knocked him into next week, but the fucker's alive. He's going to jail, though. He woke up when the police and EMTs got there, blabbering what he did to Debbie to anyone who'd listen. He kept saying it was . . .' He trailed off, his mouth pressing down in a hard line.

'He said it was my fault,' I finished for him, closing my eyes as the memories of Erik's rage and flat-out madness resurfaced, but a different worry took hold. 'Where . . . where is Jase?'

Cam looked away when I opened my eyes. 'The last I saw him he was with the police.'

'What?' I started to sit up again, but he stopped me. 'What do you mean?'

'He's not in trouble. He had to talk to them, like I'm sure you'll have to now that they know you're awake.' He paused. 'They needed a statement.'

'How long ago was that?'

Cam shifted like he was uncomfortable. 'They held him back when they took you to the hospital. I haven't seen him. I came straight here when I found out.'

He hadn't seen Jase at all? Meaning he hadn't checked on me? I closed my eyes and smacked at the useless emotions. Jase said he'd wanted to talk. He'd come and he'd saved my life. Just because he wasn't here didn't mean I needed to throw a fit. Besides, I had bigger things to deal with.

When I opened my eyes, Cam was staring at me. Several seconds passed. 'You're really in love with him, aren't you?'

I sighed. 'Yeah.'

He shifted and then cursed under his breath. 'I know you didn't want to hear this before, but you're going to listen now. The fucker is stupid, but the fucker loves you.'

I opened my mouth.

'Yeah, I know he pushed you away or whatever, but he's a guy and he's stupid. Hey, I can admit that. We do stupid shit.' Cam leaned over, lowering his voice. 'He sort of reminds me of Shortcake—of Avery—you know? She was like that in the beginning. For different reasons, but she . . . she had her own issues she had to work through. And I

341

think that's what he was doing. I don't know. I'm not him, but Jase has got some baggage.'

'I know,' I said quietly, blinking back tears. Everything about Jase was complicated. It always had been, and I wasn't sure that the only thing he needed to do was to work through his issues. Some things people just couldn't get past.

Cam lowered his gaze and then took a deep breath. 'You know, he told me a while back that you feel guilty about what I did to Jeremy.'

Surprised, my eyes widened as I stared at him.

'You shouldn't.' His head rose and he looked straight at me. 'I did that to Jeremy, and I'd do it again. It was never your fault. Okay? It doesn't matter that you kept quiet. Trust me, I know how people keep shit to themselves, storing it away until the silence fucking destroys. You were a *kid* basically, and I knew what I was doing. And the only thing I regret is that you feel guilty for something I *chose* to do.'

I don't know what it was that did it. A little bit of the weight had lifted after Jase had talked to me, but the massive gorilla with an overeating problem finally got the hell off my chest. Pure, sweet relief crashed through me, and it was like being tossed in the middle of a storm. Tears crawled up my throat and built behind my eyes.

'Teresa, don't cry.' Cam frowned. 'I didn't—'

'I won't.' I sniffed a couple of times, forcing the waterworks to stop. 'Thank you.'

'Don't thank me.'

I didn't say anything, because he didn't need to hear it but I knew it. Cam saying those words was equal to being tossed a lifeline. I grabbed it and held it close. 'I love you like I love cupcakes.'

A wide and real smile raced across his face. 'You dork, I love you too.'

It wasn't long before Mom and Dad arrived in the room. Dad looked murderous. So did Mom, but she hid it better. They all but pushed Cam out of the way and clucked over me until the police showed and I gave them my statement. Retelling the time spent in that room with Erik wasn't easy. I liked to think I was a strong person, but a fine series of quakes had taken hold of me when I got to the part of him admitting that he'd killed Debbie and staged it as a suicide. The shudders increased as I told them how he hadn't planned on walking out of the room.

Erik had planned to kill me and then himself. He'd said her death was my fault, but he had to have felt guilt if he planned to off himself. He might have buried it deep, but it was there. It had to be. I refused to believe that he'd live the rest of his life feeling completely guiltless.

Dad picked up my uninjured hand, tucking it under his chin as a young deputy closed a small notebook. 'That's all we'll need for right now,' he said, backing away from the bed. 'Get some rest and we'll call you if we have any more questions.'

'You'll call *me* if you have any more questions.' Dad straightened, eyeing the officer as he slipped into lawyers-are-the-devil mode.

The deputy nodded and left, quickly replaced by a doctor and a nurse who looked younger than me. I was poked and prodded and endured a bright light in my eyeballs. Light pain meds were pumped through the IV, and by the time they'd kicked in, my tummy grumbled and I was feeling sort of normal as Mom tucked the thin blanket around my chest. 'You'll be out of here tomorrow, and your father and I were thinking it would be best for you to come home with us instead of waiting on Cam.'

Sitting in the corner, Cam made a face at me.

'We would feel more comfortable,' Dad added, squeezing my hand. 'We really would.'

'You'd feel more comfortable if she dropped out of school and lived with you for the rest of her life,' Cam said.

Mom cast him a sharp look over her shoulder. 'After what just happened? Yes. I want her under my roof for the next three decades.'

'Only three?' I murmured.

She pressed her lips together. 'There is no reason for her to stay down here until you come up on Christmas Eve.'

There was a huge part of me that wanted to let my parents gather me up and take me home. It had been easier there when I'd visited, and I could seriously hole up in my room until Christmas Eve. It sounded really nice, but I knew if I went home with them now, there'd be a good chance I wouldn't come back to Shepherdstown. I'd want to stay where it was safe and things were familiar in a good way, but I had a life here now—college, the possibility of a career that I would enjoy. I had a future and I wasn't a kid anymore, and I couldn't rely on my parents to swoop in and coddle me whenever something bad happened. As much as this sucked to think about, they wouldn't always be there for me.

'I don't know, Mom. Let me think about it,' I said finally, knowing that would be better than telling them no flat-out. Neither she nor Dad looked happy about it, but then Cam suddenly stood.

My gaze followed his just as my dad turned, and I swore my heart might've stopped right then, if only for a second.

Jase stood in the doorway, his russet waves going in every direction and his bronze skin paler than normal. The dark blue V-neck sweater he wore was askew, showing more of the white shirt underneath than it hid. Everything about him was wrinkled, but in my eyes, he was the most gorgeous man I'd ever seen.

344

In his hands was a square, pink box.

Our gazes locked from across the room, and he stopped midstep, as if he was frozen. His eyes were a fierce silver as relief and something else, something I couldn't name, etched its way onto his striking features.

Air leaked out of my lungs as my mom stood and gently cleared her throat. 'Well, she's got some company, so let's get out of their hair.'

Dad arched a brow as he looked from Jase to me and then back to Mom. 'Maybe we—'

'We'll come back tomorrow morning, fresh and early.' Mom shot Dad a look before she bent over and kissed my cheek. 'I love you, honey.'

'I love you, too.'

Dad kissed my other cheek and reluctantly relinquished his claim to the side of my bed. As he passed Jase, he leaned in and said something that Jase nodded to. God only knew what had just come out of my dad's mouth.

Cam patted Jase's back at he strolled past, surprising me with the fact that he didn't do something immature like fist bump him or knock his shoulders.

Shit was serious when Cam was acting his age.

Jase didn't move until my parents and brother disappeared, and then two long-legged quick strides brought him to the side of my bed. Heavy silence crept into the room as he sat the box beside the pitcher of water and sat down, his hip resting again mine. My heart jumped into a racing staccato as he carefully brushed his fingers across the ridge of my cheekbone and tucked my hair back behind my ear.

He scrutinized my face slowly, the intense perusal missing nothing, chronicling what was most likely a nasty bruise that had the right side of my jaw swollen like an orange was shoved in my mouth. The corner of my right lip felt off, and the skin around my eye ached.

I bet I looked like I'd been on the losing side of a cage fight.

'Did he hurt you?' he asked, voice gruff with concern and thready with what sounded like fear. 'Hurt you more than I can see?'

At first I didn't understand what he meant and then I did. 'No—God, no.'

Jase closed his eyes as a deep breath shuddered through him. 'When I came through that door and saw him on you and you just—just *lying* there, I thought I was too late. I thought you were gone.'

'I thought I was going to die in that room with him. I really did, but you got there in time,' I assured him. 'You saved my life. Thank you.' I forced every emotion I felt into those words. '*Thank you.*'

'That's something I never wanted you to ever thank me for.' He leaned in, planting his left hand on the bed beside my shoulder, anchoring his weight. He said nothing as he bowed his head, and when he kissed the left corner of my lips, emotion swelled in my chest.

He stayed where he was as he spoke and with each word, his lips brushed mine, acting as a physical seal to what he said. 'I have been nothing but a jackass these last couple of weeks, and I know right now is not the time to talk about this, but there is something I need to say. Okay?'

I took a deep breath. 'All right.'

Jase placed the tips of his fingers against my left cheek. 'I have had issues with getting close to any girl because of Kari and Jack, but you . . . you were different. You got under my skin and dug your way into my heart. Probably that first time we kissed, you got there and I thought I could handle this—handle these feelings, but when I realized how deep they ran, it scared the shit out of me. I didn't want to get hurt again. I didn't want to lose someone like I

346

already did. But then I almost lost you today. For real. And that's what I've been scared of. I would've lost you before I even had you. And the very thought of that kills me.'

He closed his eyes, resting his forehead against mine with the slightest pressure. 'I wanted to talk to you. That's why I texted you, because I fucking missed you and I thought . . .' He pulled away, shaking his head. There was a sheen to his eyes that caused my throat to constrict. 'Anyway, we'll talk more later because you don't need this shit right now.'

I wanted to tell him that I was okay with this shit, with hearing more, because the rawness of his words was tearing me up and patching me together, filling me with hope and diminishing the events of today, but he reached over to the nightstand and picked up the pink box.

'I got this for you after music class and I wanted to give it to you when I came over to help with your dorm, so I've had it for a while. It might not be fresh.' The tips of his cheeks flushed pink as he opened the box. 'It's vanilla with strawberry icing. I, uh, know how much you like that kind of icing.'

My gaze followed the blush as it deepened. It was so rare to see him uncomfortable or unsure of what he was doing.

He peeked up at me through lowered lashes. 'You probably don't want anything to eat right now, so how about just the icing?'

My stomach grumbled, although the knots forming in my belly dampened my hunger, but he looked so hesitant that I couldn't refuse him. 'I'd like that.'

One side of his lips quirked up as he slashed his pinkie finger through the rich icing, scooping up quite a bit of the pink stuff. I wasn't expecting this method of tasting as he lifted his finger to my lips.

347

His eyes met mine then, and a flutter took root in my stomach as I opened my mouth. There was no way I could look away as I took his finger into my mouth and got my first taste of the sugary sweetness. And he kept his eyes on mine as he repeated the motions until all the icing was gone and my face felt warm.

Jase sat the opened box aside and then bowed his head to mine. I gasped as his tongue flicked out, gliding across my lower lip. 'You had some icing on your lip.'

'Oh.' I was beyond the point of forming comprehensive responses.

He drew back, eyes glimmering. 'That might have been a lie.'

My lips tipped into a grin. 'Might?'

'Okay.' He reached down, threading his fingers through mine carefully. He brushed his lips over the bruised, achy skin. 'It was most definitely a lie.'

A small laugh broke free. 'That's the kind of lie I don't mind.'

'It's a tasty lie, huh?' When I nodded, the tension in his shoulders started to ease away, but then I yawned and he stiffened. 'You need to sleep.'

Between the pain meds and everything, the allure of sleep was too strong to deny, but I didn't want to say good-bye to him. I glanced down at our joined hands, to his pinkie that was slightly stained with pink. 'Will . . . will you stay with me? As long as they let you?'

His eyes lightened to a silvery gray as his lips tipped up in a lopsided smile. 'Baby, I'm all yours if you want me to be.'

Those words seemed to be heavy with meaning, and I felt my chest spasm. 'I do.'

Bowing his head, he kissed the center of my hand and then let go. He stood with a fluid grace I envied and walked to the curtain. As he pulled it closed, he glanced over his shoulder and winked at me with a playful grin.

Jase helped me scoot over and then climbed in beside me, his long body barely fitting the bed. The two of us together made it crowded, but I didn't care. He turned onto his side, so that his head was close to mine.

Like he was dealing with fragile china, he was careful when he laid his hand over my stomach. 'Comfortable?'

Despite the dull aches and the fact I was lying in a hospital bed, I was more comfortable than I'd ever been. 'Yes.'

'Good.' His eyes met mine and held them with warm intensity that felt a lot like love. 'They'd have to pry me out of this damn bed. I'm not going anywhere.'

Chapter 30

The doctors released me the following afternoon with a prescription of pain meds in case I got any headaches or if the pains became too much, but after sleeping almost the entire night curled up against Jase in the narrow bed, my body felt surprisingly better than the day before. Sure, there were some aches and I was moving at the speed of a three-legged turtle, but I was okay.

I was better than okay. I was alive.

Mom and Dad looked like they wanted to cart me off home as I stepped out into the cold, but I wasn't going home with them when they left their hotel room later in the week. I was going back to my apartment.

Jase waited patiently by his Jeep, his hands shoved deep into the pockets of his jeans as he leaned against the door.

'Honey, I really don't want to leave you right now.'

I turned to Mom, giving her a hug. 'I'm okay. Really. I just want to go back to my place and chill out.'

'With him?' Dad grumbled, eyeing the guy that he'd always welcomed into his home without a single thought.

I sighed. 'Yes, with him.'

'Is he your boyfriend now or something?' he asked, and I had no idea how to answer that question, because I wasn't sure where we were, which did not go unnoticed by my father. A thoughtful look crept across his face. The kind of look bad things sprouted from. 'Maybe I need to talk to him again.'

'No,' I said quickly. 'You do not need to talk to him. At all.'

Dad looked like he was about to disagree, but Mom placed her hand on his back. 'Call us later, okay? Just to check in.'

'I will.' I figured I'd probably only have a couple of hours at the apartment before Cam swung by to check in. I would be facing a lot of impromptu check-ins for a while.

After another round of hugs and tears, they let me go and I joined Jase. He pushed off the Jeep and opened the door for me. 'I think your father looks like he wants to take me hunting.' He took hold of my elbow, hoisting me up. 'Like a special, scary hunting trip where I'm the game.'

I giggled. 'You know, you're probably not too far off with that assessment.'

'Great.' He closed the door and jogged around the front. Climbing in, he shot me a look. 'Your dad used to love me.'

That much was true. 'That's before he suspected there was something between us.'

'Something between us?' he murmured thoughtfully, and I tensed. He didn't speak again until he pulled out of the hospital parking lot. 'There's definitely something between us.'

I didn't know how to respond to that, because what I wanted between us was something he'd been unwilling to deal with a few weeks ago, but then there was yesterday and what he'd said before he climbed into bed with me.

Jase reached over, taking my hand, and we didn't speak

351

on the way back to the apartment. There was something soothing in the silence, and I took the time to gather my thoughts.

He found a parking spot close to the entrance in University Heights, limiting the time in the brisk, cold air since I was sorely underdressed. Cam's truck was in the lot and as we reached the landing to our level, I could hear Avery's laughter coming from inside her apartment.

'Do you think he'll propose soon?' I whispered.

Jase nodded as I unlocked the door. 'I bet he'll do it over Christmas.'

That would be perfect, but I also had a feeling that he'd just spring it on her instead of trying to plan it again. Either way, I knew she'd say yes and they would have a happily ever after.

My happily ever after? I was still praying that it was possible, that it was about to happen.

I stopped just inside Cam's apartment. Correction. Our apartment. I'd probably never get used to thinking of it that way. Looking away, I soaked in the familiar worn couch, the big-screen TV that my brother had splurged on. The game system and half the stack of games was gone, relocated to Avery's apartment. Emotion clogged my throat when I glanced into the narrow kitchen and saw the baking sheets sitting on top of the stove. I limped slowly forward, feeling heavy and weighed down by what had happened.

Jase closed the door behind us and placed his hand on my shoulder. 'You okay?'

'Yeah.' I nodded for extra emphasis. More like I needed to hear myself say it. 'It's just I didn't know if I'd ever see this place again.'

He turned me so I faced him as he cupped my uninjured cheek. His features were sharp with unspoken emotions. Fear. Adrenaline. Relief. Our gazes locked, and I knew in that moment he was feeling what I was. A future had almost been lost and we were on the cusp of a second chance, and the realization was shattering.

'I need you.' His voice was guttural with the depth of what he admitted. 'I need you right now.'

There was no doubt in my mind with what he wanted. I needed the same. 'Yes.'

Jase's hand shook as he pressed a kiss to the corner of my lip and then to the hollow of my cheek. His lips met the skin below my ear, causing me to shiver. A hot, wet path trailed down my neck and then back up. A strangled cry escaped me when he nipped on my earlobe. A throbbing ache between my thighs caused desire to blossom inside me, but it was love that was swelling, fueling the fire licking over my skin.

'I want this,' he said, sliding his hands down my sides. He gripped my hips. 'I want you always.'

I looped my arms around his neck. 'I want you.'

Jase made a deep sound in the back of his throat. 'I could *almost* live on hearing those words.'

'Almost? What could you live—?'

He lifted me up, his broad hands cupping my ass as he walked me backward. Whatever I was about to say was lost as he pressed my back against the wall beside the couch and ground his hips into mine as he kissed my throat. I wrapped my legs around his waist, the position allowing him to wedge himself between my thighs.

My eyes drifted shut as I craned my neck, giving him access. And he took it, nipping and licking as his hips thrust into mine, driving me insane with the rising anticipation.

Jase lifted his head, kissing my chin and my mouth, avoiding the area that was tender to touch. I moaned as he pushed my cardigan off my shoulders and cupped my breast through my shirt. My nipple immediately pearled, sensitive and pulsing. A spark of acute pleasure darted from the tips of my breast to my core. His hips rolled into mine, hitting a sweet spot that had me crying out.

'I'm sorry,' he growled against my mouth. 'If this is too rough, if this hurts, you've—'

'It doesn't,' I assured him, digging my fingers into his shoulders. My body was sore, but the needful ache to be with him was far stronger. 'I won't break.'

'Damn good thing to hear.' His hands trembled as they circled my waist, betraying how tightly wound he was. 'Because you're the kind of toy I plan to play with for a very, very long time.'

I arched a brow, and he sent me a wickedly mischievous wink as he extracted my legs from around his waist and settled my feet onto the floor.

'I wanted to talk to you first,' he said, tugging my cardigan off, tossing it to the floor. At this moment, talking was so overrated. 'Before it got to this, but I can't wait. I need to be in you.' He wrapped his fingers under the hem of my shirt. 'If you don't want that, you stop me now and I will back off.' His eyes, a liquid silver, met mine. 'I'll do whatever you want me to do. If you want to talk, we'll talk first. If you want me to get the fuck out of your face, I will, but if you tell me to stay, I'm going to be so deep inside you, you'll think I'll never come out again.'

My entire body dampened, liquefied at his words and his deep, husky drawl. I was out of my league with him sometimes, but I was wholly ready for him.

'But know this,' he continued, stepping closer so that our thighs touched. 'I made a huge mistake by pushing you away. I was a fucking coward, too scared of being hurt again, and I was hurting the moment you walked away. I did that to myself and to you, and I've never been more sorry in my life about anything.'

I caught my breath as I soaked in what he was saying and what it meant for us, but nothing prepared me for the rush of emotion his next words opened up in me.

He dropped his forehead to mine and with a silky soft kiss, he gently parted my lips, working his velvety tongue against mine. 'And I'm more than willing to spend the rest of my life making it up to you, because I love you, Tess. I am so fucking in love with you in a way I've never loved someone before.' His eyes glittered with hunger and love. 'Please let me prove that to you. Please, Tess.'

A flutter picked up in my stomach, and my heart rate accelerated as I stared into his beautiful eyes. He'd said he'd loved me once before, but that had come at the height of lust, and those three little words had been lost in what happened after that. These words meant everything now, and that was all that mattered. People made mistakes all the time. God knows I was a pro at doing and saying the wrong things. And Jase had made a mistake, but if he was willing to make up for it, I was willing to let him try.

I was willing to let him love me.

My knees were weak and I had no idea how I remained standing or was able to force out the one word. 'Stay.'

Jase closed his eyes briefly. 'Fuck yeah.'

My shirt came off with a startling quickness. The boy had talent when it came to removing clothes. He splayed his fingers across my ribs, just below the white lace of my bra. My skin flushed as his stare devoured my partial nakedness.

'You're fucking gorgeous, and I am so fucking lucky.' He kissed the valley between my breasts and then each swell 'But there's another part of you that's even more beautiful.'

Jase kissed my stomach and then his tongue dipped into my navel as he lowered himself onto his knees. My back arched off the wall, sucking a breath and holding it until my skin tingled.

He reached down, easing my feet out of my sneakers and then removing my socks. He grinned as he held one. 'Elves? On socks?'

'It's close to Christmas.'

'Cute.' He tossed them over his shoulder. His nimble fingers found their way under the sweats Cam had picked up for me to change into. As Jase slid them down my hips, my pulse pounded. 'There we go,' he said, kissing just below the band of my cotton panties. A rush of wetness hit me. He peered up through thick lashes. 'You know how I like to eat sweet things.'

'Oh God . . .'

With a deep chuckle, he hooked his fingers under the band and tugged them down. I was almost naked and he was completely clothed. The difference made me feel vulnerable as he rose like a predator. His hands slid around my back, unhooking my bra. With his teeth, he drew the straps of my bras down, grazing my skin in the process.

Stepping back, he admired his work. 'God, baby, you blow my mind. Look at you.' He placed a tanned hand on my hip, anchoring me as his head dipped. The edges of his soft hair brushed the swell of my breast, heightening my nerves.

But then he drew my nipple into his hot mouth, and every nerve in my body flared. I gasped as pleasure rolled through me in tumultuous waves. My fingers dug into his hair as his free hand slipped between my thighs, fingers brushing over where I throbbed with every fast heartbeat. I moaned as my head fell back against the wall.

He lifted his head, nuzzling my neck, just above my shoulder. 'I love you, Tess. I love you so much.'

My body clenched. Hot, tight shudders racked me. His fingers were barely touching me, and I was already close to falling over the edge. 'I love you, Jase.'

'Say it again,' he murmured against my cheek. 'I need to hear you say it.'

'I love you. I love you.' I repeated it over and over, lost in pure sensations. My hips surged forward, grinding against his thigh and his hand.

A satisfied smile split his lips. 'Fuck, I love hearing that.' Pleasure spiked as he slipped a finger inside. 'God, you're so wet.' He growled low in his throat as he smoothed over the tight concentration of nerves. My body jerked in response and was flooded with heat. 'You like that?'

'Yes,' I whispered, panting. 'Very much so.'

His dark hair tickled my nipples as his lips drifted over my collarbone. A tiny feminine sound caught in my throat as he knelt on his knees once more, easing my legs wide until I was completely exposed to him. Lightning rushed through me as his tongue glided from my navel to my center.

'So sweet.' He kissed my inner thigh. 'So beautiful.'

The air left my lungs as his head lowered again and he sliced me open with his tongue. I shuddered, my fingers clenching and unclenching in his hair. He captured my flesh with his mouth, alternating between determined strokes of his tongue and sucking deep as if he needed my taste to survive.

I cried out, hips thrusting against him as he worked me quickly to release. The fierce heat built and then exploded. I couldn't breathe as every muscle locked up and waves and waves of pleasure rolled through me, and he kept on, holding me up with his hand as he soaked up every response until the aftershocks died off.

Jase rose then, his lips moist and swollen as he drew me

to his chest. His eyes burned with lust and love when he cupped the nape of my neck, titling my head back. The length of his hardness burned through his clothes, pressing against my stomach.

'Now I'm going to make love to you.'

Chapter 31

Jase scooped me up into his arms and carried me back into the bedroom, gently lying me down in the mound of pillows I'd accumulated since I'd moved in.

He stepped back, his eyes riveted on mine as he undressed. Watching him reveal his exquisite body one article of clothing at a time was probably one of the most sensual and exciting things I'd ever seen.

The first time we were together had been a glorious rush. Not that it hadn't been marvelous and mind-blowing in its own way, I just knew that this time was going to be different.

Nerves stretched tight, I shook, because we were truly about to make love and I'd never done that before.

Shucking off his briefs, I felt my breath catch. Jase had the kind of body fantasies were made of. Seriously. Broad shoulders, a well-defined chest, and abs I could flip quarters off of. His hips were narrow, legs lean and long, and what hung between his thighs was pretty damn impressive. He was fully aroused and he wanted me.

And he loved me.

Jase prowled forward, climbing up on the bed and only

stopping once he hovered over me, his arms caging me in. 'Touch me,' he urged, voice dark.

He didn't have to ask me twice. I placed my hands on his chest, running them down the rigid muscles of his stomach, following the thin trail of hair until I wrapped a hand around him. He flexed against my palm, eliciting a thrill.

Kicking his head, he groaned hoarsely as I stroked his length. 'Oh God . . .'

I smiled as his chin lowered and his jaw loosened. 'You like that?'

'I like everything you do.' He dropped a kiss to my forehead and then peppered little ones all over my face—my cheeks, my eyelids, even the tip of my nose. 'Everything.'

Emboldened by his statement, I slid my hand up, squeezing gently as I reached the tip. His hips punched into the motion, and he made another deep, ragged sound.

'Yeah,' he ground out, arms shaking as he swelled against my hand. 'You keep that up and this is going to be over before it gets started and you don't want that. Trust me.'

'I don't.' But I didn't want to stop touching him.

I craned my neck as I held him, pressing a kiss to the underside of his jaw and then making my own path down his throat, tasting the saltiness of his skin. His chest rose and fell sharply as I moved my hand slowly, teasing him until he moved away.

I pouted. 'That's not fair.'

He chuckled as his breath moved down my throat. 'Be patient, baby. You'll have all of me soon enough, but first . . .'

His tongue circled the hardened tip of my breast and then closed over it, sucking deep and drawing me clear off the bed. I gripped his head, my hips moving restlessly as he moved to the other breast, paying it the same amount of attention. Rife and powerful desire built like a fierce storm.

360

He clasped a possessive hand around my hip as he lifted his head. Features strained, he took a deep breath. 'I don't think I can wait any longer. I need you, Tess.'

My heart flipped over. 'Then don't wait.'

Jase started to ease himself between my thighs, but stopped. 'Shit. I don't have a condom.'

I placed a hand on his cheek. 'You know I'm on the pill and you're the only person I've been with since, well, since like forever.'

'I haven't been with anyone else in a long time. I'm clean and I'll pull out just in case.' He paused, lining up above me. 'I'll do whatever you want.'

I slid my hands over his shoulders. 'I want you. Now.'

His lips brushed over mine as he rolled his hips forward, probing my entrance. He kissed me sweetly and so tenderly that I wanted to wrap myself around him for years. Resting his forehead against mine, he slowly pushed in, stretching me in a delicious way. I held on to him, bringing my knees up to his sides, giving him access and he slid in deeper, filling me. I let out a moan when he was in, and he shifted his weight onto his arms.

Our bodies were flush, chest to chest and hip to hip. I could feel him inside me, throbbing as he held himself still above me. 'Jase,' I whispered, dragging my fingers down his arms.

He gently kissed my parted lips. 'God, you feel so damn good.'

'So do you.' I skated my fingers back up, to his cheeks. 'It feels so right.'

'Yeah,' he groaned.

Body trembling, he slowly withdrew and then rocked his hips forward, causing my toes to curl. He set a slow pace that was both sweet and torturous. With each deep, smooth thrust, I tilted my hips to meet his. There was a seduction in the act of love, a quality missing when the heart wasn't involved. Every shift of his hips, every kiss he bestowed, and every brush of his hands and fingers meant something infinite.

He held my gaze as we made love, taking and giving to each other. The slow build went deeper than the crazy intenseness of our joining last time. I could feel him swelling and tightening inside me. I breathed every breath he took, shivered along with every shudder that coursed through his body.

But our bodies soon demanded more. My heels dug into his back, urging him to move faster, and he did. The speed of his thrusts picked up as did our breathing and my pounding heart. Wasn't too long before the headboard was hitting the wall again with the power of how he was moving.

When my body tensed up and the coil that had formed deep inside me started to unfurl at a dizzying rate, I gasped out. 'I love you.'

Whatever control Jase had at that point broke as the rawness of the act took off as his hips matched mine in a tempo that was shattering. I came, experiencing a powerful release that spread out from my core, shocking my body in tight shivers that had me crying out his name until my voice was hoarse.

He pulled out only when the last of the climax was easing through me, his arousal pulsating against my stomach as he dropped his head to my shoulder, kissing the bare skin as his hips twitched. I held him close, savoring the feel of his body on mine.

His skin was damp and his body still trembling when he lifted his head, kissing the corner of my lips. 'I love you, Teresa.'

We stayed wrapped together while our breathing returned to normal. In those moments of silence, the strangest thing happened to me. Something . . . something fragile broke inside me. Like an old, rusted-out lock finally opened.

I don't know what it was exactly that did it. Could've been the last year or so of my life and all the changes I'd gone through. From believing I only had one life ahead of me, to finally accepting there was more out there than dancing. Maybe it was seeing Jase and experiencing every up and down with him. It could've been Debbie and what her loss symbolized. It might have been Erik and the horror of that time in the dorm room and what it reminded me of.

And maybe . . . just maybe it had to do with Jeremy and the abusive relationship I'd been a part of, that *was* a part of me, and I finally fully understood that it would always be there with me, but it didn't make me who I was today. It shaped me, but it wasn't me. Before I knew it, my cheeks were damp.

Jase lifted his head. 'Tess? Baby?' He cupped my cheek, smoothing the tears away with his thumb. 'What's wrong?'

I wasn't sure how to put it into words and when I didn't answer, his face paled. 'Did I hurt? I should've waited. This could've—'

'No,' I croaked out. I tried to smile through the haze of tears. 'It's not you. It's just . . . everything and it's been a lot to wrap my head around.'

He ran his thumb under my good eye again. 'It has been a lot, Tess. And you've been handling everything. You're so strong—the strongest person I know.'

I choked out a laugh, and then the tears fell harder. Jase made a deep sound in the back of his throat, and then he gathered me up, tucking me against his chest as he held me close.

'I'll never forget what it was like to be with him,' I said, and somehow Jase knew who I was talking about. 'And that's okay, isn't it? That doesn't make me weak or a victim.'

'No.' He dropped a kiss to the top of my head. 'You are neither of those things.'

'It's not who I am now, but it's a part of me and . . . and I'm okay with that.' A shudder worked its way through me, and between the tears, we talked about Jeremy and we talked about Debbie and Erik. We talked about dancing and we talked about teaching, and he wrapped himself around me, holding me until there were no tears left, until the burdens I knew I'd carried and the ones I hadn't really realized I'd been shouldering all this time lifted and faded away.

A buckass naked Jase making soup for me so I wouldn't irritate my bruised jaw literally had to be one of the top five things in life I wanted to see in person. Even coming ahead of watching the San Francisco Ballet perform onstage.

Good God, he had the most perfect ass I'd ever seen.

We sat on my bed, the sheet tucked under my arms as we shared the large bowl of vegetable soup. One spoon and two mouths made for an interesting in-bed experience. A bit of broth escaped down my chin, and Jase caught it with his tongue. 'Hmm, how about you lie back and let me eat the rest of the soup like this?'

I laughed, feeling lighter—feeling *better* in spite of the fact that I was stuffy from all the tears. 'That would get a bit messy.'

'But it would be fun.' He swirled the spoon around, catching the tender chunks of veggies. 'More?'

Being fed seemed stupid. Unless it was a naked Jase feeding you. Then it was incredibly hot. I opened up, swallowing the broth and chewing what I could. 'Thank you.'

He shrugged a tan shoulder and lifted the spoon to his own mouth. Chewing thoughtfully for a few moments, he chased after a piece of meat. 'You know, I really planned on talking to you first before I got you naked.'

'But you did plan on getting me naked?' I couldn't resist teasing him.

'Hell yeah I did.' He grinned and then popped the meat into his mouth. Lowering his lashes, he scooped up more broth. 'Actually, I *hoped* it ended with wild, animalistic sex.' He tipped the spoon to my lips, making sure I didn't miss a drop. 'But I messed up so bad and I was expecting you to tell me to get the hell out.'

I cocked my head to the side as I wiggled closer. 'Really?'

He nodded. 'I know I'm damn charming, but I fucked up and I—'

Leaning over the bowl, I pressed my lips to his. With my busted lip, it didn't make for that hot of a kiss, but he stilled like I'd reached around the bowl and grabbed a different kind of meat. 'You messed up,' I said, as I rocked back. 'I know. You really did, you jackass. And you hurt my feelings.'

He looked contrite. 'Tess—'

'But I'm not going to sit here and hold it over your head forever. Not when I thought there was a damn good chance I was going to die yesterday. As cliché as this sounds, life is too short. I want you,' I said passionately. 'Baggage and all, Jase. And I know it's not going to be easy. I was prepared for that when I came back to you. Jack is your son, whether he realizes it or not. And it doesn't matter if you ever tell him, he will *always* be your son. And if one day you decide to tell him the truth, I'll support you in any way.'

His gaze dropped to the bowl. 'Are you seriously ready for that? What if I tell him when I graduate next semester?'

My stomach dipped a little at the prospect, but that was expected. 'You come with responsibility that I'm willing to be a part of. I don't know how good I'll be at anything that has to do with him, but I'll try hard.'

Jase lifted his gaze, eyes wide. 'You'd be perfect, Tess.

He already likes you a lot and he . . . well, one day, you'd make a great mom.'

I flushed, and instead of being skeeved out by the idea of motherhood, I warmed with the compliment. 'Thank you.' I took a deep breath. 'And you're really ready for this?'

'I've done a lot of thinking, Tess, and I am. I think I've been ready but didn't want to acknowledge it. What I feel for you, it blew my mind. At first I thought it was wrong because of Cam, but when I realized that wasn't it, that I was afraid of losing you, I knew I needed to work through it all.' He thrust a hand through the mess of hair. 'And you were right. I hadn't fully moved on. I know I need to visit her grave. I wanted to. That was what I was going to tell you.'

'When you texted me that you wanted to talk?'

He nodded again. 'That wasn't the only thing, but it was a part of it. I think by doing that, it's like closing the door, you know? Not forgetting, but truly moving on.'

I tried not to show my shock. That was a huge step for him. Maybe not to some people, but for Jase it was a big deal. 'I think that's a great idea and if you need me there with you, I'll be there.'

He smiled a little as he shook his head. 'You . . . you are amazing, Tess.'

'No, I'm not. I just love you, Jase.'

It appeared that he stopped breathing for a moment, and then he leaned around me, sitting the bowl on the night-stand. As he settled back, he touched the bruise on my jaw lightly. 'I'm not sure I deserve you.'

I closed my eyes. 'I don't like hearing you say that.'

'And I don't like thinking it, but I can't help feeling it.' The touch of his lips was butterfly soft. 'Though I'm going to do everything to change it.' Placing his hand on my shoulder, he gently guided me down until my head rested on the pillows. He settled beside me, lying on his side as he propped his cheek up on his elbow. 'I promise that.'

'I believe that.'

A soft smile appeared on his lips as he trailed his finger over my shoulder. Several quiet moments passed. 'When are your parents going back home?'

'Tomorrow, I think. They wanted me to go home with them, but I'm not.' I shivered as his finger danced over my collarbone.

'What about Christmas? I know it's a week or so away, but what've you got planned?'

I closed my eyes, blindly seeking the featherlight touch. 'I'll go up with Cam as planned. He leaves on Christmas Eve or the day before.'

'Christmas is a big deal at my house too.' His finger dipped, following the line of the sheet. 'Jack still believes in Santa, so I need to be there with him in the morning, but I want to see you. Maybe you can spend Christmas Eve with me and then I can come up to your house on Christmas? I'd drive you up later that morning. I mean, if you want me there, that is and your parents are cool with it.'

My eyes popped open. 'I'd love for you to come up.' A big, goofy smile crossed my face at the thought of spending Christmas Eve with his family and then Christmas night with mine. 'But I don't want you to make an unnecessary trip.'

'You can always stay the night with me.' He tugged the sheet down, exposing the length of me. 'If that's cool with your parents and you.'

'It's cool with me and they'll be okay with it because it's what I want.' I bit my cheek as his gaze left mine and traveled down. A muscle flexed in his jaw. 'Do you think your mom and dad will be okay with it?'

'Of course.' He sounded distracted.

'It's our first.' I giggled, flushing as I let my head fall back against the pillow. 'That sounds stupid, doesn't it?'

'It doesn't.' He rolled on top of me, and I felt his hardness nudging me as he settled between my thighs. 'And it won't be our last.'

My breath caught as I arched, clutching his hair. '*This* or spending Christmas together?'

He chuckled as he reached between us, wrapping his hand around his thick base. 'Both.'

'Oh.' My ability to form comprehensive sentences had flown out the window. He slid into me in one deep roll of his hips. '*Jase.*'

He groaned as he gathered me close and then shifted onto his back, staying inside me. Astride him, I braced myself with my hands flat against his chest. 'Yes?' he said, grinning.

'You are so bad.'

His hands circled my hips. 'And you haven't seen anything yet.'

Chapter 32

Tiny flakes of snow had begun to fall the moment we'd left Shepherdstown. It was in the late afternoon, and the chilly air seemed to seep through every crevice in Jase's Jeep and no matter how high he had the heater cranked, it didn't get warm enough.

Jase held my hand as we drove in silence. My knuckles were still swollen from when I hit Erik, but the rest of the scrapes and bruises had healed for the most part.

The first couple of nights after Erik had snapped had been the hardest. Thank God Jase had attached himself to my hip, being there when I'd awoken from a nightmare and staying up when I was too antsy to fall back asleep. He'd put those wee hours in the middle of the night to good use, distracting me from the dark memories that lingered from those hours spent with Erik.

I glanced over at him, and my heart did a little flip. He loved me. He was *in* love with me. My brain still whirled with all the possibilities of what that meant in the long term for us.

Squeezing his hand, I smiled reassuringly when he glanced over. Worry deepened his eyes to a steel gray. When he'd woken up this morning and asked if I'd do this with him before we went over to his parents for Christmas Eve, I'd been shocked but glad that he was taking such a huge step.

'You okay?' I asked.

Locks of brown hair flipped out from the gray knit toboggan. 'It feels weird that you're the one asking me that.'

'True.' From the knee injury to Debbie's death and Erik's breakdown, all his concern had been focused on me. 'But I'm asking you.'

'I'm . . . I don't know.' He paused as he turned right, cutting through a gas station. 'I'm sad. Confused. Weirdly happy, like I'm proud of myself, and that sounds stupid.'

'It's not stupid. You should be proud of yourself.'

A quick smile appeared and then vanished. 'I guess I'm just feeling everything.'

Which was understandable. It had been years since Kari's death, but this was a first for him. I squeezed his hand again.

By the time we arrived at the cemetery, a light dusting of snow blanketed the grounds. Based on his parents' directions, he turned right into the cemetery and followed the curve until the large, bare oak tree came into view.

Kari's gravesite would be near the tree—five gravesides over to be exact.

He parked on the shoulder. Only then did he pull his hand free to turn off the engine, but he made no move to exit the vehicle. Instead, he stared over, toward the tree. Branches swayed in the gentle wind.

A knot formed in my chest. 'You really ready to do this? Because we can do it another time.'

'I'm ready,' he replied quietly after a few moments. 'I need to do this.'

I agreed. Jase had moved on, but he hadn't fully let go. All these years he'd treated Kari's death like she'd broken up with him. That she was out there somewhere, living a life, and maybe that had helped him get over her loss, but he hadn't completely come to terms with it. It was why he'd pushed me away after admitting that he'd loved me. I got all that now. It was the fear he'd carried for years of loving someone and losing them.

Several minutes passed and then he nodded. 'Okay.'

'Okay,' I whispered.

He opened the car door and a blast of cold air rushed in. I did the same, pulling my gloves out of my pocket as he grabbed the poinsettias we'd picked up at the nearby grocery store on the way to the cemetery.

My boots crunched over the frozen grass and light snow as I joined him on the other side of the Jeep. He stopped and glanced down at me. The uncertainty and vulnerability in his expression tore at my heart. With his free hand, unprotected from the elements, he reached between us. I immediately gave him my gloved hand. Through the wool, the weight of our joined hands seemed to give him strength to move forward.

We were silent as we passed the stones, and I tried not to think of Debbie's funeral and how Erik had blamed me for her death in front of the entire procession, but it was hard. She was buried here too, but on the other side of the main road.

Cemeteries were supposed to be peaceful, but the stillness—the utter lack of life—always gave me the creeps. Today was different though. As we got near the great oak, I wasn't thinking of the *Night of the Living Dead* or the fact there were a whole bunch of bodies under our feet.

I was only thinking about Jase and how hard this was for him.

When Jase suddenly stopped, I knew we were at Kari's grave. Following his gaze, I drew in a shallow breath.

The gravestone was made of polished, gray marble and the head was shaped in a heart. An angel praying had been engraved in the stone, and below the kneeling figure was the name Kari Ann Tinsmen, and the birth and death dates were unfairly close.

This was her. No face. No body. Her whole life was summed up in the calligraphy below the dates, *Loving sister, daughter, and mother, asleep with the angels.*

Mother.

A knot formed in my throat. Kari never really had a chance to be a mother. Hell, she really hadn't the chance to be any of those things.

Jase shook his head slowly as he stared at the gravesite. I couldn't even begin to imagine what he was thinking. Probably a little of everything as he stood there, going through their short life together.

A lot of things Jase had said in the past made sense now. How he'd sworn that beautiful things could come from tragedy. He'd known that firsthand. An unexpected pregnancy had given him Jack, and a tragic death had pushed him in the right direction.

The same could be said about losing the ability to dance. I hoped that through teaching, I could actually make a difference in the world and wasn't that why people became teachers? Sure as hell wasn't for the money. The reasoning was deeper than that, more substantial. Teachers molded the future. Dancers entertained. And it wasn't like I would never be a part of that world again. I had my goal of getting Avery back in the studio and could help out with the really young dancers if I wanted to.

And I wanted to.

That's the thing about death that makes it useful. Death was always a reminder to the living to *live*—to live in the present and to look forward to the future.

'She was a really . . . good girl,' he said finally, breaking the silence.

My smile felt watery. 'I'm sure she was.'

He stared at the tombstone for a stretch. In his hand, the red poinsettias petals trembled. I doubted it was from the bitter cold. 'She loved winter and the snow.' He paused, throat working as he looked up. Flakes of the white stuff fell in heavier patches. His words were thick as he spoke again. 'This is kind of fitting, I think.'

I watched a rather large snowflake come to rest on the curve of the marble stone.

Jase drew in a deep, shuddering breath. 'I think Jack gets that from her. You know, the love of winter. It's his favorite season. Might be because of Christmas, but I like to think it's because of her.'

I squeezed his hand. 'Winter isn't a bad season.'

One side of his lips moved up. 'I'm a summer kind of guy.' He eased his fingers free from mine and stepped forward. Kneeling down, he placed the pretty red flowers at the base of her headstone.

Silent, I watched him tug off his toboggan and bow his head and I didn't know if he was praying or if he was talking to Kari. Either way, I felt like I was eavesdropping; it was such an intimate, sad moment.

Blinking away tears, I fixed my gaze on the tree and swallowed hard. Snow coated the bare branches, causing the thin tips to turn down at the edges.

When Jase returned to my side, he'd pulled the toboggan back on and the tip of his nose looked as red as mine felt. 'Do you mind if we stay for a few more moments? I know it's freezing and you can wait—'

'I'm okay.' If he wanted to stay here for a month, I'd be right beside him. 'We can stay as long as you want.'

'Thank you.' His spine lost some of its stiffness as he

373

draped his arm over my shoulders. Tugging me against the shelter of his body, he rested his cheek against the top of my head and sighed. 'Thank you for being here with me.'

The Winstead farm was decked out.

It looked like Santa threw up holiday cheer all over the grounds, but in a good way. Multicolored lights covered the split-rail fence lining the driveway. Red, green, and blue twinkled off the barn, and the entire front of the house glimmered like a giant, square disco ball.

Jase chuckled as my eyes widened, which made me smile, because it was the first he'd laughed since we'd left the cemetery. 'My parents go a little crazy during Christmas, especially because of Jack.'

A little? There was an inflatable Santa sitting off the right of the porch. On the roof, there were eight plastic reindeers. Rudolph, the ninth and most important reindeer, was MIA. A plastic Santa was perched on the chimney, complete with a bag of gifts.

There was a giant frosty snow globe, bubble thing in front of the porch. Through the large windows, I could see the lights from the Christmas trees. My parents tended to stick to the one Christmas light color theme, but I liked this better. There was something warmer about the chaos of lights.

'We're going to leave the presents in the Jeep,' he said as we climbed out. 'You know, Santa hasn't arrived yet.'

I grinned. 'Santa looks a little drunk on the roof.'

He looked up and laughed as the wind caused the plastic Santa to spin on the chimney. 'That's my kind of Santa.'

I lingered at the steps, dragging my boot in the dusting of snow. 'Are you sure it's okay for me to be here?'

Shooting me a look, he placed his hands on my shoulders and lowered his head so that we were eye level. 'Of course.

Mom and Dad are happy that you're spending Christmas Eve with us, and they know you know the truth.' He smoothed a hand over my head and tucked my hair back behind my ear. 'I think they're more excited about you being here than me.'

I laughed. 'That's because I'm pretty damn amazing to have around.'

'That's true.' Jase slanted his head, and his warm breath danced over my lips. I shivered, and his lips curled up. 'Thank you for today. Seriously. I can't say it enough. I don't think I'd have been able to do it without you.'

I leaned forward and stretched up a little, brushing my cold nose against his. 'You would've done it with or without me, but I'm glad I could be there. Really.' Having left my gloves in the Jeep, I placed my bare hand against his cheek, loving the feel of the slight stubble against my palm. 'Are you okay?'

His thick lashes swept down. 'You know, I didn't think I'd feel any different, but I do. It's not huge, but I feel good about it.' He placed his hand over mine as his other curved around the nape of my neck. 'I think I owe you a thank-you kiss.'

'You don't owe me a thank-you, but I'll take the kiss anyway.'

He smiled as his lips brushed over mine once and then twice, as soft as the snowflakes falling around us. His hand held me in place as he coaxed my mouth open, teasing the seam with his tongue. Heat flowed through me, causing my muscles to tense when he flicked his tongue over the roof of my mouth.

This was the kind of thank-you kiss I could get behind.

And Jase, well, he simply didn't just *kiss*. He tasted. He devoured. He promised pleasure with his lips and teased of more to come with his tongue. The boy could offer a class on kissing. He made it an art form when he drew a soft moan from the depths of my core.

'Now, come on, son. I taught you better than to kiss a pretty gal out in the cold.' His father's voice interrupted, spreading a hot flush across my face as Jase pulled back.

'I'm keeping her warm,' Jase replied, grinning. As I turned to shield my flaming face, because there was nothing like getting caught by your boyfriend's parents when your knees were weak from kissing, I saw the lightness in Jase's expression, a gleam to his silver eyes that had never been there before. 'Right?'

I blinked slowly and murmured, 'Right.'

His father grinned. 'Come on. Yer mom has Jack in the kitchen, baking cookies for Mr. Santa.'

Jase winced as he reached down and took my hand and led me up on the porch. Oh. There was the ninth reindeer, standing guard by the door. 'Is it a disaster?'

'Boy, it's about as bad as you being in the kitchen.' He turned, holding the door open for us. 'So, yeah, it's a disaster.'

I laughed at the face Jase made. 'Come to think of it, I've never seen you cook anything besides soup from a can yet.'

His father laughed as we stepped into the house. The room smelled of cookies and evergreen. 'Honey, that is not something ya'll want to see.'

'It's not that bad.' Jase frowned as he stripped off his jacket. 'I only melted the spatula in the Rice Krispie treats once.'

'Once?' I draped my jacket off the hook of a coat rack. 'I think that's more than enough.'

'What he ain't telling you is that he also tried to feed it to his cousins.'

I laughed at the sheepish look that crossed Jase's face. 'Oh my God, are you serious?'

'What?' He shrugged as he dragged his toboggan off. 'They didn't eat it.'

'Only because it was as hard as a brick and could have killed someone,' his father replied, smiling. 'My son is a lot of damn good things, but a cook ain't one of them.'

'Thanks, Dad.'

'Jase!' shrieked Jack from the kitchen. 'Tess!'

We turned just as Jack came barreling through the dining room. 'Whoa, buddy! Slow down,' Jase said, stepping forward as Jack almost head butted the dining room table. 'Jack, you're gonna—'

Sensing that Jack was about to make a kamikaze dive attempt, Jase knelt and caught his son the second he launched himself at him. He wrapped his arms around the boy, standing up. Jack clung to him, sinking his tiny hands into Jase's hair.

'I made cookies for Mr. Santa!' Jack announced, holding fistfuls of hair. 'They have chocolate in them and walnuts!'

'Is that so?' Jase turned slightly, holding his son close. My chest tightened at seeing them together. Even though Jack didn't know the truth, you'd be hard-pressed not to see the love between them. 'What about peanut butter cups? You know that's my favorite kind.'

'We have them, too. I ate a lot of them.' Jack grinned as he put his head on Jase's shoulder.

'A lot?' Mr. Winstead snorted. 'The boy ate about half the batch.'

The grin on Jack's face spread, and then, seeing me, he let out another squeal. 'Lemme down! Lemme down!'

Smiling, Jase lowered the kid's swinging feet to the ground. The second he landed, he took off, wrapping his arms around my legs.

'Hey,' I said, messing up his already out-of-control hair. 'You excited about Santa coming?'

'Yes! Daddy said Mr. Santa would be leaving soon!' He pulled back, grabbing my hand. 'Come!'

I glanced over at Jase. He smiled and shrugged, lingering back with his father as Jack tugged me through the dining room.

The kitchen *was* a mess. Cookie batter covered the island and the countertops. Flour was on the floor and the egg shells filled bowls, but the smell of sugar goodness had me anticipating a heavenly sugar rush.

'Lookie who I found! Lookie!'

Mrs. Winstead turned, wiping her hands along the Christmas trees lining the bottom of her red apron. 'Oh, honey, I'm so glad you're here.' She strode over to me in the same long, purposeful strides Jase made. 'Look at you,' she clucked, brushing a finger along my jaw, where I knew a bruise was still fading. 'How have you been, honey?'

'Good.' I smiled as Jack slipped free and climbed up on a step stool that was pushed again the counter. He sunk his hand into cookie batter. 'I'm doing really good.'

'I'm happy to hear that.' Her strong arms went around me, and she nearly squeezed the air out of me. 'When Jase told me what—' She glanced over to where Jack was rolling dough into balls. She lowered her voice. 'I don't want the little one to overhear, but I'm glad you're okay and that—' her voice dropped low—'crazy son of a bitch is in jail.'

My lips twitched. 'Me too.'

Mrs. Winstead shook her head sadly as she watched Jack plop a ball of batter onto a cookie sheet. 'Just that poor girl . . .'

'I know.' I bit down on my lower lip. 'I keep telling myself that at least there's justice for Debbie now.'

Jack looked over his shoulder, a frown of curiosity on his cute face. 'What's justice?'

'When bad people have their comeuppance, baby. And that's the good thing.' Mrs. Winstead smiled at me, and the lines around her eyes deepened. Her voice lowered again. 'But that . . . that's not all.'

Placing her hand on my shoulder, her chest rose with a deep, heavy breath. 'I'm glad that you *know*—that Jase told you.'

I didn't know what to say. All I could do was nod, and Mrs. Winstead's smile spread as Jack snuck a piece of dough. 'Jase used to do that as a little boy too,' she said, blinking rapidly. 'He ate more dough raw than he did cooked.'

'That's when it's at its best.' My voice was surprisingly hoarse.

She patted my shoulder. 'You're good for my boy, so damn good. He hasn't gotten close to anyone since Kari, and you've gotten him to open up that heart of his. I know we haven't had a chance to really get to know each other, but for that, you'll always be like a daughter to me.'

Oh dear, I was going to cry.

Blinking back tears, I smiled and then I laughed. 'I'm sorry. I don't want to cry.'

Jack was turned around again. 'Why you sad?'

'I'm not sad,' I quickly told him, smiling for his benefit. 'I'm happy, really happy.'

He took my word for it and went back to the cookie dough. I wiped at my eyes and pulled myself together. 'Thank you. That means a lot to me, and I would never jeopardize him,' I said, nodding at Jack's back. 'Or Jase's heart.'

'That's my girl.' Her eyes turned misty, and she cleared her throat. 'Now, look at me. I'm about to start shedding tears, and that ain't gonna do us any good, not when my boy is coming right in here.'

'Hey, Mom.' Jase strode across the cluttered but homey kitchen, leaned in, and kissed his mother's cheek. As he pulled back and glanced between us, he frowned. 'Is everything okay?'

'Everything is good,' I said, smacking my hands together. 'Jack is pretty busy over there.'

He glanced over at him quickly, before eyeing both of us closely. 'Are you sure?'

'Yes, hon. Us gals were just chatting. All good things.' Mrs. Winstead turned, opened the oven door, and peeked in. 'These are almost done.'

Appeased, Jase went over to where Jack was and snuck a ball of dough off the cookie sheet.

'Hey!' Jack giggled as Jase popped the whole thing in his mouth.

Kissing his little boy's cheek, Jase then pivoted around, coming up behind me from around the kitchen table. He slipped his arms around my waist and hooked his hands together. 'Can I steal her away now? Want to show her the tree.'

Mrs. Winstead winked at me. 'Only if she wants to be stolen by you.'

'Oh, she wants to be stolen by me,' Jase replied, and I smacked his arm. He laughed. 'Don't be embarrassed.'

His mom shook her head as Jase spun around. Moving his arm to my shoulder, he led me back through the dining room. His father was no longer in the hall, and the large living room was empty.

The Christmas tree was huge and real and reminded me of home. Full of different and mismatched bulbs, the lights blinked every few seconds. Stockings hung above the fireplace.

'Look at this.' Stretching forward, he unhooked a red stocking and held it up. 'What do you think?'

'Oh!' The stocking had my name on it, written in red glitter. 'That's mine? Are you serious?'

'Yes.' Jase laughed, hooking it back up. 'Jack made it for you this morning.'

I don't know what it was about the stocking with my name on it, but it made my heart swell like the Grinch's had done. I thought it might burst.

'You like it?' he asked, sitting down on the floor with his back against the couch. Tugging on my hand, he waited until I sat. 'I'm thinking you love it.'

'I do.' I laughed and then swiped at my face again. 'I swear. I'm an emotional baby.' Lowering my hands, I let my gaze wonder over his striking face. 'I really do love it.'

'I wonder what Santa will put in your stocking.' The way he said it made me think of dirty things. 'And under your tree.'

I lifted a shoulder and then put my hands on the hard-wood floor. Leaning forward, I kissed his lips. 'I already have everything I want for Christmas.'

'Mmm.' His hands settled on my hips and he swept his lips over mine. 'I don't,' he murmured. 'Because I'm greedy, I want to wake up with you tomorrow morning. That's what I want.'

'But—'

'Cam's already left with Avery and I was taking you up late tomorrow morning. So why should I take you back to the apartment tonight?' He kissed the corner of my lips. 'You can stay here with me. My parents wouldn't care. We can pretend we're sixteen and having quiet, dirty sex so no one hears us.'

I laughed. 'You're such a perv.'

'I am.' He kissed the other corner. 'Stay with me?'

Kissing him, I pulled back just a little. 'Like I'd say no.'

Jase wrapped his arms around me, situating me so that I sat between the vee of his legs and my back was to his front. I felt his lips curve against the side of my neck when Jack let out a high-pitched laugh at something Jase's father had said in the kitchen.

'You know what?' he asked.

I turned and his lips then grazed my cheek. 'Chicken butt?'

Jase laughed under his breath. 'That was really dorkish.'

Giggling, I snuggled closer. 'Yep. But you love me, so . . .'

'That's true.' He kissed my cheek. 'Which brings me to what I wanted to say.' There was a beat of silence, and his chest rose against my back. 'In a way, you've already given me my best gift ever.'

'This morning?' I twisted so I could see him. 'When I woke you with my—'

'Well, that was great, but no.' He grinned. 'It's bigger than that.'

I held my breath.

His gaze searched mine. 'I never could picture myself married, you know. After what happened with Kari and spending these last couple of years watching my parents raise Jack, I didn't see a family for myself in the future.'

My heart rate picked up.

'But that's changed,' he continued, holding my stare, and those silvery eyes became my entire world in that moment. 'And it changed because of you. Now I can see myself married, and I can see myself having my own family. With you. And that's the best gift I could ever have.'

I opened my mouth, but I was beyond words. What he said was like basking in the August sun and had stolen my very ability to speak.

'Hey.' He cupped my cheeks. 'Say something.'

I needed to say something, because what he said was so wonderful and so beautiful. My heart was pounding, and my thoughts were a mess of so many things. Elation rose deep inside me. Us. Together. Marriage. A family. One day. I fell in love all over again.

'God, Jase,' I breathed, closing my eyes. 'I love you. I love you so much.'

He made a deep sound in the back of his throat and closed the tiny distance between us, fusing our mouths together. We kissed as if we were desperate for each other, pouring how we felt into it. And even when the swell of passion subsided just enough for us to breathe, we stayed close. Forehead to forehead. Lips brushing every so many seconds. Neither of us spoke, because everything that we needed to say had been said.

We stayed like that until the sound of pounding little feet forced us to break apart. Jack plopped down beside us, precariously holding a plate of cookies in one hand and a tablet in the other. He looked up at us with eyes that matched his father's and tugged at my heart.

'Cookie?' Jack held out a half-eaten chocolate chip cookie.

I took it and broke it in half, holding one half up. Jase's lips brushed my fingers as he took the whole thing in his mouth, causing Jack to burst into giggles. I ate mine a bit slower.

'These cookies are the best,' I told him.

A proud smile puffed up his round cheeks. 'Cuz I made them.'

'That's right.' Jase rested his chin on my head as he reached out, messing up his son's hair with a large hand. 'You've got mad cooking skills.'

'I wanna make Krispie treats next year for Santa.'

Jase groaned. 'I don't have good luck with those things.'

383

'That's okay,' I said. 'I can teach you. I make some really good Rice Krispie treats.'

Jack's eyes widened. 'Really?'

'Promise.' I grinned as I glanced up, seeing his parents standing in the doorway. Tears glistened in his mother's eyes as Mr. Winstead squeezed her shoulder. As my gaze fell back to Jack, who had moved on from the cookies to the tablet and was already engrossed in his game, I realized what his parents were seeing.

Because I was seeing it too.

The future.

The three of us.

So much had changed for us in a little over four months. Back in August, I never thought I'd be here on Christmas Eve, with my lips still tingling from Jase's sweet kisses. Our future together wasn't something any of us planned. I'd always thought I'd be a dancer. Jase always believed he'd never let himself fall in love again. None of this was expected, but I wouldn't give any of this up to dance again.

My dream had been shattered, but then re-created, fashioned into something with more meaning and becoming more precious.

Holding the game high, Jack whooped as he smiled up at Jase. One day, he would know the truth about his father and his mother and I knew deep in my soul, I'd be standing next to Jase when that day came, there for the both of them.

I slid my hands down Jase's arms, coming to where his hands were nestled just below my belly button. I spread my fingers over his, and he flipped his up, threading our hands together.

'Do you want to play the next round?' Jack asked with hope in his beautiful gray eyes as he looked up at me.

'I'd love to.'

Appeased, Jack returned his attention to the game, and Jase pressed a kiss to my temple, and then, against my skin, he mouthed the words I'd never grow tired of or used to hearing.

He whispered *I love you*.

Keep reading for an exclusive look at

*Jase and Teresa's
first kiss*

The Kiss

I can do this.

Standing a few feet from the guest bedroom door, I said those four words one more time to myself, hoping they'd give me the courage to knock. *I can do this*.

Inhaling deeply, I forced the lungful of air out very slowly. My knees were knocking together and sweat dotted my palms.

So not hot.

I couldn't remember the last time I was this nervous, which was freaking ridiculous. I'd been dancing in front of crowds of hundreds since I was knee high to a cricket and I didn't get this anxious. Like I'd keel over at any given second, pass out face down in the carpet like a giant dumbass.

But this was about Jase—Jase-Hot-as-Hell-Winstead— and if one thing was sure, when it came to him, nothing about me was expected.

I shouldn't want him like I did. He was older than me, my brother's best friend, and I knew from the conversations I'd overheard—er, eavesdropped on—between him and Cam, Jase put the "play" in player.

Who would blame him though? If I was a dude and looked like him, my bedroom would be like a bus stop, but the ugly flash of jealousy told me that I wasn't really happy with the idea of Jase being so, um . . . active.

But it wasn't just his looks. Jase . . . well, he was like a superhero in my eyes, the only person who'd been capable of pulling my brother out of his depression. Jase saved Cam and in a way, saved *me*. Because of Jase, I'd been able to let go of some of the guilt that crowded my thoughts on a daily basis. He'd become a friend to me and somewhere over the time, he'd become something else.

Jase hadn't left the sad excuse for a poker game that was still going on downstairs that long ago, so I knew he wasn't asleep.

And I also knew I shouldn't be standing outside his bedroom door.

Especially considering what I was wearing or lack thereof.

I glanced down at my painted toes and flushed hotly. I'd changed into sleep shorts, the kind that barely covered my ass. My shirt flashed a great deal of my belly and was pretty tight. No bra. And it was kind of chilly upstairs. If Cam or my parents caught me flouncing around dressed like this with Jase in the house, someone would get hurt.

Probably Jase.

This might've been a bad idea.

My attempt at seduction felt a wee bit . . . lame. Like a little girl playing dress up . . . or dress down. But I knew if I went back to my bedroom to get changed I wouldn't leave. I'd lose my nerve. It was now or never or the next time he randomly showed up with my brother, and who knew if we'd get this chance again?

Cam was *always* cock-blocking like a mofo.

I can do this.

Taking another deep breath, I rapped my knuckles off

the door and then stepped back, fighting the urge to take off running down the hall, giggling like a twelve year old. But this was such a bad idea. A totally bad idea. I needed to leave, because Jase had better things to—

The door swung open and there Jase stood in all his glory. And boy, it was a lot of glory. Like sexy angels harking and all that jazz.

His hair, a messy bronze color fell over his forehead in careless waves, the color of skin deep, hinting at something interesting in his bloodlines. He was still wearing what he had on earlier—faded blue jeans that hung low on his hips and an old tee shirt that stretched taut across his broad shoulders.

I'd had the pleasure of seeing him shirtless once before, when he'd been visiting Cam. It had been early and he'd stumbled out of the bedroom, making his way to the bathroom. All he'd worn was flannel pajama bottoms, and all I had done was stared at the kind of stomach dreams were made of.

So I knew what he was hiding under the old Nirvana shirt.

'What's up?' he asked.

I almost closed my eyes and sighed. His voice . . . Nothing compared to the deep, rolling sound. He could read dishwasher-operating instructions and I could listen forever. Before I could answer or stand there like an idiot, Jase stepped aside in silent invitation.

Such a good guy.

My bare feet sunk through the carpet as I stepped into the guest room. A small duffel bag sat on the armchair in the corner by the window. Other than that and the slightly rumpled pillow at the head of the bed, it didn't even look like Jase was here.

The door hadn't shut all the way behind me, but only a sliver of a space remained open. Swallowing hard, I turned to face Jase. Nervous, I raised my arm and ran my fingers through my hair, brushing it back from my face.

Jase had magnificent eyes. They weren't really blue or gray, more like a cross between the two. Silver. Framed with heavy black lashes, those eyes were really quite striking. Right now, they weren't focused on mine.

His gaze drifted from my face, all the way down to the tips of my painted blue toenails. His stare got a little hung up on my stomach. When I brushed my hair back, it had caused the shirt to rise up. My hands itched to pull it down, but that would've defeated my whole purpose of being here, right?

I wanted Jase to not see me as a little girl—as Cam's little sister.

He looked up, the hollows of his cheeks a deeper color than the rest of his face, and then he looked way, scrubbing a hand along his jaw.

Jase's gaze dipped again, this time to my chest, before bouncing back to my face. 'So what's going on?' His voice was deeper, more gruff.

My heart pounded against my ribs as I walked around the corner of the bed, so I was back in his line of vision. His stare seemed to find mine. Our eyes locked for a brief moment and then his gaze went south once more, and this time his stare was so intense it felt like a physical caress. Certain parts of my body really, *really* liked that, got all tingly and noticeable. A flush crept across my cheeks when his eyes met mine.

He drew in a deep breath. 'What are you doing, Tess?'

My breath caught as I shifted my weight from one foot to the next. He was the only person who called me Tess. No one else did. I loved it. 'I was just checking to see if you needed any extra blankets or pillows.'

He glanced at the bed—at the mini mountain of blankets

and pillows Mom or someone had obviously dropped in here—and then back at me. His brows rose.

Damn it.

'Well, I guess you don't need any of that.' I bit down on my lip. 'Do you need anything?'

Jase stared at me a moment and then he moved. His long-legged, fluid stride carried him to the bed. He sat on the edge. 'That's very sweet of you to ask.'

My heart was beating so fast it was like the jackhammer of hearts. 'I'm a very sweet person.'

One side of his lips tipped up. 'That you are.' Eyeing me from behind thick lashes, he grinned at me. 'I'm on to you.'

Stomach dropping, my eyes went wide. 'What do you mean?' Was it that obvious? Uh, hell, I was dressed like a porno was about to start filming. Yes. It was obvious.

He patted the spot next to him. 'Come on.'

Feeling a bit spacey, I hurried over to the bed and sat beside him. Not right on him. There was a healthy distance between us.

'So what do you want to talk about?' he asked, flipping onto his back.

My tongue worked around words, but nothing came out. Realization set in and my muscles relaxed. Okay. It wasn't so obvious why I was here. He thought I wanted what I always wanted when he came around. Or at least what he thought. To talk. We always talked when he visited—about school, dance, friends, everything and anything.

Except I really didn't want to talk. 'Um, how is school?'

He folded his arms behind his head. His shirt inched up, exposing an expanse of hard lower abs. A fine trail of hair ran under his navel, disappearing beyond his jeans. Yum. 'It's going good.'

I bet it was.

'How's school for you?'

I had no idea what he was talking about. My gaze shifted to him. 'Huh?'

'School.' That grin of his spread. 'I was asking how school was going for you.'

'Oh. Yeah. Great.' I twisted toward him, dragging a leg up on the bed. A muscle ticked along his jaw, snagging my attention for a second. 'How's your brother?'

'Jack's good.' His brows lowered a fraction of an inch. 'Do you always run around dressed like that?'

Honestly? No. I shrugged a shoulder, somewhat happy that he was vocalizing that he'd noticed me. 'Yeah.'

'Cam doesn't have a lot of friends visiting, right?'

I thought that was an odd question. 'No. I mean other than you, sometimes Ollie swings by.'

Those brows came down even further. 'And do you wear *that* when he's here?'

My lips twitched, but I fought the smile wanting to form. 'I don't know.'

'I hope not,' he muttered.

'Why?'

'Why?' Surprise colored his tone. His gaze slid down my face to my chest and lingered there until it felt like he was touching me. My body reacting swiftly, and I wasn't sure if he noticed, because his gaze swept back to mine. 'That's why.'

Oh my.

A giddy feeling pooled low in my stomach. 'I don't know what you're talking about.'

His eyes rolled. 'You shouldn't be dressed like that when your brothers' friends are here, especially freaking Ollie. The boy has sperm for brains.'

My brows shot up. 'I shouldn't be?'

'No.'

Caught between feeling offended and wanted to clap for

394

joy, I wasn't responsible for the stupidity that flowed from my mouth. 'I'm not a little girl, Jase.'

'Uh. I think I know that.' He paused. 'Trust me.'

An unsteady breath swelled in my lungs. 'What does that mean?'

His gaze shifted toward me. 'I can *see* that you're not a little girl.'

A pleasant warmth swept through my veins. 'And what's wrong with that?'

Jase opened his mouth and then snapped it shut. He rose up on his elbows, tipping his chin down. 'There's a lot wrong with that.'

Well, that's not what I wanted to hear. 'Care to explain?'

'Not really,' he said, and I swore it looked like he was struggling to keep his gaze on my face.

Part of me wanted to tuck tail and run, but there was a part of me—the reckless side, the other half that never shied away from anything—drove me forward. 'I'm sure most guys wouldn't have a problem with the way I'm dressed right now.'

His mouth dropped open.

'Actually, I'm pretty sure they'd enjoy it. There're a lot of boys in—'

'Boys. Exactly.'

I flushed. 'Boys. Men. Whatever.'

'I'm not a boy, Tess.' His eyes met mine, and the color was deeper, like quicksilver. 'And neither is Ollie.'

Back to Ollie? What the fuck? 'I don't dress like this when Ollie comes around.'

His head tilted to the side as he studied me. He started to look like he was about to say something, but changed his mind. 'Good.'

We were at an impasse. How did I respond to that? My gaze drifted to his mouth and then down, over the long length of his body. I felt like I was in a buffet line and he was the main course and the dessert.

'And you shouldn't dress like that when I'm here,' he said, and his voice was deeper again. Raw.

My lashes swept up and something had changed in him, in the way he watched me and how tense his body was. 'Why?' I asked.

Jase didn't answer.

I'd probably look back on the next couple of moments for the rest of my life and I'll never know what provoked me to do what I did, but I knew I'd never regret it, even if he dropkicked me off the bed.

I moved, drawing my other leg up on the bed, resting on my knees as I leaned forward, easing my weight on my hands. Jase froze like an animal that had scurried out into traffic and was now staring into glaring headlights.

He didn't move as I drew in a breath and leaned closer, coming within a scant inch of his mouth. His breath was crazy warm on my lips. My heart thumped and my pulse pounded throughout my body. My hair slipped over my shoulders, falling in the space between us. We were close, closer than we had ever been.

'Is it because you look?' I asked, my voice breathy.

Jase didn't answer again, but I heard him swallow.

'I don't mind if you do,' I told him, my fingers curling into the blanket. 'In fact, I like it.'

The breath he took was audible. His chest rose swiftly. 'Tess . . .'

'Jase?'

He made a sound in the back of his throat, something that was a cross between a groan and a growl, and was completely a hundred percent man. 'You have no idea what you're doing.'

'Yes. I do.' I wetted my lips. 'I thought about it. A lot. All the—'

Jase rose up and with how close we were, the distance between us vanished. His lips brushed mine, and a riot of sensation flooded my senses. It was such a quick and soft sweeping of his lips, but I felt it zing all the way to my toes.

He kissed me first.

And that was all the validation I needed.

I pressed my lips against his, silently demanding more, and that sound rose from him again. Our lips lingered together, moving slowly, tasting. His hands landed above my hips, his fingers gently pressing against the bare skin of my waist, eliciting a series of shivers from me. His hands, they were so warm and felt so large, and I knew he was strong.

I wanted to feel him against me, his arms around me, and my chest flush against his, our legs tangled. And I wanted the kiss to go deeper, so that I could really taste him.

But then he tasted me.

His tongue slid over the seam of my lips and I gasped. The kiss deepened and his hands spasmed along my sides. A gasping moan rose up.

Then the kiss was over.

When he lifted his mouth from mine, he hauled me forward, against his chest, into his lap and in his arms. He held me tight, squeezing me as he breathed into the hair at my neck. He said something, murmured too low for me to hear beyond the blood pounding in my ears, and then he lifted me out of his lap and stood, carefully placing me on my feet. His hands lingered on my sides for a moment or two longer and then slipped off, trailing down my hips.

I opened my eyes, flushed and dazed and a thousand other things.

Jase's eyes were like molten silver, burning bright as they drifted over me and then latched onto mine. Several seconds passed before he spoke. 'I think . . . I think you should go back to your bedroom. Now.'

I blinked. 'But—'

'We'll talk tomorrow,' he said, coming toward me. I tensed up in the most delicious way. He placed the tips of his fingers on my cheeks and tilted my head back. 'I promise. We'll talk tomorrow.'

'Okay.' My heart swelled so fast in my chest.

Jase closed his eyes and then pressed a kiss to my forehead and that kiss was the sweetest thing ever. He drew back, dropping his hands. 'Goodnight, Tess.'

I hesitated a moment and then backed up toward the door. Wrapping my fingers around the knob, I stopped. Jase watched me much like a hawk, and I briefly considered closing the door completely and locking it, just to see what he would do, but I thought that might be pushing it.

'Goodnight,' I whispered, and then stepped out into the hallway.

Cam's head appeared at the top of the stairs as I slipped inside my bedroom, closing the door quietly behind me. I walked backward until the backs of my thighs connected with the bed. Sitting down, I raised my hand to my still tingling lips and closed my eyes.

It really had just been one kiss.

One endless, beautifully perfect kiss.

'Oh God,' I murmured, and then I grinned. Thank baby Jesus in a manger that no one was here to witness what was most likely the goofiest grin this side of the mountain.

But the grin didn't fade and I knew I would *never* forget that kiss and I would be damned if it was going to be our last one.

I was a Hamilton.

And we got what we wanted, one way or another.

Acknowledgments

First and foremost a big thank you to Kevan Lyon and the team at Marsal Lyon Literary and Taryn Fagerness Agency. Tessa Woodward—I'm so glad you love these characters as much as I do and your editorial hand is priceless. Thank you to Jessie, Abigail, Jen, Molly, and Pam—you're the peeps beyond the scenes, getting the word out and making my job as an author a hell of a lot easier.

Jen Fisher—thank you for letting me turn you and your cupcakes into a fictional character. You're the bomb and so are your cupcakes. *Be With Me* would've never happened without Stacey Morgan. Not only is she a great friend and assistant, she's the poor soul who has to read the first drafts of these books. Another big shout-out to the ladies (in and out of writing) who rock: Laura Kaye, Sophie Jordan, Molly McAdams, Cora Carmack, and Lisa Descrochers.

Last and most important, a huge thank you to all the readers and reviewers out there. Books wouldn't be possible without you guys. You're the most integral part in all of this and THANK YOU from the bottom of my little heart.

If you liked *Be With Me*,
you'll love J Lynn's first novel

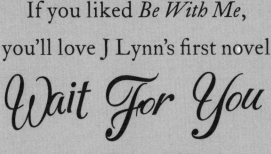

Wait For You

New York Times #1 bestseller

Avery knows she should stay away from Cam Hamilton:
he might be the hottest guy on campus but she really
doesn't need that sort of drama right now. Love is best left
in the past – along with her troubles. But sometimes, the
last thing that you want is just the thing you need…

Turn the page to read an extract!

Chapter 1

There were two things in life that scared the ever-loving crap out of me. Waking up in the middle of the night and discovering a ghost with its transparent face shoved in mine was one of them. Not likely to occur, but still pretty damn freaky to think about. The second thing was walking into a crowded classroom late.

I absolutely loathed being late.

I hated for people to turn and stare, which they always did when you entered a classroom a minute after class started.

That was why I had obsessively plotted the distance between my apartment in University Heights and the designated parking lot for commuter students over the weekend on Google. And I actually drove it twice on Sunday to make sure Google wasn't leading me astray.

One point two miles to be exact.

Five minutes in the car.

I even left my apartment fifteen minutes early so I would arrive ten minutes before my 9:10 class began.

What I didn't plan for was the mile-long traffic backup at the stop sign, because God forbid there be an actual light in the historical town, or the fact there was absolutely no parking left on campus. I had to park at the train station adjacent to the campus, wasting precious time digging up quarters for the meter.

'If you insist on moving halfway across the country, at least stay in one of the dorms. They do have dorms there, don't they?' My mom's voice filtered through my thoughts as I stopped in front of the Robert Byrd Science Building, out of breath from racing up the steepest, most inconvenient hill in history.

Of course I hadn't chosen to stay in a dorm, because I knew at some point, my parents would randomly show up and they would start *judging* and start *talking,* and I'd rather punt-kick myself in the face than subject an innocent bystander to that. Instead, I tapped into my well-earned blood money and leased a two-bedroom apartment next to campus.

Mr. and Mrs. Morgansten had hated that.

And that had made me extremely happy.

But now I was sort of regretting my little act of rebellion, because as I hurried out of the humid heat of a late August morning and into the air-conditioned brick building, it was already eleven minutes past nine and my astronomy class was on the second floor. And why in the hell did I choose astronomy?

Maybe because the idea of sitting through another biology class made me want to hurl? Yep. That was it.

Racing up the wide staircase, I barreled through the double doors and smacked right into a brick wall.

Stumbling backward, I flailed my arms like a cracked-out crossing guard. My overpacked messenger bag slipped, pulling me to one side. My hair flew in front of my face, a sheet of auburn that obscured everything as I teetered dangerously.

Oh dear God, I was going down. There was no stopping it. Visions of broken necks danced in my head. This was going to suck so—

Something strong and hard went around my waist, stopping my free fall. My bag hit the floor, spilling overpriced books and pens across the shiny floor. My pens! My glorious pens rolled everywhere. A second later I was pressed against the wall.

The wall was strangely warm.

The wall chuckled.

'Whoa,' a deep voice said. 'You okay, sweetheart?'

The wall was *so* not a wall. It was a guy. My heart stopped, and for a frightening second, pressure clamped down on my chest and I couldn't move or think. I was thrown back five years. Stuck. Couldn't move. Air punched from my lungs in a painful rush as tingles spread up the back of my neck. Every muscle locked up.

'Hey ...' The voice softened, edged with concern. 'Are you okay?'

I forced myself to take a deep breath—to just breathe. I needed to breathe. Air in. Air out. I had practiced this over and over for five years. I wasn't fourteen anymore. I wasn't there. I was *here*, halfway across the country.

Two fingers pressed under my chin, forcing my head up. Startling, brilliant blue eyes framed with thick black lashes fixed on mine. A blue so vibrant and electric, and such a stark contrast against the black pupils, I wondered if the color was real.

And then it hit me.

A guy was holding me. A guy had never held me. I didn't count that one time, because that time didn't count for shit, and I was pressed against him, thigh to thigh, my chest to his. Like we were dancing. My senses fried as I inhaled the light scent of cologne. Wow. It smelled good and expensive, like *his* ...

Anger suddenly rushed through me, a sweet and familiar thing, pushing away the old panic and confusion. I latched on to it desperately and found my voice. 'Let. Go. Of. Me.'

Blue Eyes immediately dropped his arm. Unprepared for the sudden loss of support, I swayed to the side, catching myself before I tripped over my bag. Breathing like I'd just run a mile, I pushed the thick strands of hair out of my face and finally got a good look at Blue Eyes.

Sweet baby Jesus, Blue Eyes was …

He was gorgeous in all the ways that made girls do stupid things. He was tall, a good head or two taller than me, and broad at the shoulders, but tapered at the waist. An athlete's body—like a swimmer's. Wavy black hair toppled over his forehead, brushing matching eyebrows. Broad cheekbones and wide, expressive lips completed the package created for girls to drool over. And with those sapphire-colored eyes, holy moly …

Who thought a place named Shepherdstown would be hiding someone who looked like this?

And I ran into him. Literally. Nice. 'I'm sorry. I was in a hurry to get to class. I'm late and …'

His lips curved up at the corners as he knelt. He started gathering up my stuff, and for a brief moment I felt like crying. I could feel tears building in my throat. I was really late now; no way could I walk into that class late, especially on the first day. Fail.

Dipping down, I let my hair fall forward and shield my face as I started grabbing up my pens. 'You don't have to help me.'

'It's no problem.' He picked up a slip of paper and then glanced up. 'Astronomy 101? I'm heading that way, too.'

Great. For the whole semester I'd have to see the guy I nearly killed in the hallway. 'You're late,' I said lamely. 'I really am sorry.'

With all my books and pens back in my bag, he stood as he handed it back to me. 'It's okay.' That crooked grin spread, revealing a dimple in his left cheek, but nothing on the right side. 'I'm used to having girls throw themselves at me.'

I blinked, thinking I hadn't heard the blue-eyed babe right, because surely he hadn't said something as lame as that.

He had, and he wasn't done. 'Trying to jump on my back is new, though. Kind of liked it.'

Feeling my cheeks burn, I snapped out of it. 'I wasn't trying to jump on your back or throw myself at you.'

'You weren't?' The lopsided grin remained. 'Well, that's a shame. If so, it would have made this the best first day of class in history.'

I didn't know what to say as I clutched the heavy bag to my chest. Guys hadn't flirted with me back at home. Most of them hadn't dared to look in my direction in high school and the very few that did, well, they hadn't been flirting.

Blue Eyes's gaze dropped to the slip of paper in his hand. 'Avery Morgansten?'

My heart jumped. 'How do you know my name?'

He cocked his head to the side as the smile inched wider. 'It's on your schedule.'

'Oh.' I pushed the wavy strands of hair back from my hot face. He handed my schedule back, and I took it, slipping it into my bag. A whole lot of awkward descended as I fumbled with my strap.

'My name is Cameron Hamilton,' Blue Eyes said. 'But everyone calls me Cam.'

Cam. I rolled the name around, liking it. 'Thank you again, Cam.'

He bent over and picked up a black backpack I hadn't noticed. Several locks of dark hair fell over his forehead and as he straightened, he brushed them away. 'Well, let's make our grand entrance.'

My feet were rooted to the spot where I stood as he turned and strolled the couple of feet to the closed door to room 205. He reached for the handle, looking over his shoulder, waiting.

I couldn't do it. It didn't have anything to do with the fact that I had plowed into what was possibly the sexiest guy on campus. I couldn't walk into the class and have everybody turn and stare. I'd had enough of being the center of attention everywhere I went for the last five years. Sweat broke out and dotted my forehead. My stomach tightened as I took a step back, away from the classroom and Cam.

He turned, brows knitted as a curious expression settled on his striking face. 'You're going in the wrong direction, sweetheart.'

I'd been going in the wrong direction half my life, it seemed. 'I can't.'

'Can't what?' He took a step toward me.

And I bolted. I actually spun around and ran like I was in a race for the last cup of coffee in the world. As I made it to those damn double doors, I heard him call out my name, but I kept going.

My face was flaming as I hurried down the stairs. I was out of breath as I burst out of the science building. My legs kept moving until I sat down on a bench outside of the adjacent library. The early-morning sun seemed too bright as I lifted my head and squeezed my eyes shut.

Geez.

What a way to make a first impression in a new city, new school … new life. I moved more than a thousand miles to start over and I had already mucked it up in a matter of minutes.